THE CORVETTE TOOK OUT TWO GUNNERS, THEN SCREECHED TO A ROCKING STOP

As if in continuation of the motion already in progress, the driver's-side door opened and a man stepped out. He was dressed in black and wore a duster that hung to midcalf.

Brognola saw a wry grin split the man's grim features, sensed the spark in the ice-blue eyes that glinted as hard as gunsights. The man moved with an economy of motion, lifting a long tube and placing it across his shoulder as he stood behind the Corvette's door.

For the first time since the attack had begun, the big Fed felt hope come alive inside him. He stood taller beside his wrecked sedan and took a firmer grip on his .38. He could imagine the surprise and puzzlement racing through the minds of his foes as they wondered who the new arrival was.

Then the tube belched flame. A heartbeat later the middle pursuit car exploded, chased by sheets of bright flame.

Brognola had seen the calling card before. There was no mistaking the Executioner's handiwork. And once introduced to it—as the hitters tonight were about to discover—a person never forgot the experience.

Other titles available in this series:

STONY MAN II
STONY MAN III
STONY MAN IV
STONY MAN V
STONY MAN VI
STONY MAN VII
STONY MAN VIII
#9 STRIKEPOINT

DON PENDLETON'S

MACK BOLAN®

STONY MAN™

SECRET ARSENAL

A GOLD EAGLE BOOK FROM

WORLDWIDE®

TORONTO • NEW YORK • LONDON
AMSTERDAM • PARIS • SYDNEY • HAMBURG
STOCKHOLM • ATHENS • TOKYO • MILAN
MADRID • WARSAW • BUDAPEST • AUCKLAND

First edition May 1994

ISBN 0-373-61894-8

Special thanks and acknowledgment to Mel Odom
for his contribution to this work.

SECRET ARSENAL

Printed in U.S.A.

SECRET ARSENAL

CHAPTER ONE

Near Aix les Bains, France
11:14 p.m.

Belted in the passenger seat of the Bell Aerospace UH-1D helicopter, U.S. Army Captain Chris Wardlow studied the broad expanse of the fields below. Even before tonight's assignment, he'd heard of the LeCourbe vineyards. The family had maintained its own label for well over one hundred fifty years. That sense of tradition didn't fail to leave an impression on him.

The H&K MP-5 gripped loosely in his right hand also made an impression. Whatever happened tonight at the LeCourbe vineyards, he was sure things wouldn't be the same. And if Major D'Orsay's Intelligence reports were correct, relations between the NATO forces inside France and the French government would be stressed to the breaking point.

The Huey's rotor throb continued to fill the cabin around him as the chopper rolled over the final hill and skimmed the last bits of dark forest that gave way to the sculpted fields of grapevines.

Wardlow cradled the subgun against his chest and wiped his hands on his trouser legs. He'd been stationed in the France-based NATO unit for almost eighteen months. Until tonight he'd never deployed on anything other than routine patrols or surprise inspections. He was acutely conscious of the combat cosmetics staining his features and the weight of the field pack strapped across his shoulders.

"Two minutes, Captain," the pilot said laconically.

Wardlow gave the man a tight nod and loosened the seat belt. "Our shadow?"

"Ahead of us now, sir. About two o'clock and four hundred yards out."

Squinting, Wardlow scanned the dark night sky, barely making out the dim outlines of the other Huey as it skated only a few feet above the earth, as well. Both aircraft ran without lights, navigating by instrumentation. "I suppose that Major D'Orsay intends to be the first team on the ground."

"Yes, sir." The pilot turned his head and flashed a white grin. "Unless the captain would rather have that privilege."

"No. It's the major's show. Let him run it. We're primarily here for observation and confirmation. Backup only if he needs it."

"Yes, sir."

Wardlow checked the walkie-talkie rig over his shoulder, slid the ear-throat harness into place and switched it on. He dangled a foot out the open door, feeling the slipstream slam against his boot, and tried to loosen up.

It was an eyes-only mission. He knew what they were there looking for. The rest of his team were to follow whatever orders he gave them. But they knew there was every chance that the situation could go ballistic. His sergeant, a seasoned veteran who'd been in a handful of hot spots around the world, had suggested bayonets while they were in the vineyards because of the possibility of close-quarters fighting. Wardlow had quickly relayed the suggestion to the rest of the team, heard the hollow clicks of the fighting knives sliding into place on the M-16s and tried not to think too clearly of what things might be like down there in the darkness of the vineyards.

He hoped French Intelligence was wrong, but he knew the GIGN was tied pretty tightly to political events that were changing the face of Europe and the rest of the world. The old hostilities with Great Britain hadn't been forgotten, but the French and Germans appeared to be drifting into ever-closing spheres of influence. And part of what the GIGN had stumbled on had come from the opening portals of Eastern Europe, where the Germans had a decided advantage. American military Intelligence hadn't seemed to give too much credence to the rumors circulating throughout the area, but the NATO arm had had to respond to French demands for an investigation.

"One minute," the pilot said.

"Roger." Wardlow tapped the transmit button on the headset. "Sergeant."

"Yes, sir?" Culpepper was calm, neutral.

"Get your team ready."

Wardlow envied the sergeant his disposition, at the same time grateful that the man was with him. The eight other members of the team were purely peacetime Army. Wardlow had been blooded in Desert Storm, but though that had involved months spent in a state of constant vigilance, it was nothing like spending months in battle the way Culpepper had.

"Yes, sir."

"From this point on, I'm Halo Leader. You're Halo Two. Name the rest of your team as you see fit. Two-man teams. You'll be relaying my orders. The French group will be working on our main tac channel, reserving one for private communications as we are. They're designated the Harp Group. The major is Harp Leader."

"Understood, sir."

"We'll all be wearing red, Sergeant, and they're treated to show up that way on the NVGs."

"Yes, sir."

Wardlow cleared the channel, changed it to the main tac freq, then slipped his red scarf from his pocket and secured it around his left arm.

"Halo Leader, this is Harp Leader. Over."

"Go, Harp Leader. Over."

D'Orsay spoke in French. The Second Foreign Parachute Regiment major was well versed in English, but had been delighted that Wardlow spoke French so well. As a division of the French Foreign Legion, the soldiers in the 2e REP often spoke no more than what was necessary to follow orders because they were drawn from sources outside France. During the tentative friendship Wardlow had struck up with the major over the past months, D'Orsay hadn't minded saying he was starved for the language. "Your team? Over."

"Ready." Wardlow took a fresh grip on the subgun and scanned the terrain below. Nothing had changed. "And yours? Over."

"Ready. Best of luck to you and yours when we touch the ground, my friend. Over."

Wardlow felt a smile crease his face. "Maybe we're just chasing the worries of maidenly aunts tonight." The main house came into view, and the helicopter pilot drastically cut his speed and settled toward the ground. Ahead of them the other Huey did the same. "If so, the first beer is on me when we get back to base and debriefed. Over."

"I'll hold you to that," D'Orsay said. "But don't go into those fields tonight thinking you're in for a cakewalk. I'd hate to lose such a learned conversationalist. Harp Leader out."

"Okay," Wardlow said to the pilot, "dump it, and let's get this show on the road." He raised his voice and thumbed the transmit button on the walkie-talkie. "Halo Two. Over."

"Go. Over."

"Ready for debarkation. Over."

Metal shrilled along the side of the Huey as the door was forced open. The helicopter listed to one side as the cargo weight shifted. Working the yoke in a confident grip, the pilot instantly compensated, bringing the aircraft back on an even keel.

"Ready, Halo Leader. Over."

"On my go. Over." Wardlow took out a pair of night-vision goggles and scanned the target zone.

The vineyard's main house was a three-story white structure that had to be as old as the LeCourbe family business. It was rectangular, with squared-off corners and a red tile roof that looked blood dark under the sliver of moon showing in the grayed slate of the sky. Four other buildings formed an outer perimeter.

Wardlow had been briefed on all of them, shown satellite pictures. In the northeast quadrant closest to him, the big, rambling structure held the tractors and other farm equipment necessary for taking care of the century-old vineyard. The workers' quarters were in the most modern-looking building in the northwest quadrant. A few vehicles, mostly old cars and pickups, were parked on the two sides graveled for that purpose. The buildings in the south quadrants housed the massive kegs and bottling supplies, built into the ground to help maintain the necessary temperatures.

Nothing appeared out of place or suspicious.

Wardlow's only hope was that they didn't scare the LeCourbe family too badly. He tapped the transmit button. "Move now. Halo Leader out." He pulled on a pair of leather gloves.

The helicopter bobbled as the team deployed. Three rappeling ropes were thrown over the side, and the soldiers slid down in quick succession. Culpepper was the first to touch down, instantly waving his group into position as each man made his landing.

Wardlow pulled his NVGs into position and saw part of the color drain from the night as the images suddenly sharpened. He stepped out onto the skid, caught the rappeling rope the last man tossed him, then quickly went down, the nylon thickness hissing through his gloved palms. As his boots thudded into the soft loam, he released the rope. He tapped the headset button and cleared the pilot for withdrawal as he pulled on his Kevlar helmet.

Rotor wash swirled around them, raking invisible fingers through the leafy foliage of the forest and the outer perimeters of the vineyard. The helicopter swung out, stayed low and disappeared behind the rolling hills in the distance.

"Sergeant," Wardlow said quietly, "deploy your troops."

Culpepper nodded and gave hand signals to his men. One went to the point position, flanked by two wingmen, who quietly faded into the rows of grapevines. The communications man took up position directly behind Wardlow, carrying the big set that had a broadcasting range far beyond their needs. NATO officers were awaiting word back in Paris, but avoided any direct communication until events were confirmed one way or the other.

The captain slipped off his leather gloves and zipped them in an oversize pocket of his camo pants. He tapped the transmit button. "Harp Leader, this is Halo Leader. Over."

"Go. Over," D'Orsay called back in English.

"We're in and on our way. Over."

"As are we. Harp Leader out."

Culpepper kept the NATO team up to a slow jog, and the soldiers moved like shadows through the grapevines.

It took only moments for perspiration to thoroughly soak the NATO captain's fatigues, and an irritable uncomfortableness settled over his skin under the gear. His imagination, honed by his own love of reading and research, of plotting and counterplotting, conjured myriad images as he moved through the rows of grapevines. The possibilities were so tangible, spurred on by the information gathered by his senses. The smell of the grapes hovered like fog, tainted with the scent of insecticides and fungicides. The vines themselves were well over six feet in most places, formidable walls in their own right.

He glanced around self-consciously, wondering if Culpepper had seen him shiver. The sergeant had a very disturbing habit of reading a man through body language. He caught sight of Culpepper just in time to see the man raise his rifle and aim it in his direction.

Before Wardlow could react, Culpepper's M-16 banged out two rounds. The muzzle-flash flamed out over the vines, leaving spots hanging in the captain's vision. For a sick instant he waited for the bullets to smash into him.

Then a body fell from the row of grapevines and sprawled at Wardlow's side. A 9 mm pistol spilled from the corpse's gloved fist.

"Holy shit!" the communications man said.

Wardlow stepped away from the row, already sensing further movement inside the dark recesses. He brought up the H&K MP-5 one-handed to waist level, flicked it over to full-auto, then tapped his headset transmit button. "Halo Leader to Halo group. Fan out. There are unfriendlies here. Halo Leader to Harp Leader."

The last echoes of Culpepper's rounds were only now beginning to fade. Before the last strains could disappear from hearing, more gunfire erupted. The tribursts of the NATO-issue M-16s were almost drowned out by the full-throated roar of autofire.

A cluster of grapes only inches from Wardlow's head splattered and jerked as bullets slammed into them. Warm grape juice slicked over the captain's face and neck as he went to ground. Someone leapt through the tangled mass of grapevines over his head.

Whirling on the ground, scrabbling furiously with his free hand, Wardlow tracked the attacker, brought him into his sights and squeezed the trigger. He cut a figure eight across his target's chest and saw the man go staggering back to be swallowed by another row of grapevines. The Uzi the man held chopped a line of holes across the flattened ground between the rows but touched none of the Halo group.

"Halo Leader," D'Orsay transmitted, "you have Harp Leader. Over."

"We're under attack," Wardlow replied. "Unidentified forces." He scrambled on his knees and free hand to the man Culpepper had dropped. Both of the sergeant's rounds had taken the man in the face, making it hard to even guess at his nationality. "I'm also unsure how many of them there are. Over."

"Affirmative. We've evidently run into some of them ourselves. Let me know if we can be of assistance. Harp Leader out." The sound of transmitted gunfire broke off with the connection.

Wardlow ran his hands over the corpse. There was a chain around the dead man's neck, but no dog tags. The pockets were empty of everything but a few notes of paper currency, coins and a book of matches. The tag in the shirt had been removed.

"Captain," Culpepper called out.

Wardlow released the dead man and looked up. He shoved the matchbook and the money into an empty pocket of his fatigue shirt, then glanced at his second-in-command. "Yeah."

"We can't stay here."

"Get us moving." Wardlow shoved himself up into a crouch.

"I can't reach the point or the left wing," the sergeant said.

"Do you know where they were?"

"Yes."

"Let's find them first."

Culpepper nodded and took the lead position.

Wardlow followed, sweeping his gaze from side to side, ready to react. The communications man stayed at his heels. "The chopper?" he called out to the sergeant.

"No," Culpepper replied without hesitation. "If we bring it into the immediate area, chances are that they'll put it down and leave us without a means of exfiltration if we need it."

Wardlow jogged right, following the narrow walkway created by the rows of grapevines. "Makes me wonder."

"Yeah?"

"If the choppers were going to be sitting ducks for these people, why didn't they take us down when they had the chance while we were all together?"

"It's something to think about."

"I know." Wardlow felt an anticipatory shiver course through him as he reflected on how close he'd come to dying before Culpepper even had the opportunity to save his life.

"Damn," the sergeant said softly as he came to a stop.

Glancing down at the man's feet, Wardlow saw the sprawled body of the pointman. A line of blood bisected the soldier's neck.

"Garrote," Culpepper said as he knelt and examined the fallen man's weapon. "Never had a chance to get off a round."

The surging roar of a racing engine slashed through the silent vineyards. Harsh, bright light thrust fingers through the leaves and vines.

Wardlow backpedaled, catching his communications officer on his back as if he were back on his high school basketball court using an illegal moving block. He heard the man's breath whoosh out as he drove them backward. Culpepper was already in motion, throwing himself out of harm's way.

A pickup came flying through the vines, transmission whining as it lost traction for an instant. The rear wheels spun, then dug into the black loam and sent the vehicle hurtling forward. It bounced across the open area between the rows, slamming into the next and was momentarily blocked.

"Move, soldier!" Wardlow shouted to the communications officer. He shoved the man roughly, getting him in motion. Bringing up the H&K MP-5, he bracketed the pickup and squeezed the trigger. A burst of 9 mm rounds tore through the back glass as the truck rocked free and went shooting back toward the NATO captain.

The driver's face was scarred, twisted into a snarl as he gazed through the empty back glass and tried to steer the truck.

On the move, the subgun blown empty by the last burst, Wardlow tried to run but found himself betrayed by the loose soil. His foot went out from under him. Instinctively, he raised his empty hand and the subgun, using them to make contact with the truck. The impact sent shivers up both arms, tore skin on his gun hand, but kept him from slipping under the churning wheels. He fell away and rolled, continued until he was in the relative safety of the nearest grapevine. By the time he came to a stop, he had a fresh magazine shoved into the MP-5.

Before the driver could do more than shift gears, Culpepper was ahead of him, the M-16 locked to his shoulder. The sergeant fired in single-round mode, as regular as a metronome.

The pickup bucked, jumped forward a few feet, then the engine died. Twin yellow headlights probed the darkness.

Shoving himself upright, Wardlow closed on the pickup. There were two men inside, but Culpepper's bullets had found them both. Most of the driver's head was gone, looking as if it had been worked over by a carrion crow.

"Henderson," the sergeant said as he yanked the driver's side door open and let the body fall out, "the wingman, he's dead, too."

"Same way?" Wardlow asked.

"Yeah."

"This doesn't make a whole hell of a lot of sense," the captain commented.

Culpepper expertly made his way through the dead man's clothes while Wardlow and the communications man stood guard. "Can you tell me what the assignment was now?"

Wardlow shook his head. "No." Security was going to remain tight on the operation unless the teams found what was hoped wouldn't be there. Even gossip later about what they were there looking for could create international repercussions.

"These guys aren't carrying anything," Culpepper said. He didn't take any offense at his superior officer's reticence. "No ID, no personal effects."

"Same thing for the other guy." Wardlow scanned their surroundings. The sounds of gunfire were dying away now, becoming more sporadic. But that only meant the shooters were taking more care with their targets, making each shot count.

"Means they were prepared for possible discovery," Culpepper said as he went on to the passenger side.

"Any idea about where they're from?" Wardlow asked.

"The States," the sergeant replied without hesitation.

A worm of anxiety twisted in Wardlow's stomach. "You're sure?"

"Yeah. Sure enough to guess." A penlight flicked on in Culpepper's hand, a tunnel of narrow light that touched an arm of the first dead man. "Special Forces tattoo. Been there for a while."

Wardlow stepped closer, took in the sinewy form of a black panther twisted around a combat dagger on the inside of the dead man's forearm.

"This guy," Culpepper said, "had bad teeth that somebody took care of." He opened the second corpse's mouth, shining the penlight inside. "Whoever did the work used ceramic polymers. That tells me it was an American dentist. European dentistry still uses silver and gold fillings." He released the corpse's head, and it dropped and twisted. "That tell you anything?"

"Yeah." Wardlow dug in his kit, pulled out his gas mask and the rest of his chemical protective clothing. There'd been some eyebrows raised when the team had found the clothing in their packs, but he hadn't allowed any questions. "Count your team down and get everyone into their jumpsuits."

"Yes, sir." Culpepper didn't hesitate about compliance, directing his orders along the Halo private freq.

Wardlow keyed the headset as he pulled his gear on. "Halo Leader calling Harp Leader. Over."

"Go," D'Orsay called back.

"We've got two possible American agents here," the captain said, feeling as if he'd betrayed his country. "They're either military or ex-military. It looks like the Glass Badger's Intel might be on the money. My team's taking the necessary precautions now. Over."

"Acknowledged," the French major radioed back. "We'll do the same here." His voice softened. "And know that I'm sorry, *mon ami.* Neither of us wanted things to turn out this way. Harp Leader out."

Wardlow cleared the channel, glanced around, saw that Culpepper and his communications officer were ready and waved them into motion.

Only two men of the Halo team had been lost. Three were dead in D'Orsay's group.

Six minutes later Wardlow encountered his first enemy soldier since the incident with the pickup. The man was a flickering shadow against the grayed-out backdrop of the grapevines, lit briefly by the muzzle-flash of his weapon.

The NATO captain returned fire, joined by Culpepper, but was sure neither of them had hit anything. When the pulsing cordite smoke cleared, the man was gone. Wardlow gave the order not to pursue. Halo's target was the farmhouse and outbuildings.

"These guys aren't defensive guards," Culpepper observed. "More like a covey of quail. Something flushed them from their hidey-holes. They weren't expecting us."

Wardlow silently agreed. They pressed on, having to hold back cautiously with the lure of their objective pulling them on.

At the edge of the vineyards, coming up on the barn, Wardlow scanned the fifty yards of cleared land separating his team from the structure. There were no lights inside, only the dark, cavernous mouth of the open double doors.

Culpepper fanned a man into the point position, and the rest of the Halo team set themselves to provide covering fire.

The NATO soldier covered the distance at a dead run.

No one fired at him.

Wardlow breathed a sigh of relief when the man made the relative safety of the barn. Culpepper went next, and he was hard on his sergeant's heels, expecting the harsh crack of gunfire at any moment.

Culpepper took another man and raced across the open double doors, flattening out into position immediately. The four remaining Halo soldiers covered the rear exit from the barn.

"Harp Leader to Halo Leader. Over."

Wardlow answered. "Go."

"We have secured the farmhouse without hostile engagement. The LeCourbe family appears to be more confused by events than anything else. However, we will be checking to make sure everyone in here is who they say they are. Over."

"Affirmative. We're taking the barn now, and we're encountering no resistance. Talk to you in a moment. Out."

A tight nod sent Culpepper inside.

Wardlow whirled around the corner at the same time, the H&K MP-5 on full-auto and held steady at waist level.

Nothing moved inside the barn.

Farm equipment was neatly arranged and put away. Rakes, hoes, coiled water hoses and hedge trimmers hung on the walls. The only things that jarred the symmetry of the workplace were the two one-ton transport trucks parked in the center of the barn. Olive-drab tarp covered the cargo areas.

Once the immediate vicinity was secure, Wardlow moved forward, a cold chill spreading through his chest.

"Halo Leader," D'Orsay called. "Over."

"Go," Wardlow replied softly as he reached for his sheathed Ka-bar combat knife.

Culpepper opened the driver's-side door on the truck, and a body tumbled out to flop on the hard-packed earthen floor of the barn. Death had been caused by a single bullet, entering at the base of the skull and exiting through the forehead.

"Have you secured your target?" D'Orsay asked. "Over."

"That's affirmative, Harp Leader. Come ahead. Halo Leader out." Wardlow clicked out of the loop and slashed the Ka-bar through the first of the tie downs. The hemp parted easily. He prepared to flip the tarp back as the 2e REP people filled the doorway, clad in biochemical protective gear, as well.

D'Orsay joined him at once and helped to pull back the tarp.

Wardlow took his flashlight from his combat harness, flicked the halogen bulb to life and played it over the truck.

Gleaming canisters sat huddled in the center of the cargo area, lashed together by double strands of bright chains threaded through eyebolts mounted in the sides of the truck bed. The markings were in Russian, glared warnings in the red-and-yellow markings alone.

The French major cursed in his native tongue, then slowly heaved himself aboard the truck. "It is true, then," he said.

D'Orsay had spoken in French, so Wardlow knew only he and maybe two or three others understood his words. Even through the lenses of the gas mask, the major's glance was accusatory.

"If it is," Wardlow said grimly, "I wasn't aware of it."

"You had no orders to cover this up?" the Frenchman demanded.

"No."

"Perhaps whoever is behind this thought these people would be gone by now. The LeCourbe family was frightened out of their minds when we showed up. They appeared to know nothing of the armed men camped in their vineyards."

Pulling himself into the cargo area of the truck, Wardlow knelt and traced his gloved fingers over the warnings painted onto the canisters, letting the physical realization sink into him while his mind struggled with it. "I've got to report this to my superiors," he said in a hoarse voice.

"As do I," D'Orsay replied. He fixed the NATO unit captain with his masked stare. "I suggest we leave members of both teams on guard here. As a show of mutual trust."

"Agreed."

"Captain."

Wardlow glanced at the rear of the truck. One of his corporals was standing there. "What is it?"

"One of those canisters, sir," the corporal said. "Hinkle found it outside, empty."

"Any casualties?"

"A few cows. Some chickens."

"Any evidence of what the cause was?"

"No, sir."

"Don't touch anything."

"Yes, sir."

"And make sure the rest of the team understands those orders apply to them, as well."

"Yes, sir." The man fired off a quick salute and jogged into motion.

"It would be best," Wardlow said as he swung his attention back to the major, "if this was handled quietly. If the press gets wind of this, we could have even more casualties. This area needs to be contained until whatever agent was released is neutralized."

"I agree," D'Orsay said as he stepped from the rear of the truck, "but it will be done by French biochemical teams."

Wardlow bit back a retort, remembering that he had suddenly gone from a NATO army captain to the ranking member of the U.S. Army representing an international incident implicating the United States of America in an act of possible subversion.

Once on the ground again, he called for the corporal carrying the communications gear and gave the order to radio the emergency control waiting to hear from them in Paris.

"Captain."

Wardlow glanced over his shoulder and saw Culpepper walking toward him. Blood gleamed on one of the sergeant's gloves. "Yeah?"

"We got a problem."

Stepping over to one side so they could have some privacy, Wardlow said, "I'm listening."

"That dead man back there wasn't alone. I found two guys in the other truck. All of them look to have been killed with the same-caliber weapon—a .45. I've seen enough wounds over the years to know the kind that weapon makes, and that's definitely a .45, not the little 9 mm popguns we're using over here. And the major's people aren't using anything heavier than 9 mms, either."

"Fuck." Wardlow didn't bother to chide himself for the slip. He maintained a professional image at all times, and cursing wasn't part of that image. "Were any of those men armed with .45s?"

"No, sir. My first thought, too. They carried nines, all three of them."

Meaning there had been a fourth group among the chaos scattered across the LeCourbe vineyards tonight. Wardlow settled the H&K MP-5 in the crook of his arm and turned to look at the French and American soldiers taking up guard positions around the two trucks.

"Could be this whole thing's a setup," Culpepper said.

Wardlow nodded. As a student of history, he knew of the impact past events had on the present, how it seemed that endless patterns cycled through the ebb and flow of human decisions, but never before had he really had the chance to stand in the middle of something that was going to be as historically significant as he felt the discovery of the Russian biochemicals here tonight would be. The only thing in his mind was how big of a disaster future historians would have to write about. And he wondered how many more people were going to have to die as a result of that discovery.

CHAPTER TWO

Department of Justice, Washington, D.C.
3:08 a.m.

Hal Brognola sat in his office in the Department of Justice watching CNN and waiting for the phone to ring. He felt tired, and a headache had already taken root between his temples hours ago when the first news of the Russian biochemicals discovered in France had been reported. It had promised to be a late night anyway, and he'd already called Helen to let her know he wouldn't be home for hours—if at all.

He sighed, tried to find a comfortable spot in his swivel chair, then gave up because they'd all been worn away years ago. Acid burned in his stomach.

Palming the remote control for the TV-VCR combo, he walked to the couch, where he tossed his jacket, and raided his pockets, coming up with a half-empty roll of antacid tablets. He popped two of them into his mouth and chewed, sat on the edge of the sofa and unlaced his shoes. Once they were loose enough, he pushed them off with his toes and flexed his feet.

The phone rang, drawing him to his feet instantly.

He fisted the receiver. "Brognola."

"You dropped a quarter in a few places," Mack Bolan said without preamble.

"It felt like the time to get in touch with a few old friends." Despite repeated efforts at sweeping his office for electronic surveillance devices, the big Fed was painfully aware that things did get through. And there was more than one covert agency jealous and curious about the power and attention Brognola seemed able to exert at times.

"Expecting some heavy farm work in the near future?" Bolan asked.

"I think so," Brognola replied. "No official word yet."

"Unofficially?"

"I'm drawing blanks."

"Interested in wines these days?"

Brognola wasn't surprised that his old friend was in tune with the situation. Bolan kept himself apprised of international and domestic situations at all times. The war books he kept in different places throughout the world would have provided staggering data bases for Intelligence communities if they could have gotten their hands on them. "There seems to be an interesting squeeze brewing over there these days."

"I agree. Before I got your call, I was thinking about calling myself to see if some kind of transport and a jacket could be arranged. I could get there on my own, but it would take a little longer."

"Captured your attention?"

"To say the least," Bolan said. "How much of what I'm hearing is true?"

"The merchandise was there."

"The real thing, or copycat?"

"Haven't heard either way for sure yet. I'm told the packaging is for real."

"Any ideas why it was there?" Bolan asked.

"A few. But we can't limit any of the options. The media is bringing out a few of them. Inquiring minds are pointing out the others."

"The alphabet people are interested, too?"

"Yeah. You couldn't turn sideways over there right now without bumping into some of them."

"Should make things even more dicey," Bolan said dryly. "Did this operation have the big bear's seal of approval?"

Brognola knew the soldier was asking if it was a Russian operation gone awry. "Not officially. Unofficially the Man has talked to the biggest bear and gotten a thumbs-down on the project. If it comes from them, he wasn't aware of it."

"How are relations over there these days?"

"Strained. Things keep trying to come apart at the seams. They're kept busy with patchwork."

"But can the Man count on what he's being told?"

Brognola hesitated. The President's current stance with the Russian president was good these days, and things seemed to be building toward an even more promising future between the United States and Russia. Although that should have been viewed as a relief to the rest of the world, the nations caught between the squeeze of the East and the West appeared to be more concerned than ever. And the economic foundations being shoved into place by Japan and a united Germany were quietly threatening, creating a greater chasm between the haves and have-nots.

"He believes he can be," the head Fed replied. "But as you and I both know, things over there can hardly be called stable. Big bear might be running into some domestic competition on this thing."

"True."

"When I get more," Brognola said, "I'll let you know."

"I'll hold you to that."

"Where are you going to be?"

"Around," Bolan said. "I like the feel of this city at night."

"You're local?"

"Extremely."

The answer took some of the knots of pain from Brognola's stomach. "I didn't expect that."

"Like I said, I was on my way in the back door. If you need me, call me." Bolan read off a number.

Brognola instantly memorized the digits, translated them by the simple code he and the Executioner had worked out for conversations over an open channel and recognized the real number as a mobile phone.

"See you when I see you," Bolan said.

"Soon," Brognola promised, and broke the connection. He set the phone back on the desk and turned to the TV and CNN. The anchors had slid through reports concerning South African unrest and Wall Street reaction to the confusion going on in France. Then it cut to a live broadcast from Paris. He lifted the remote control, cut the sound back on and walked toward the television.

"—going live soon to a speech given by Barnabe Siffre at the Paris city hall," the CNN anchor said as he touched the earphone at the side of his face. "Siffre had called this meeting to speak with his countrymen concerning the night's events, and our reporters on the scene don't expect he'll be supporting Russian and American sympathies."

A squared block of computer imaging flipped into place over the news anchor's left shoulder, blurring quickly into focus. The three-quarter-profile shot revealed a dark-haired man with silver staining his temples. His teeth were white against his deep Mediterranean tan and gleamed in a generous smile. Other photos cycled through the computer window, showing Siffre engaged in conversations in boardrooms, at building sites and at public schools. He looked equally at ease in three-piece suits and hard hats.

The camera blinked, filling the screen with a new anchorperson. This one was blond, petite and less relaxed than her peer. She stood in morning sun that unkindly showed the beginnings of dark bags under her eyes. She was dressed in a professionally cut blue business suit. "Thank you, John. Siffre is due to begin speaking in just a few moments inside city hall. My contacts suggest that he's here to begin the public outcry against what is believed to be a joint subterfuge by the United States military forces and Russian espionage units that has endangered French citizens."

Winking again, the camera shifted images, recreating the night before as French troops secured the outer perimeters of the LeCourbe vineyards against international reporters. There was a lot of confusion, hands waving, soldiers digging in their heels against the onslaught, with the broad white farmhouse sitting peacefully in the background as more soldiers in chemical protective gear moved around in bright tunnels created by klieg lights mounted in the backs of trucks.

Brognola had already seen this a half-dozen times. It didn't prove to be any more enlightening on this go-around. Just the same, his stomach rumbled threateningly.

"Siffre is a principal negotiator in the new Franco-German relations," the reporter said. "He's been involved in government talks between what were then three countries in 1986, and has since spearheaded the French interest in German industry and politics since the Berlin Wall fell in 1989."

Another picture took over the screen, this one showing a modern building in downtown France with the Eiffel Tower in the distant background.

"Barnabe Siffre has been likened to the United States' own Donald Trump. When new business, or the promise of new business, has presented itself to France, Siffre or his people have been there to bid or negotiate on it. But Siffre has one distinct difference, that being his war-hawkish mentality."

Footage rolled, showing a parade down one of the old streets in Paris. The avenue was narrow, flanked by tall buildings with sidewalk cafés and balconies. A handful of children carrying baskets of flowers scattered petals in front of a solid wall of men dressed in the Franco-German uniforms representing Europe's recent answer to NATO military bases. The men marched crisply, proudly, all smiles to an appreciative crowd.

"Barnabe Siffre and Siffre Industries has been instrumental in forming the Franco-German military and espionage arm linking the interests of the two countries," the reporter went on. "It's thought that he'll be using some of his influence in that organization to urge an immediate investigation of last night's mysteries."

Brognola didn't have any doubts of that. Franco-German units had been some of the first on the scene at the farmhouse, and they'd been very militant about American involvement there. The NATO team that had been in place at the vineyards had been impolitely given the bum's rush. Although the Franco-German espionage and military units were under the control of their respective governments, the head Fed had already ascertained that Barnabe Siffre's opinion counted a lot. Politicians owed him favors, and he had his thumb on the pulse of the emerging European economic bloc. For now, people across the European mainland, even the Eastern European satellites, were listening to what Siffre had to say. Brognola knew that even America was listening now.

The camera moved back onto the reporter. "We're taking you inside now, via the special hookup CNN has arranged with Paris news channels."

A brief footer ran across the bottom of the suddenly gray screen, identified the news channel cooperating with CNN in English and in French, then opened onto a large conference room filled with seated men and women. The camera played over the audience for just a moment, swept along the high walls, then closed in on the podium at the front of the room.

A collection of somber men stood talking among themselves, gesturing wildly. French policemen stood in the background with holstered side arms. It also became apparent to Brognola's trained eye that Siffre had bodyguards of his own. Hardmen in clothes cut extremely well hung in a loose perimeter around the French financier. The big Fed didn't doubt for a moment that some of the Franco-German militiamen had been recruited for the morning address.

Less than thirty seconds passed, then Siffre approached the podium. Flashbulbs sparked in increasing waves as he took his place behind the microphones. Silence drifted over the crowd. He tapped one of the microphones experimentally, and the hollow noise filled the large room. French and German flags hung behind his left shoulder, reflecting the solidarity his presence signified.

Siffre spoke in French. An interpreter lagged only a heartbeat behind on a voice-over. "Ladies and gentlemen of the press. I wish that we could have met this morning under more auspicious circumstances. But Europe has clasped wolves to her breast, and we need to speak of that."

The reporters were galvanized into action immediately, scribbling furiously.

"We stand," Siffre said imperiously, with a pause for effect, "on the threshold of a new world. Old thinking has fallen by the wayside for the most part. No longer does central Europe have to be caught in the middle of war games promoted by countries divided by an iron curtain. No longer do our children have to grow up in the shadow of nuclear arsenals well out of our control. Much of the influence of the superpowers has collapsed." He darted a look around his audience as if daring any to disagree with him.

Personally Brognola thought the man was laying it on a bit thick. There were any number of things out in the world that had yet to be resolved.

"Soviet Russia has fallen apart like an ill-made machine," Siffre said, "unable to afford the doctrine and dogma that drove her for almost eighty years. And the United States—self-proclaimed policeman to the world—is but a pale shadow of its former glories. People living within the U.S. are selling out, giving up on dreams for cash offered by foreign investors. How long will it be before other foreign powers start directing the moves made by America and the powerful army at her disposal?"

Unease touched Brognola. Siffre wasn't hesitating about pulling punches at all, going for all the vulnerable points.

"I don't worry about that question so much," Siffre went on. "That is only a question of 'when,' not 'if.' The question you should be concerned with as Europeans is, what will be left for Europe once this happens?"

French policemen had to tighten their ranks to keep the reporters at bay.

"The two once-superpowers are struggling to redefine their status in the world. Russia is starving from within. People of the United States have forgotten how to dream the American Dream. The governments of both these countries have legions of enemies within and without their borders ready to take advantage of their weaknesses and fears. I have to ask myself as a European, as the Europeans among you must ask, when will it be that the Russians and Americans reach out to us to try to seize the promise of an opportunistic future?" The French financier swept the crowd with a challenging gaze. "And make no mistakes, my countrymen, both of those nations will rip their needs from Europe as it becomes necessary."

Behind Siffre a large-screened television monitor was lowered into position and switched on. Color pictures of the Russian biochemical canisters filled the screen.

"We've heard much about *glasnost* these days," Siffre said, "about how the Russian bear and the American eagle are putting away their differences. But they are both predators. They've spent years warring against each other to perfect those skills. I ask you, what is a predator without prey?"

Brognola knew the still of the canisters was damning.

"I present to you an example." Siffre pointed at the large monitor. "Russian bacterial agents. From the reports I have received, these materials were liberated from the Ukraine by a joint force of American and Russian special forces, shipped through the Black Sea by submarine, through the Mediterranean Sea, and transported up through France for safe destruction with agents in Great Britain."

And that, Brognola knew, summed up what most of the people of the European community were paranoid about these days. Siffre had managed to unleash myriad fears in a relatively small number of words. He'd also managed to hit on an option of where the biochemical agents had come from that Brognola hadn't been privy to before.

"The continuing liberation of the Eastern European satellites is hurting Russia," Siffre went on. "Primarily economically now. With the dispersion of the nuclear and biochemical weapons, those satellites have managed to maintain their freedoms, but espionage sources I am close to indicate that the United States and Russia are working to take those weapons away from the satellite countries like the Ukraine.

"I see the Americans and Russians as being jealous of their lost influence in the workings of the world." Siffre leaned into the microphones now, face sad as if he were talking about the failings of a close friend. "And they're going to work to bolster each other to maintain their positions of power. I am told that there are U.S. Special Forces working with Russian espionage units to track down the biochemical weapons and nuclear arsenals out of Moscow's direct control, then remove them from the countries that possess them. Once they have them, the American and Russian teams are transporting them by the route I have described, across France, and to Great Britain, where they are being disposed of. From what I have been able to learn, this has been going on for at least fourteen months."

Brognola jotted down a short list of notes, basing questions on what Siffre said. If any operations like that were being undertaken by U.S. covert forces, he wasn't aware of it. But Aaron Kurtzman and Barbara Price at Stony Man Farm could start researching the possibility.

"At the LeCourbe vineyards last night," Siffre said, "joint forces of the French Foreign Legion and NATO soldiers discovered a shipment of biochemicals presumably on their way to Great Britain. This hasn't been confirmed, but it is believed to be true by ranking espionage officials."

Brognola knew those officials might well be within the ranks of the Franco-German forces that Siffre had so much influence with. It wasn't a lie, but it might not be the truth, either. But it was a powerful statement that hit all the fear buttons in the European community.

"Just as a drowning man will grasp at a straw," Siffre said as he reached up with one hand and clutched at an imaginary object, "I'm thinking that the United States and Russia will grasp at all of Europe to halt their economic backslide. Before they have that opportunity, I want to see France and Germany lead the way to shaking the shackles the superpowers would force us to wear and forge our own destinies."

More than half of the audience surged to its feet and started clapping thunderously. The roar of approval almost drowned out the echoes of the high-caliber rifle.

Brognola's trained ear noted them instantly, and he scanned the crowd.

The camera jostled, as if battered by the sea of people suddenly moving in fear, but the cameraman remained professional and locked onto his subject.

Three clusters of spiderwebs centered in midair over Siffre's face and upper body. It took Brognola a moment to realize the podium had been placed behind a sheet of bulletproof glass and that the rounds had been halted inches from Siffre.

A pair of guards were in motion at once, diving on the French financier and dragging him to the ground. Two more shots rang out, and the bulletproof glass webbed in another pair of spots. When the next shot sounded, it chopped out a fist-sized section of the glass and dropped a security man moving toward the cluster of people surrounding Siffre.

The cameraman worked with jerky professionalism, zoomed in even closer, made sure Siffre was okay, then whirled around dizzyingly as if remembering the financier was only half the story. The camera swept the walls as it searched for the sniper, trailing across the sea of pointing hands.

An excited voice-over by the American affiliate inside the meeting room began at once, restating the events of the past thirty or forty seconds.

Vertigo swirled around Brognola, but he was unsure if it was caused by what he'd just seen happen or by the wildly swinging camera. His attention was seized by the ringing phone. He scooped it up automatically, clasped it to his ear, muted the television and said, "Brognola."

"Are you watching?" There was no mistaking the voice.

Brognola stood a little more erect as he responded to the President of the United States. "Yes, sir."

"No matter who pulled that trigger," the Man said, "the U.S. and the Russians are going to be blamed."

"I'd say that's a good guess," Brognola replied, knowing it was more than a guess. It was a fact just awaiting confirmation.

"Put your people on alert, Hal," the President said. "There have been some things that have come to light that you need to know about. The French aren't going to sit still on this situation. And whoever is ultimately behind this isn't going to be easy to smoke out."

Brognola agreed.

"How soon can we meet?"

"I'm on my way now."

The President broke the connection.

The big Fed thumbed the cradle buttons, then punched in a number. He listened to the beeps in his ear as he shouldered the phone, sat on the couch and pulled on his shoes and laced them. The clicks signified the cutouts making the transmission untraceable. If his office phone was bugged, the guy working surveillance would track the call to Mei's Chinese Takeout, San Francisco.

The call was really answered at Stony Man Farm in Virginia by Barbara Price, Stony Man's mission controller. "Yes," she said.

"Me," Brognola stated, knowing she'd recognize his voice immediately. He stood, pulled on his coat and quickly reknotted his tie. "You've seen the news?"

"I'm still seeing it."

"We're on a yellow alert, pending assignment," Brognola said as he stepped toward his desk and took out the .38 snub-nosed revolver he kept there. He shoved it into a paddle holster, then slipped it into his waistband. "The teams?"

"Able is here," Price replied. "Phoenix is in Paris working the black market areas trying to get a lead on whoever helped ship those biochemicals in-country."

"Have you got anything solid on that?"

"No. But it seems to be the most logical place to start. Those chemicals aren't made in France, so someone had to bring them in. If the black market movers and shakers aren't involved, chances are they might know who is."

"I agree."

"So far," Price went on, "Katz has kept his team on a short tether, not wanting to muddy the waters over there. I'm thinking that with the hit that just went down against Barnabe Siffre, we could move a little harder and be covered by the general fallout."

"Do it. One other piece of good news—Striker's in town."

"Your side of town?"

"So he tells me."

"That's unexpected."

"Not really. He was already looking in that direction himself."

"Is he coming here?"

"Soon. We're supposed to meet first."

"Let me know."

"I will." Brognola rang off, punched in the mobile phone number Bolan had left and skated past the mobile operator.

The Executioner picked up on the first ring. "Yeah?"

"Things are in motion."

"So I've heard."

"It already has radio coverage?"

"Yeah. And I've got a television set keeping me company."

"The Farm's on yellow alert."

"We're going in on this?" Bolan asked.

"I'd say it's a safe bet. We'll meet, go down together."

"You have a place in mind?"

"How about the dead Frenchman's?" Brognola suggested, knowing Bolan would understand that he was talking about Lafayette Square behind the White House.

"It seems fitting."

"That's what I thought," the big Fed said. "And I have to make a short stop to see someone in the neighborhood first."

"When do we meet?"

"I'll have to call."

"Okay." Bolan broke the connection.

Satisfied that everything was put into the play that could be, Brognola left the office, locked the doors behind him and took the elevator down to the parking garage.

After a thorough inspection of his unmarked sedan, he rolled out of the garage and took Ninth Street north to Pennsylvania Avenue.

When he made the left-hand turn onto the thoroughfare, he made the first tail in the rearview mirror.

The car was an older Lincoln Continental, black and nondescript, built back when Detroit still used a lot of heavy metal in the machinery. It pulled onto his trail from Ninth Street, amber signal blinking a slow metronome. As it made the curve, the wall of lights from the waiting traffic on westbound Pennsylvania Avenue lit up at least four silhouettes inside the car.

Brognola freed the .38 from the paddle holster and tucked it into the crease between the passenger seat with the butt foremost. He opened the glove compartment, took out a carton of ammo and dumped the rounds in his jacket pocket. Before he could do more than start planning his next moves, a blocker car slid into position in front of him. The brake lights flared briefly in warning.

Cursing, the big Fed tapped his own brake pedal and slowed. A glance in his rearview mirror showed the tail closing the distance. Then he was aware of flanker action along the inside lane. Before he made the corner at Tenth Street, he was neatly boxed in.

His eyes swept the two new entries. At four heads apiece, at a conservative estimate, that bumped the ante to twelve guns. He berated himself for not having had backup with him. There were people in Washington, D.C., who had him pegged as the guy the President called when things had to be handled quietly and efficiently. And there was plenty of reason to believe that knowledge went beyond national boundaries.

He lifted the car phone, punched a number to Justice, then realized there was nothing but white sound coming from the earpiece. When he checked the two-way radio mounted under the dash, he found it had been tampered with, as well. Angrily he dropped the handset to the floor.

When he glanced over to the flanker car, he saw the window roll down.

A big man with a gunslinger mustache and an Uzi leaned out of the window and waved Brognola over to the curb.

The big Fed gave the man a grim smile. "No fucking way, pal." Then he applied his foot harder on the accelerator and got himself ready to make the play of his life.

CHAPTER THREE

"Are you all right, sir?"

Barnabe Siffre peered through his fingers and stared up at the security man's face only inches from his. His voice, when he answered, was more strained than he'd thought it would be, and it bothered him. "Yes."

"We're going to need to get you out of here," the security man said.

"Of course," Siffre replied, suddenly conscious of his heart hammering under the combined weight of the men he'd hired to take an assassin's bullet for him. He wondered if any of them had hesitated before moving to his rescue, made a mental note to check the news videos and the private tapes his people had shot for reticence on the part of any of the security personnel.

The security man pushed himself off Siffre. The financier noted the man's breath smelled of garlic, then absently brushed away the sparkling bits of bulletproof glass that clung to his clothing. More shone from the dark and curly locks of his would-be rescuer.

"Easy now," the security man advised. He held a 9 mm Beretta in a scarred fist. "We make these next few moves smooth and sure. If we hurry, we could be dead men."

"Okay." Siffre pushed himself into a crouched position on his feet. He glanced up at the bullets smashed into misshapen cones and suspended in the special glass shield that had been almost invisible to the human eye before the destruction that had marked it. Although he'd been prepared for the sight, had seen it himself in laboratories he owned, an unexpected shiver raced down his spine. The hole blown through high and to the left was as big as both his fists together.

Wondering where the stray round had gone, he glanced over his shoulder and saw another security man downed. Two other men were hurriedly stripping off his coat and shirt in an attempt to get to the wound. Siffre assumed they were going to try to staunch the bleeding, because it seemed rather excessive. He leaned forward, intending to get a look as the shirt ripped away. The wound would surely prove fatal.

"Sir."

Siffre looked up.

"The car is around back. Are you ready?"

The financier nodded.

The security man took charge, commanded three other men to cover Siffre, then took the lead through the back-stage area.

Walled by human flesh he'd bought and paid for, Siffre made his way toward the waiting car. Groans of pain attracted his attention to the stage area, and he turned in time to see other members of his security team physically repelling the more ambitious media people. One of them was thrown bodily back into the crowd as a warning to the others. Policemen surged forward, blowing their whistles furiously and waving their white-gloved hands.

Out of sight of the cameras, Siffre took the walkie-talkie from the lead guard's belt and keyed the transmit button. "Trudaine?"

"Yes, sir." The voice was crisp, professional.

"The assassin?" Siffre asked.

"Regretfully I must report that the man—or men—made their escape."

"That's too bad. One of my guards was killed."

"I'm aware of that."

"I want a story to hit the press by early this afternoon. Full bio. Good employee, good father, if he was. That sort of thing. The kind of person who will be grievously missed by Siffre Industries."

"Yes, sir."

"I want to see some roughs on that by the time we make the airport."

"Yes, sir. I took the liberty of already beginning such a project. I anticipated your decision. I trust that you're not offended."

"Not offended at all, Trudaine. That's what I pay you for."

"Yes, sir."

The morning sunlight when they entered the alley was harsh and gleamed against the silver-gray finish of the stretch limousine. Two of the security men sandwiched Siffre between them, kept him hunkered down, hands on his shoulders as they hurried him to the open door of the car. They tucked him inside, left him alone as he'd requested and jogged toward the cars waiting for them.

"Mr. Siffre?"

The financier looked forward, catching the chauffeur's eyes in the rearview mirror, almost colorless and flat behind the amber-tinted aviator glasses. "We wait. Just a few moments until everything is in place."

"You're taking chances, sir." The driver shrugged lightly, his corded muscles moving under the black livery. "If the guys who tried to whack you are carrying anything with antitank capabilities, they might get you. No disrespect intended, but you're paying me to do my job."

"Indeed, Victoir, and I trust your advice in that capacity. But today, in the face of my enemies, I want to make a show of strength, not run from the fight like a coward."

"Yes, sir." A crooked smile touched the chauffeur's thin lips. "I understand the gesture and compliment you for having the brass to make it."

Siffre gave the man his patented wink of disarmament. Victoir had been handpicked to fill the job he currently had, trained arduously, and further trained by the antikidnapping tactics perfected by the Italian chauffeurs for their wealthy employers. As far as the financier was concerned, there wasn't a better driver, nor one with more nerve in all of France. The chauffeur had learned his first hard lessons of life on the streets of Paris and had only been yanked up out of that existence after his path crossed that of Barnabe

Siffre. Victoir felt he owed his life to the man, and that was something the financier took great delight in knowing.

One of the security cars, bulletproofed and armor plated so that it rode low to the ground despite the special suspension, appeared in the mouth of the alley ahead of them.

Siffre sat forward on the edge of the seat, peered at the crowd as they noticed the security car and started surging for it. "Okay, Victoir, let's go."

The driver nodded, then leaned down briefly to lift up the SPAS-15 automatic shotgun from the sliding rack under the seat and slam it home into the retaining clips mounted on the dashboard for quick access.

The limousine accelerated smoothly, rolling forward between the lines of trash bins. Within seconds it was riding the bumper of the security car and cutting a swath through the crowd of media people and the curious. Newspaper reporters of both sexes banged on the windows of the limousine, pleading looks and anxious lights in their eyes.

A line of uniformed policemen materialized out of the crowd and started creating a break in the mass of people. There was a brief flurry of movement, then a male reporter with a microphone in his hand stepped in front of the limousine.

Victoir didn't hesitate, keeping his hands locked securely on the wheel, his foot level on the accelerator.

The reporter's eyes widened when he saw the big car wasn't going to stop as he'd expected.

Siffre permitted himself a slight smile at the journalist's sudden fear, certain that no one, including Victoir, would see it.

Human flesh smacked against the nose of the limousine. The reporter, frozen by his own fear, rolled the long length of the luxury car's hood, then spilled over the side.

Glancing back, Siffre saw two policemen step forward quickly and seize the reporter as he scrambled drunkenly to his feet. Sunlight gleamed on the bright metal skin of the handcuffs one of them brandished.

"Damn fool," Victoir commented quietly.

Siffre disagreed. The reporter displayed a certain tenacity for his job, or perhaps for his own measure of success, that few people had these days. It was a facet of the man that was certainly worth exploring, maybe even worth capitalizing on.

He leaned forward and lifted the receiver on one of the five telephones built into the spacious back of the limousine. He punched one digit, heard it quickly race through the number already programmed into its memory. "Trudaine?"

"Yes, sir."

"A reporter just assaulted my car."

"Yes, sir. Our men had him covered. If there had been any sign of a weapon, rest assured he would have been dead before he had the chance to use it."

"I never doubted that for a moment," Siffre said with a grin. "Find out who he is."

The sound of computer keys clacked over the connection. "I already know who he is, Mr. Siffre. A Mr. Didier Lobineau. He's with *Paris Drummer,* a weekly newsmagazine specializing in the lighter elements of the city. Movies, books, plays, that sort of thing. He's also been a stringer for *Rolling Stone* regarding French musicians."

"*Rolling Stone,*" Siffre repeated.

"Yes, sir."

"That definitely has possibilities." The financier rubbed his chin, took another look over his shoulder and saw Lobineau being hustled between the two policemen to a waiting car. "Arrange Mr. Lobineau's bail, Trudaine, and his medical needs if any. Have him cleaned up and at my table by eight o'clock tonight. I think I see a firebrand waiting the chance to spread the truth to the masses. If he's polishable, I want to see that he receives that chance."

"Eight o'clock should be no problem."

Siffre let the matter of the reporter slip from his mind. Trudaine was far better than any personalized notebook he might have carried. "Trudaine?"

"Sir?"

"You saw Lobineau rush the limo?"

"Of course."

"Where are you?"

A ghost of the man's smile sounded over the connection. "As always, Mr. Siffre, I'm just where you need me to be when you need me there. Is there anything else?"

"No."

"Then I'll see you on the plane."

Siffre hung up. Trudaine had his own methods for doing things. That was the reason Siffre had hired the man all those years ago. And now perhaps Trudaine allowed himself a few indulgences with that expertise he wielded so adroitly, but he was well worth the self-stroking he applied to his ego.

Checking his watch, Siffre found they were well within the time frame established for the exfiltration from the city. One of the phones rang. He answered it, flipped it over to speaker-phone function and arranged his clothing. It was a safe bet that at least part of the media would know about his private Learjet awaiting him at the airport. "Siffre."

"Barnabe," a well-modulated German voice said in heavily accented French, "you're alive."

"Yes."

"I'd heard that you were." Johann Gruber sounded pleased, one of the few times Siffre had actually detected emotion—other than anger and belligerence—in the man's words.

"You've been watching CNN again," Siffre admonished.

"Guilty. It is one of those Western luxuries that I find myself too weak to resist."

The German manufacturer had been trapped on the wrong side of the Berlin Wall for most of his life, but with the reunification of the Germanys in 1989, he'd pushed himself to the forefront of developing what had been the East German market. As a result, he was a very wealthy man, and he was one of the men Siffre desperately needed to hold the Franco-German bloc together to create a European solidarity. That need was great enough that Siffre made sure Gruber knew how to reach him at all times despite his usual operating procedures.

"Do you know who tried to assassinate you?" Gruber asked.

"No." He'd learned to lie with expert calm while still a child. "But our people are working on it. I expect them to know something in very short order."

"And if it is the Americans or the Russians?"

"Then we will retaliate," Siffre said without hesitation.

"Is that wise?"

"We've discussed this, Johann." The stretch limousine slid through the private gates of Orly Airport with only a heartbeat of slowed motion before the guard waved it on through. An airport security car immediately fell into the lead and took them around the concourse toward the waiting jet. "The United States and Russia are no longer what we've always believed them to be. They are failing countries. Both of them. Like drowning men, they will flail blindly to retain their positions, and they will pull down all within their reach. Europe has too long been at their mercies. We strike back now at each threat they bring to us just to let them know we can no longer be cowed. We must earn their respect, and if necessary, we will earn their fear."

"Those are harsh words, my friend."

"Only more sad because I fear these are only the beginning."

"Perhaps we can salvage the situation," Gruber said.

"Perhaps." But Siffre knew he wasn't even going to try, other than to give the effort lip service. Things were progressing nicely in the direction he'd intended. He said his goodbyes to Gruber as the limousine came to a smooth halt beside the silver Learjet painted with the Siffre Industries logo, a stylized Gothic silver *S* on a field of sky blue.

Bodyguards flanked him on both sides as he jogged up the carpeted steps leading into the belly of the jet. The whirling cherries of the airport security people and Parisian police warned everyone else away. Media people, some already in place and others just arriving, formed a semicircle around the jet's entry ramp some one hundred yards distant.

The copilot pulled the ramp closed and locked it. "When will you be ready to leave, Mr. Siffre?"

"Now." He adjusted his jacket and looked at the plush seats.

Trudaine sat in one of them, looking as bony as ever. He was pale, lantern-jawed and bespectacled, his blond hair so colorless it was almost white, unruly so that it stood out in a near Mohawk cut. Though in his midtwenties, his brow was already furrowed like a man much older by the intent fashion he stared at the laptop computer balanced like a newborn infant across his angular knees. The chambray work shirt and jeans bagged on his thin frame, and his feet, encased in cross trainers, looked incredibly long.

Taking a seat across from the computer expert, Siffre watched as Trudaine finished entering a list of commands on the computer keyboard.

The thin man gave a slight smile of satisfaction, then unhooked the mobile telephone from the laptop's add-on modem. Beside him the compact laser printer spit out a sheet of paper. Trudaine glanced at it for a moment, then handed it across.

Siffre accepted it and studied it briefly. A picture of the dead security guard as he'd been in life had been digitized in the upper left corner, showing a man proud to be in the Siffre Industries Security uniform. The picture in the lower right corner showed the man's crumpled form behind the podium as the two men worked to save his life. Between the two pictures were four columns of neatly spaced type that gave an overview of the man's career with Siffre and quotations from fellow employees who remained anonymous.

"I pulled the latest photo off the AP wire," Trudaine said. "The photographer is being sought for his permission to use it, and there should be no problem."

"If there is, there were plenty of photographers at the city hall. Someone will sell you the rights to their picture."

"Exactly."

"Good work," Siffre said. "It should evoke public sympathies for Siffre Industries and pave the way in forgiving the next steps we take. Run it."

Trudaine reconnected the mobile phone to the computer modem and started transmitting his information.

Watching the man in silence, Siffre studied his second-in-command. Of all his employees, Trudaine was the one he had the least information on, yet had managed to ingratiate himself into the position of highest trust. He'd been with Siffre for only six years, young enough at that time that there couldn't possibly have been any time for formal tutelage at university. Yet there was no one who knew cybernetic systems better than Trudaine. The young man had found his way into and out of espionage networks like a ghost, never touched and seldom seen. Having little in the way of hard data, Siffre had had to trust his instincts with the younger man. But it had largely been those instincts that had brought him this far in his plans. As long as he could trust Trudaine, he would. Any time after that, Trudaine would be a corpse just like anyone who crossed him. One comforting thought was that Trudaine was driven by passions of his own to succeed at Siffre's game, though the industrialist would have felt better if he'd known what they were.

The jet rolled forward, leaned into the acceleration and jumped lithely into the sky. As it leveled off, Siffre lifted the telephone mounted on the wall beside him, punched in a single digit and accepted the glass of champagne from the copilot while the phone rang at the other end.

Jacques D'Anton answered on the second ring. "Yes," he said in a neutral voice.

"Close out that account," Siffre stated, then hung up.

D'Anton was one of the captains of the Franco-German militia striving to take the place of the NATO units scattered across Europe. He'd been handpicked by Siffre and knew his place in the scheme of things. There would be no hesitation as he carried out his assigned strike.

"What about the American Justice Department agent?" Siffre asked Trudaine as the man closed the lid on the laptop. "This Harold Brognola."

"Provided your men are very good," the computer expert answered, "he should be dead or dying by now."

"They're good," Siffre said.

"So is Brognola," Trudaine pointed out. "The man has survived in his present capacities through two American presidents and a lot of American military action overseas, as well as some very complicated work in the espionage fields."

"What about his covert team?"

"From what I've been able to discover, they were put on yellow alert by the President only a few moments ago."

"Hardly enough time to be effective. They'll be days fielding units over here, or assembling the people they want to use from groups already here."

"They've got an international arm operating within Paris already," Trudaine said. "I just found out."

"Do you know who they are?"

"No."

"Or where?"

"They'll turn up. These people are more the smash-and-grab type, although they can work with finesse."

"Americans?"

"One of them. The rest are a mixed bag of threats. An Israeli with French roots, a Briton, a Cuban and a Canadian."

"A Frenchman, you say?"

"Jewish. He was raised in France."

"Maybe we can appeal to his sense of patriotism," Siffre pointed out.

"I don't think this man can be bought."

"If he's already switched allegiances from France to Israel, and is now working for the Americans, I'd say our chances look good."

Trudaine shrugged.

"When will you know about Brognola?"

"As soon as it's done."

"And this will destroy this agency he heads?"

"No. But it should delay them getting into motion. And whoever steps in to fill his shoes as liaison to the President will be highly profiled. Our American-based teams will have no problems taking that person down, as well."

"Good. Let me know when you get word."

Trudaine nodded, then turned his attention back to his computer.

Reaching over into the seat beside him, Siffre switched on the small color television set and watched the news coverage of the attempt on his life at the Paris city hall. He smiled as the camera panned in on the bullets frozen in the pane of bulletproof glass. It was definitely one of his better productions. But it had to be, because the stakes had certainly never been higher.

CHAPTER FOUR

Washington, D.C.
4:27 a.m.

Even though he was prepared for the collision and belted in,
as well, the impact of his sedan striking the rear bumper of
the blocker car made Hal Brognola think he'd been hit by a
three-hundred-pound linebacker. The seat belt made a line
of fire diagonally across his chest and knocked his breath
from his lungs. Grimly he hung on to the steering wheel,
cutting hard right when the intersection with Tenth Street
came up.

Rubber skidded and metal grated as the sedan twisted free
of the bigger blocking car. A shotgun boomed, and shards
of glass from the rear side window of the Justice car hurtled across the back seat. The Uzi he'd seen earlier chimed
in a heartbeat later, knocking holes in the metal bodywork
of the head Fed's vehicle.

He twisted the steering wheel violently, shook free of his
attackers for just a moment, then noticed the set of oncoming headlights swinging in his direction from the other side
of Tenth Street. A muzzle-flash seared a white-hot yellow
cone from the driver's side of the approaching vehicle. A
bullet tore through the windshield on the passenger side of
Brognola's car, then ripped into the seat.

Brognola jerked the wheel again. The front end of the
sedan cut too sharply, jerked over the curb, then came down
with a jarring bounce. He knew someone had cut his front
tires out from under him. More bullets sparked off the
quarter panels, leaving long scars in the metal.

His mind worked furiously, going over his options. There
was no doubt the team had been waiting for him. Whatever
ties they'd discovered between him and possible U.S. retal-

iation for the events unfolding in France had obviously been enough to move him up near the top of someone's list.

He floored the accelerator and felt the steering turn into a jarring struggle. Glancing in his rearview mirror, he saw the two cars that had been beside and behind him cut across the traffic and begin pursuit along Tenth Street. The car he'd rammed had applied its brakes, then backed into a position where it could circle around, taking briefly to the sidewalk on the wrong side of the street as it came after him. The remaining car that had attacked him from Tenth Street itself had crashed into another vehicle in its attempt to come around too quickly and was only now freeing itself from the wreck.

The J. Edgar Hoover Building was tantalizingly close, but he knew he'd never make the distance on foot. With the way the sedan was shimmying as he pushed it hard, he realized he wouldn't be much better off than on foot for long. He glanced at the .38, making sure it was still there. The butt poked from between the seats as token security, but it was a grim reminder that he was definitely outclassed.

The sedan sagged as bullets took out the right rear tire.

Brognola fought the wheel as the car fishtailed and lurched across the center line. Horns blared as drivers of oncoming traffic dodged and signaled their anger. He pulled it back onto his side of the road with difficulty.

Ford's Theatre came into view at the intersection of Tenth Street and E Street. The head Fed was already acknowledging his chances of disappearing into the building when the sedan's engine died. He slipped the transmission into neutral, taking advantage of the movement left in the vehicle before abandoning it. He checked the rearview mirror as he curled a fist around the .38.

One of the pursuit cars came up fast on the left, rushing out into the intersection against the light. A handful of cars were frozen in the cross lanes, waiting their turn to zip across. Behind the other three Lincolns, a low-slung sports car blazed forward in a zigzag pattern that took it through the line of cars in the oncoming lane. Horns blared and brake lights flared as puzzled drivers were treated to a new threat.

Cutting his wheels toward the curb before Ford's Theatre, Brognola ducked instinctively as the attack car came up beside him. Bullets ripped across the driver's side of the sedan, smashing through the windows and showering cubes of safety glass over the head Fed.

Rubber shrilled out on the street as the echoing blasts of autofire faded against the surrounding buildings.

Brognola pushed himself up, found the emergency release on the seat belt with his free hand and dropped the .38 into target acquisition on the attack car as it spun around in the street. Vehicles that had been waiting to cross were now backing away, retreating the way they had come. The big Fed was waiting for the friendly sound of an approaching police siren, but heard none.

The lead attack car swung around like a bird dog on point.

Brognola dropped the hammer on the .38, kept it on target and put all five rounds through the windshield on the driver's side.

The Lincoln started to creep forward aimlessly, then rocked to a jerky stop. Figures moved on the other side of the glass as doors flew open.

Cracking open the cylinder of the .38, Brognola dumped the empty shells into the floorboard, then craned his neck around to look at the rear guard.

The three attack cars skidded to stops in a semicircle.

Brognola finished loading the pistol by feel, slammed the cylinder closed and reached for the passenger-door release. It clicked, but he had to slam a shoulder into it to get it free.

He stared at the dark glass framing the theater's windows. The lower level contained a museum with items that had once belonged to Abraham Lincoln and John Wilkes Booth. Above it was the 700-plus-seat theater where Lincoln had been shot. He knew it didn't provide much in the way of cover, and it was already a proved ground for assassins.

He swept the neighborhood as his attackers gathered. Across the street was the Petersen house where the dying President had been taken. The immediate environs were shabby compared to most of downtown Washington, D.C., and it wasn't an area of the city where the dwellers were likely to lend a hand even if they could.

He scrambled across the seat and got to his feet at the side of the car. Snap-firing a round at the window of Ford's Theatre, he kept his head low and watched as his attackers went to ground.

The window smashed, then the strident shrills of a burglar alarm filled the night. It took only seconds for the attackers to realize he hadn't fired at them at all. He gripped the .38 in both hands in a kneeling Weaver's stance and hoped the local precinct would react to the alarm when it reached the security network.

Just as the first few bullets started chipping away at the sedan and made Brognola realize he had no hope of holding his present position, the low-slung sports car he'd noticed earlier came roaring into view.

It was a black Corvette, totally unmarked except by a mobile phone antenna jutting from the rear fender. Smoketinted windshields kept the interior from view. The driver rocketed across the intersection, then tapped the brake and turned the sleek vehicle into a snarling monster. It came around sideways, slamming the tail end into the stalled Lincoln Brognola had initially targeted.

The fiberglass body of the Corvette gave way instantly to the heavier car, the taillights scattering in broken pieces as the bulbs died. Still, there was enough weight and force behind the sports car to push the Lincoln several feet. The move caught the gunners in that vehicle by surprise as they stood behind the doors taking cover. All of them were knocked down and away as the big car rolled backward.

The Corvette rocked to a stop facing the other three cars. As if a continuation of the motion already in progress, the driver's-side door opened and a man stepped out. He was dressed in black and wore a duster that hung to midcalf.

Brognola had an impression of a wry grin on the man's grim features, saw the spark in the ice blue eyes that glinted as hard as gun sights. The man moved with an economy of motion, lifting a long tube from under the folds of the duster and placing it across his shoulder as he stood behind the Corvette's open door.

For the first time since the pursuit had begun, Brognola felt hope come alive inside him. He stood straighter beside his wrecked sedan and took a firmer grip on the .38. He could imagine the surprise and puzzlement racing through the minds of his foes as they wondered who the new arrival was.

Then the tube belched flame. A heartbeat later the middle pursuit car exploded, blowing apart like a defective Tinkertoy, chased by sheets of bright fire. Men in the immediate vicinity were killed instantly. Others were knocked down or took cover.

Brognola had seen the calling card before. There was no mistaking the Executioner's handiwork. And once introduced to it—as the hitters tonight were about to discover—a person never forgot the experience.

MAC BOLAN DROPPED the empty LAW to the street. The antitank weapon had performed its job and couldn't be traced back to him. The rumbling roar of the 95 mm grenade's detonation bounced around the buildings. The hardmen would be disoriented long enough for him to turn the tables on the battlefield for a few precious moments.

He was dressed in a combat blacksuit and wore a Kevlar vest, which he'd slipped on when he saw Brognola being tailed from the Justice Building. The duster had been pulled on to cover the rest of his personal armament from casual inspection. The .44 Magnum Desert Eagle rode his right hip, while the 9 mm Beretta 93-R was snugged into shoulder leather. Two smoke grenades were clipped to his combat harness, while military webbing held extra magazines for both pistols. A Cold Steel Tanto knife was in a sheath on the combat rig opposite the Beretta.

The gunners who'd survived the blast were starting to become mobile.

While they were still hesitant, he jerked the smokers free of his harness, pulled the pins and tossed the bombs at the two cars. The grenades hit the street in front of the vehicles with an unmistakable metallic clang.

At least two people called out warnings, and the group scattered for cover again. The grenades popped loudly and spun in circles on the smooth concrete as they spewed out their contents. A dark, black cloud gathered, thick enough to blot out the yellow-and-orange flames clinging to the battered frame of the middle car.

The Executioner raked the Desert Eagle from his hip, hearing the sound of hurried movement coming from behind him.

"Striker!" Brognola yelled out in warning.

Bolan whirled. That his friend was able to call a warning took away the thought that he'd arrived too late. The hardteam had slid into position faster than he'd believed they would and had inadvertently blocked him out of the action without even knowing he was there.

The warrior raised the heavy length of the big .44 automatic and fired from the point. His first three 240-grain rounds slammed into his target's upper chest, knocking the man from his feet and sending him sliding lifelessly backward.

Two men remained standing, crouched over their weapons as they faced him.

Bolan shifted to the man on the left when he recognized the Uzi in the guy's hands as a greater threat than the 9 mm held by the other man.

The Uzi spit a line of bullets that skimmed the top of the Corvette. At least two impacted against the Executioner's Kevlar vest with punishing force.

Without losing his focus, the warrior triggered two rounds that zipped into the man's face and sent his corpse sprawling.

The surviving gunner of the team fired on single-shot as fast as the slide would move, but his bullets never touched Bolan.

Swinging the big .44 into target acquisition, Bolan fired a single round that caught the man in the center of his chest.

Hammered by the force of the 240-grain bullet, the hardman staggered backward, caught his balance as he dropped his weapon and covered his chest with both arms. He fell to his knees, then tumbled forward.

Bolan leathered the Desert Eagle, unlimbered the Beretta 93-R and flicked it to triburst. Shadows drifted out of the coiling strands of smoke. He targeted them, put some of them down and chased others away. He looked at Brognola, saw the head Fed firing judiciously into the group of attackers and heard the flat crack of the .38 Special rounds as they were touched off. He raised his voice, yelled, "Hal!"

Brognola looked at him.

"Come across."

The Justice man nodded, paused long enough to thumb fresh cartridges into his revolver, then came around the wrecked sedan and threw himself into a dead run.

Bolan ran through the rest of the Beretta's clip, providing covering fire. The pistol blew back empty with Brognola's hand on the passenger door. The warrior freed the clip, dropped the empty into a pocket of the duster and slid the fresh one home. Then he climbed into the bucket seat behind the steering wheel.

He leathered the Beretta, shifted into first gear, put his foot down on the accelerator and slipped the clutch. The Corvette's high-performance engine twisted the drive shaft, and the tires dug into the street. Bolan cut the wheel hard, and the rear end floated around in a tight turn. The sound of tortured rubber overrode the scattered banging of pistols and autofire. None of the bullets touched the car. He headed north on Tenth Street and blew by the F Street intersection on a yellow light.

"Where?" Bolan asked.

"We've still got a meet," Brognola replied, gazing through the Corvette's back glass.

"If we drive up in this in the condition it's in, we're going to attract some attention."

"We're going to attract attention, anyway," the head Fed replied. "You go on in. Tonight, after this, I've got an umbrella big enough to carry you, too. I've got a feeling the Man's going to be writing a blank check on this operation."

Bolan checked the rear and side mirrors. Only one of the cars had managed to fall into pursuit, but it was blocked by the cross traffic.

Brognola punched in a number on the mobile phone, then slipped his pistol into the paddle holster at his waist.

"Washington, D.C., Police Department," a confident male voice answered. "How can I help you?"

"Hal Brognola. I'm with the Justice Department."

"Yes, sir." The guy was obviously underimpressed.

"The trouble down by Ford's Theatre," Brognola said, "that's me. I'm going to be fielding a team into that area and I want them to handle the investigation."

"I don't know," the cop said. "We've already got units rolling on that."

"You keep them back out of the way."

"You'll need to talk to the watch commander about that." A surly tone had crept into the voice now.

"Find him," Brognola said in a harsh voice, "and find him damn quick. He's liable to be one pissed-off son of a bitch when he finds out you were the reason for his demotion."

"Yes, sir."

"And when you find him in the next five minutes before it's too damn late to get a handle on this thing, have him call me at—" Brognola looked at Bolan.

The warrior gave him the mobile phone's number, then made the left-hand turn onto H Street without spotting signs of the pursuit car.

Brognola relayed the number, then broke the connection. He punched in another number. A sleepy voice answered at the other end. "Craig?"

"Yeah," the man replied. There was a beat, and the voice sounded like dominoes clicking into place. "Hal?"

"Right. Get up, guy. You got things to do." In terse sentences, he described the situation that had just gone down, leaving Bolan's name out of the report.

"Are you okay?" the Justice agent asked. The noise in the background let Bolan know the guy was getting dressed as he listened and talked.

"I'm fine," Brognola replied. "You just get hold of the situation down there and don't let anyone else screw it up. Whatever information we can recover from that scene, I need. I'm going straight to the Man with this one."

"Understood. You'll have it as soon as I do."

"Get Robeson, Gibson, and Stockbridge to cover the forensic stuff. I want prints made immediately of everyone you find there. Run them through NCIC and get back to me soonest. I want the information downloaded into the Justice computers, filed under whatever password you choose, as long as I know what it is. You'll have FBI types there, too, since the J. Edgar Hoover Building is close to the scene. Keep them brushed back. This isn't going to be a domestic issue, and I don't want them peeking over my shoulder while I'm trying to work."

"I'm on my way."

Brognola broke the connection.

Bolan coasted along the northern boundary of Lafayette Square, stared at the lighted front of the nation's capital and made the left-hand turn on West Executive Avenue. He kept to the outside lane, watched the traffic moving in his wake, but didn't see anything of pursuit. He used the pause at the light to shove a fresh magazine into the Desert Eagle.

Brognola dumped out two empty shells of his own, scanned the side mirror and twisted his head around to look out the back glass. He thumbed in new rounds and kept the pistol in his fist.

"Are we going in the back way?" Bolan asked as he crept over into the left lane.

"Yeah," Brognola replied. "Soon as I make a call." He reached for the mobile phone. "When things start happening this soon, I have to wonder what else is going to get dropped onto the field before we make it out of the huddle."

Bolan nodded. He knew the feeling. And from the way things were shaping up, it was promising to be a hell of a ride.

CHAPTER FIVE

Stony Man Farm, Virginia
4:10 a.m.

Aaron Kurtzman blinked his eyes tiredly at the computer monitors arranged neatly before him on the horseshoe-shaped desk.

He tapped the computer keyboard and sealed off the window he'd been examining. Obediently the multicolored rectangle snapped closed, corkscrewed into a black dot and disappeared. When he lifted his coffee mug, he found it was empty.

Setting the mug in his lap, he unlocked the brakes of his wheelchair and coasted backward down the ramp that led to the desk. At the bottom he locked one wheel, expertly made a one-hundred-eighty-degree swing and powered over to the coffeemaker perched on a long table against the wall.

He poured himself a cup of coffee that had remained in the pot long enough to get thick and black, a consistency that no one on the Farm seemed to appreciate but himself. Then he reached for the pastry dish. With one big hand, he scooped up an apple-and-lemon danish and two cookies.

Swiveling back around, he surveyed the room and the work in progress and tried to let his mind relax for just a moment. So much of what he did required ultimate concentration. Often he didn't know how truly tired he was until he took a break. He inhaled the danish, hardly tasting it at all, and took his time with the cookies.

The Farm's computer lab resembled something from a futuristic world depicted in a science-fiction movie. Below the raised dais of his own desk were three other workstations, facing the outer walls. An impressive array of computer hardware was neatly arranged at each station, and

monitor screens fanned out around them. The walls were
covered by floor-to-ceiling screens that traveled the hori-
zontal length of the walls, as well, reflecting different scenes
from the work done at each station.

Carmen Delahunt occupied the first desk. She was red-
headed and compact, old-line FBI whom Kurtzman had
liberated from Quantico under the noses of her superiors.
At present she was working with news footage coming out
of France, compiling a data base of every face that had been
in every scene since the opening shots at the LeCourbe
vineyards.

Next up was Akira Tokaido. The young man had a steel-
trap mind capable of off-the-wall thinking and wild what-
ifs. He sported a Mohawk haircut and wore a sleeveless
neon pink Red Hot Chili Peppers concert sweatshirt and
winter-styled camo pants. A portable CD player jutted out
of one of the thigh pockets of the pants, and a thin wire
snaked into an earphone on one side of his head. His head
bobbed slightly as he listened to the thrash metal music, and
his jaws moved as he worked the wad of bubble gum he ha-
bitually chewed. The wall screen in front of him was filled
with the dead faces of the supposed Russian and American
soldiers who'd been gunned down in the vineyards. Many of
them had already been identified, and the clues provided by
those confirmations were leading in puzzling directions. But
they were damning ones, as well. Some of those men had
once been American soldiers and Russian agents, just as the
rumors had indicated.

Seated at the third workstation, Huntington Wethers still
looked like the Berkeley cybernetics professor he'd been a
handful of years earlier. He was lean and black, hair carefully styled and gleaming, and wore a dress jacket and tie.
An empty pipe was clamped between his teeth, and he sat
erect as his hands teased information from various sources
available to the Stony Man computers. His wall screen
showed digitized representations of the chemical makeup of
the biological agents taken out of the LeCourbe vineyards.
So far, no one had identified what it was. Wethers had
voiced the opinion that it was some kind of agent geared to
infect plant life, based on his own observations. That line of

thinking had been echoed by botanists Hunt Wethers knew, and some of them—like him—had enjoyed Defense Department clearances that made them privy to a number of State secrets and research still on the drawing board. But no one Wethers had talked to so far knew for sure what the agent was or what it was supposed to do.

The phone at Wethers's side rang. He answered it quickly, shouldered it to his ear for a moment, then shoved it into the modem. A heartbeat later new information surged across the wall screen and the central monitor.

"Now, that's a look of bewilderment if I've ever seen one."

Kurtzman glanced up at the speaker, a smile already twisting his lips.

Barbara Price was a honey blonde with big eyes that a man could lose himself in. She was lean and athletic, and had a face that national magazines had once paid for the privilege of plastering across their covers. But her stint as a model had been only to help her pay the university tuition bills that the scholarships hadn't covered.

Kurtzman never knew what Price's major had been. He'd never seen her file. She'd been recruited by Brognola through the head Fed's own sources to become the Farm's mission controller, and the big computer wizard made it a point never to sift through personal data on his friends and co-workers unless it became a necessity.

"At least," Kurtzman observed, "I know I'm not the only one around here who looks like death warmed over."

"You're bad," Price said with a smile. She bent over the ice bins, retrieved a can of orange juice, took an oatmeal muffin from the pastry dish and removed a foam cup from the stack beside the coffeemaker.

"Did you get Able Team off?" Kurtzman asked.

"An hour ago."

He looked at his wristwatch, amazed to see the time. "Has it been that long?"

"Yes. I've been on the phone working out a Justice Department cover for them while they're in Washington, D.C., looking for the mercenary connection you turned up."

"Nation's capital could be crowded damn quick," Kurtzman commented.

Price raised an arched eyebrow.

"You said Striker's already inside the city."

She nodded.

"Sounds to me like a powder keg just waiting for a match. And Ironman's not too shy about lighting them."

"I know. He worked out his own liaison with a homicide detective who's crossed Able's trail before."

"And the guy was still willing to sponsor them?"

She gave him a wry grin.

It was a joke and they both knew it. In order to fight hard, the teams—as well as their support system—had to play hard, as well. But Carl "Ironman" Lyons had a history of taking the bull by the horns no matter how much damage it caused to the area around the combatants.

"Brave soul," Price said.

"Either that or he has a death wish."

Price sipped the orange juice. "So why the bewildered look?"

"Got a new wrinkle in developments." Kurtzman refilled his coffee mug, propelled himself toward the horseshoe-shaped desk, then tugged the keyboard into easy reach again. "During the last few months, there have been three attempts to breach the security of the computer systems here."

"You'd told me about that," Price said as she studied the computer monitor with serious intent. "But you also said you were certain whoever it was hadn't made their way into our files."

"I'm still sure the security's intact." Kurtzman tapped out commands on the keyboard. "However, I keep the access codes changing on a rotating basis, and I've programmed some fail-safes into the software that shouldn't allow alien programming to immigrate into our data bases. Let me review the files for you." He finished the commands to initiate the files he'd lined up for inspection. "It's code-named Jester. You'll see why."

A window exploded onto the center screen, filled with brightly colored spots that coalesced into the figure of a man wearing a single-piece suit made up of red-and-white diamonds. The figure was poised on one foot, raised to its toes like a ballet dancer. The shoes curled up on the ends, with a bell sewed to the exaggerated toes. A cowl closed in tightly around the head, still carrying out the red-and-white diamond-patterned motif. The arms were outflung to its sides, empty palms turned upward. The side of the face presented in profile was covered in white greasepaint, the sparkling eye outlined in black mascara, the cruelly smiling thin lips painted bloodred. A row of odd-shaped cones jutted out across the head.

"A clown," Price said.

"A king's jester," Kurtzman corrected. "As close as I can figure it, that representation's from the court of Louis XIV, judging from the clothes and the makeup. I did a lot of research after the first encounter with this guy. The white patches clowns paint over their eyes and nose originated back in eighth century, B.C., in China. There was a governor named Bo Bi who used his power and position to take advantage of everyone he could for money." He resettled himself in the wheelchair and sipped more coffee. "A lot of clowns today copyright their faces, so a lot of work goes into creating a clown's stage identity. Even back when copyright infringement hadn't even been thought of, clowns were particular about their style and their faces. I traced this look back to the palace at Versailles."

"So we've got a French connection?"

"So to speak."

"That wasn't intended as a pun," Price said as she folded her arms across her breasts and studied the garish caricature.

"I know." Kurtzman tapped a series of keys. "But it is true. And it gives me more of a direction to look in now that this thing has started over there."

The jester went into motion, turning to face his audience. The face was unmistakably male, bisected by a green line that never failed to make Kurtzman think of witch's skin. While the right hemisphere was white, the left was ebony. White liner covered the eyelid and made the gaze harsh and sadistic. A crazed smile twisted the bloody lips. It froze again in midwhirl.

"You said it always brought a warning," Price said.

"Yeah." Kurtzman allowed the program to run.

The clown went into motion, drawing in its arms and whirling madly. Kurtzman had often thought it looked like a Tasmanian devil. Without warning, the jester stopped, left hand pressed tightly to its chest while the other hand was thrust out clasping a bouquet of purple-veined white flowers.

"Fleurs-de-lis," Kurtzman supplied.

"Another tie to France."

"Yep." Kurtzman froze the clown again, its pose this time coming close to something very sinister. "It's thought to have been used by Charlemagne as a heraldic design. It was used from the latter part of the eleventh century on in the coat of arms of the French kings, and was appropriated for a short time by England's Edward III when he claimed the French throne."

"That lasted until the French Revolution."

"Pretty much," Kurtzman agreed.

Price's eyes narrowed. "Somebody's using this as their calling card."

"I'd say so, and they've been knocking at our door for some time."

"When did the first transmission reach you?" Price asked. "I'm trying to refresh my memory."

"Two and a half months ago."

"And this is it?"

"Yeah." Kurtzman hit the keyboard again and let the programming run through its course.

The garishly colored court jester spun again, a whirl of color.

When he came out of his mad pirouette, the flowers had gone, and in their place was an impossibly long-barreled pistol. Somehow he managed to twirl it around his finger, his bloody smile baring yellowed fangs. The weapon's muzzle came to a rest pointing out at the front of the screen, then became a tunnel so big it took up over half of the space.

Above the muzzle, the hammer dropped toward the firing pin.

Lightning sizzled in the pistol barrel, and a loud explosion crackled from the monitor speaker.

Price involuntarily flinched.

Smoke filled the screen. When it cleared, the jester stood there with the pistol hanging at his side. A word balloon floated up over the pointed cones of his cowl. "Bang! You're dead!" It laughed, silent and mocking, then reached behind itself and grabbed a handful of its cowl. A black hole irised open behind the jester. With a powerful tug, it yanked itself into the black hole and disappeared. The last thing to go were the curling shoes with the bells.

"You've got no idea where this came from?" Price asked.

"Only the things I've pointed out to you," Kurtzman replied. "Nothing concrete in the way of tracing the programming. Whoever's seeding it into our cybernetics systems is aiming the transmissions at us and popping them across in bursts."

"What do the others look like?"

Kurtzman ran through the other two in the file. The second one showed the jester again, this time carrying an umbrella as it crossed a high wire between buildings. It toppled from the wire in an exaggerated burst of motion that made the jester look as if it had at least nine arms flailing for its balance. It tumbled, scratching at the air for purchase. A long word balloon trailed from its lips. "Help me! I've fallen and I can't get up!" Then it unfurled the umbrella, and the fall stopped. It soared toward a full yellow moon that had a face and winked at him. A small word balloon popped from the jester's evil grin. "Not!" A footer trailed under the graphics display. "You couldn't catch a cold, *mon ami*. I'll live to piss on your grave."

"Whoever it is deliberately used French that time," Price said.

"I know. The guy's good, but he's a gamer. He's addicted to the thrill of possibly getting caught. In the end that's going to cause him problems." Kurtzman set the third installment into motion.

It opened on the jester hunkering in front of a door guarded by thick electronic locks and surveillance devices. Obviously it was protecting something of monumental importance. Top Secret was stamped across the steel surface. The jester turned toward the screen, gave a full frontal smile and pointed at the keyhole he'd been peering through. The view was pulled in as if sucked through the keyhole. The monitor blinked. When it refocused, the keyhole was the only thing visible. Then the jester's white-rimmed eyeball in the center of its black face moved into view, glowing malevolently. A header rapidly printed itself in blazing keystrokes across the top of the screen. "I know who you are. I know what you do. Now you're going to die."

"Have you tried a retina print?" Price asked.

Kurtzman was impressed. Even though she'd been briefed on the transmissions, she'd never seen them. And he could still feel how disconcerted he'd been. It had taken him most of half an hour to think of a retina scan. Price had thought of it instantly. "Already been done," he said softly, staring at the beady gaze frozen on the screen. "That eyeball you're looking at belongs to the President of the United States of America."

"Funny guy," Price commented.

"If it is a guy," Kurtzman pointed out. "All we know so far is that it's a very gifted hacker of some sort. There's no real connection between this person and the events that are going on over in France now."

"But you think there is a connection?"

"Oh, yeah." Kurtzman played the keyboard again. "This came in only a few minutes ago, which is why I asked you to come by when you had a second."

The monitor scene changed again, focusing on the interior of a car. A familiar-looking man sat behind the wheel as it drove toward the viewer. The background was dark with night, obviously animated in a cartoonish cityscape of buildings.

"That's Hal," Price said in a hoarse whisper.

"Yeah."

An arm covered in the familiar red-and-white-diamond pattern flopped casually over the seat from the back. The cartoon-Hal didn't notice, keeping his eyes on the road. Then the jester's coned head popped up behind the cartoon-Hal and grinned. A straight-edged razor flipped open in his other hand. Reaching forward, the deadly clown gripped the cartoon-Hal under his chin and pulled his head back, baring his throat. Then the blade winked and flashed across its victim's neck. A gaping, obscene second mouth appeared, vomiting blood violently.

Cartoon-Hal's eyes rolled up in his head, and he turned a ghostly white. The jester pushed the body away and shoved himself toward the windshield, skewing his face into impossible dimensions. None of the makeup smeared. Word balloons surfaced like dead fish floating to the top of a lake. "Brognola's dead," the first one read. "And you're next."

The scene ended and disappeared with an audible pop.

Kurtzman looked at Price, her face set in grim, hard lines. "I was thinking we should let Hal know they had his name."

Price shook her head. "A team already made a try for him tonight."

"And?" Kurtzman's heart sped up.

"They missed. Striker was on hand for the fireworks. Hal's fine. He's also got a Justice team on-site at Ford's Theatre picking up the pieces. Once they get the data collated that we can use, we're supposed to be able to access it from Justice Department files. Password Protean."

"Hal must be brushing off his Latin," Kurtzman commented. "Protean" referred to something that readily took on different shapes and forms, which was exactly the situation going on over in France.

"Maybe. But it fits." Price turned her gaze to the big computer wizard. "Back to the clown."

"Okay."

"You say he's a gamer."

"Yeah. He fits the profile of a lot of self-taught hackers I've met. Akira agrees. Assuming there's some organization behind what we're seeing coming out of France these past couple of days, I'd say the jester is somewhere near the top, but he isn't calling the shots. That's not his style. Maybe he's even at the head of their cybernetic Intelligence network, somewhere so that he doesn't have to fear reprisals if he's caught baiting us. It's possible whomever he's working for can't catch him, or it's possible that he's clever enough he figures no one will ever know. Either way, he's drawn to the game he's designed for himself."

"An ego trip?"

"Yeah," Kurtzman scratched his chin. "Hackers I know, they like the attention of their peers. When the phone-phreaking started in the computer groups, the only way Ma Bell and her enforcement arm was able to find those guys was because they started bragging to their friends, who in turn started telling other friends. And once you tell a secret to one other person—"

"It's no longer a secret."

"Right. I think our clown is pulling a scam under the noses of his employers. He's been hired to ferret out any espionage forces they might run into, and he's probably been paid damn well for his time and trouble, but he wants more out of it than that."

"He wants the game."

Kurtzman nodded. "He—or she—wants the game. If he or she just wanted to pull down the big bucks and be a good little employee, there are plenty of research centers and businesses out there looking for those kinds of people." He worked the keyboard, bringing up the Protean file from the Justice computers.

"Can you find this guy?" Price asked.

"I think so." Kurtzman glanced at the names on the monitor, swiveled forward the mouthpiece to his ear-throat apparatus and keyed the headset. "Carmen."

Delahunt looked over her shoulder at him, tapping her own headset. "Yes?"

"I've got a batch file coming at you," Kurtzman said. "Mix it in with what you've already put together and let's see what comes out."

"Okay." Her hands got busy on her keyboard, and the wall screen changed, becoming a reflection of the information contained on Kurtzman's central monitor.

"I'll work on the clown as the opportunities arise," Kurtzman told Price. "I can't guarantee anything, but I might be able to get some leverage there."

"That's all I'm asking for, big guy."

Kurtzman opened other windows on his screen and started to archive the information being gleaned from the Justice Department files. He thought about the personality at the other end of the clown's appearances. The guy was cocky, yeah, and sure of himself, but the golden rule in any kind of con game was that even the players could be played. However, part of Kurtzman's mind had to wonder if that facet hadn't been planned on, as well.

"If they know about Hal," Price said, "we have to assume they know about Phoenix Force and Able Team."

"I know. Makes you wonder how far wrong this thing can go in one night."

Price didn't say anything. She didn't have to.

Kurtzman could tell by the pinched white line between her eyes that she was already turning those possibilities over for herself.

CHAPTER SIX

Paris, France
10:21 a.m.

The operation was going smoothly, which pleased Yakov Katzenelenbogen. He checked his watch and found they were well within the time frame he'd established for the mission.

Dressed in a lightweight tan suit and a dark red beret, he knew he didn't attract much attention standing on the corner of Rue de la Ferronerie. The street bordered the south side of the Square of Innocents. It had begun as a market during the reign of Philippe August, with many plans in the years since detailing what should be done with it. But despite the plans of monarchs and men, it had become Les Halles all on its own. Instead of the towering office buildings that were supposed to fill the famous hole created by the excavation of the original marketplace, Les Halles Mark 2 became a striking and stylish shopping center. There was plenty of room between the shops, boutiques and outdoor cafés to roam and look at everything, but damn little room for traffic. Which was why Katzenelenbogen had chosen the area after learning of their target's affinity for it.

He took out a pack of unfiltered Camel cigarettes, shook one out, put the pack away and tamped the tobacco tight in the paper against the metal prosthesis that was his lower right arm and hand. He'd been wounded in the Israeli Six Day War years after leaving his native France.

Breathing in the smoke from the American cigarette, he observed again that Oscar Wilde was right: a man could never truly go home again. He had fond memories of the city and of Les Halles, both old and new, but today he only saw it as a potential battleground.

"Phoenix One, this is Phoenix Four. Over."

The voice came from the earphone over Katz's left ear. He shoved the wire-thin mouthpiece from the concealment of his jacket collar, covering the movement easily as he brought his cigarette up to his mouth. Phoenix Four was Rafael Encizo, the Cuban-born member of the team. Like Katz, Encizo carried scars from previous wars before linking up with the Stony Man Farm teams. He'd had a stay at the infamous El Principe prison as a young man after the Bay of Pigs fiasco. "Go, Four. Over."

"I have the little general in sight. Over."

Katz scanned the crowds moving slowly through the narrow streets. "Where? Over."

"By the fountain. Over."

Focusing his visual inspection of the area, Katz homed in on the mark.

Cordell Fauborg was a mover and a shaker in the black market business that moved through the underbelly of Paris and the city's environs. He had connections that could reach any border within minutes. And it had been those connections, Kurtzman and Price had discovered, that had allowed at least some of the false American and Russian soldiers entry into the country on forged passports. No one believed that Fauborg was the brains behind the operation, but the man definitely had some answers they were looking for.

"I see him. Over."

Fauborg was tall and lean, a well-kept man in his late thirties. His hair was dark with styling gel, swept back from a hatchet face with a knife scar scoring one cheek. His suit spoke of money and self-importance, tailored well enough to almost conceal the pistol he carried at his hip. He carried a charcoal gray outer jacket draped over his arm. There was enough intangible menace clinging to him that most pedestrians automatically gave way before him.

"He's not alone, mate. Over."

The new man in the communications loop was David McCarter, code-named Phoenix Two. The lanky Briton was ex-SAS, skilled in the deadly hand-to-hand combat arts of the paratroopers. He was also an excellent pilot and driver.

"How many?" Katz asked. "Over."

"I see three," McCarter replied. "One running blocker. The other two bringing up the rear. Over."

Katz swept the people around Fauborg. Studying the pattern of movement around the black marketer, he quickly picked out the bodyguards.

The lead man was a rail-thin Pakistani with a short-clipped mustache and military haircut. He wore a three-piece suit and carried a briefcase. One of the rear guards probably would have been six and a half feet tall if he didn't walk with a stooped, round-shouldered posture. His corduroy jacket had patched elbows and hung badly on him. His face was marked with acne scars, and he squinted against the morning sun. The third man was built like a boxer, broad shouldered and lean waisted, his skin the color of coffee with cream. He carried a sports bag over one shoulder and held the straps easily in one big hand.

Thumbing the transmit button on the headset again, Katz said, "Phoenix One to Phoenix Five. Over."

"Go, One. You have Five."

Phoenix Five was Calvin James, an ex-SEAL and the newest member of the antiterrorist team. Besides his military experience, James had also worked the police game and was the group's medico.

"We're in motion," Katz said. "Bring the car around now and be prepared. It is a safe bet that the three men we see guarding Fauborg are not the only people he has in the area. Over."

"Affirmative," James called back, then cleared the channel.

"Phoenix Three?" Katz radioed. "Over."

"Here. Over." Gary Manning was Phoenix Three. The barrel-chested Canadian had earned a Silver Star during a tour of duty in Vietnam as a "special observer" attached to the Fifth Special Forces. He was a demolitions expert, and no one knew more about combustible materials than Manning.

"Are you ready?" Katz asked. "Over."

"That's a big roger," Manning replied. "I've seen about all of this damn fountain today that I care to see the rest of my life. Over."

A brief smile flickered over Katz's lips. Of all his team, Manning was probably the least patient. McCarter ran a close second, but usually took the edge off his nervous energy by running a dry and derisive social commentary.

"When this goes down," Katz said, "there is going to be some concern from the general populace. You and I speak the language, so we'll run interference for the others as they take Fauborg away." He took a stick of gum from his pocket, carefully unwrapped the foil and stuck the gum in his mouth. Opening his wallet, he smoothed the foil with skilled fingers, then folded it into a rough diamond shape and placed it carefully inside the wallet. The silver foil caught the sun briefly when he opened it, satisfying him. At first glance, with everything that would be going on in the marketplace, the gum wrapper inside his wallet should pass inspection.

The French black marketer had crossed the esplanade. His posture was very erect, and Katz had seen pictures of the man in the South African military uniform he'd worn for most of one year when the governments in that country had seesawed back and forth in the early eighties. The position had been granted by one of the nationalist governments trying to push itself into power in return for Fauborg's ability to supply their efforts. He'd never been called on to fill out the role, but the espionage circles interested in South African events had acknowledged his pride in the appointment.

Katz waited, measuring the distance Fauborg traveled against the parameters he'd marked in his mind. He tapped the transmit button on the ear-throat headset, said, "Get it done," and reached under his jacket for the Beretta.

David McCarter moved away from the fountain and into full speed without giving an appearance of being in a hurry. The distinctive yellow cover of the *National Geographic* he'd been perusing settled over his right hand as if keeping his place. Though Katz couldn't see it, he knew the fox-faced Briton held his Browning Hi-Power there now.

Keeping the Beretta concealed, Katz started for Fauborg, ignoring the Pakistani running blocker.

Unusually light on his feet for such a big man, Manning made his way through the crowd with long strides, an intent look on his ruddy features.

"Phoenix Five," Katz said softly over the open channel.

"I'm there, buddy," James responded.

The Israeli glanced over his shoulder and saw the big Fleetwood Cadillac glide to a stop at the near curbside of Rue de la Ferronerie. It was painted a nondescript brown, with wheel panels that would provide a little protection from bullets if it came to that. James sat easily behind the steering wheel, both arms wrapped around it as he hunkered down to watch the action.

"Hey," the Pakistani said, changing course to intercept Katz.

Fauborg's gaze flicked to the Phoenix Force commander with only a little concern showing.

Katz never broke stride.

"Hey, man," the Pakistani said in French. "Where the hell do you think you're going?" He put out a palm toward the Israeli's chest, his other hand filled with the briefcase.

Before the Pakistani could act, Encizo was on him. The stocky little Cuban seized the Pakistani's outstretched hand from the side and pinched nerves designed to deaden the arm muscles. Katz knew that from the way the Pakistani's face suddenly contorted. While still holding the man's hand, Encizo twisted, forced the Pakistani around, then kicked him three times rapidly in the stomach and chest. The last kick lifted the man off the ground. When he came down, Encizo rolled him over, then dropped a knee into his back and shoved the barrel of his SIG-Sauer P-226 into the man's neck.

"Don't move," Katz said in French as he walked past the fallen guard. "Otherwise he'll kill you."

Fauborg started to retreat, glancing behind him in time to see McCarter thrust the Browning into the side of the stooped man's neck.

The remaining guard was almost able to get his sports bag off his shoulder when Manning caught him full in the face with a short hook that had all of his weight behind it. The Canadian managed two more short jabs that tumbled the guy to the ground. Manning relieved him of the sports bag and the automatic holstered beneath his arm.

"If you run," Katz told Fauborg in a quiet voice that carried a deadly earnestness, "I'm going to shoot you in the legs. Maybe more than once." He unleathered his Beretta and aimed it.

Fauborg froze, automatically raising his hands and locking them behind his head. "Who the hell are you?"

Tucking the Beretta under his right arm, Katz opened the wallet and flashed it at the curious crowd, then put it away in an officious manner. "Police," he said in a loud voice. "Do not worry. Everything is under control. No one will be hurt." He tucked the wallet out of sight and fisted the pistol again.

"What do we do with these blokes?" McCarter asked, maintaining his hold on the stoop-shouldered man.

"Leave them," Katz said in English. Then he switched to French and addressed McCarter's prisoner.

"Down on your stomach." He gestured with the Beretta so the Briton would know the man was moving in response to an order he'd been given.

The man went down and a moment later had his hands secured behind his back with disposable plastic cuffs.

"Hands behind your back," Katz ordered as he stepped toward Fauborg.

"Bullshit," Fauborg said. "You're not cops." He turned to yell at the crowd. "They're not cops. This is some kind of kidnapping. Call the real police. Do it now!"

Katz leathered the pistol and reached for the black marketer, closing his hand in the man's clothing. Just as he started to pull, he felt Fauborg yank away from him.

Blood pooled out from a wound high on the left side of Fauborg's chest. Then the crack of a high-powered rifle became audible.

"Sniper!" James called over the headsets.

With his hand still gripping Fauborg's clothing, Katz shoved his body into the other man's and bulled him toward the fountain less than five yards away. The walls of the fountain and the statues around it would provide some cover until they were able to organize a game plan. Fauborg's legs slammed up against the low wall, and the men tumbled over into the water.

The black marketer struggled to get to the surface at once, letting Katz know he wasn't dead or in shock. The Israeli controlled his prisoner, didn't let him up until he had the man pressed up against the relative safety of the low wall. Splashing water fell over Katz as he peered over the wall.

Encizo and Manning had gone to ground, taking shelter behind large cinder-block flower boxes that framed the outer perimeters of sidewalk cafés. McCarter slid an Ingram MAC-10 from the black bodyguard's sports bag. Hunkered on his knees to make a smaller target, the lanky Briton slipped the safety and worked the action to ready it for firing. On his feet now, running toward the sluggish crowd, he emptied the clip in rapid bursts that went over their heads but created a lot of noise.

Self-preservation kicked into the crowd's mental circuitry. They stampeded, fleeing into the outskirts of the Square of Innocents.

Before McCarter could take cover, a bullet cut him down.

Katz watched the Briton stagger, then fall. Beside him, Fauborg struggled to get away. Katz barely spared the man a moment's notice, lashing out with his metal prosthesis and smashing the man unconscious with a slap. He peered back over the wall, saw McCarter on the move, sprinting, then diving over the wrought-iron fence in front of a dress boutique. He tapped the transmit button on the headset. "Phoenix Two?"

"I'm okay," McCarter radioed back. "The vest stopped the slug. Bloody bastard must be using an elephant gun."

"I've got him," James said in a voice filled with deadly focus.

Katz shifted fields of view, disregarding the relief he felt that McCarter was still intact. His mind was churning with the new information the attack had brought. Fauborg was bait. In snapping closed their own trap, they had merely triggered another. Someone, somewhere, knew about the team, knew they were in the area.

Out on the street, James had taken up position behind the Fleetwood, a Beretta M-21 sniper rifle snugged into his shoulder. The rifle recoiled, then the crack of thunder rolled over Katz's position. He looked in the direction James was aiming, saw the body come tumbling from a third-story window to land in a spread-eagled crash atop a Volkswagen minibus. The top gave out immediately, and the windows exploded from the crushed frames.

Turning his attention back to his prisoner, Katz fisted Fauborg's shirt and pulled the man's head back above the water. The black marketer coughed and spluttered weakly. Crimson streaked the water from Fauborg's shoulder wound.

Katz braced a knee against Fauborg to hold the man in place while he wadded up two handkerchiefs and shoved them under the man's shirt to work as temporary pressure bandages for the entry and exit wounds.

Fauborg moaned.

"We've got more company coming, lads," McCarter said grimly.

The harsh bark of motorcycle engines slashed through the screams and shouts filling the marketplace.

Looking over his shoulder, through the white spray spumed off by the ornate fountain, Katz saw a half-dozen cyclists burst through the small alleys cutting through Les Halles. They were dressed in one-piece leather motorcycle suits, their faces concealed by helmets. They rode two to a machine, the rear man carrying a subgun that opened fire as soon as they were in range.

A line of bullets chopped into the fountain.

Katz targeted the driver of the motorcycle bearing down on his position. The line of bullets closed in as the rear gunner reassessed the range. Holding true to his target, the Israeli squeezed the trigger.

A crack split the face shield of the motorcyclist driver, and the guy's head wobbled on his neck like a helium balloon caught in a stiff wind. Out of control, dipping back and forth as the rear man tried for the handlebars, the motorcycle slammed into the fountain and both men and machine tumbled into the water.

Katz got to his feet at once, keeping track of the live man and the dead one. When the rear gunner tried to scramble up from the water, the Israeli fired the Beretta twice, point-blank at the assassin's chest. He took cover behind the spewing mouth of the fountain and surveyed the battle zone.

The Fleetwood took out two more of the cyclists before they knew James was there. One of the bikes hit skidded up over the nose of the big luxury car, then spun off to one side. The other went under the wheels, providing bumpy traction. James brought the car to a sliding stop beside the fountain and flung open the passenger door.

At least a dozen people in the crowd had been cut down by the assassins' wild rounds. Some of the braver among them were busy trying to drag the wounded to relative safety.

Manning stepped from concealment as one of the surviving motorcycles drifted in too close to his position. Striking without warning, the big Canadian swung a wrought-iron chair from a sidewalk café. The chair swept the motorcycle clear, sending the two riders sprawling. Before they got their feet under them, he had his SIG-Sauer in his hands. The first assassin went down before he could fire. The second one got off a handful of rounds that ripped through the colorful awning over Manning's head. Then the Canadian's deadly aim put him down, as well.

Tracking the last two motorcycles as they hit the end of the marketplace only a few yards shy of Rue de la Ferronerie, McCarter and Encizo took up positions behind the idling Fleetwood. The cyclists dropped their legs, leaned into the turns, then were forced to slow as they came around. Knowing they were more vulnerable now, the rear gunners sprayed bullets into the marketplace on full-auto.

Katz leathered the Beretta, then grabbed Fauborg by the back of his jacket collar as he stepped from the fountain and headed toward the Fleetwood.

Without pause, Encizo and McCarter stood their ground, squeezed off their shots and made every round count. When they stopped a few seconds later, none of the assassins was left alive.

Katz shoved Fauborg into the Fleetwood's rear seat and followed the man inside. Manning bracketed him on the other side. Encizo and McCarter took the front seat beside James.

Rapping the Beretta's barrel against the top of the car, Katz said, "Go."

The team took a moment to recharge their weapons as James made a tire-shredding turn that completed a one-eighty around the fountain. Part of the crowd started to surge out at them, then quickly gave way when they saw the big car wasn't slowing down.

Katz disconnected the prosthesis, then dropped his artificial hand into the equipment bag at his feet.

"How are we going to handle this?" James asked as he momentarily moved into the oncoming lane to negotiate stalled traffic.

"The same routes we've already discussed," Katz replied.

Fauborg was more aware of his surroundings now. The black marketer gripped his wounded shoulder and grimaced in pain.

Delving into the equipment bag, Katz took out his hook, clicked it into place and flexed it. The twin hooks moved in a slow, hypnotic fashion, catching Fauborg's attention at once.

"I've got a van," McCarter said, peering back out the passenger-side window.

"Where?" James asked.

Manning passed over a Heckler & Koch MP-5 SD-3. The silencer at the end looked like a stainless-steel bratwurst.

McCarter took the subgun, checked the action and freed the safety. "Maroon Econoline pulling up behind us. Aerials suggest it's wired for mobile phone and shortwave."

"They'll have made the car, then," Katz said. "We'll have to dump it." He watched the van as it closed, saw figures moving on the other side of the dark tinted glass.

James nodded, then pulled hard left, turning the Fleetwood onto Rue Coquilliere, ignoring the red light. The big car brushed up against a delivery van edging out into traffic, shivered, then recovered when James put his foot harder on the accelerator. The delivery driver braked hard and stalled.

The van slowed only for a moment, then accelerated again, racing in pursuit of the Cadillac. It was obvious the power plant under the Econoline's hood was more than standard equipment.

"What do we do with the van?" McCarter asked.

"Take it out," Katz answered. "I'll tell you when."

He looked at Fauborg, switching to French. "Somebody must really think you know something, my friend. You'd better be well worth our investment."

Fauborg looked grayish, whether from the wound or from the dizzying pace of the chase through the streets Katz didn't know.

"Coming up on Montmartre Street," James called back.

Katz glanced at McCarter. "David?"

The Briton nodded, moving into position, bringing the H&K MP-5 up to his shoulder.

"Take the van out as it starts into the turn. The tires. We don't know for sure who's inside."

The light at the intersection was green, but a line of cars was only now getting under way.

"Hang on," James said. He cut the wheel hard, tapping the brake.

Katz braced himself against the seat ahead of him, his good arm thrown across Fauborg.

The Fleetwood caught the curb and bounced crazily for a moment, struggling like a swordfish breaking the ocean surface in an attempt to free itself from the hook that held it. Then it landed on its wheels, powered over a street sign posting the legal speed and shot for the clear area.

Hot brass spilled from McCarter's H&K, the Phoenix Force warriors automatically shielding their faces and the open parts of their clothing. The autofire, softened by the silencer, sounded like a brief flurry of hail.

Katz glanced at the maroon van. Both front tires blew as it attempted to take the same path James had chosen. The driver lost control, and the vehicle smashed into plankboard shelves supporting rows of colorful flowers in pots and baskets.

"Clear," McCarter reported as he slid back into the Cadillac. He passed the subgun back to Manning, who put it away.

"We'll dump the car at the prearranged spot off Hausmann Boulevard and Richelieu Street," Katz said. The team had two more cars waiting at Place Vendome, buried in the thick confusion of cars left there by the all-day shoppers that flocked to the ladies' boutiques located in the large octagon. Barbara Price had arranged for a Learjet to be waiting for their use at Roissy Airport under a diplomatic umbrella—provided they made it there without any more interference that would draw the attention of the local police.

James made the left turn onto Hausmann Boulevard. Nothing appeared in their wake.

Katz turned to the black marketer. "Now, my friend, as you have no doubt guessed, there is something we wish to talk to you about."

Manning crowded in on the other side, taking away their prisoner's private space. McCarter turned around in the seat and smiled a mirthless grin under the blank lenses of the aviators.

"We don't have a lot of time," Katz went on. "So when I ask you questions—" he settled the hard metal hook against Fauborg's Adam's apple ""—you will do your absolute best to answer them not only as truthfully as you can, but as quickly, as well. As you can see, we are truly desperate men." The Israeli stared hard into the man's eyes. "Do you understand?"

Fauborg nodded carefully, very aware of the hook. "Of course."

Manning flicked on a small microcassette recorder as Katz began the interrogation.

CHAPTER SEVEN

Washington, D.C.
4:36 a.m.

It *was* a plan, Carl Lyons thought again as he crept through the night, sort of. The problem with his teammates was that they'd been brought up on the Special Forces way of doing things. Everybody had a part to play, and a time to play it. A Special Forces mission—now, that was like baseball, with every option covered and every player knowing what he had to do when the ball was hit, no matter where it was hit. Police work, Lyons had argued only a few minutes earlier as Able Team had left its van a few blocks back, was more like football. It didn't matter how many plans had been laid, once the ball was snapped they were all subject to change.

Personally Lyons liked the uncertainty. He'd been a cop for the LAPD for a number of years before making the move to Able Team. Uncertainty could be a liability at times, yeah, but it could also be a hell of a weapon.

He cradled the SPAS-12 in his hands as he paused at the corner of the warehouse Barbara Price's Intel had led them to. He crouched in the shadows, knew from the eastern sky that dawn wasn't so far away.

To the north, the Potomac glittered in the last vestiges of moonlight. Key Bridge was to the east, already filled with a line of headlights as the work force began their daily trek into D.C.

Lyons tapped the transmit button on his ear-throat headset. "Gadgets. Politician."

"Go," Hermann "Gadgets" Schwarz said. He'd earned his sobriquet in Vietnam. Then he'd been assigned to Pen-Team Able and to Special Forces Sergeant Mack Bolan. Schwarz was gifted with an intellect geared for figuring out things mechanical and electronic, and his stint with the Executioner had turned him into a veritable flesh-and-blood nightmare when it came to booby traps, surveillance and sudden violent mayhem with things normally considered safe in the average kitchen.

"Here," Rosario "Politician" Blancanales answered. Also assigned at one time to Pen-Team Able, the Politician had a knack for getting to the heart of a discussion—any discussion, and from any side of it. Where Schwarz held sway over things of the physical world, Blancanales was a master of emotions. He could change the mood of a lynch mob with a few well-chosen words, or give fighting hope to a group of warriors ready to give up in the face of an overwhelming enemy.

"I'm in place," Lyons said. "I'll give you the go."

"Are you sure we shouldn't do more recon?" Schwarz asked.

"By the time we finished even a half-assed recon effort," Lyons pointed out, "it'll be daylight. Take a look at Key Bridge. The city's already starting to come alive. I don't want to do this with a bunch of citizens hanging around waiting to get caught by the cross fire."

"Ironman's right," Blancanales said. "It would be nice if we had more time to do this thing right, but we don't. Phoenix is probably taking down the other end of this little travel agency right now. Could be someone's even trying to tip these guys off. If we move fast enough, chances are we can put this one out of business, too."

"You call it, Carl," Schwarz said. "And don't bother looking over your shoulder because I'll be there."

Safe-T Warehouse was a small storage company that catered to some of the shops in Georgetown Park. The owners stowed overstocked merchandise for the stores and carted them into the neo-Victorian shopping center for a monthly stipend and freight charges.

The business was legit, even turned a tidy profit at the end of each fiscal year. But the people behind it weren't. According to information Price had turned up, the man behind Safe-T was Peter Fawcett.

Fawcett had taken a couple falls during his twenty years of crime, nothing really heavy. The man always had something to negotiate to cut a deal. NCIC had logged him as a one-time distributor of federally controlled substances, but he appeared to have gotten out of the field shortly after that. Kurtzman's reports had revealed that Fawcett hadn't been deterred as much by local and federal law enforcement as he was by the rival drug gangs willing to shoot it out in the streets over territory. Since drugs had become too hot to handle, Fawcett had moved into another lucrative field that involved a lot of the same connections he'd already established: moving people.

From what Price and Kurtzman had been able to discover, Fawcett had been responsible for transporting at least four of the dead American "soldiers" into France a few weeks before the recent fiasco. The CIA had most of the information in their computers, but Price had put the rest of the Intel together from the military files she had access to.

And the rest, Lyons figured as he looked at the Safe-T, was about to become history.

The warehouse was two stories tall, and had probably looked old and weathered when it had first been built thirty years earlier. It had a small set of bay doors opening onto the Potomac, complete with a block-and-tackle rig for taking loads from small boats. The largest bay doors were on the east side, opposite an eight-foot fence topped by three strands of barbed wire. Trucks had become more important than boats when it came to transportation, since the building had been erected. At the fence line the blacktop street turned into a graveled lane with several washed-out areas nearly a foot deep. There were no guards posted, but then Fawcett had no reason to believe he'd been found out.

A snitch borrowed from Lyons's contact in the Washington, D.C., PD had confirmed Fawcett's location less than an hour before. Then the snitch had been quietly transferred for the night to a detox center for a mandatory twenty-four hours so he wouldn't be near a phone to try to line up some side action on the information. The guy hadn't been happy about it, but he hadn't put up much of a fuss.

Lyons was dressed for action. The Kevlar vest was too damn hot, but he'd learned to trade the discomfort for the safety. Beads of perspiration collected along the bands of combat cosmetics coloring his face, arms and hands. In addition to the combat shotgun, he carried his Colt Python .357 at his right hip and a Colt Government Model .45 in shoulder rigging. A gravity knife was in the pocket of his black jeans. A black T-shirt and dark blue running shoes completed his ensemble. A waist belt with military webbing held spare magazines for the SPAS and the Government .45, and speed-loaders for the Python.

The exit door beside the bay doors in front of Lyons opened, and a man stepped out.

Lyons shifted, moving closer to the hedge he'd chosen for cover. He tapped the transmit button and whispered, "I've got movement."

"I see him," Blancanales replied.

The man shrugged and stretched, then reached into his jacket for a pack of cigarettes. A lighter flared briefly, then the cigarette became a glowing orange coal.

"Anybody we know?" Lyons asked.

"No." Blancanales had a Star-Tron scope mounted on the CAR-15 he carried.

"Okay, cover me while I see about putting him down quietlike." Lyons slithered forward when the man turned and gazed out over the river.

The man appeared content to relax, the wind pulling a curling strand of gray smoke from his lips.

Lyons reached into his webbing and took out the roll of ordnance tape he carried there. He slid the roll onto his wrist, then took out the gravity knife with his other hand. The blade flicked into place with a small snick. Then he was in motion, pumping his legs hard as he pushed his speed up to a full run.

The man obviously heard the shifting gravel under Lyons's feet and started to turn, his hand going to his mouth for the cigarette.

Lyons leapt, his left foot catching the six-inch sill thrusting out from the barred window on the lower level. As he pushed off, his free hand gripped the support arm for the sign above the fence advertising the bay area for trucks. The metal shrieked in protest as it took his weight. He threw his legs forward, arching over the barbed-wire strands.

The man's cigarette dropped from his mouth as he reached under his jacket.

Some of the tines raked the Kevlar vest as Lyons came down flailing for balance. At least two others dug into the flesh of his upper arm, drawing blood. He felt it gather and flow warmly down his skin as he landed.

The hardman extended a Smith & Wesson .44 Magnum and thumbed the hammer back professionally.

Jarred from the landing, Lyons focused on the man's gun hand. His foot lashed out, catching the guy's wrist with enough force to send the pistol spinning way. Before the man could make a move to retrieve his weapon, the big Able Team warrior was on him.

Lyons caught the guy like a linebacker sacking a quarterback and trying to force the fumble. Only an agonized wheezing erupted from the guy's mouth as Lyons dumped him on the ground and dropped a knee in the middle of the man's chest. He showed the guy the gravity knife, then held it under his throat.

"One word," Lyons warned in an Arctic whisper, "and you don't get to stay around to see how all this turns out."

The man nodded, still working on drawing his next shuddering breath.

Working quickly, Lyons taped the man's wrists and ankles together with the ordnance tape. He added a final piece to seal the guy's lips, then dragged his body up against the warehouse.

The big ex-LAPD cop unslung the SPAS, clicked off the safety and approached the side door. He put a hand on the knob. It was unlocked.

He opened the door and passed through into more darkness. The strong odor of industrial-strength pine cleaners filled the still air. Voices, muted and distant, carried hollowly through the cavernous vault of the warehouse. Huge stacks of skids piled high with boxes sat on either side of the exit, reaching nearly to the ceiling. A narrow catwalk ran around the building, but no one appeared to be there.

Soft fluorescent light glowed around the corner in front of Lyons, almost white enough to turn the yellow safety lines painted on the floor to an off-orange color. Someone switched on a radio, and the noises trapped inside the warehouse became stained with top 40 tunes.

"We're past the fence, Ironman," Schwarz called out. "We've got the bay doors covered. First sign of trouble, we're on your heels."

"Affirmative." Lyons moved forward, the combat shotgun held at waist level, seeking the source of the radio and the conversations. Peering around the corner, he spotted a small office built into the upper southwest corner of the warehouse. Angle braces left the warehouse floor clear below.

The large plate-glass window stretched across the front of the office was dingy from accumulated cigarette smoke. Lyons counted five men inside.

Fawcett was a balding, short fat man. He was dressed in a golf shirt and Day-Glo green golfer's pants, and leaned against a desk. The conversation didn't appear to be anything serious. According to the snitch, Fawcett was there only to pick up the weekly take from the business done under the table around the Safe-T Warehouse. Dope was out, but Fawcett was picking up pocket change selling guns to the street gangs determined to kill one another.

Pulling back, Lyons reached for the headset, ready to call it. The box beside his head exploded, and he automatically dropped to one knee.

At least two more rounds tracked him as the gunner shifted aim.

Lyons brought up the SPAS and aimed it in the direction of the muzzle-flashes. He touched off two rounds, watching as a dark silhouette carved itself from the shadows and went spinning away. The double-aught buck he was using made sure the guy stayed down.

A quick glance at the second-story office let him know Fawcett and company were in motion. He started to give pursuit, but the sudden blat of a big diesel engine behind him drew his attention.

A forklift erupted through a wall of stacked boxes, barreling straight at him. A skid of crated boxes rode the forks ahead of it.

Lyons fired three rounds as it closed in, but the buckshot didn't penetrate the boxes at all, just left pie-sized holes leaking glass and electronic hardware. The driver was intent on smashing him against the row of crates behind him.

The Able Team leader threw himself to one side, rolled and came up on his knees with the shotgun pointed in the right direction. The forklift driver tried to make a course correction one-handed and brought up an Uzi with the other. Unable to get a clear shot at the driver, Lyons shot the outside tire.

The rubber unraveled immediately. With the load the forklift was carrying at the height it was carrying it, the machine wobbled and tipped over.

Boxes scattered, raining down on Lyons before he could move. Somewhere in the general confusion he lost the shotgun. For a moment he thought the load was going to bury him. Dazed, thinking he was fighting for survival, he forced himself into a standing position.

Movement near the forklift signaled danger.

Lyons cleared a final box out of his way, drew the Colt Python, dropped the sights over the heart of the forklift driver and fired as the man squeezed the trigger on the Uzi.

The gunner went down and stayed that way.

"Ironman!" It was Blancanales, worried.

Lyons tapped the transmit button. "Holding my own, buddy, but we're definitely off to a bad start."

"Fawcett?" Schwarz asked.

"Here," Lyons replied as he fished the shotgun out of the mess, "somewhere." The upstairs office was empty.

A small explosion went off, and the truck bay doors crashed in. Blancanales and Schwarz entered the warehouse through the fog of rolling smoke and dust.

"Got me?" Lyons asked as he thumbed fresh rounds into the SPAS.

"Got you," Schwarz answered.

Blancanales waved, then peeled off toward the front of the building, jogging along the outside of the warehouse floor.

Schwarz held the center line.

Anxious, knowing Fawcett might hold information the Stony Man teams could find useful, Lyons broke into a run, holding the SPAS in both hands. He headed toward the rear of the warehouse where the building butted up against the Potomac River, trusting the cop instinct that had developed over the years. It was only after he was in motion that he realized the river might afford Fawcett the only wild-card exit they hadn't planned on.

A man stepped out of the shadows, moving furtively, apparently unaware of his pursuer until Lyons was practically on top of him. The Able Team leader swung the SPAS in a blistering arc, catching the guy on the point of his jaw with the folding steel butt of the combat shotgun. The man managed a single bleat of pain while he fell backward, then slumped unconscious to the warehouse floor.

Shots rang out in the front portion of the warehouse, interspersed with the composed tribursts from Blancanales's and Schwarz's CAR-15s.

The rear exit was open beside the smaller bay windows overlooking the river, and a figure stood in the doorframe. A muzzle-flash appeared from somewhere near its center.

Lyons dropped, diving to safety behind a stack of crates. The rough pine of the skid raked a line of splinters along his cheek. Pushing himself up as a line of bullets ate into the crates, some of them chewing through, the Able Team leader pointed the SPAS in the direction of the door. Before he could squeeze the trigger, a concussive warhead took out the bay doors.

The man who'd stood in the exit was killed immediately, his body coasting past Lyons like a flambéed and bloody rag doll.

Lyons tapped the transmit button. "Pol?"

"Intact." Blancanales sounded winded.

"Gadgets?"

"Standing. What the hell happened back there?"

"Somebody nuked the back of the warehouse," Lyons answered. "I don't think it was Fawcett. He'd have been too close to the blast. I figure a rocket launcher. Maybe from across the river." He scanned the opposite riverbank, disoriented by the lights around Georgetown University and the residential area along Prospect Avenue.

"Somebody cleaning up loose ends," Blancanales suggested. "Could be the French and U.S. connections were leaked to draw out anyone interested. Turned them into stalking horses to up the level of confusion."

"Yeah," Schwarz commented, "but then you have to start asking that nasty little question of who would do such a thing."

"Got to remember," Blancanales pointed out, "that if somebody somewhere wasn't already asking that very question, me, you and the Ironman wouldn't be here now."

A spark flared at eleven o'clock on the north riverbank.

Lyons identified it at once. He hit the transmit button as he dropped to the ground behind the stacks of merchandise. "Incoming!"

The second warhead slammed into the warehouse higher than the first, catching the main roof section of the two-story building. The whole structure shuddered. Beams split, cracked, broke in two and came tumbling down end over end. More sky appeared through the sudden holes in the ceiling.

Knowing the numbers were falling faster than ever on the play, if they hadn't come to a stop already, Lyons broke cover and charged the bay area. It was wreathed in fire, the flames curling up from under the shattered lip of the bay. The block-and-tackle assembly had been blown away.

Movement on the water attracted Lyons's attention.

When he glanced down, he saw a small powerboat. Fawcett and three other men were scrambling aboard, backlit by the flaming debris scattered over the surface of the river. The powerful engines sputtered, then caught. One of the men seized a fire extinguisher and hosed down the burning sticks and splinters aboard the boat. Another man threw off the mooring line.

Lyons surveyed the lower section of the warehouse. It was twenty feet to the river surface, too far to drop and hope to be effective against four men. The swaying wooden stairway leading down to the Potomac caught his eye. He wasn't certain if it would hold his weight.

He leapt, landed haphazardly because the staircase was no longer stable against the warehouse and nearly flipped over the edge. He caught himself with his free hand, stabilized his movement and went down the stairs two at a time. His feet pounded, loud and drumming.

Two of the men in the back of the powerboat looked up and saw him.

Lyons fired the shotgun on the run, aiming at Fawcett. Before he got there, another rocket detonated against the nose of the boat.

The concussion tossed Lyons from the staircase. He hung on to the SPAS by its sling, willing his body to go limp to absorb the coming impact. He had a brief impression of the powerboat blowing apart as it was enveloped in a sheet of flame. Then the river smacked into him and covered him over.

He remembered touching bottom, the greasy feel of the Potomac mud sinking into his clothing. His lungs were empty, seared with a need for oxygen so intense that at first he was afraid he'd inhaled the flames. Lyons regained his equilibrium, put his feet down solidly and stood in water that was barely waist deep. He raked his wet hair back with a muddy hand and blinked the water from his eyes.

Where the powerboat had been a moment earlier, only flotsam and flames remained.

Lyons retreated from the wreckage in case the rocket team had snipers among their ranks, as well.

"Carl?"

The Able Team leader reached for his headset, realized he'd lost it somewhere in the blur of events, and realized also that Schwarz was calling from overhead. "I'm here."

"In one piece?"

"Seems like." Lyons checked himself, finding nothing more than bruises and cuts that could wait until later. "How are things up there?"

"Burning. Pol's taking a look at the office files, scavenging anything that looks interesting, but he's not going to have a lot of time. This place is coming down."

"Get what you can," Lyons instructed, "then get clear. I'll call the Farm, see what kind of deal we can work with the PD and the local Feds about hanging on to everything we can recover here. I'll meet you back at the van."

"Right."

A body floated out of the wreckage toward Lyons. It was Peter Fawcett. He knotted a hand in the dead man's drenched clothing and pulled him to shore. "Hope you got all your money up front and there was a lot of it, 'cause it looks like the bennies aren't for shit, guy."

He left the corpse well away from the burning building, now spread out over the graveled road. He paused long enough to lift the gate key from the man he'd overcome earlier, then moved the guy to safety.

Lyons jogged the three blocks to the van, already the center of attention as residents and the early shift spilled out into the street, wanting to know what was going on. A glare kept everyone back.

Using the van's cellular phone, he apprised Price of the situation, wasn't offended when she cut the chat short and went to work. He was used to her ways and her methods. If any deals could be cut with the local people, the Farm's mission controller was just the person to cut them.

Lyons punched in the next number from the card Detective Sergeant Rollie Maurloe had given him only a few hours earlier, using the hand-scrawled number on the back rather than the official line on the front. Maurloe was Lyons's sort of cop, big and rough around the edges because he'd refused to be worn down by the endless episodes of violence and sudden death that took place every day in the city he'd signed on to protect.

The phone was answered at the other end of the third ring. "Gilley." The voice was thick and sharp.

"I'm calling for Detective Maurloe," Lyons said.

"Hold on."

The sergeant came on the phone a few seconds later. "Yeah?"

"It's me," Lyons said, depending on the detective's keen memory for voices. Every time he'd met the D.C. lawman, he'd been using a different alias. To remember who he was this time out, he'd have to sort through the wet wallet in his muddy pants.

"Ah," Maurloe said, "my favorite mystery man. How are things with you?"

Lyons looked at the curling black smoke gathered above the Safe-T Warehouse. "We're really cooking now."

"I'll bet."

Sirens sounded, drawing closer to the warehouse.

"What's that?" Maurloe asked suspiciously.

"Fire engines," Lyons answered. He saw the first of them now, barreling down the street, swinging wide to make the corner.

"Fire engines," Maurloe repeated. "Going to be a lot of them?"

"Yeah. Part of the Potomac's on fire, too."

"The river. You set the damn river on fire?"

"Not me. I'll explain when you get here. This is going to make a hell of a report."

"What about the Safe-T Warehouse that you were going to check out?"

Lyons watched as the roof of the warehouse suddenly caved in and disappeared behind a row of houses. "Probably won't be a stick left standing."

CHAPTER EIGHT

Paris, France
10:58 a.m.

"Count it down," Jacques D'Anton ordered.

The eleven men in his command quickly counted down their numbers over the radio frequency they used, signaling their readiness.

D'Anton was tense, as he always was when he knew there would be gunplay. He sat in the passenger seat of the lead van, checking the side mirror for the van following closely behind. It was there, barely two car lengths back, a nondescript tan with markings that identified it as a coffee-service vehicle. The van he was in carried advertising about a popular linen service. Neither was involved in those fields.

"Captain."

D'Anton glanced over at his second behind the steering wheel. First Lieutenant Racine was as composed as always. The captain had often thought the man relished the thought of physical action. He certainly had no compunctions about killing. "Yes."

"Might I suggest a cigarette?" Racine said, shaking one out of his pack and passing it over. "We have time."

Taking the cigarette, D'Anton studied his second through slitted eyes. Though Racine would never—correction, *had* never—crossed the line that would undermine his superior's authority, he'd come awfully close at times. D'Anton lit the cigarette with his own lighter.

Racine drove the van across the Seine River on the Pont de BirHakeim, staying in the more sedate right lane to avoid attention. Since the attempt on Barnabe Siffre's life earlier, and the armed assault in Les Halles by as-yet-unknown forces the French police had put on extra shifts. The traffic thinned out still further when the tourists made the turn at Quai Branly to see the Eiffel Tower. The two vans rolled easily along Boulevard de Grenelle.

It helped that every man in the Franco-German unit had been in a firefight before—in some part of the world. Exactly where was a mystery even to their captain. One of the first things the special forces groups had been warned against was asking one another too many personal questions. It reminded D'Anton of the romance of the old French Foreign Legion. But there was a more military reason for withholding information from one another. If apprehended, none of the team could tell much about the other members. But nothing was said about who for sure might do the apprehending.

D'Anton himself had come from French Intelligence services. On one hand, the sanctions made sense, but on the other, he knew that the command of silence could be used for more than one purpose.

Racine was an enigma to him. The man was about five years older than D'Anton, and had the scars to prove that he'd seen more combat. Yet he was relegated to a number-two position and seemed happy with it.

When he'd first joined the Franco-German army after an impassioned speech delivered by Siffre two years earlier, D'Anton had been enthusiastic, fired by the man's words, so sure that France would lead the rest of Europe onto a path of equal footing with the superpowers. Only now there was only one superpower, and even that one was waning.

And today he'd been given the assignment to kill someone.

"Thinking, sir?" Racine asked quietly. He made the left turn onto Avenue de Lowendale.

"Yes."

"About the Americans?" Racine asked.

D'Anton looked at the man, but Racine didn't look back, his attention fully on the traffic around them.

"After last night there should be no doubts in your mind," Racine said. "At this point we have to assume the Americans and the Russians are working against our efforts here."

"I know." D'Anton had already had those arguments with his superiors during the night. It hadn't done any good, and he didn't really care to go through it again with Racine.

"It's your first termination mission, isn't it?"

The captain stubbed out his cigarette. "Yes."

"You have to believe the Americans are already heavily involved in sabotaging our efforts to rebuild Europe," Racine said.

"You make it sound like it's France against the world."

Racine nodded solemnly. "Perhaps it is. Like Mr. Siffre says, this country—all of Europe—is poised between two hungry sharks eager not to lose their positions of domination in the world."

"The Commonwealth of Independent States is hardly in any position to dominate anyone."

"True," the lieutenant replied. "But they have the armament to destroy much of the world if they so choose. There is a saying, and I think of it when I consider Russia's supposed weakened state now—in the country of the blind, the one-eyed man is king."

"But the Americans? They have always supported France."

"Have they? Maybe to justify their own ends. Remember, sir, that America has never really had her empire days, her years of colonial expansion. Perhaps now, with this new, bleaker future dawning over us, the American government will feel quite differently about such matters. Everything these days turns on money."

"You sound like Barnabe Siffre."

Racine nodded. "He's a smart man. Mr. Siffre has a vision."

They were now less than ten minutes away from their target. Picking up the oversize sports bag that carried his equipment for the operation, D'Anton unzipped it and made a final inspection. His lead weapon was the little French military MAS 5.56 mm assault rifle. Less than a meter long, the weapon looked like a combination ray gun and child's toy with the unique bullpup design and long carrying handle-sight channel. He'd worked with NATO weapons before, and had a fondness for the American M-16, which was more than twenty-five centimeters longer. Still, the MAS was a good rifle. His side arm was carried in a hip holster under the loose Windbreaker. He preferred a SIG-Sauer 9 mm pistol, but what he'd gotten was a Model D MAB, chambered for the 7.65 mm Longue cartridge. Like the MAS rifle, it was a good weapon, just not what he would have wanted. Four packs of incendiaries were in the bottom of the bag under the three extra clips for the assault rifle.

The engagement wasn't supposed to last long, but it was supposed to produce as much devastation as possible in the minute and forty-two seconds allowed.

D'Anton pulled on the thin leather gloves the team had been assigned. No fingerprints were to be left behind.

The Faubourg Saint-Germain region was southeast of the Rodin Museum housed in the Hotel Biron. The area was filled with palatial private mansions from the eighteenth century. Great care had gone into maintaining the facades and courtyards of the buildings. Very few people could afford to live in that kind of splendor anymore, and even fewer would make the attempt. Most of the mansions, when rented out at all, housed foreign ministries and embassies.

The covert NATO team that the Americans had tried to slip into the country only a few weeks earlier had rented one of those mansions to use as a base.

D'Anton didn't know what assignment the Americans had. He had asked, but no answer had been given, and he was admonished by his superiors for his curiosity.

In light of the proof the NATO and 2e REP teams had uncovered last night, though, he knew the Franco-German divisions had every right to move into the area and shut the American operation down. They were suspect. Secretly he felt deportation would have been enough. It would have let the American military know they were being watched, and it would have turned the eyes of the world onto the President of the United States.

He didn't want to have to kill anyone.

Racine parked the van in a small alley little more than a block from the target house. The second van drove a block farther on, then parked. The lieutenant grabbed his bag and slung it over his shoulder as he got out.

They divided into two teams. Racine took one of them, then hustled them off at a jog.

D'Anton and the two men with him moved at a slower pace, intent on taking the more direct route while the other three teams worked on a more forcible means of entry into the building.

No one spared them a second glance as they passed through the immaculately kept grounds.

The bacterial agents found in the vineyard were what D'Anton concentrated on as he walked up the ornate steps to the front door of the mansion. If Russia and America wanted to continue to play their little spy games when there was no prize left to be won, let them. But they had no business bringing their dirty laundry onto French soil—especially when that dirty laundry could injure or kill hundreds or thousands for years if those agents had been released accidentally.

No, the captain decided, one way or the other, the American influence—primarily through UN intervention and NATO in particular—needed to be leveraged free of France and Europe for a time until all this could be sorted out.

Though he couldn't confirm it with any of his physical senses, D'Anton knew there was movement in the house.

It was large, three stories tall and covered with gingerbread architecture that made him think of Grimms' fairy tales and Walt Disney movie interpretations of the same. From the blueprints he'd studied, he knew the house had only a few scattered rooms of any great size. The rest were small and enclosed, which had been the popular style in those days. Most of those rooms would be walled off, the furniture left there covered by dustcloths. It would be a simple matter to find out what rooms were being used.

The satellite dish on top of the roof might be there to pull in television stations, but D'Anton knew that wasn't its only function.

He walked to the front door without hesitation and pressed his gloved thumb to the doorbell. The two men with him waited farther down the stairs, talking as though they were more engrossed in their conversation than they were in anything going on around them.

When the door opened, they reached inside their sports bags, pulled out their MAS 5.56 mm assault rifles and charged up the stairs.

The man who answered the door was American military. His hair was cut short, and he had the hungry, lean look so many of the young ones had these days. He glanced over the Franco-German army captain's shoulder at the two approaching men.

Before the man could move, D'Anton freed his autopistol and pressed it into the American's stomach. "Don't," he warned in English.

The man froze, his eyes narrowing to slits as he turned his gaze back to D'Anton.

"Inside," the captain instructed. When the American stepped back, his arms lifted at his sides, D'Anton followed him inside the foyer. His two teammates charged inside.

"What the hell are you doing here?" the American demanded.

"I'm asking the questions," D'Anton replied. His gaze swept the great room beyond the foyer as he ushered his captive ahead of him.

"If you're French Intelligence," the man suggested, "maybe there's been some kind of mix-up."

"Your people are the ones who made it."

They turned right, found their way into a spacious kitchen still styled in elegance, but now sporting the latest in electronic technology. Two men were there. One lounged at a table reading the sports pages of an imported American newspaper, while the other microwaved a cup of coffee.

"What's going on?" the man by the microwave demanded.

"No sudden moves," D'Anton said clearly. "No foolish heroics, and no one has to die."

According to the dossier he'd seen on the American occupation of the house, there were supposed to be eight men. There were five of them left unaccounted for.

"I don't know what you're doing here, pal," the man behind the sports pages said, "but you picked the wrong damn house to roust."

Though there were no body moves behind the open newspaper to betray the man's attempt, D'Anton knew from the American's eyes that he was going for a gun concealed somewhere on his person. Just as the Franco-German army captain was about to shift his pistol from his initial prisoner to the man sitting at the table, several bursts of autofire screamed down from the upper stories.

The men in the kitchen went for their weapons.

Without hesitation but with a lot of regret, D'Anton put two rounds through the man in front of him, then shifted to the man behind the newspaper.

The American came to his feet yelling in rage as his two comrades slumped to the bloody tiled floor. D'Anton's pistol rounds and at least three or four bursts from the MAS assault rifles kicked the dead man's body through the floor-to-ceiling paned windows and into the flower garden on the other side.

D'Anton reloaded his pistol, holstered it and took his MAS from his sports bag as he raced for the great hall. He had the assault rifle up, canted against his shoulder, as he took the winding staircase to the second floor in two and three steps at a time. The autofire continued rattling inside the big house in bursts that echoed in the dozens of empty rooms.

Racine met him at the second-floor landing, his face speckled with red dots of blood attesting to how close he'd been to the men he'd killed. "They're all dead," he growled to his commanding officer. "Five men upstairs."

"There are three dead in the kitchen," D'Anton said.

The rest of the teams came up behind the lieutenant.

"We got them all, then," Racine said as he started hurrying down the stairs. "Good. Our incendiaries have already been placed in the upper stories." He pointed at the two men who'd followed D'Anton. "You men see about setting yours."

They hurried off at once.

D'Anton passed his explosives packages to one of the men around him and went after his second-in-command. He caught up to Racine as the man stood inside a small room filled with electronic gear. Closed-circuit TVs and top-of-the-line communications hardware were spread out over three desks. "Who started the shooting?" he demanded.

Racine turned to face him, his eyes cold and as hard as ice in a Siberian winter. "Begging the captain's pardon, sir, but does it really matter? These people were the enemy. We were sent here to kill them. We did."

"You were to wait until my signal."

"And then what, sir?" Racine asked, his eyes burning.

"You broke orders."

"No, sir. My orders were to kill the enemy. I did." Racine let the silence hang for a moment. "What are your orders, sir?"

The old intuition that had helped D'Anton through college and military school, through the Intelligence training that came afterward, hit the captain with a flash of insight. Racine hadn't really been sent on the mission as his second. The lieutenant had been assigned to him to evaluate his performance. "We've found nothing here to lead us to believe any kind of conspiracy was being arranged here by the Americans."

"Trust me, Captain. The proof will be found in the rubble left by the fire."

"You mean it will be planted?" A raw, cold, greasy spot formed in D'Anton's stomach. As an Intelligence officer for the French government back before the fall of communism, he'd had his hands on some truly dirty deals. But never before had he encountered something like this.

"I meant what I said," Racine said. His voice carried a harsh edge to it now. He worked quickly, affixing the adhesive-backed incendiary package to the small mainframe computer shelved against the far wall.

"We killed innocent men this morning," D'Anton said. His fists tightened around the MAS as he considered his own words.

"Nobody's a complete innocent in this world."

"How much of this whole scenario is being engineered?"

"Wrong question, Captain."

"We're setting these people up."

"There's some who would say the Americans and Russians set themselves up." Racine glanced at his watch. "I happen to agree. And we're operating in the red right now."

"How many people in command positions know about this?"

"Enough," Racine replied. "After this morning's action at Les Halles, the Franco-German army is a couple of commanders short in the special-strikes divisions. It was thought you might be able to fit one of the billets. Evidently the higher-ups were mistaken."

The lieutenant's words twisted and turned sickeningly inside D'Anton's head. Someone was obviously running a cell within the Franco-German army, masking their real intent by the flood of goodwill initiated by the joint effort between the two countries. For the first time in his life, D'Anton felt truly betrayed. Siffre's words had accounted for nothing. The financial wizard's dream of a unified Europe taking the helm of the world was built on feet of clay. People had to be told. He took a firmer grip on the assault rifle.

"And it's a shame," Racine said.

D'Anton glanced up at the lieutenant and saw the French military pistol curled into the man's fist. The muzzle never wavered from D'Anton's eyes.

"A shame that, in uncovering another festering plot engineered by the American military, we had to lose such a gallant soldier." Racine grinned. "You will be martyred, Captain."

D'Anton tried to move, shifted to bring up the MAS, but he knew already he was doomed to failure. The pistol in Racine's hand boomed, and D'Anton thought he saw fire jump from the barrel. Then an inkblot slammed into his forehead, swam around until it filled his brain and he knew nothing more.

The White House
5:11 a.m.

MACK BOLAN stood beside the President's desk in the Oval Office and watched as the story unfolded on the television across the room.

"Rescue workers," the male anchor said in accented English, "are unsure how many bodies are inside the palatial home. Neighbors insist that perhaps as many as a dozen young American men had rented the house. No one, it appears, knew exactly what they were doing there. This news staff is still awaiting word from the French state department."

Behind the yellow-slickered news anchor, two French fire trucks were angled across the narrow street, effectively blocking traffic from both ends. Uniformed firemen brandished hoses that writhed like serpentine monsters and spewed torrents of silver-white water against the burning house.

Bolan didn't allow himself to think about the loss of life. There would be time to grieve for those who had been lost later, when it was a certainty that no more such losses were going to happen.

"That," the President said as he muted the television set with the remote control from behind his desk, "was an Intelligence-gathering team culled from military Intelligence and briefed by the CIA. Two weeks ago the team was inserted into the area, given the few facts we had to go on concerning the bacterial agents and told to keep a low profile while they hunted around and set up a communications network. Quietly. They were under orders not to engage anyone while they were in place."

"Didn't keep them from being engaged," Brognola observed quietly from the coffee service lining one wall.

"That," Bolan said, "was a warning. Whoever's staging this thing is just letting you know they're on to your game plan. If they take out a couple of small operations like this along the way, you have to think your whole program is suspect. It'll cause you to think about every move you make before you make it.''

The President sat back tiredly in his chair. "I feel like we're already running around in circles on this thing.''

Bolan sipped black coffee from his cup. In his mind he'd already started assessing the information they'd received since their arrival. Phoenix Force was still in motion, working on squeezing information from the source they'd captured. Able Team was trying to manage something of a save from the Washington PD investigation of the site they'd covered.

"If you don't mind my saying," the warrior said, "you don't have a whole lot of choices about what you're going to do next.''

"If I minded," the President responded, "you and Hal wouldn't be here now.''

"You start hitting these people back," Bolan said. "So far, they've got NATO where they want them. The U.S. and Russia look like the villains. Unless there was a covert operation between us and the Russians to recover bacteriological and nuclear armament from the outlying satellite countries.''

"No. We haven't been doing anything like that. It's all hogwash.''

The Executioner could see a softening in Brognola's face that told him his friend was relieved to hear that. Bolan knew that his country, as much as he loved it, was at times guided by people who acted from personal motivations that weren't in the best interest of the nation. It didn't make the country any less loved, but it had prompted him to undertake his arm's-length relationship with anyone connected directly to the government. That way he could still do what needed doing without worrying about everyone else involved.

"But who do we hit back?" the President asked. "France? Germany? I refuse to believe those governments are behind the attacks against the United States.''

"But it's been confirmed that the attack on that house," Brognola said, pointing at the television set, "was done by members of the Franco-German army.''

"Yes. But we don't know under whose orders they were acting."

"Barnabe Siffre was responsible for the formation of the Franco-German army, wasn't he?" Bolan asked.

"Primarily," the Man replied. "But he wasn't alone in the effort. This new group doesn't operate entirely under government sanction. The French and German business interests pull a lot of weight with them, as well."

"Which puts Siffre in the driver's seat, as well as the political leaders," Bolan commented.

"Along with a number of other financial investors of both countries who've shoved money at the project. If you're expecting to be able to trace whoever gave the order to take that place down, you won't be able to. The Franco-German army's top brass is shielded from us so far."

"I wasn't considering that," Bolan said. "If there had been a way inside the Franco-German army Intelligence network that was worthwhile, I know a way would already have been made."

"Then what are your suggestions?" the President asked.

"We take whatever leads are available to us and we start a chain reaction back to the source," Bolan said. It was a method he'd used a lot in his Mafia war days, rattling cages just to see what would panic and fall out. "Phoenix and Able have turned over a couple of rocks that we can start with. We'll put it together from that."

"The United States can't appear to be a part of this," the Man warned.

Bolan nodded. "That's understandable at this point."

"It's also regrettable," the chief executive said. "For you, as well as the other Stony teams. But things between all of the countries involved are extremely tense. And it seems all the problems and pitfalls facing the U.S. haven't been laid out on the table yet."

Bolan wasn't surprised. Even the best plans didn't cover every contingency.

"Judging from the surface appearance after Able Team was nearly killed along with its target," the Man said, "whoever is framing America and Russia with the bacterial weapons has also got considerable influence inside the borders of this country. There's no telling how much damage those groups will be able to cause inside national boundaries, or how it might look to international parties watching what develops in Europe." The President sighed. "But you're right. We can't sit here and hope for the best. We've got to take action."

"It'll help once we figure out more of what they're after," Bolan said.

"I'd say what they're after is pretty obvious," the President replied. "More control in Europe, unsupervised by the United States."

"Yeah," Bolan said, "but that's not all of it. What kind of control? How are they planning on attaining it? What will they settle for if they can't have it all?"

"Knowing that is going to help?"

"Yes." Bolan faced the chief executive. "Once you put a goal into terms of a military objective with the rules of engagement attached, there are steps you have to undertake to achieve that objective. Once we can see those steps, understand them, then we can take a more direct action. Without being able to directly confront whoever is behind this, we're talking about guerrilla warfare. That's fine. Stony Man Farm was designed with that in mind. We draw the final line, and nobody crosses it. As soon as we think we have a fix on their game plan, we can take them down before they can get entrenched."

"And if they're already entrenched?" the President asked.

"Then," Bolan said, "it takes a little more time."

CHAPTER NINE

Stony Man Farm, Virginia
6:33 a.m.

"Sarge."

Mack Bolan came out of the light doze he'd willed himself into earlier. He blinked his eyes against the early-morning sun pouring in through the Plexiglas bubble of the military Huey he and Brognola had boarded at a secure area at Washington National Airport. Taking a deep breath, he cast out the last chill that prolonged fatigue had caused to take root in him. His eyes felt grainy. Even though he'd been trained by circumstances and himself to take the most from whatever respite he was offered, the jump had taken less than forty-five minutes. It wasn't enough rest.

"Coffee." Seated in the pilot's chair, the yoke of the Huey comfortably in hand, Jack Grimaldi pointed at the two foam cups sitting in a mounted cup caddy between the seats.

Bolan reached out, took one of the coffees and peeled out the preformed sipping tab. "Hal?"

Grimaldi jerked a thumb over his shoulder. "Rear deck, logging phone time."

Shifting in his seat, Bolan felt the rest of his body come sluggishly alive. It was one thing to come up out of a full sleep in the middle of a hellground suddenly gone volatile. Then adrenaline covered all the squeaks and aches of past injuries and old wounds. Waking up when he wasn't in a fight-or-flight mode was sometimes less than pleasurable. He looked down at the Blue Ridge Mountains. They were covered by a carpet of emeralds that swooped and fell with the land.

"It's beautiful out here," Grimaldi said. "Sometimes I take an extra ten or fifteen minutes for myself when there's nothing pressing."

Bolan nodded. He knew. There were memories buried in those hills, some good, some bad. Some of them still ached. Fighting men had a history of dying along that terrain, striving to protect or serve an ideal. American mountain men had perished there while trying to fulfill the idea of manifest destiny. Brothers, fathers and sons had lost their lives during the Civil War.

And Stony Man Farm had buried some of its dead there, too.

He turned in the seat, cast off thoughts of the past and concentrated on the shape of the coming mission. From his own estimate, landing was less than ten minutes away.

The radio crackled.

Grimaldi lifted one of his earpieces and clapped it to his head. Bolan did the same.

"G-Force, this is Stony Air. Over."

"Go, Stony Air. Over."

The voice of Stony Man Farm's air-operations man was taut, professional. "We've gone to alert status here on the ground, G-Force. It appears you've acquired a hitchhiker the last five minutes of your flight. Stony Base requests that you make no further moves toward the Farm till that has been dealt with. Over."

"Whereaway is our hitchhiker?" Grimaldi asked. "Over."

Bolan took a pair of Zeiss binoculars from his kit, uncapped the lenses and swept his gaze across the sky. His combat senses came on-line, pushing away the last of the sloth caused by fatigue and the lack of sleep.

"At five o'clock from your present heading. Over."

Grimaldi moved the stick, stopped the forward motion of the Huey and gained altitude like an express elevator, coming around in a slow spin. "The way I see it, Sarge, we can stop dead in the water at about tree level and play possum—let them figure out what the hell we're doing—or we jump right in there among 'em and find out damn quick what they're up to. Me, I don't feel like waiting."

Brognola came forward. "What's going on?"

Bolan explained with an economy of words. A heartbeat later he found the other aircraft, focused on the silver sheen of it and brought it closer with the glasses. "I've got it."

"Me, too," Grimaldi said. His arm moved, and the helicopter locked into position like a cobra poised to strike. "Looks like a midrange Cessna." He held their position. The rotor beat steadily.

Brognola seized an extra headset from the mounts overhead and slipped it on, then hunkered between the seats.

"Can you get any numbers on that thing?" Grimaldi asked.

Tracking the Cessna's flight pattern, Bolan zoomed in on the identification numbers along the airplane's tail, calling them out as he made them.

"Stony Air, this is G-Force. I've got a number on your bogey." Grimaldi repeated the letters and numbers the Executioner had given him.

Panning in closer, Bolan studied the occupants.

The Cessna made a slow, lazy half circle in front of the helicopter.

Grimaldi held his ground, turning slowly to the right as he kept the Huey's nose pointed at the Cessna.

Bolan counted six people inside the plane's cabin. The small cargo room behind them could have held more. The ones he saw were men. Something about the cut of their hair suggested military backgrounds. The pilot wore a shoulder rig. Bolan caught a glimpse of it as the plane banked to the left, floated farther out in the one-hundred-eighty-degree path it was taking.

"What are they doing?" Brognola asked.

"Trying to figure out where the Farm's airstrip is," Grimaldi replied. "They've been following us for a while, maybe since Washington. Must have an on-board radar because there's no way anybody slipped a homer on this baby. I took care of the maintenance myself."

"They'll have trouble spotting the Farm for what it really is unless they've been briefed," the Executioner said. Camo netting that took advantage of the natural terrain around the Farm would make it hard to spot unless the searcher knew what to look for. The outpost had been located where it was so that it wouldn't be easily found. He pulled back the focus and swept the Cessna's line again. Something was scratching at the back of his mind, demanding his attention.

"G-Force, this is Stony Air. Over."

"Go, Stony Air. Over."

"Drawing a blank on your numbers, son. That bogey floating around you hasn't filed a flight plan with any airports close enough to make the jump here possible. And those numbers don't belong to any legally listed aircraft in the United States. Over."

"Understood, Stony Air. What does Stony Base suggest we do about the bogey? Over."

"That's your discretion, G-Force. We're standing down here, but we're ready to back your play as long as we don't compromise our position here. Over."

"Tell the lady I'm going to knock on this guy's door. See what he's up to. I don't especially like the feel of hanging around out here like a clay pigeon. G-Force out." Grimaldi moved the yoke. The helicopter dipped its nose, then shot forward, veering toward the Cessna.

Apparently the pilot noticed his approach immediately. The Cessna came around in a tight circle, climbed for more altitude, putting the sun at its back until Bolan could see only a two-dimensional black silhouette against the glare. But in that time he'd seen what his subconscious had been warning him about. "That plane's armed," he announced.

Bolan stuffed the binoculars into a side pocket of his duffel and unzipped the main compartment.

"What's it got?" Grimaldi asked in a tight voice.

"Cannon mounted under the belly. Molding covers most of it, but it's there if you look."

"Twenty mil?"

"I think so."

"Shit." Grimaldi broke off his approach.

Reaching into his duffel, Bolan took out a Mini-14 Ruger Ranch Rifle Model 5RF and two 30-round clips. A long strip of ordnance tape secured the clips together facing different directions, then he slammed the first magazine home. He worked the action, throwing the first .223 round into the breech. The folding stock snapped into place.

Something sizzled by just outside the Plexiglas windows, then an explosion blossomed in the forest of trees off to one side. An oak crashed to the side, blown out of the ground by the explosive round.

"Obviously playtime's over," Grimaldi said as he swung around the tail of the Huey. "Since we're not going to cooperate, I guess they don't think they need us anymore."

"Can we lose them?" Bolan asked.

"Not in this," Grimaldi said. "We're not as outclassed as if they'd had a Learjet, but we'll definitely come in second in any kind of footrace."

More 20 mm cannon rounds streaked by the helicopter and smacked into the ground and forest with echoing, booming thuds that rolled over the mountainous terrain.

Grimaldi zigged and zagged, struggling to become a difficult target. The problem was, Bolan knew, that being a difficult target was the best the pilot could hope for. The Huey wasn't carrying any armament. And the Mini-14 wouldn't provide much of an edge, especially after the initial surprise wore off. He reached into the duffel again and took out a wide-lensed sniping scope.

Brognola made room as Bolan worked his way into the cargo area. Together they slid the doors back. The slipstream reached tangible fingers into the open area and tore at their clothing. The warrior tapped his headset, opening the frequency connecting the helicopter crew to Stony Man Farm. "Stony One to Stony Base. Over."

The Cessna burned up along the Huey's back trail. The cannon rounds sailed by above and below, on both sides, scarring the forest below.

"Go, Stony One, you have Stony Base," Barbara Price said. "Over."

The Executioner stood at the side of the cargo opening and attached the sniper scope to the rings of the Mini-14. It clipped into place easily. "We have two options at this point, Stony Base. Staying in the air isn't one of them. Either we land there or we put down here." He quickly explained the

Cessna's mounted cannon. The detonation of the explosive rounds transmitted along the frequency.

"Buy us some time," Price replied calmly. "We're not leaving you people out there to hang. Stony Base out."

"Jack," Bolan called as he sighted through the sniper scope.

"I heard," the pilot responded. "I don't know how long I'm going to be able to juke these guys around. That pilot's pretty good, and this Huey stands out real well against the forest below."

"I'll give them something else to think about," Bolan promised. He took up the slack on the trigger. "Give me a platform until I tell you to break."

"You got it." The Huey stabilized.

Keeping both eyes open, his breath coming in steadily through his nose and emptying through his mouth, Bolan put the Cessna's cockpit inside the cross hairs of the scope.

The airplane was a steel-and-fiberglass predator almost three hundred yards behind them, slightly elevated. A white fog puffed out from the cannon mounted under the Cessna's belly.

The cross hairs settled over the pilot.

Another round from the 20 mm cannon streaked by, amputating the top of a tree less than fifteen feet below the helicopter's landing skids.

Bolan concentrated on his shot. The airplane pulled to within two hundred fifty yards.

"At this range, Sarge," Grimaldi said, "we're sitting ducks."

The Huey skimmed along the treetops.

The Executioner fired his first round, the Mini-14 banging against his shoulder. He tracked the shot immediately, knowing the pilot's response would be in a heartbeat or less. He took in the round hole in the center of a white spiderweb spread over the glass slightly above the pilot's head, brought the rifle's barrel lower and squeezed off seven rounds at the cockpit.

Abruptly the Cessna dropped a wing and heeled over, turning belly outward as it broke off pursuit.

The Executioner went through the rest of the clip in quick succession, aiming at the body of the plane. With the whipping slipstreams working against both aircraft, as well as the prevailing winds in the area, it was no surprise the 62-grain boattails jumped inches in their approach to the intended target. Bolan felt confident at least some of the bullets struck the Cessna, letting the hardmen aboard know the Huey was capable of fighting back in some capacity.

"Okay, Jack, break." Bolan switched magazines.

The helicopter juked left. "You bought us some time," Grimaldi said, "and maybe a little breathing space. But they'll be back. They'll just stay out of range of your rifle."

The Cessna gained altitude, coming around again. The 20 mm cannon broke the tree line, starting small fires on the ground.

"Tenacious little bastards, aren't they?" Brognola said.

"Skilled," Bolan replied. "And they must be paid well if they're willing to risk themselves like this. They have to know they're looking for a ground base, using themselves as bait."

"Somebody's not pulling any punches."

"Yeah, but once we get a fix on this thing, neither will we."

The Cessna clung to the helicopter's back trail with dogged determination.

"G-Force, this is Stony Base. Over." Price's voice was clipped, professional.

"Go. Over," Grimaldi called back.

"You are approved for flyby. Over."

"Roger that, Stony Base, but be acknowledged that G-Force is coming in steaming hot. Out."

The Huey spun in the air, taking a new course.

"You guys better strap in back there," Grimaldi called out. "Things are going to get dicey."

Sitting across from Brognola, Bolan belted himself in, listening to the rotor throb overhead and scanning the visible parts of the sky for their attacker. The forest sometimes less than a yard below became a rushing, verdant river. He keyed his headset. "Stony One to Stony Air. Over."

"Go, Stony One. Over."

"Are there any other aircraft within the vicinity? Over."

"Negative, Stony One. Everything else on-screen checks out clean. Over."

"So if this team is relaying the information they have, they're transmitting to a ground-based communications net. Can you jam their signal? Over."

There was a brief hesitation.

Grimaldi zigzagged like a broken-field runner looking to pick up a moving blocker.

"That's affirmative, Stony One. Stony Air can do. Over."

"During the final approach," Bolan said, "jam their signal. Maybe we can keep from compromising your twenty. Over."

"Roger," the Stony Air communications officer responded, "but Stony Base looks like she's got us covered, sir. Stony Air out."

Brognola raised his eyebrows in grim, silent mirth. "That's the way I feel," he shouted across to Bolan, "when I start trying to do Barb's job for her."

"Okay, gents," Grimaldi called out, "we're going in."

Bolan saw the Cessna heeling over, tracking onto the latest course correction. The 20 mm cannon had fallen silent. Evidently the team realized the Huey was going home to roost.

"Stony Air, you have G-Force on the flyby. Over."

"Bring it on, G-Force. Here at Stony Air, we're loaded for bear. Over."

For an instant Bolan caught sight of the landing strip north of the Farm. Then it was gone.

"Loaded for bear, eh?" Grimaldi radioed. "Well, skin this one and I'll bring you another. G-Force out."

The Huey never faltered, never veered.

Bolan watched the Cessna break into the Farm's airspace. For a moment it was there, and he doubted the pilot ever knew he or his craft was in serious trouble. Then a roiling orange-and-black fireball enveloped the small plane, crunching it to pieces as if enclosed by massive jaws. The flaming bits of wreckage rained toward the ground.

Grimaldi brought the Huey around. Below, a dozen men moved along the outer perimeters of the landing strip, getting ready to drop the camo netting back into place. At least that number of jeeps and four-wheel-drive vehicles were plunging into the forest with Stony Man blacksuits clinging to the seats. The equipment thrown into the jeeps that Bolan could see included fire extinguishers, axes, camo netting and shovels.

Monitoring the blacksuit frequency for a moment, the warrior found out the standing orders were to seek out the debris left by the Cessna and bury it or cover it over where they found it. Night excursions would be made later to get rid of it once and for all.

On the ground, he ducked out of the Huey, followed by Grimaldi and Brognola. He paused long enough to grab his duffel and sling the Mini-14 over his shoulder. The ground crew working the airstrip were oblivious to them. That was part of the team's job.

"Yo, homeboys," a raucous voice called out.

Bolan stopped, recognizing the voice at once. He felt a smile touch his lips when he saw Leo Turrin piloting a Jeep Cherokee through the organized confusion littering the landing strip.

"Yo, homeboys?" Grimaldi repeated in obvious derision.

Turrin pulled the Cherokee to a stop in front of them. He grinned. "My bit for mixing the cultures. What can I say?" He was stocky and broad, smiling under a scraggly gunslinger mustache. He'd been in the hellgrounds with Mack Bolan in the Mafia days, a rising young capo with a future and a job moonlighting as an undercover cop for the Justice Department. Somehow he'd made the mixture work, with occasional help from Bolan, and had been able to walk away from most of it when the time came. Now he managed another duality as a semiretired Mafia golden boy and a covert Justice Department agent named Leonard Justice.

"Hey, Leo," Bolan said, shaking hands. He shoved his gear through the open rear door while Grimaldi added his flight bag and personal effects. Brognola took the shotgun seat beside Turrin, leaving the other men the rear seat. They clambered in and Turrin headed back to the farmhouse.

Bolan never failed to be affected by the sight of it. A lot of memories were housed there. And—in a sense—it would always be home, even though he'd rejected the shelter it offered so he could live his life on his own terms.

The Farm was a working industry. Apple and peach orchards produced a bountiful crop every year, as did the fields of vegetables. Some of the crop was canned and stored for Farm use, but the bulk of it found its way to local produce distributors, providing a legitimate cover for the counterterrorist installation.

The main house was three stories tall. Beneath the whitewashed exterior were steel walls that had withstood direct hits from armor-piercing rounds. Besides the main house, there were two outbuildings and a tractor barn that held surprises of their own.

During the daylight hours, denim-clad farmhands worked the orchards and the fields. No one ever saw the Uzis and pistols they carried as part of their everyday equipment. After work hours the woods were alive with black-clad warriors wearing camo combat paint, pulling night patrol.

"How long are you in town this time, Sarge?" Turrin asked.

Bolan showed his old friend a small smile. "Not for long, buddy." He never was.

CHAPTER TEN

"My, my, they're certainly energetic," Barnabe Siffre said as he stared at the thrashing couple on the television screen across the room. He sat at the big mahogany desk he'd had handmade and imported from the West Indies. He felt refreshed from the trip in from Paris. He'd taken time to shower, shave and change suits before he returned to his home office. He continued to study the frantic coupling on the television.

The view was obviously shot through the window from somewhere outside. Though the cameraman was steady, the scene jiggled occasionally, and when it did the magnification necessary to relay the images became apparent.

Trudaine ran a hand through his unruly hair, blinked behind his glasses, then swallowed a yawn. "I guess so. Want something to drink?"

Siffre glanced at his Intelligence specialist with renewed curiosity. "You don't find yourself the slightest bit titillated by this?"

"No." Trudaine's gaze never faltered, nor did it go back to the television.

"Have you ever had a woman?" Siffre asked, suddenly curious in spite of himself.

"Sure. There are plenty of them out there. Can't avoid them all." Trudaine crossed the room to the wet bar in the corner, took down a heavy glass, splashed whiskey into it and added water. Then he reached underneath to bring out a diet Pepsi. He set the drink on a coaster on the desk and kept the soda for himself.

"And how was it?" Siffre asked.

"The woman?"

"Yes."

Trudaine shrugged. "Okay. Except that she talked too much."

"They all have a habit of doing that," Siffre said. "That's why I so rarely trust them, and usually find out some of my best information on competitors through their own secretarial pool." He paused. "Haven't you ever found one woman who really made you feel alive?"

"Maybe."

"And?" Siffre felt as though he were pulling teeth.

"She couldn't keep up with me."

The financier laughed. "That sounds pretty egotistical. Not something I would have expected from you."

Trudaine blushed. "Not in bed. In programming. That's how we met. Through an international BBS."

"It was love at first sight?" Siffre checked the television scene, saw that the woman had clambered on top of the man in the center of the bed.

"No. She was bright. But I'm careful about who I show my work to. For a while I thought she might be able to help. I was wrong." He sipped the soft drink.

"She didn't measure up."

"Not even close."

"Your work means a lot to you."

Trudaine didn't bother to respond.

Siffre felt himself grow irritated. He accepted a certain amount of insolence from the younger man because Trudaine's abilities with cybernetic systems were nothing short of uncanny. "In the years that we've been associated," he said after a moment, "I've never known you to be with a woman."

"That's because I haven't been. There are more important things to do."

"And I've never seen you drink anything stronger than diet Pepsi."

Trudaine dropped into one of the two plush chairs in front of the long desk. He sipped his drink again. The moans and groans of the couple on the television punctuated the silence.

"Every man has passions," Siffre said. "It's the one thing that I've been able to count on, to use in my business. However, with you I find myself mysteriously without leverage."

"Why are we talking about this?"

"Because you are an enigma to me."

"You're worrying for no reason. You give me everything I could ever ask for. There's no reason I would go anywhere else."

"None?"

"No." Trudaine's gaze remained level.

"There are depths to you that remain unplumbed."

"Mr. Siffre, have you ever thought that perhaps you might be the slightest bit paranoid?"

Siffre stared into the other man's face.

Trudaine held up his hands. "No offense intended. I'm just pointing out something here. In the years I've known you, I've seen you peel away layers and layers of ruses and counterruses business people and politicians have wrapped themselves in. You're used to dealing with people who are playing a variety of angles every time they do business with you. It could be that I'm really just more shallow than you want to believe. Perhaps if you discovered I had a hidden agenda, you would be more accepting of me. Paradoxically if I had the seeds of disloyalty with me, maybe you would even find me more trustworthy in your eyes because you'd know what it took to buy me off."

Steepling his fingers together in front of him, Siffre leaned back in his swivel chair. "Maybe you're right."

Trudaine smiled easily. "I know I'm right."

Siffre nodded and turned away from the cybernetics specialist. There was *something* there. He'd almost had a glimpse of it just then. Trudaine, though the man would never admit it, was being more protective than usual. He glanced at the television screen. "Who are these people?"

Turning to look at the television, Trudaine said, "The man is Horst Wessel. One of your German coconspirators. Your agents have gathered proof that Wessel has been hiring people to spy on you, and has, in fact, activated an espionage cell in German Intelligence to investigate you."

"We knew about this?"

"Not until it was too late. What we're attempting now is damage control."

"Every time I've met with my partners," Siffre said, "Wessel has always been a mouse. He had resources, yes, but he's never figured into the scheme of things in a large way."

"He does now," Trudaine replied. "Your agents found out this morning that Wessel has become aware of Dr. Simmy."

"How much does he know?" A knot of concern formed in Siffre's stomach. At this point things were balanced like a house of cards. One shove in the wrong place could precipitate actions on his part that he was unwilling to make, yet would have no choice in making.

"Enough so that he became dangerous to us."

Siffre considered that. "Then why is he still alive?"

"He isn't. Not really." Trudaine uncrossed his legs, stood and walked to the other end of the desk. His eyes on the television screen, he punched a number into the phone.

Siffre knew it was an international call from the number of digits entered. It didn't bother him. The line the cybernetics specialist was using could never be traced back to this building.

Wessel's face contorted in completion, and the woman leaned down heavily over him, her own face covered with disgust she didn't bother to conceal once she was out of his view.

A high-pitched whine bleated from the television speaker. Both Wessel and the woman glanced at her purse, sitting on the nightstand beside the bed.

Trudaine hung up the phone. "The woman is Jennifer McGill. She's in your employ, though she doesn't know about you."

With a real smile on her face, McGill reached under the mattress and brought out a small, bright automatic. Moving with a calm grace, she jammed the barrel of the little gun under Wessel's chin and pulled the trigger four times. The reports of the weapon were almost muffled by the contact with flesh.

Standing, McGill wiped the fingerprints from the pistol and dropped it onto the bed beside the corpse. A fine crimson spray of blood stained her breasts. She poured water from a pitcher into a washbowl on the bureau, cleaned herself quickly, then dressed. For a moment she disappeared, out of view of the camera. When she returned she was a brunette instead of a blonde. She threw a golden-tressed wig onto Wessel's bloody chest. Then she disappeared.

"Show's over," Trudaine said with a sardonic smile. He placed another international call, and the televised transmission winked out a heartbeat later. "Mission accomplished. No fuss, no muss."

Siffre took a pencil from the caddy beside his phone and tapped it on his desk calendar. "The cameraman?"

"Jorgensen. You've used him before."

"Yes." Siffre sat forward as Trudaine switched the television off with the remote control. "I apparently hire good people."

Trudaine resumed his seat. "Yes, you do."

"It also appears that you know a lot about my business. You've been exceeding your responsibilities of late."

A wry grin twisted Trudaine's face. "I choose not to view it as exceeding them, Mr. Siffre. Instead, I congratulate myself on being able to anticipate them better than I used to." He paused, looking deep into his employer's eyes. "I could never take your place, if that's what's crossing your mind right now. I lack the ambition in that field. I couldn't do what I do without you."

"You seem to be doing okay for yourself."

"I know my limitations. Isn't that what Dirty Harry always said in those American movies? A man's got to know his limitations. Well, I know mine. You're the dreamer in this relationship, Mr. Siffre. You figure out the goals, find the emotion within yourself to invest to seek those goals out. My interest in this is just to figure out the ways I can help you attain those goals. I enjoy playing the game by the rules you set up. I've never been able to create a game all by myself. That's what keeps me working with you. The fact that you're driven. It inspires me in ways you can't even begin to imagine."

"You know what I'm ultimately after."

Trudaine nodded.

"And none of that interests you?"

"No. In fact, when the time comes that you are successful—and I believe that you will be with my help—I'll have to find a new game to play. And it depresses me because I know nothing I could hope to find could ever be as grand as this one."

Siffre nodded, understanding at least part of Trudaine's motivations. There was nothing he could think of that could compare with the coup he was aiming for. "What about the Justice agent?—Brognola?"

"The teams missed both times," Trudaine said.

"And where are they?"

"For the most part," the cybernetics specialist said, "they're dead. These people don't fuck around when it comes to gunplay. And their computer-systems people might just be the best I've ever encountered. I haven't been able to break into their files."

"And Brognola's missions base?"

"Remains unknown. Though we're sure it's somewhere in the Blue Ridge Mountains."

"That's a lot of territory to cover."

Trudaine nodded his agreement. "They've had years to dig in. Even if the ground search teams found it, they might not recognize it for what it was."

"We'll back them off the search for now. Our primary targets will shift to Brognola's agents themselves. If the unit has only a small enforcer arm, as our information suggests, taking them out will cripple their effectiveness, leaving the President of the United States no choice but to employ military troops if he wants to stop us." Siffre grinned. "However, by then it will be much too late for him to stop us."

CHAPTER ELEVEN

Stony Man Farm, Virginia
8:58 a.m.

"I'm going to be bringing Phoenix on-line in just a few minutes, Hal," Aaron Kurtzman said. The big man sat behind stacks of computer equipment at his desk, his hands trailing over the keyboard in front of him.

Mack Bolan took a foam cup from the stack at the refreshment table and filled it with coffee. He glanced around the War Room, finding it surprisingly empty without Katz and the rest of his team on hand.

Able Team had made the scene nearly a half hour ago. Blancanales and Schwarz were engaged in one of their seemingly endless animated conversations that usually held the potential of entertaining only themselves. Lyons sat beside them, rubbing his temples and flipping through the hard copy Price had given him on his arrival concerning information Able had turned up from police files.

Turrin and Grimaldi sat on the other side of the long conference table and talked in low voices. Cowboy John Kissinger—the Farm's armorer—sat with them, more observer than participant.

Bolan sat at the other end of the table, opposite Brognola.

The head Fed unwrapped a fresh cigar and slipped it into his mouth, not bothering to light it. A thick stack of papers and documents covered the table in front of him.

The War Room was state-of-the-art. Behind the plain white walls were cybernetic enhancements that turned the room into a communications studio capable of international transmission in an eye blink. Different than Kurtzman's work lab, the War Room literally surrounded the people inside with a wealth of information.

Barbara Price was at Brognola's right hand. The slacks and shirt she wore were professionally cut but couldn't help showing off the well-rounded body beneath. Her eyes moved restlessly as she scanned the information she was receiving on the laptop computer in front of her.

The lights in the room dimmed, and panels slid away from the walls to reveal cream-gray glass surfaces that reached from floor to ceiling and side to side. Without warning, rainbow-colored novas ignited on the screens and burst into four identical pictures of David McCarter's face, ten times its normal size.

Kurtzman looked up at the wall screen at the other end of his workstation. He adjusted his headset and cleared his throat. One of the half-dozen minicameras wired into the ceiling along track bars rotated and fixed on him. "Phoenix, this is Electron Rider. Do you read? Over."

"Phoenix reads, mate," McCarter replied. "Over." The picture blurred briefly as gray lines raced across it.

Kurtzman glanced at the gauges and dials before him. "Adjust your telemetry to these coordinates, Phoenix." He read them off quickly.

Within seconds the broadcast cleared, no longer interrupted by the gray lines and the blurring static.

"Okay, Phoenix, I have your transmission locked. Stand by to scramble." Kurtzman's hands tapped out commands on the keyboard.

Bolan sipped his coffee and thumbed through the stacks of pages and photographs before him, memorizing the hardlined faces he found there. From what Kurtzman and Price had been able to ferret out, the organization they were dealing with had insinuated itself deeply within several layers of government and private industry in Europe. It was going to take key moves in the right places and at the right times to break loose their stranglehold.

The image of the wall screens became redefined and enlarged to encompass all of Phoenix Force. The team sat in chairs and a sofa in the safe house Price had arranged in Paris. McCarter sat cross-legged in front of the compact satellite transceiver-computer on the coffee table. The minicamera broadcasting their images was somewhere before them.

Scanning the men of Phoenix Force, Bolan realized they were looking ragged around the edges, too. They'd all been immersed in the dynamics of the present situation for a few days, but it didn't seem things were going any better.

Brognola stood. One of the cameras moved overhead, buzzing almost silently as it focused on him. The cigar shifted to one side of his mouth. "We've got a situation brewing in Europe," he said without preamble. "At this point, we're uncertain about where it's heading. As you know from your assignments and from the briefs you've been given to look over, someone has framed the United States and the Commonwealth of Independent States, making it look like we're responsible for transporting biochemical weapons across Europe to be disposed of off the coast of Great Britain."

"The frame has been confirmed?" Yakov Katzenelenbogen asked.

"The President gave me his word," Brognola replied.

The gruff ex-Mossad agent nodded.

Bolan understood why the Phoenix commander had to ask. In the past couple of decades, it often seemed that there were two layers to any international event. One that skimmed along the surface of politics where nothing wrong was ever done. And one that quietly flirted with the military aspect of things, in which anything that was done was perceived as the right thing to do, no matter how wrong it might be morally or politically. Stony Man Farm was a clearcut example of the latter kind of thinking. The decision not to try to deal with those two levels and accept only the missions he saw before him had been the major reason the Executioner had left the Stony Man fold.

But trust had to start somewhere, and Bolan trusted the man who presently held the office of chief executive.

"There has been a move within the past few years to gradually push American interests out of Europe," Brognola went on, "or at least to curtail the position American interests have in those countries. It's our belief that someone is taking advantage of that and shoving current paranoia to the breaking point in those nations."

"A Europe First mentality isn't something we can fight against," Encizo said. "It might be true that we can uncover who is framing the United States and the Commonwealth, but the choice about NATO's place on the European continent still belongs to those people living there."

"If that's going to be our operation over here," Manning replied, "it'll take a little time to cut into this thing and figure out who all the players are."

"Unfortunately," Brognola said, "that's not all that's involved here." He glanced at Kurtzman. "Aaron."

Kurtzman nodded, his hands tapping commands into the keyboard.

Brognola continued. "We were able to run a series of tests on the bacterial agents recovered in France. What we encountered was something Intelligence sources had never seen before."

The big cybernetics whiz finished his keyboard adjustments and turned to look expectantly at an area above a flat black mat on a table by itself.

Bolan watched half-inch-wide bands form only inches above the black mat. They were silvery at first, then took on a multitude of colors. It seemed to turn sideways, blinked, then became a three-dimensional collection of corkscrews that looked like giant pasta. They were a bilious green, looking vile enough that the battle-hardened warrior expected them almost to writhe and strike out without warning.

"What the hell is that?" Turrin asked. The tight grimace on the little Fed's face showed the effect the hologram had on him.

"Some of the bacteria found in the canisters recovered from the LeCourbe vineyards," Kurtzman explained. "One of my people has a friend who's a specialist in genetic engineering. Recombinant DNA, that sort of thing. What you're looking at here was created in a lab, by one very clever, twisted son of a bitch. There are supposed to be guidelines against research like this, but like mushrooms, this kind of thing grows in dark places where nobody sees."

The fear and outrage in Kurtzman's tone were evident to Bolan. He leaned forward in his chair, set his coffee to one side and asked, "What is this?"

"Basically it's a biological time bomb."

The bilious green corkscrew shapes continued to slowly spin along in an invisible axis above the black mat.

"I raided files from top-secret U.S. installations after I found out about this," Kurtzman said. "Even hit DARPA."

"But you didn't find anything?" Lyons asked.

"No. I found some research conducted along the lines of what this little monster is supposed to do, but nothing developed anywhere near like this."

Bolan considered that. DARPA was the Defense Advanced Research Projects Agency within the U.S. government. He'd already encountered some of the space-age weaponry those people had been responsible for producing. They were chiefly interested in esoteric means of killing an enemy. He'd heard and read about electromagnetic bombs capable of killing millions of people, yet leaving the buildings standing. If DARPA wasn't aware of the strain of bacteria found in France, it had to be something really nasty or new—possibly both.

"I also checked with Russian research facilities I have taps into," Kurtzman went on. "They had some of this stuff on the drawing board there, but hadn't done any real development on the hypothesis."

"What does this do?" Bolan asked.

"That," Kurtzman said, looking at the slowly revolving holo of the bacteria, "is a potential famine waiting to happen. Let loose, that bacteria would kill every green and growing thing on the face of the earth within its sphere of influence."

Letting his mind run with the information, Bolan sifted back through the facts, figures and photos in front of him. It put an entirely new face on things. "Those bacterial agents were supposed to be discovered."

"Yeah," Brognola said heavily. "That's what we think, too."

"It wasn't just a red herring to the European communities," Bolan said. "Those canisters were meant as a warning to the United States."

"That's how the Man sees it," the head Fed agreed.

"How does this thing work, Aaron?" Calvin James asked. The ex-SEAL also had a background in medical arts and chemistry.

"As I said," Kurtzman explained, "this is a bacterium. Usually bacteria come in one of three shapes. You got your rod-shaped ones—called bacillus. Your ball-shaped ones are called coccus, and then you got these. The corkscrew-shaped ones are called spirillum. Everybody's familiar with designer drugs. This is a designer bacterium. The concept isn't new. It's been around for years. One of the most common examples we have of designer bacteria is insulin shots for diabetics. The basic function of any bacteria is to break something down. It's bacteria that cause dead animals and plants to decay. The digestive system wouldn't work without bacteria. Plants depend on bacteria that live in the soil to change nitrogen into substances the plants can use."

"They also use bacteria in industry," Schwarz added. "Without them you wouldn't have paints, plastics, cosmetics, candies, along with other drugs besides insulin. Businesses use bacteria to cure tobacco leaves, tan hides, dissolve the outer coverings of coffee and cocoa seeds and separate fibers for the textile industry. They even have bacteria that help refine metal and petroleum products by eating the impurities in them. Sewage-disposal plants are another chief user of bacteria."

"This bacterium was years in the making," Kurtzman told them. "It had to be. Specialists I've talked to this morning tell me something like this would have to be babied along through a lot of gene-splicing to get the end result. But in the end, they got it." He tapped computer keys.

The corkscrew shapes melted from view, replaced by a three-dimensional green-and-blue image of the world turning on its axis.

"Hey, mate," McCarter said, "I think I've seen this soap opera."

Brittle laughter went around the table and echoed into the War Room from the scrambled transmissions. Bolan knew the cause for their grim chuckles in the face of adversity. They were all hard men doing a hard job, and when the opportunity presented itself, they played hard, too. He got up from the table long enough to get a coffee refill.

"You haven't seen this one," Kurtzman said. "The bacterium you just saw was designed to attack green, growing things, particularly grain- and fruit-bearing plants and trees. Bacteria that attack specific fruits and vegetables are already known to us."

"Like fire blight in pears," Lyons said.

"Yes," Kurtzman responded.

"Way to go, Ironman," Blancanales said in mock appreciation.

"Hey," Lyons said, "I'm just putting this into perspective so I can get a handle on it." He shifted his attention back to Kurtzman. "I spent a couple summers when I was a kid working orchards with migrant farm families to pick up extra money. I learned about a few things then. Learned how to slip melons like they were newborn babies because you were paid for the unbroken ones. Learned about fire blight in pears, too. What I was told, fire blight is caused by bacteria that live in the bark of trees. The pears we've got over on the West Coast are the European variety. They're real susceptible to the fire blight we have in the States, but the effects are small on the Pacific coast. That's why California, Oregon and Washington grow almost ninety percent of the pears in the U.S. They imported pears from Asia because they were resistant to fire blight."

"Right," Kurtzman said. "The genetic coding is different in those species."

"Yeah," Lyons went on, "but the Asian pears were hard and gritty. They were called sand pears for a reason. People worked with them for a while, crossed the Asian pears with the European ones and came up with a pear that had a better taste appeal and was still resistant to fire blight. But even if somebody came up with a super fire-blight bacteria, there are ways to keep it from hurting the produce."

"You're right and you're wrong," Kurtzman said. "You're correct when you say a bacterium can be fought. Breeders have to figure out new strains all the time. For better flavor, better texture, to get a hardier species. But that all takes months and years of planning and research. If someone unleashed the bacterium that we've discovered here, we're talking about a major famine that could envelop the world."

The revolving holo image of the earth stopped with the North American continent facing the table. A fiery crimson line quickly zipped across the land mass and inscribed the United States.

"The bacterium we're talking about here is a real vicious bastard," Kurtzman said. "It covers a broad-based spectrum. Unlike fire blight, or black rot in cabbage, this bacterium can destroy an as-yet-untold number of grain- and fruit-bearing plants and trees. If enough of it was unleashed in the United States alone, can you imagine what the results would be?"

Without warning, the area within the red lines turned black and died.

"Famine," Brognola said. "Pure and simple. The United States is the world's single largest producer of farm products in the world. We supply almost half of the corn that goes on the world's tables every day."

"If you postulate a little, as Barb and I have done," Kurtzman said, "add in Canada because it's outside the European sphere of influence, too. They produce a lot of grains and timbers, as well as beef."

A red line raced around the Canadian borders, and the ten provinces and territories died.

"We're facing problems with global hunger now," Brognola said. "If something like this got loose in the world, there'd be no stopping it for years. And during every one of those years, the attrition rate would increase. It would take years to develop new strains of plants and trees that could withstand the bacterium Aaron has described. And even more years before those new plants and trees could be planted and start bearing." He took the cigar from his mouth and tossed it into an ashtray beside him.

"Has the President been contacted by anyone?" Bolan asked.

"No," Brognola replied. "Not yet. But we're expecting the ransom notice at any time."

Barbara Price stood. "We're not waiting for the ransom notice, though, gentlemen. By the time we get it, if we're not already in motion, we're dead in the water. For right now, we've got a blank check to operate. But we have no Intelligence umbrella, either, so you're going to have to cover your butts out there as well as you can. You can depend on the Farm to give you as much support as we possibly can, but that will mainly consist of Intelligence and weaponry. Whoever we're up against has a timetable. Bet on it. Our key offensive here is to take that timetable away, make the opposition start covering holes by putting the pressure on. If we're successful, they'll start making mistakes we can capitalize on."

"We have two goals here," Brognola added. "First and foremost we have to find out how much of this bacterium has been made and get it out of unfriendly hands. Second we need to clear up the confusion about American and Russian duplicity in the European theater."

"What have we got to work with?" Bolan asked.

Price looked at Kurtzman and nodded.

The room dimmed a little more as the holo of the world popped, exploded and faded away. All four wall screens were lit up with a handful of images concentrating on a slim, elderly man. He stood with military erectness, the polished head of a cane gleaming between tapered fingers. Except for a short-cropped fringe of gray hair around his head, he was bald. A monocle ringed his left eye, serving as a counterpoint to his hawkish nose.

"You're looking at Dr. Gustav Simmy," Kurtzman told his audience.

"He's a Russian microbiologist," Schwarz said. "I've read some of the articles he's written for international science digests."

Kurtzman nodded. "He's also the man we believe to be responsible for the bacterium. While he was still working with the KGB out of Directorate 13, a lot of his research was grounded in molecular restructuring that would have resulted in the bacterium found in France. Like some of the things hypothesized in our own country, Dr. Simmy's works were considered too terrible to be given a physical reality."

"Could be the Russian politicos took great delight in pointing out to the military mind-set that destruction of the free world's ability to feed an international market wasn't exactly the brightest of ideas," Manning said.

"Yeah," Kurtzman agreed, "but someone paid for it to happen."

"Are you sure Simmy created the bacteria?" Bolan asked.

Price fielded the question. "Simmy is the best lead we have for now. If he didn't create the bacterium as we believe, then it's very probable he might know who did. Whoever is responsible for the bacterium, they had to use Simmy's research."

Bolan studied the flat, harsh face. "His ties to the KGB aren't going to stand up very well in the light if he is the one."

"He's not with the KGB or its successor anymore," Price replied. "Since 1989 he's been in Germany. Leipzig. The CIA monitored his defection there but hasn't been able to get close enough to him to figure out what he's been working on."

"And now we have the Franco-German army moving onto the scene in a big way," James said. "That sounds like no coincidence to me."

A tight smile turned up the corners of Price's mouth. "We're betting it isn't, either, Calvin."

More faces drifted across the wall screens.

"Those are the people we put down this morning," Lyons said, straightening in his chair.

"They're mercs," Price replied. "Most of them. A number of the ones you see here usually hole up in New Orleans. And others, from what we've been able to trace, were paid through funds from Stoccard Industries, a company in New Orleans. Reports we scanned in the FBI files suggested that Merle Spurlock runs a large percentage of the merc brokerage business down in New Orleans. Some of these people were known to associate with him."

The wall screens wavered and changed, refocusing on a broad, beefy man. Merle Spurlock looked to be in his early fifties, with salt-and-pepper-colored hair tight against his skull in small ringlets. His beard in subsequent pictures was of varying lengths and always looked darker when it was shortest. He wore wire-rimmed glasses and clenched a pipe between his teeth in most of the outdoors pictures.

"The connection's loose," Price admitted, "but it's enough that I'm sending Able down to investigate." She glanced at Lyons. "With a low profile if possible."

Price looked at the wall screens. "Katz?"

"Yes."

Kurtzman tapped commands into the computer. A heartbeat later Spurlock cleared from the wall screens and was replaced with Phoenix Force.

"What did your questioning of Fauborg turn up?"

"A man named Pasquale Crivello," Katz replied. "I'm working through some old contacts in Paris now to find out what I can about the man."

Bolan sipped his coffee. Katz had been Israeli Mossad before being recruited to lead Phoenix Force. The man believed in his people's struggle, but his views had shifted over the years. He still fought for Israeli freedoms, but from an international standpoint rather than a national one. The Israelis were sometimes too blinded by their own passions to be effective on an international level, and that was where the whole world was turning. In past missions, Katz had worked with and against Mossad agents. There was no guarantee what his reception would be once he attempted contact.

"Have you negotiated a meeting?" Price asked.

"Yes."

"How necessary is it?"

"Aaron was unable to identify Crivello," Katz replied. "If we are to pursue the leads we've established, we need to know more about the man."

"Agreed," Price said. "How honest are you going to have to be with your friend concerning the present problems in Europe?"

"I think it can be managed. They might try to take an active interest, but I'm confident we can stop that before it becomes a problem."

"I'll leave that in your hands. If there's anything I can do from this end, let me know."

Katz nodded.

Price turned to Bolan. "Striker, your mission begins in Leipzig. Jack's going with you to maintain aerial transportation. I've worked out some details with the German government regarding your freedoms inside the country. It's not much, but you do have some latitude. According to your cover story, you're on the ground investigating high-tech industrial espionage regarding American businesses trying to establish themselves over there. Try to remain in the shadows, because once this situation goes ballistic, all bets are off. I might be able to extricate you from the country, but we need Simmy or his research notes if we can get them."

"Understood."

"John."

Cowboy John Kissinger looked up. "Yeah?"

"You're on the ground with Striker on this one."

The big man nodded.

"The Russians are interested in clearing themselves of any wrongdoing, as well," Price added. "Chances are you'll encounter some of their teams who'll use Simmy as a way of proving their own innocence and leave the United States to take the rap. You'll be providing ground support."

"Got it."

Leo Turrin glanced up with a lopsided grin on his face. "Still leaves the sarge running solo."

"Any suggestions?"

Turrin glanced at Bolan. "Want to take a chance on a guy who used to know how to play the game before he got settled behind a nine-to-five desk job? When I was in the Army, I pulled a stint in West Germany. I know the lingo enough to get by on the street."

"I think Leo's just lining himself up for one of those cheap European vacations," Schwarz commented. "But what the hell, Sarge, take him along with you and air him out a little.''

"The way I remember it," Bolan said, "there was a time when you and I made a hell of a team." He glanced at Price. "Any problem with a second cover to go along with the first?"

Price smiled. "I can't think of one." She shuffled her papers and files together in front of her. "For the moment, gentlemen, that's all we have to go on. At this point it's up to you to help bring information into our network so we can figure out the next steps to take. Whoever's behind this, you can bet they're not waiting for us to make the next move. They'll be making moves of their own. So when we do move, let's make sure each step we take is designed to shake their damn house down." She locked eyes with every man at the table and with the camera relay to Phoenix Force. "We're adjourned. Let's get to it."

CHAPTER TWELVE

Leipzig, Germany
4:46 a.m.

"Lot of movement around a place that's supposed to be conducting top-secret research."

Mack Bolan lay quietly in the shadows and kept the light-amplified binoculars roving across the target area. Beside him, shielded by the foliage and the tall grasses filling the area, Leo Turrin used his own binoculars to scan the blacktop road leading up to the complex in the valley before them. The main highway was seven klicks away. They'd hidden their car along the road, then hiked the rest of the way, arriving almost an hour ago.

"They're not working under any illusions that they're anywhere near a secret installation," Bolan said quietly. "Looks like someone's given them the order to abandon the site."

On the surface Konigsalle Laboratories had been a legitimate business for almost thirty years. After World War II, with the poverty levels that had quickly been reached under Russian rule, cutbacks had closed the complex for eight months. Shortly thereafter it had reopened, this time as a camouflage for East German Stasi operations. Once the Stasi had become a thing of the past in the reunited nation, the complex had been taken over by agents fleeing the Communist purge in the Commonwealth. Aaron Kurtzman's information search had been extensive.

But then it had to be because the two warriors were staking their lives on it.

The complex was almost four hundred yards away, in the heart of the valley. It consisted of five buildings. The four outer buildings were designed to support the central structure: two of them were storehouses, a third housed a cafeteria, the fourth held the staff cars and transport trucks. A dulled gray fence with coiled barbed wire across the top enclosed the area, leaving at least twenty yards of barren ground between the fence line and the nearest wall of any building.

"It's not going to be easy to get in," Turrin commented.

Bolan grinned. "You and I never signed on for the easy assignments."

Turrin grinned back, his face masked by combat cosmetics, as was Bolan's. "Yeah, that's why I figure we're owed."

"Let's close it in." The Executioner pushed himself to his feet and took advantage of the brush and trees as he eased down the gentle defile. He was clad in a blacksuit, the Desert Eagle holstered on his right hip, counterweighted by the Beretta 93-R leathered under his left arm. His lead weapon for the night's probe was an East German made MPiKMS-72 assault rifle. A Gerber Mark II combat knife was sheathed in a breakaway holster on his combat harness. Equipment pouches carried smoke and explosive grenades, extra magazines for the pistols and rifle and other deadly tools of the warrior's trade.

Turrin was similarly clad and wore two .38 Special Mauser revolvers in a double shoulder holster. He carried a MPiKMS-72, as well.

A dark Mercedes sedan pulled to a halt at the electronically controlled double gates. A guard jogged to the driver's side, rifle slung over his shoulder. He used a penlight, glanced hurriedly at a sheaf of papers thrust out at him, then waved the car through.

The guard in the security booth acted immediately, and the gates slid back smoothly on well-oiled casters. The car eased through and accelerated at once. The ruby brake lights flared briefly as it made the corner farther down the blacktop road.

"Chances look kind of grim about finding Simmy still here," Turrin commented.

"Tonight," Bolan said, "we'll take what we can get." His body was still fatigued from the ten-hour jump from Virginia by the pair of F-111s he and Grimaldi had piloted into the American base in Berlin. The Stony Man pilot had remained with the planes. Kissinger was waiting in a Volkswagen van borrowed from the military base and specially outfitted with armament and bulletproofing.

Less than a hundred yards away, Bolan came to a stop and raised the binoculars to his eyes again. He scanned the complex grounds, working through quadrants he'd marked off in his mind. Though the men were dressed in dark maroon security uniforms, their movements were unmistakably military.

Bolan looked at Turrin as he slipped a pair of wire cutters from his gear. "Ready?"

Turrin nodded. "As I'm ever going to be."

The Executioner took the lead, creeping through the grass as he made his way to the east fence line, opposite the main gate. Dawn was only minutes away, already lightening the sky behind their approach into the compound. Strands of shadows twisted through the long grass, wet with dew.

The warrior's face was damp by the time he reached the fence, and droplets fell from his chin. He flexed the wire cutters, choosing his first link. Security had definitely lapsed. A number of the guards had lit cigarettes, and none of their commanders cared.

"You've got the watch," the warrior whispered.

Turrin settled into position at the Executioner's back. "Do it."

Reaching forward with the wire cutters, Bolan clipped the first strand. The metal parted with a distinct ping. Others followed in quick succession. His hand cramped from the effort, but he ignored the pain. Within minutes he was halfway around a square big enough to let them through the fence.

The sound of approaching footsteps reached Bolan's ears a heartbeat before Turrin's hand dropped to his shoulder.

"Wait a sec," Turrin warned.

Bolan moved back, looked at the way the section of fence listed in its moorings but didn't think it would be enough to give them away.

The guard gave the appearance of stretching his legs more than being on patrol. A cigarette dangled loosely from his lips, burning bright orange as he drew on it. His rifle was strapped over his shoulder, out of easy reach.

Bolan drew the Beretta and waited, breathing slowly through his mouth. He lay prone in the grass, hoping the darkness and the shadows would effectively mask his presence.

For a moment it seemed the shadows and their clothing would be enough. The guard passed by, then caught himself and turned around. Cupping his cigarette in his palm, he shrugged and dropped his shoulder, catching the Heckler & Koch HK-91 as the strap slid free. He moved back toward the cut section of fence.

"Shit," Turrin said softly.

The guard's eyes widened in surprise, and the cigarette tumbled from his lips.

Lifting the Beretta from the protective shadows of the grass, Bolan triggered three silenced rounds. One of them skated across a link in the wire mesh and threw out a stream of sparks that quickly vanished. All three 9 mm rounds took the guard in the face.

The man's head jerked backward, pulling the rest of his body behind him, and sprawled him in a loose heap.

Leathering the 93-R, Bolan went back to work on the fence, clipping the remaining strands in quick succession. Activity at the main gate had picked up, drawing more attention from the bored security staff.

Once the fence was cut through, Bolan reached for the dead man, grabbed his foot and pulled. Turrin helped. The corpse went through the opening with only slight difficulty, and they cached it in a pool of shadows and brush along the uneven ground.

Bolan took the lead and clambered through the fence on his belly, followed by Turrin. The stocky Fed squirmed through a little more slowly, pausing to pull the cut section of fence back into place and secure it with a piece of tape from his kit.

Pushing himself to his feet, Bolan unlimbered his assault rifle and jogged for the nearest outbuilding, shielded by a wide-bodied transport truck. He came up against the

building and glanced at the main structure. Only a few lights
gleamed within. He looked at Turrin.

"Whenever you're ready," the stocky Fed said.

Bolan drove his feet hard against the packed earth, kept
the assault rifle high and dodged into the recessed doorway. He reached up and smashed the dim security bulb
above his head as Turrin joined him.

"Got it," Turrin said as he slid into place.

Glass broke under the Executioner's boots as he plunged
through the door. Beyond, the hallway was dark, broken
only by a few squares of light coming from doors and windows of the lab rooms. He moved forward, grimly aware
that there was no time to waste. If anything remained of Dr.
Gustav Simmy or the biologist's research, he had to act
quickly.

The first room was sterile white. Long lab tables in the
middle of the floor looked like rectangular black islands. A
half-dozen stools sat haphazardly around them. Two white
lab smocks hung on hooks mounted on the wall, and a lone
Bunsen burner sat on the middle table, its flame a wavering
blue arc. A confusion of chemical smells overlaid the room.
The big warrior couldn't identify them, but there was one he
did know.

"That's gasoline," Turrin said.

"Yeah." Bolan took out his penlight, flicked it on and
played it over the room. Shallow pools of liquid shined under the tables, creating gleaming streaks across the black
surface of the countertops. "Scorched earth. They're not
leaving anything behind."

Voices sounded out in the hallway, carrying into the lab.

Bolan waved Turrin to one side of the door and took the
other for himself. He lifted the heavy assault rifle, keeping
the safety on.

Two men stepped into the room. The lead man carried an
H&K MP-5 and swept the room with a casual glance. The
man behind him was dressed in a silvery thermal suit and
heavy boots. A flamethrower was cradled in his arms, the
spout leaking a yellow torch varying in length from six
inches to a foot of flame.

"Okay," the lead man said in German. "Fire the lab." He started to turn around and make his way out of the room, then his eyes locked with Bolan's. His hand dropped for the muzzle of the H&K MP-5.

Stepping forward, the Executioner swung his rifle and caught the maroon-uniformed guard on the chin. The guy sailed backward with only a harsh groan of pain, unconscious before he hit the gas-soaked floor.

The man with the flamethrower hesitated only a moment, then raised his weapon. Black smoke snarled from the end of the barrel, the flame wavering like an angry ghost.

Bolan flicked off the rifle's safety, knowing he couldn't cover the distance between himself and the man before the flamethrower was unleashed. He paused for a moment when he saw Turrin step up behind the man.

The little Fed screwed the short barrel of one of his Mauser .38s into the guard's neck. "I really wouldn't do that if I was you," he said with quiet authority.

The flame winked out at the business end of the flamethrower. The guy let it hang at the end of the support straps as he raised his hands.

"Down," Turrin commanded.

The guard dropped to his knees, then fell forward onto his stomach and put his hands behind his back as Turrin told him to do. Keeping the .38 tight against the guard's neck, the former capo took a pair of disposable handcuffs from his equipment pouch and put them on his captive. Bolan did the same to the other guard.

Grabbing the conscious guard by the loose material of his silver suit, Turrin dragged him toward the wall by the door.

Bolan gave him a hand, reaching out long enough to partially close the door. Other voices sounded out in the hall, but they were farther away.

"We're going to have us a chat," Turrin said in a hard voice. "If I feel like you're telling us the truth, maybe you don't end up fricasseed in the next few minutes."

"What do you want to know?"

"Where's Simmy?"

"Gone."

"Where?"

"I do not know. He was taken late last night."

"By who?"

The man hesitated.

Turrin leaned in close to the guy, taking away his personal space and whatever feelings of security might have remained. "I get the impression you two weren't the only ones out starting wienie roasts tonight. You want to tell me about how much time I got to waste staying here asking you questions?"

"Schleswig took him."

"Who's Schleswig?"

"The overseer for this project. Leopold Schleswig."

Bolan turned the name over in his mind. It didn't mean anything to him, but Price and Kurtzman could use the name to perhaps leverage free another part of the puzzle facing the Stony Man teams.

"Where was Simmy taken?" Turrin asked.

"I do not know. I swear to God, I do not."

"What kind of work was being done here?" Bolan asked.

"Research."

"The biological agent was created here, wasn't it?" Bolan's dark gaze was unrelenting.

"Yes."

"Who is Schleswig working for?"

"I do not know. Measures were taken to make sure none of us knew anything more than was necessary."

"How much of the biological agent is still here?"

"Some. Most of it is gone. They have been shipping it out for months."

Bolan moved away from the man and scanned the walls again. The time frame was greater than Stony Man had guessed at. Provided all that was wanted was a weapon to intimidate the United States, as well as frame America and Russia, that could have been arranged in weeks. But if they had been shipping the agent for months, there had to have been a specific purpose and destination in mind. The image of the blackened world Kurtzman had revealed hung heavily in the warrior's mind.

Turrin gagged their prisoner with material ripped from his own fatigue shirt.

Switching on his penlight again, the Executioner swept it across the walls, following it to a mounted reproduction of the lab area. A blue dot identified the room they were in. He quickly memorized the various rooms and hallways leading to them.

The level of voices outside continued to grow. A man roared orders in German, adding curses when those orders weren't carried out quickly enough.

"Anything?" Turrin asked.

"A storage area inside the building," the warrior said as he snapped off the penlight. "If we get a little luck breaking our way, maybe we can take out whatever reserves are on hand."

"I'm game."

Bolan took the lead, starting down the hallway at a jog, conscious of the other movement in the corridors ahead of them. In the dim light provided in the hallway, though, they didn't stand out much from the maroon-clad guards.

He took the second right, stepping the pace up. Smoke cloistered in the corridors now, streaming from other rooms that had already been fired. They passed a guard in the wide hallway but drew little attention. The smoke made it hard to see anything clearly.

Bolan's eyes watered, and he made the doorway he was searching for more from memory than from visual inspection. When he tried the knob, it was locked.

Drawing the silenced Beretta, the Executioner hammered two 9 mm parabellum rounds through the locking mechanism. He tried the door again, and it swung inward. A dim light in a recessed mounting glowed weakly over the narrow stairs that led down into a womb of darkness.

Three guards were on their way up, freezing uncertainly as they tried to make out the new arrivals. "What are you doing down here?" one of the men demanded. "Everything here has been attended to."

Bolan kept on moving, feeling Turrin fall back behind him to give them more room. He eased his hand around the pistol grip of the MPiKMS and slid his finger through the trigger guard. Less than ten feet separated him from the men.

"Not us," another man said desperately. "They're not us!"

The Executioner brought up the assault rifle and swung it into target acquisition. Before he could squeeze the trigger, an explosion rocked the lab, sending tremors deep into the earth around the structure.

The metal stairway came loose at both ends and dropped sickeningly. Startled yelps came from the Germans. Someone loosed a short burst that dug concrete chips from the wall.

Off balance, Bolan jumped away from the falling staircase, stretching out an arm as he tried to gain control of his fall. The darkness inside the room was all consuming, keeping him from getting his bearings. More explosions rattled the interior of the room, carrying enough force to shake loose ceiling tiles and light fixtures. He felt them hit his back and shoulders, muffled thumps against the Kevlar vest he wore under the blacksuit. He almost had his feet under him when the floor came up from seemingly nowhere and smashed into him.

"Son of a bitch," Turrin said off to the warrior's left.

A fire-bright riff of a muzzle-flash carved a vicious arc at eleven o'clock from Bolan's position, nowhere near where Turrin had come to a rest. The continued explosions erased most of the sound trapped in the room, but the sonic pressure still beat at the warrior's ears.

Breath tight in his battered chest, Bolan raked the MPiKMS-72 forward, bracketing the suspect area, and blazed a deadly figure eight toward his target. The rifle bucked in his hands, then he was rolling out of harm's way.

The 7.62 mm rounds struck their target, catching the gunner as he was unleashing another burst. The muzzle-flashes abruptly jerked skyward, cutting a swath into the reinforced ceiling at least twenty feet above them.

Bolan heard one of the ricochets go whining past his ear as he rolled to a stop against a wall nearly ten feet from his previous position. He pushed himself up and tried to find the remaining two Germans but couldn't. He freed a small grenade from his harness. The explosions pummeling the building from the outside continued to slam into the structure. More ceiling tile rained down, creating a dust that irritated his eyes and stuck to the greasepaint on his face.

He ran his free hand along the wall, discovering it was a concrete pillar jutting from the smooth surface. Almost a dozen inches thick, it provided some defense.

"Leo," he called out.

"Here." Turrin coughed.

A fusillade of bullets tore into the wall and the pillar Bolan was taking cover behind. Stone splinters pelted his face. "Are you mobile?"

"Hell, yes. I just can't see where I'm going."

Bolan pulled the pin on the grenade and cradled the bomb in the palm of his hand. "Stay low. I've got a Thunderflash going in. Things are going to be confusing for a moment."

"Do it. One way or another, we need some relief down here." Although the words were meant to be playful, there was real stress in the stocky Fed's voice.

Bolan pitched the grenade underhanded, aiming for what he thought was the center of the large room. Between the slower pace of the explosions still shaking the complex, he thought he heard the metallic thump of the grenade striking the floor.

One of the guards recognized the sound for what it was and tried to cry out a warning. The grenade exploded, swallowing his words.

Even with his eyes screwed tightly shut, Bolan could see the harsh bright light given off by the Thunderflash when it detonated. Created for the British Special Air Service, the grenade wasn't designed to kill or maim, only to disorient an opposing force.

The Executioner swung around the pillar with the assault rifle at waist level as soon as the initial flares cast off by the Thunderflash had died away. Embers hung in the air like fiery snowflakes. Enough light was available to see the security people.

One was sprawled in the middle of the floor, obviously in no shape to provide more fight. The other two were in defensive postures that did no good at all in the light.

Turrin was up against a wall to Bolan's left, both hands wrapped around the Mauser .38s.

The Germans focused on Turrin at once, raising their weapons up to their shoulders.

Switching the East German assault rifle to selective fire, Bolan stroked the trigger twice for each man, putting them down with head shots.

The Executioner knew neither man would be getting back up. He looked up at the yellow rectangle of the door set into the wall ten feet overhead. Eddying clouds of dust rolled in the light falling into the room.

A shadow stepped into the doorway, the familiar lines of an assault rifle canted on its hip. A man's voice called out for anyone who might be listening. When he moved, the light revealed the maroon coloring of his uniform.

One of Turrin's .38s barked, spewing a muzzle-flash that licked out eagerly for its target.

The man in the doorway stiffened for a moment, then seemed to come apart like a child's puppet with the strings cut. The body tumbled into the room, hit with a muffled thud that stirred up a cloud of dust and coasted into the light pouring into the room.

The explosions had died away, but were replaced with sounds of small-arms fire.

A shadow moved in the darkness as Bolan switched on his walkie-talkie. He slipped on the ear-throat headset. A moment later Turrin called out in the darkness filling the storage room. "He's dead."

Two other people in the maroon security uniforms raced past the doorway, but neither attempted to stop.

Bolan slung his assault rifle over his shoulder, then dug his penlight from his pocket as he keyed the headset's transmitter. "Striker to Thunderer. Over."

"Go, Striker. You have Thunderer. Over." Kissinger sounded tight and tense.

Switching on the penlight, Bolan adjusted the beam, spreading it out into a wide-angled glow that lighted a large portion of the storage room. "What's the situation? Over."

"You're under attack, buddy," Kissinger growled. "Seems to be as much of a surprise to the home team as it is to us. I'd say a fair amount of panic is about the only thing these people are capable of at the moment. Two helicopter gunships aided in a land-based mortar attack that must have crept in after we did. Over."

"What's your situation? Over."

"I can make my way in if you need me. Over."

"No." Bolan glanced at the doorway overhead, well out of reach. "When the time comes, we'll make our own way out. Then we're going to need wheels ready to move. Any idea who's doing the hitting? Over."

"They're military, but that's all I can tell you. Evidently they had this place staked out by the numbers, because they haven't made a hesitant move yet. Over."

"What kind of resistance is the complex security staff putting up? Over."

"Too little too damn late. I'd say you and Sticker are going to wind up in the eye of the storm in a matter of heartbeats. Over."

Bolan acknowledged, then cleared the channel, leaving the frequency open so Kissinger could apprise them of any new changes.

He moved forward, stepping over the dead bodies in the center of the floor and avoiding the twisted wreckage of the metal staircase. Wooden skids held more than a dozen stainless-steel canisters. Coming to a halt beside them, he adjusted the penlight again and played the tighter beam over the painted characters around the necks of the canisters.

Reaching into the thigh pocket of the blacksuit, he brought out his war book, flipped to the pages he wanted from memory and compared the sketches he found there with the characters on the canisters. He'd done the sketches himself before leaving the Farm, recording the Russian Cyrillic alphabet as it had been found on the canisters found in France.

"The same?" Turrin asked.

"Yeah." Bolan closed the war book and slipped it back into his pocket.

Turrin plucked at a cardboard rectangle secured to one of the canisters by a thin wire. The words were in German. "Can you read it? I learned the lingo when I was over here, but I didn't get around to the written word except for legends on the men's-room doors and the occasional menu."

Bolan shook his head. "Some of the easy words, yeah. But most of these seem to be scientific terms. The presence of numbers indicate measures, but I can't be sure what of." He took a micro-sized infrared camera from his kit and started taking pictures of the canisters, moving in to focus on the Russian and German markings.

On the way back toward the door, he took more frames of the dead men. At the wall below the doorway overhead, he cupped his hands and prepared to take Turrin's weight as the man stepped up.

The pale illumination streaming from above lit the rueful expression that twisted the stocky Fed's lips. "Between you and me, Sarge, I think I got a better chance of hoisting you up to the door than hauling your butt up after me once I made it." He made a stirrup of his own hands and waited.

Bolan stepped into it, pausing while Turrin adjusted to his two-hundred-plus pounds, and drew the .44 Desert Eagle. With a grunt of effort, Turrin pushed the Executioner up to within reach of the doorway's lower lip. The warrior curled the fingers of his free hand over it, levering the elbow of his gun arm over, then took his own weight and pulled himself up.

A layer of smoke floated through the corridor, swirling as if stirred by an invisible spoon. At the bottom of the hallway, the air was relatively clear and free of smoke. Traces of acrid pain bit into Bolan's lungs when he breathed.

He stayed low, cognizant of the sound of gunplay at both ends of the corridor. Unslinging the assault rifle, he grasped the weapon by the sling and extended it down to Turrin. He felt his friend grab the rifle, then use it to climb the wall. Seconds later Turrin was on the floor beside him, breathing harder because of the climb.

Bolan got to his feet, reached into his equipment pack and took out two blocks of plastic explosive. He stabbed self-powered timers into each of the blocks, set the first one for two minutes and tossed it in the general direction of the biological-agent canisters. Setting the second timer for ninety seconds, he reached inside the doorway, stretched as far as he could and slapped it into the overhead wall.

He ran the diagram of the building through his mind again, made certain he still retained his sense of direction and moved into a jog. Holding the assault rifle at the ready, he took a gas mask from one of the pouches secured to his battle harness and slipped it on, careful to keep the headset in place.

"Duck!" Turrin shouted. "We've been made."

Flattening against the wall to his left, Bolan glanced back through the smoke shrouding the hallway and saw two figures dressed in night cammies drop into firing positions. A burst of 5.56 mm tumblers chewed into the walls and drummed against the floor.

The Executioner freed another Thunderflash from his harness, armed the grenade and flung it toward the advancing soldiers. A double set of doomsday numbers flipped through Bolan's head as he counted down. The Thunderflash blew as the new arrivals jumped for cover. The magnesium flares inside threw out a glare that filled the corridor and painted bent and twisted shadows across the walls. Then the dying light was punctuated by autofire that ripped into the warrior's position.

At least two of the rounds skated off Bolan's Kevlar body armor, leaving bruises that would be felt and seen for days. Dropping the Desert Eagle into target acquisition, he fired four rounds over the heads of their attackers. The situation was confusing enough without making enemies of possible allies. During the scramble from the bouncing grenade, Bolan had heard at least one of the men shout a warning in Russian. There was every possibility that the Commonwealth had fielded teams into the area to do the same thing the Stony Man teams were trying to do.

The two Russians were hunting cover as the last number in Bolan's head reached zero.

The doorway leading to the storage area erupted, belching smoke and flames into the corridor. Chunks of mortar and drywall smashed against the opposite wall. The concussive wave that swept down the hallway caught Turrin by surprise and knocked him from his feet.

Braced against the wall, anticipating the blast, Bolan remained upright. He kept the Desert Eagle in his fist, reaching down with his other hand to grab a fistful of Turrin's shirt, and helped the man to his feet.

"Striker, this is Thunderer. Over."

Bolan barely heard Kissinger's voice through the ringing sound filling his ears. He released Turrin, sure the man could make it under his own power now, and thumbed the transmit button. "Go."

"You're covered over now, old son," Kissinger said tightly. "If you and Sticker hang around much longer, you're going to have to pull some kind of rabbit out of your hat to do a fade. The complex security has been breached all to hell. The opposition's got motorized troops pulling up to the front door. Over."

"Acknowledged, Thunderer. Use your discretion about staying in the area. We've got to make the effort here before everything is lost. Striker out."

"I'm not leaving you people in that hellhole, guy," Kissinger said. "The lady would put my ass in a sling. Thunderer is in for the duration. Out."

Bolan ran, skirted fallen masonry where he could, leaping over it when he couldn't. Turrin pounded away behind him.

A maroon-uniformed man swelled out of the smoky miasma staining the corridor, leveled an Uzi and fired a stream of bullets.

Twisting violently, the Executioner dropped to one knee and raised the .44 Magnum into target acquisition. The pistol bucked in his hand.

The 240-grain boattail zipped across the intervening distance and caught the guard in the forehead. The bullet's momentum picked him up and slammed him to the floor.

A heartbeat later the second C-4 charge in the storeroom went off. Kurtzman's information concerning the biological agent was that it would be rendered inert if there was no foliage for it to infect within the first sixty minutes of exposure. Inside the sealed storeroom, there was nowhere for it to go. Unable to bond with living organic matter and the chlorophyll it needed to survive, the bacterium would die, leaving no further threat because it needed to reproduce before it could leave spores behind.

Smaller explosions vibrated through the complex. Bolan knew they were from concussion grenades used by the invading forces. They weren't as threatening, but they made him grimly aware that the deadly circle around them was tightening.

Two turns farther on, he came to the office he was searching for. It was fronted by an unmarked steel door that didn't even come close to being camouflaged by the coats of white paint that covered it.

"Where are we?" Turrin asked as they pressed up against the wall beside the door.

"Simmy's personal offices," Bolan replied. He tried the door and found that it was open. When he twisted the knob and pushed, though, it didn't budge. From the way it was blocked, he could tell someone had secured the door from the inside. Delving into his equipment pouch, he pinched off a small amount of the last block of C-4, leathered the .44 and rolled the explosive between his palms until it made a white worm a little over a finger length. He pressed it into the crack between the door and frame, added a timer, set it for ten seconds and initiated the sequence.

It blew with a dulled thud that echoed inside the room.

Whirling instantly, the Desert Eagle once more in hand, Bolan slammed into the door and followed it inside.

The outer room was an office, filled with a small desk, a couch, an end table and a chair. No one was inside. Another door was set in the back wall. Dim illumination from a flashlight snapped off in the open doorway, fading from the beige walls and the clouds of smoke filling the rooms.

The Executioner moved into the other room cautiously but quickly. When he peered around the corner, he saw a slim figure dressed in black rifling through the filing cabinets that lined two walls of the office. Deft hands finished stuffing documents and computer disks into a vinyl pack strapped across the figure's chest.

Though Bolan was sure he'd made no noise, the figure spun and reached for a weapon holstered behind its back. There was a brief impression of golden tresses under a hood the color of midnight. The eyeholes were large and generous, revealing arched eyebrows that couldn't belong to a man. The skin beneath was pale. Gloved hands brought up a Heckler & Koch VP-70 Z 9 mm automatic in a sudden sweep.

It wasn't just that he didn't know if the dark figure was friend or foe that kept the Executioner's finger from the trigger. There was something about the way the hooded person moved, the way the head was held and the way the Weaver stance came so readily.

Slowly he lowered the Desert Eagle, then held his arms away from his body. It wasn't surrender, but he made it an offer. Staring through the dust-covered lenses of the gas mask, he locked eyes with the figure.

The gun never wavered. "Striker." The voice was feminine.

A grim smile twisted the warrior's lips, amazed that she had been able to recognize him despite the gas mask and the combat cosmetics. They'd had only a few days together, and that had been a lifetime ago in the kind of work they did. Striker had been the only true name she'd known him by. Before he could say anything, he heard Turrin's assault rifle drum out a deadly beat behind him.

"Incoming!"

The woman raised her pistol so that it pointed at the ceiling. She made a final few desperate grabs at the pile of papers and computer disks in the filing cabinet drawer she'd broken open. "Come on," she said in English. "There is a way out."

A grenade mushroomed into an explosion in the outer office, throwing a concussive wave into the room.

Turrin's assault rifle cycled dry, and he fell back to allow Bolan to take over his position while he reloaded.

Using two hands on the Desert Eagle, the Executioner placed his shots with expert skill. One of the 240-grain rounds ripped into the exposed knee of a man in a maroon uniform, yanking the man away from his position along the corridor wall and dumping him to the floor. Bolan followed up with another round that smashed through the bubble-faced gas mask he wore, shattering plastic and drilling through one eye. Another round splintered a shoulder as a guard leaned around the corner to hose the office with his assault rifle. He emptied the rest of the clip into the walls, hoping they were thin enough to allow the .44 loads to pass through.

Evidently they were, because the assault force backed away in seconds as the rolling booms of cordite thunder filled the room.

"Grenade," Turrin said calmly.

The Executioner pulled back, dropped the empty magazine from the Desert Eagle and shoved a fresh one in place. Turrin leaned forward and lobbed a spherical grenade underhanded into the office. Glancing back at the blacksuited woman, Bolan saw her running her hand along the wall under a Dali print. A loud click sounded, swallowed by the sudden explosion of the grenade Turrin had tossed.

Plaster ripped off the walls, and the Dali print tumbled from its mountings beside a hidden door that had opened up in front of the woman.

The silence that followed the explosion was sudden and sharp, and the big warrior knew it was only the calm before the storm. Gunplay outside the building was more sporadic now, but he knew it was no less deadly.

The woman paused, her free hand chasing the zipper along her chest pack, securing the stolen documents inside. She was framed by the deeper black of the cavern yawning behind her in the wall. "Don't just stand there," she said sharply. "The Russians are heavy-handed, but they are thorough. If you try to get past them that way, you'll never make it." Without hesitation she took to the shadows.

"Sarge?" Turrin said.

Bolan knew there was no decision to be made. The woman was right. And the Stony Man team had no protection from the Russian Intelligence squad swarming over the laboratory. Also she had seemed knowledgeable about what was in Gustav Simmy's files. Whatever there was to be had, she'd probably gotten most of the important stuff. Whether she would be willing to share remained to be seen.

"We go," Bolan said tersely.

Turrin nodded, racing for the hidden door.

Bolan was at his heels, the assault rifle canted at his hip as he swung inside. He was conscious of warm, feminine flesh pressed against his and realized she'd been waiting just inside the entrance.

She reached out and pressed against the wall behind him. A motor hummed, then the door slid silently closed until it became a part of the wall once again.

"This way," she said. A flashlight blossomed in her hand, throwing a cone of light down the darkened tunnel that was so low Bolan had to duck to navigate within it.

The warrior ripped off the gas mask as he fell into step with her. The air here was clear, cold. The incline downward was slight but noticeable. The woman adjusted her chest pack and moved into an athletic jog.

The tunnel was wide enough for two people if they were careful. Stepping up his own pace, Bolan dropped into place beside her. He kept the Desert Eagle up and ready, took out his own flashlight and added its beam to hers.

She reached up and took the mask away from her head, letting her shoulder-length ponytail fall to her back. She was just as beautiful as Bolan remembered, high cheekbones and well-rounded lips. Her gray-hazel eyes sparked with the same vitality he recalled.

"The way we are going will not be easy," she said. "I was planning only on seeing myself free of the area."

"We can take care of ourselves," Bolan replied.

A smile twisted the woman's lips, showing a hint of cruelty that he didn't remember. "You don't trust me?"

"As much as is necessary," the big warrior replied. "The last time our paths crossed, we very nearly killed each other. It's something to keep in mind."

The smile seemed more genuine now. "Yes, I suppose it is."

They raced on, reaching for greater speed when they heard the explosion behind them that blew the hidden door to pieces.

CHAPTER THIRTEEN

New Orleans, Louisiana
9:52 p.m.

"I've been thrown out of better places than this," Hermann Schwarz said with sincerity.

Carl Lyons sat hunched over the steering wheel of the Dodge van issued to Able Team for the operation in Louisiana. It was three years old, colored a two-tone sandy brown that the big ex-LAPD officer thought would have allowed it to pass as a camouflaged military vehicle in the Middle East. The tinted windows would make it difficult for anyone to see inside. Licensed with local plates that could be traced back to a nonexistent apartment a few blocks from Jefferson Downs Racetrack, it wouldn't attract attention from the local constabulary or the crew they were after.

"Probably doesn't have a place on the local restaurant guides, either," Rosario Blancanales added. "You'd think, with as many hours as we've logged in this little burg, that we'd have had the chance to sample the native cuisine by now. I could really go for some gumbo right about now. Or maybe something really spicy."

"Spicy?" Schwarz repeated. "With the Ironman around, you want something spicy to eat? Let me remind you that most of this mission has been a closed environment. That is definitely not an idea worth pursuing."

Lyons ignored the byplay. For the most part he was able to ignore the chatter the two men seemed to insist on inflicting on whomever they were with.

The subject of the latest conversation was dead ahead, and he kept his attention focused on it.

The tavern was built like a 1940s shanty, and it listed slightly to the east. Weathered wood the color of cigarette ash made up the walls, at intervals broken by small windows partly covered by faded curtains. A single door that allowed entrance into the building looked out of place to Lyons's practiced eye because he knew the vinyl exterior concealed a steel-plate core. He also knew that the barrier was there only to dissuade small-time thieves. The doorframe hadn't been reinforced to take the door, so if someone really wanted in, the door could be ripped from the frame.

Lyons had been thinking about how easy it would be to do, while he took pictures of the tavern's patrons with an infrared camera. He then faxed them to Stony Man Farm through the cellular phone and computer equipment they had stashed in the back of the van.

A battered and faded sign ran the length of the tavern's peaked roof. The Royal Deuce was written in cursive letters that had at one time flowed with a flourish and had possibly been navy blue. Now, peeling paint and the elements had gotten the better part of the sign. Only one of the trio of spotlights trained on it worked. A cluster of moths and other flying insects buzzed through the beam like miniature World War I flying aces engaged in heated battle.

Most of the earlier hours of the day had been spent trolling along the riverfront of the city. New Orleans had a long and checkered career as a seaport. Sailors from all parts of the world drank in her bars and taverns, which Lyons had glumly figured were probably innumerable. The Yellow Pages hadn't been much help because they didn't list every mom-and-pop watering hole the men of Able had discovered in their search for Merle Spurlock. The dossier Price and Kurtzman had listed some of the merc rep's usual hangouts, but Spurlock hadn't turned up in any of those.

Lyons had decided to take the Royal Deuce on a flyer, from information gleaned from past inquiries. The problem was that by this time Spurlock's own Intelligence network within the city had doubtlessly clicked into play and had registered Clay Legend—ex-cop turned mercenary—as a man looking very hard for Spurlock.

A Lincoln Continental slid into the graveled parking area before the tavern and cruised to a stop at the entrance. Its lights glared over the ash-colored exterior, turning it alabaster.

Using the infrared camera, Lyons focused on the license plate, memorizing the numbers on the sheet of vehicles Spurlock was known to own. His forefinger came to a rest on the fifth number down, and he glanced back up to confirm it when Blancanales said, "That's our guy."

Lyons put the file away and watched as Spurlock cautiously climbed out of the back seat of the Lincoln.

Two burly men approached from the front of the Royal Deuce, making no bones about the cut-down 12-gauge shotguns they carried under military ponchos that were too damn hot for the present weather. They took up position on either side of Spurlock and kept him between them all the way to the tavern. The Lincoln didn't pull away until Spurlock had vanished inside.

"Okay," Lyons said as he pushed himself out of the driver's seat and walked to the rear of the van, "let's see if we can smoke that son of a bitch out and take him downtown." He shrugged into a khaki vest that would conceal his Kevlar vest and his hardware. The Colt Government Model .45 was in shoulder leather, and the Python .357 was at his back in a paddle holster. He carried a lock-back Spyderco knife in his jeans pocket in case he didn't have time to reach for the spare magazines and speed-loaders in his vest pockets.

For added insurance, Lyons snugged a Semmerling .45 derringer into its wrist holster and fitted it to his right arm. Flexing his hand the right way sent the deadly little blaster sliding into his palm.

Schwarz slipped on a faded and patched jean jacket. The two Beretta 92-Fs he wore didn't show at all. "I got the back door," he said, then slid the van door open and stepped out into the night.

Lyons gave him thirty seconds, starting a mental countdown.

Blancanales moved from the passenger seat and took the wheel. He slid the CAR-15 assault rifle out from under the seat and shoved it into the clips mounted on the dash. The ear-throat headset monitoring the special frequency Able was using for the operation was pulled into place. A flick of a switch juiced up the police radio they'd appropriated for backup in case things got tense.

When he reached thirty seconds, Lyons glanced at Blancanales. "You've got the conn, Rosario."

The Politician gave him a thumbs-up and a white-toothed grin. "Engaged, buddy, and you watch your ass out there."

Lyons navigated the sliding door and closed it behind him. The parking lot was uneven, filled with potholes and water from the brief thunderstorm that had blown in from the coast earlier.

Lyons took a final deep breath, held it a moment, then released it and hit the Royal Deuce's front door. As he passed through, he was assaulted by a whirling maelstrom of cigar and cigarette smoke, the smell of stale beer and the odor of unwashed flesh.

The bar lined the entire left side of the room, except for a set of bat-wing gates that allowed the cocktail waitress to pass back and forth. The patrons who occupied the bar stools missed few opportunities to pinch and pat the women as they whipped by. Most of the response from the working girls was laced with boredom and practiced sarcasm that lacked real feeling.

The right wall of the long interior of the tavern was covered with stuffed and mounted fish that seemed to be frozen in mute horror. Pictures of sailors and fishermen holding up other prize catches filled in the empty spaces. Less than a handful of the pictures were in color. Some of the older ones depicted movie stars from the 1940s and early 1950s.

At the far end of the bar, by the twisting stairway that led to a second floor, was a group of pinball machines and arcade games. Raucous laughter and good-natured cursing from that area of the tavern provided a counterpoint to the other low conversations. Money switched hands in front of an electronic dart board, and the discussions there seemed more intense.

It wasn't the kind of place where the proprietor kept pool tables in the back. Lyons knew that from experience. Blood would have been quickly spilled on the green felt for a fist-ful of dollars.

There was no sign of Spurlock or the two men who'd escorted him into the tavern.

Lyons dipped his hand into the pocket of his Windbreaker and tapped the transmit button of the miniature sending set he carried. The receiver was mocked-up to resemble a hearing aid and was settled into his left ear. It blocked his hearing on that side, but it was better than having something obvious. And it put Blancanales and Schwarz only heartbeats away if he needed them.

Lyons whispered into the button-sized microphone clipped to the collar of the Windbreaker as he approached the bar. "Pol."

"Here, *hermano,* reading you five by five."

"Gadgets."

"Ready."

"There's no sign of Spurlock," Lyons said as he took a bar stool at the end of the long counter. "But there's some rooms upstairs. Could be Spurlock's hidden himself up there."

"I see a window back here," Schwarz said. "Lighted. Yeah, a couple shadows are moving back and forth inside."

The bartender, a rail-thin young man with greasy hair pulled back into a ponytail, threw his bar towel over his shoulder and walked toward Lyons.

"Eyeball it," the Able Team leader said, "and let me know what goes. We'll try to do this one without a fuss."

Blancanales and Schwarz acknowledged and dropped out of the circuit.

Lyons ordered a draft beer and gazed around the room. A number of the hard-fisted, hard-eyed men had noticed him now and were giving him the once-over. He relied on his cop's instincts to warn him of someone giving him too much attention. He didn't think he'd been made, but the possibility was there.

The bartender placed a foaming mug of beer in front of Lyons. The glass was already sweating. "That'll be a buck."

Lyons took a five-dollar bill from his shirt pocket and dropped it on the bar.

"You want the change, or you want to run a tab?" the bartender asked.

"The change," Lyons replied. Seasoned veterans of watering holes like the Royal Deuce counted every dollar bill and spent every one as if it might be the last. It was one of the first lessons he'd learned when he'd started working undercover for the LAPD. He'd also learned to keep his flash money in a shirt pocket, away from his main stash.

The bartender stuck four worn dollar bills near the mug and started to walk away.

"Hey."

The bartender looked up at Lyons.

"I'm new in town, and I'm looking for some action."

"You a cop?"

"I look like a cop?"

"You ain't from around here, pal. You don't wanna answer the question, just say so. I get paid for the service, not the conversation I provide."

Lyons reached into his pocket, took out a twenty-dollar bill and snapped it out straight between his hands. "I'm not a cop, but I am a fan of Andrew Jackson. You want to be a member of the fan club?"

The bartender took the bill and laid it on the counter, covered it with his palm and made no move to put it away. "Action?"

"Action."

"This covers a room upstairs. You work out your own deal with the girls."

"Not girls," Lyons said. "I never paid for women in my life."

"If you're looking to hustle beer money, you take it up with the guys in the back. You don't need me. You ask around, you'll be able to drum up a game of darts."

"I'm not a hustler, either. I'm looking for a guy. I was told he might be here."

The bartender shrugged. "You see anybody in here you're looking for?"

"Merle Spurlock."

"I get another club card?"

"They come one to a customer."

"Mr. Spurlock's not somebody who likes to be bothered much. He might not even like me bothering him."

"I'm looking for work," Lyons said. "I was told Spurlock was putting some people together for a couple operations. If I get an interview, and it goes good, maybe there'll be something more in it for you."

"I'll get back to you." The bartender made the twenty disappear in his jeans pocket and curled a forefinger at a brunette waitress. They talked for a moment, then the waitress nodded, took two bottles of Michelob and walked up the stairs.

Lyons took a polished stainless-steel cigarette case from his Windbreaker pocket and cupped it in his palm, turning it so he could keep track of the woman's reflection without being obvious.

The bartender went back to polishing glasses. From the way he hovered around the cash register, careful never to get more than arm's reach from the counter, Lyons guessed he had some kind of weapon there.

The waitress went to the second room down. Lyons could barely see her in the polished surface of the cigarette case. She knocked on an unmarked door. A man with a tangled growth of beard and a camo T-shirt answered the door. A S&W .357 with an 8-inch barrel was holstered under his left arm, obviously for effect because the guy's beefy build precluded any chance of a quick draw.

The waitress talked, pointing Lyons out.

The bearded guy ducked back into the room and re-emerged with one of the bodyguards who had escorted Spurlock into the Royal Deuce. They descended the stairs together, not bothering to conceal their weapons.

Lyons pocketed the cigarette case and sipped his beer, holding the mug tightly in his left hand in case he needed it as a weapon.

The bearded guy sat on the bar stool next to Lyons. "You looking for Mr. Spurlock?"

The big ex-cop looked him in the eye, noticing the way the other man had dropped into position a few feet away, out of reach. "Yeah."

Almost every eye in the Royal Deuce was focused on the unfolding events.

"Do I know you?" the bearded man asked.

"I don't know you," Lyons said.

A mirthless grin split the beard. The beefy forearm on the countertop had a tattoo of a flaming skull with a Special Forces dagger thrust into one empty eye socket. "If you want to meet Mr. Spurlock, I'm somebody you should get to know."

Lyons made his voice hard. "The bartender cost me a twenty, and money's kind of tight right now in my part of the world. How much are you going to cost me?"

"I don't cost you nothing, boy, unless you don't measure up. Then we get to find out what you're really made of. And don't plan on getting funky with me. That good old boy standing behind you has got himself a 'ported Casull .454 he's just dying to use." His hard eyes glittered dangerously. "You just put your hands flat on the counter and keep 'em that way."

Lyons put his hands out.

"You carrying?"

"Does a frog bump his ass when he hops?"

"Where?"

"Shoulder leather. A Colt Government .45. I got a .357 Magnum in a paddle holster along my spine."

"Anything else?" the bearded man asked.

"A folding knife in my pants pocket. Sometimes I clean my nails when I get bored."

"You're a funny guy. Mr. Spurlock, he don't cotton much to funny guys. They don't listen to orders so well."

"I did my time in the Nam, pal," Lyons said in a tight voice. "When I hear a righteous order, bet your ass I know how to respond to it."

"I'm taking your hardware."

"Fine. As long as we understand that I'm expecting it back."

"Only way you're going to meet Mr. Spurlock." The man expertly slid the two pistols from the leather and dropped them into a canvas bag the bartender handed him. "Give me the knife, too. Slow and easy."

Standing, Lyons added the Spyderco to the confiscated weapons.

"Let me have your ID."

Lyons passed it over.

The man never made more than a cursory check over the rest of Lyons's body, didn't run his hands along his arms at all. The sending set, dummied up to look like a cassette player with the switch off, attracted only a moment of attention.

"What are you doing looking for Mr. Spurlock?"

"I heard he was hiring. Doing some international stuff and needed experienced people."

"And you figure you're experienced?"

Lyons shrugged. "Enough so that I can't go back to the states of California, Washington and Nevada for a while."

"You got paper floating on you?"

"Some."

"How heavy is it?"

"Heavy enough that I got in touch with a few buddies who turned me on to Spurlock for a chance to work East Coast for a while, maybe even make a jump across the big pond."

"Who?"

"You figure me for a rube? I don't name names in this business. Not if I want to keep on working and keep my throat intact."

The bearded man fingered the faked driver's license carrying the Clay Legend name. "This for real?"

"Run it through NCIC," Lyons said. "Get you a rap sheet. A couple stints early on, before Nam, nothing since. I took the training Uncle Sam gave me to heart. My only problem right now is I backed some small-time players in big-time action and got hung out to dry for my trouble. There's some pissed off Triad people in Seattle, and a couple connected families in Los Angeles who wouldn't mind having my guts for garters."

"You working part of a pirate operation?"

Lyons knew the man was referring to pirate gangs that stole dope and money from drug runners transferring the merchandise and cash from one point to another. "At the time it was work."

The bearded man waved an open hand. "That's chicken shit compared to what we're into now. You check out okay, you'll be getting top-flight equipment and square meals three times a day."

"So show me where to sign up."

"Follow me."

Lyons fell in behind the bearded man, easily matched his awkward waddle as the guy climbed the stairs.

"Ironman," Blancanales whispered in his ear, "are we chill here?"

Lyons reached down, squeezed the Morse code sender attached to the false lining of his jacket. He clicked it once, signalling yes.

The bearded man rapped on the door, a quick tattoo that evidently filled a prearranged signal. The door opened, allowing the sweet smell of marijuana to drift out into the hallway.

Four men were seated around a small table in the center of the room. A light hung down from the cracked ceiling, surrounded by a gaudy green lamp shade that dimmed the illumination considerably over any part of the room but the table. Spurlock sat across the table, sizing up Lyons with a professional glance devoid of any warmth. The other three men were hired muscle, but dressed considerably better than the two men who'd brought Lyons up. Scars on their arms and faces spoke volumes about the kind of work they'd been accustomed to doing for years.

A fifth man was handcuffed to a chair, his mouth covered by strips of tape that formed an X.

The bearded man tossed Lyons's false ID onto the table, jarring the poker chips stacked there. A deck of cards rested at Spurlock's left elbow. The mercenary broker picked up the wallet and thumbed through it quickly. "Clay Legend," he said.

Lyons nodded, crossed his hands over his chest and tried not to look into the frightened eyes of the man manacled in the chair. "That's me."

"And what do you want?"

"Work."

Spurlock glanced up over the wallet, his eyes hard and suspicious. "What kind of work?"

"The kind that pays well. I've been experiencing a personal drought lately."

"You know what I do, Mr. Legend?"

"Yes, sir." He considered trying for the Morse code clicker and informing Blancanales and Schwarz about the man in the room but couldn't take the chance. Any one of the men sitting at the table might recognize it for what it was and kill him before he had a chance to do either of them any good. Taking another quick glance, he saw that the man had been severely beaten. The man's right pant leg had been hacked open with a knife. Torn tatters of adhesive tape hung from the leg underneath. Just about where an ankle holster would be worn by an undercover officer working real deep, Lyons thought.

"For an impoverished man," Spurlock said as he tossed the wallet back to the tabletop, "you've got a new wallet. Not something I'd expect from a man strapped for cash."

Lyons mentally kicked himself. His usual wallet was back in the van, filled with documentation identifying him as a Justice agent operating out of the Bureau of Alcohol, Tobacco and Firearms. He hadn't wanted to try to keep up with switching the IDs every time it became necessary. He dropped his eyes a little, as if he was embarrassed.

"Actually," he lied, "it was cheaper to buy a new wallet than a new wardrobe. I didn't hit town with much more than what you see right here."

Spurlock's blank gaze held him, measured him, showing nothing of what went on in his mind. "I'll buy that. At least for now. I find out you ever lied to me, you're a dead man. And you can make book on that."

Lyons kept silent. It was the merc broker's show.

"As it is, I'm involved in something that could use a few more good men. If you check out, if you're good enough, the pay and benefits are something that could see you through your present difficulties." Spurlock's gaze never wavered. "However, there is a down side. If you *ever* cross me, you'll end up like that asshole over there."

Knowing he was supposed to notice the other guy for sure now, Lyons looked. The sour taste of bile rose in his throat.

"That's Drew Claridge, one of the New Orleans Police Department's brightest young undercover officers. Called himself Hank Tait when he joined my crew. Checked out, too. For a while. He was working a small sideline I have, moving a few arms deals through the bike gangs in the Southwest. The last six weeks, he's drawn pay off me and the city. Had himself a good time while he worked to put a case together against me." Spurlock grinned. "But hell, there hasn't ever been a case against me. This is my town. People here have a long memory when it comes to remembering who did them a good turn. My captains missed the meetings old Drew was having with his ranking officers, but some other people I do business with didn't. Made him tonight, and it looks like it was just in time. The D.A. will never have a case against me with their star witness gone."

The receiver in Lyons's ear buzzed. "Oh, shit, Carl," Blancanales said. "I'm on my way now."

"I'm kicking in the back door," Schwarz added.

Perspiration covered Lyons's skin under the Kevlar vest, trickling down the small of his back where the .357 had been leathered.

A shark's cold grin fitted itself to Spurlock's face. "The way I see it, I got a double bonus tonight. This prick gets iced and put away so he can't touch me, and I find out damn quick which side of this thing you're coming down on."

A lemony dryness tightened Lyons's throat. It didn't do any good to curse whatever fates had conspired to put this kind of spin on the situation, so he didn't waste his breath or his concentration.

"Harper," Spurlock ordered, "waste this son of a bitch cop so I can get back to winning the salary I pay you."

One of the younger men at the table stood and unbuttoned his jacket. He drew a Colt Woodsman .22LR from a hip holster, took a silencer from his pocket and threaded it onto the barrel.

Every eye in the room darted back and forth between Lyons and the undercover NOPD cop. Lyons was grimly aware of the attention.

Then women's shouts of warning rang out below, punctuated by the sound of breaking glass.

A troubled, uneasy look spread across Spurlock's face. "Find out what that is."

The bearded man gave a quick nod, unleathered the .357 and went out in the hallway for a quick peek.

Harper hadn't wasted a moment. Once the silencer was in place, he lowered the Woodsman into target acquisition and aimed for the NOPD cop's face. The young detective's eyes were wide, but he didn't flinch in the face of certain death.

Knowing there was no way he could sit by and watch a cop die, Lyons whirled into action. He swung out with his left elbow, caught the man standing beside him flush in the face and sent the guy reeling backward with blood gushing from his broken nose. A swift shake of his hand sent the Semmerling derringer kicking out into his palm. He closed his fingers around the skeletal body of the gun and thumbed the trigger back.

Harper saw him and struggled to bring the Woodsman to bear. Spurlock and the other two men were springing for cover and bringing out weapons of their own.

Lyons squeezed the trigger, sent a 185-grain round screaming into the center of Harper's chest. He added another to make sure of the kill as the man fell backward over his chair and went down in a tangle of flailing arms and legs. Then he shifted his sights immediately to Spurlock, hoping to wound the man and put him safely away. He fired again as the merc broker came into focus, saw the card table topple as Spurlock used it for cover.

A heartbeat later it felt as if a Missouri mule tried to kick in Lyons's ribs. He heard the sound of gunfire as if he were underwater, then realized he'd been spun around and thrown against the wall.

"Ironman!"

The voice belonged to Schwarz. Lyons knew that. It seemed to come from inside his head, and it took him a moment to remember the receiver. Black spots swam in his vision. He forced himself to his knees as hurried gunfire from the other two men slammed through the drywall.

He brought up the Semmerling, tracked across the room for Spurlock and found him swinging a chair through the window. Glass exploded from the casement as a bullet whipped only inches from Lyons's cheek. Cursing, he aimed the .45ACP derringer at the man who'd fired at him, going for the low-percentage head shot because the little hideout gun had only two rounds left.

Without waiting to see how his comrades were doing, Spurlock hurled himself through the broken window and out onto the slope of the peaked roof.

Lyons dropped the hammer. The Semmerling kicked against his palm, and the round smashed through the shooter's left eye. The man dropped like a poleaxed steer.

Picking up the remaining man in the room, Lyons fired his last shot. The bullet caught the man in the neck, which made him drop the Dan Wesson Super .38 he held and grab his throat. A bellowing roar from the man still alive behind the Able Team warrior nearly deafened Lyons. Before he could turn and meet the challenge, a pair of massive arms had encircled his chest and arms with crushing force.

Schwarz tried to hail Lyons again.

Knowing he needed to warn Gadgets that Spurlock had escaped, Lyons tried to break free but couldn't. Visions of Schwarz getting gunned down in the alley danced in the big warrior's head, adding desperation to the flow of adrenaline already charging his system.

Lyons stomped his boot on the instep of the man's foot with bone-breaking force, felt and heard something go with a satisfying snap. The man howled in pain. Taking advantage of the leverage he suddenly gained, Lyons fired an elbow into the man's face again, sensing the crunch of bone and cartilage under flesh.

Free, Lyons wheeled around and kicked the man in the crotch. When his opponent doubled over, the Able Team leader grabbed the back of the guy's head with both hands, then brought his knee up into the man's face three times in quick succession. The man went down without another sound.

Gunfire banged in the hall, punctuating the noise of breaking glass and screams.

"Gadgets." Lyons knelt, grabbed a gun from the floor and checked the load. It was a Glock 17 with a Plus-Two extender on the full magazine, which gave him twenty rounds of 9 mm ammunition.

"Go, Ironman."

"Spurlock's loose. The son of a bitch lit a shuck out the window and headed across the roof. I lost him." Lyons fisted the textured polymer grip and ran across the room, pausing only for a second to kick the overturned card table out of his way.

"If I find him, I'll let you know."

"Yeah, well, make sure you check before you cut loose because I'm making my way out there, too." He threw his leg over the sill and pushed out of the room.

"Pol."

"Go."

"Trouble?"

"What there was of it has up and surrendered. I think one of the waitresses made a call to 911, so this party might not remain private for long. I got your back if you need me, but if I leave, these guys are going to pull a fade."

"Stay there. Me and Gadgets will cover this end." The shingles were slick underfoot. Lyons slipped twice and almost fell, forcing him to slow down. The rain earlier had made the chancy going even more treacherous. His feet thumped across the roof as he made his way toward the peak of the building. Spurlock was nowhere to be found. Lyons figured he needed the highest vantage point possible to salvage the play.

As he neared the crest of the roof, Lyons felt vibrations tremble just ahead of him, heard the sound of running feet drumming against the shingles. He redoubled his own efforts, but lost a precious few seconds when his foot smashed through the roof up to his ankle. By the time he freed his boot, he could hear the sound of the approaching engine at the front of the tavern.

He tapped the transmit key. "He's headed for the front."

"You got a visual?" Schwarz asked.

"No," Lyons said as he lunged for the peaked roof near the billboard. He slipped and fell, but managed to snare the ridge with his free hand. He threw his other hand over, still holding on to the Glock, and pulled himself up. His forearms were abraded by the rough wooden shingles. Once his eyes were clear of the ridge, he had a relatively unimpeded view of the parking lot. "Wait. I got a visual on Spurlock now."

"I'm on my way."

"Keep your eyes peeled, buddy. There's rolling armor waiting for him out there."

The same Lincoln Continental that had dropped Spurlock off less than half an hour earlier pulled to a halt in front of the tavern.

The aging merc commander was scrambling over the eave of the roof, clinging to a drainpipe that Lyons hadn't guessed would hold the man's weight.

The Able Team leader raised his voice as he pushed himself over the roof's center-beam ridge and got his feet under him. "Spurlock. You're under arrest. Stop where you are and I won't shoot."

"Fuck you, pig," Spurlock yelled back. "If you were gonna shoot, you'd have shot by now." His head vanished over the edge of the roof.

Shoving himself into an awkward jog, Lyons hit the transmit button. "Gadgets."

"Go."

"He's on the ground."

"I'm turning the corner now."

The banshee cry of wailing sirens split the night. In the distance the whirling red-and-blue lights of the New Orleans Police Department cruisers rocketed up Lakeshore Drive.

The Lincoln Continental came to a rocking stop in the clear, and the back doors opened in tandem, spilling a handful of men onto the graveled parking area. Spurlock dashed toward them, yelling wildly.

Lyons came to a halt at the edge of the roof and gave the drainpipe a kick. It rang hollowly but held. He thought it might hold his weight.

He lifted the Glock in both hands and took aim. "Spurlock."

The merc broker didn't break stride.

Two of the men at the rear of the Lincoln reached into the back seat.

Lyons opened fire and pumped round after round at the car's tires, hoping to cut the rubber from under the vehicle and disable it. On his sixth round, counting dispassionately, coolly making his shots with the unfamiliar gun count, he punctured the right front tire.

The Lincoln sagged as air hissed out.

Small-arms fire cracked, and muzzle-flashes stained the shadows enveloping the luxury car.

Lyons knew he was backlit by the billboard sign behind him. He took up the trigger slack again and aimed another round at the right rear tire.

Spurlock shoved his way through the small cluster of men, ignoring them as he climbed inside the Lincoln.

A cold chill rolled down Lyons's neck when he recognized the long, hard shape two of the men were attempting to bring to bear. The 7.62 mm M-60 Maremont lightweight machine gun had a distinctive shape to it that the big Able Team warrior could recognize even from his position.

While one of the men snapped the ammunition belt into the feed system, the other man settled the big weapon into his arms, holding the pistol grip and the forward grip. Once the first man had the ammo belt in place, he clapped the machine gunner on the head.

The Maremont unleashed a chattering roar of 7.62 mm rounds.

Lyons gave way before the raking line of fire that chewed into the wooden shingles. He turned and ran, unable to return fire effectively without exposing himself and being a stationary target. He slapped the transmit button. "Gadgets."

"I see it. Get the hell off that roof."

Bullets chopped at Lyons's feet, whipping around him and cutting back toward him. He threw himself into a dive behind the advertising billboard. A heartbeat later the machine-gun fire slashed through the thin wooden sides of the billboard and shattered the baby spots into glittering shards that cut the big man's face. He covered his head with his arms and waited out the onslaught.

Schwarz's Beretta banged out a retort, joined seconds later by Blancanales's CAR-15. The exchange was brief. The Maremont didn't leave much room for discussion.

When Lyons uncoiled from the shelter of the ragged billboard, he caught a glimpse of Spurlock's Lincoln speeding through the parking area. The brake lights flared briefly before it took to the street. Lyons stood, grabbed the Glock in both hands and fired the weapon dry. It didn't have any effect, and the flat tire didn't appear to be slowing the vehicle much.

He ran for the drainpipe, slid down and managed to slice open one of his fingers. Warm blood flowed over his left hand as he ran for the Dodge van. Blancanales and Schwarz were a half step ahead of him. He yanked the door open and crawled behind the steering wheel. He keyed the ignition and put it into gear, spinning the tires as he hurtled in pursuit of Spurlock.

Before he could gain the street, two NOPD cruisers skidded in from different directions and blocked his path. He slipped the transmission in reverse, tried to back up, only to find a third cruiser moving into position. He closed his bleeding fist and banged the steering wheel in silent frustration.

CHAPTER FOURTEEN

Paris, France
5:11 a.m.

"You were followed," Karla Hirschfeld said, her tone one of mild accusation.

Yakov Katzenelenbogen smiled at the woman and accepted the cup of tea she offered. He was dressed in street clothes, the Walther P-88 tucked out of sight by good tailoring. He was also freshly shaved. "It is only Yuri Mitroff. He will cause us no trouble."

"He will cause me no trouble," Hirschfeld said confidently. "You, however, I do not know about. You have your own agenda these days. There are some who didn't want me to talk to you."

The Israeli agent was in her late thirties, Katz knew, but she remained supple and fit. Her hair was black as a raven's wing, her eyes the color of glacial ice. She wore a two-piece bikini in neon pink and orange and looked like a woman ten years younger. Her tan was coffee with cream except for the thin white mark a knife blade had left on her left bicep eight years ago.

"But you did agree to speak with me," Katz said gently.

Hirschfeld smiled into his eyes, trailed her fingers under his chin and nodded her approval at the smooth skin she found there. "Only because I was given permission."

They stood in the cockpit of the powerboat she maintained in a slip along Quai de la Tournelle, rocked gently by the waves made by passing boats. The woman sat in the fighting chair facing Katz as he leaned against the ladder leading up to the flying bridge.

Katz nodded his understanding. Despite the fact that he'd once worked with the woman for a time, and despite the fact that they'd once been lovers, he knew there was no way she would have talked to him without approval. "And now that you've been given permission, do you have anything on the man I asked you about?"

She gave him a sweet smile, and it took Katz back to a handful of lazy Sunday mornings spent between killing fields. "Of course I do. There is a reason you came to the Mossad for this information." She got to her feet lithely, adjusted her bikini in a move that Katz recognized as being more seductive than necessary, then knelt in front of the small freezer by the live-bait well. She took out two bottles of beer and passed one over, then used an opener attached to the freezer handle by a length of cord on both.

Hirschfeld took a pull and walked barefoot into the cabin.

Holding his beer under his prosthesis against his stomach, Katz reached up and tapped the transmit button on the headset. "Phoenix Two?"

"You've got Two, mate."

"Your security parameters?"

"Complete," David McCarter radioed back. "You're as safe as houses."

"The Russian?"

"At this point he's stationary, content to watch. Five tells me there's no evidence of long-range surveillance equipment. If Five sees anything, he'll close the man down."

"Gently," Katz admonished. "The man is something of a friend. One of the few trustworthy opponents I've ever faced."

"Understood, One."

Katz cleared the frequency and followed the woman into the cabin. The eastern skies were turning maroon and purple now as dawn started to break over the city, but inside the cabin it was still dark, dank with shadows and the heady smell of the river and fish.

"Give me a moment," Hirschfeld said. She stood beside the bank of radio equipment.

Without hesitation, Katz turned his back and looked out over the river. He heard her rustling around behind him, heard a hidden lock snap open and well-oiled hinges whisper as they moved. There was a rustle of papers, the snap of a rubber band. He took a drink of his beer. "I've not known you to be a morning drinker."

"Worried about me, Yakov? Thinking that the stresses and pressures of this job have finally done it for poor little Karla?" Her laughter was delicate. "Thank you for your concern, but I assure you it's misplaced. This is not morning for me. I've not been to bed in almost thirty hours. When we finish here, I intend to sleep. The beer just helps me unwind. You can turn around now."

He did, and found her spreading papers and photographs across a small table. There was no sign of the secret hiding place she'd retrieved them from. He approached the pile of documentation.

She placed a hand over the papers and gave him a hard look. "You know how it is with the Mossad. They give nothing away. They want to know what you can give me in return."

Katz returned her gaze in full measure. "Nothing."

"You're a hard man."

"They knew that before they told you it was all right to talk to me."

"They are afraid of you these days."

"There is no reason to be. I have never worked against Israel."

She looked at him, and the expression on her face softened. "They told me to ask you to come back into the fold, Yakov, to become fully Israeli again instead of working with the Americans. Too many things have happened of late, and the American politicians are eager to point out the faults they want to find within the Israeli nation. We need you."

"I can't."

"You mean you won't."

"I believe in what I'm doing, and I believe what I'm doing allows me to help Israel in ways I wouldn't be able to elsewhere." He paused. "Since I have nothing to barter with, does this mean I don't get to see what information you have on Pasquale Crivello?" He didn't like thinking he and Phoenix Force had wasted hours fruitlessly searching through the Parisian black market in vain while awaiting the Mossad Intel.

"No." Hirschfeld removed her hand. "I'll dip into some information I've been storing up, and credit you with it. Of course, they'll know what I did, but it will save face on all sides. They know you wouldn't try to take the information from me.

"Besides," Hirschfeld said, "the team you are with is not exactly a low-key effort. Mossad knows you are involved with the Russian bacterial agents that are supposed to be getting transferred through Europe. They're working on angles of their own to get involved. Since you asked about Crivello, they've been able to add to their own store of knowledge anyway."

"Will anyone from Mossad attempt to intercede?"

Hirschfeld shook her head. "As you'll see from these reports, Crivello is too well buried to be gotten at easily. It will take a wrecking crew to pull him out, and at this point the Mossad is willing to let you and your team take the risks."

Katz sorted through the pile until he found a full-face photograph of Pasquale Crivello. It was four years old, according to the legend typed on the back.

Crivello looked piratical in the picture, with a big, beefy build, a wedge of a jaw that was nearly always covered with reddish blond stubble, and a scarred leather eye patch covering his right eye. His hair was nearly shoulder length and fluttered around his head in sun-bleached curls. In most of the pictures he wore casual nautical attire and favored whites and sky blues.

"What do you know about this man?" Hirschfeld asked.

"Only that he's involved in the operation I'm working on," Katz replied as he sifted through the pages and pictures. "He's been involved in black market dealing for a number of years, and has done some gun and drug running in his past."

"He's a good businessman these days." Hirschfeld sorted through the pictures with him, found the one she wanted and laid it on top of the pile. "He still operates in the munitions and drug empires as a conduit into and out of countries, but he stays away from the hands-on stuff as much as possible. Whenever he's directly involved, you can bet there's a lot of money to be made quickly. A number of Intelligence agencies use him to transport people and supplies. The only reason he does it is to earn points in his favor that he can call on later. This is his boat."

Katz lifted the photo and studied it carefully. It was a large sailboat, and the name—*Jade Falcon*—was written in Italian in flowing emerald script on the hull. Her sails were in full swell in the picture, and her prow cleaved the water cleanly. Peering closely, he saw Crivello standing on the foredeck, one hand knotted in the rigging.

"Do you know where to find him?" Hirschfeld asked.

"I was told Milan."

She shook her head. "Not anymore. Less than two hours ago the *Jade Falcon* was tied up in a slip in Venice. My people have confirmed that Crivello is aboard."

Katz scanned through the rest of the information quickly, learning in only moments that the Italian black marketer had racked up some impressive scores over the years and had suffered less damage than most people would have expected. He indicated the documentation. "Does this have to stay with you?"

"No. That's yours. With the blessing of the Mossad, Yakov, so you needn't worry about interference for a while."

"Meaning they'll be watching as much as they can."

She shrugged. "The world is changing, but that doesn't mean everyone is ready for it. World peace is a great and noble thought, but Israel is going to wait to see what all that entails before they blindly accept it. Even the Russians and the Americans haven't completely called in all their espionage forces. Otherwise, you and your people wouldn't be here now."

Katz didn't make a reply as he gathered the pages and pictures.

"I wish you good hunting," Hirschfeld said when he was finished and everything was tucked away in a manila folder under his jacket. "But stay on your toes. Crivello is a dangerous man, and he doesn't hesitate to kill."

"I'll keep that in mind." He started to go past her, but she stopped him with a hand on his chest.

Her eyes were open and honest as she gazed up at him. "Remember, too, that the Mossad is aware of the bacterial agents that are believed to be shipped from the Ukraine by American and Russian forces. They'll be watching you, and if they suspect you and your team—if you are involved in some kind of cover-up—they'll kill you and bury the evidence. These days even though the threat of war has subsided, it seems that no one is more interested in anything other than their own survival."

"You've become a cynic," Katz said with a smile on his lips and a heaviness in his heart as he grieved for the young dreamer the woman had once been.

"Not true. I've just had my eyes opened a time or two. It hasn't killed me yet."

He held her hand in his. "God willing, it won't."

She stood on tiptoe, brought her mouth up to his. He relished the taste of her and embraced her tightly. Reluctantly he broke away.

Her breath came quicker, and there was a shine in her eyes that took him back years. "That was for luck, my love, and something to reawaken memories that might give you comfort."

Still holding on to her hand, Katz raised it to his lips and pressed them against her warm skin. "Thanks again, Karla, and I hope that we may soon meet again under less tense circumstances. It would be nice to become reacquainted." Then he turned and walked up the steps, already setting up the exfiltration with the rest of Phoenix Force.

Stony Man Farm, Virginia
10:26 p.m.

SEATED AT HIS DESK in the computer lab, Aaron Kurtzman handled the inquiries from the New Orleans Police Department himself rather than assigning it to any of the three people working the main floor. He'd scheduled overlapping twelve-hour shifts that gave him access to two of his three key people at any one time. At the moment Akira Tokaido and Carmen Dalahunt occupied their usual places, while Keith Rush held down Hunt Wethers's post.

He worked the inquiries with a few keystrokes, verified the information coming from the NCIC computers and the Department of Justice system that verified Lyons and his team as members of the Bureau of Alcohol, Tobacco and Firearms. There were three department heads who were being contacted by other people Price had buried within the division to make sure Able's cover held if they were called personally.

Within a matter of minutes, the inquiries shut down.

He pushed himself back, surveyed his team and let a moment of pride fill him. Price did her job well, creatively pulling a coherent missions-op out of a confusing blend of fact and fiction.

But the jester was proving to be the joker in the deck.

Whoever the computer specialist ultimately proved to be, the guy was damn good—and very dangerous. Every fact, every little glimmer of the financial machinations that had gone on through the pipeline shipping the bacteriological canisters through Europe had been carefully concealed. The designer had known there were going to be traces, just as there had been traces back to Fauborg and Fawcett, and ultimately back to Spurlock. Instead of working to eradicate those traces, other trails were tied into the real events. Following the progress of monies deposited into Fauborg's and Fawcett's Swiss bank accounts was like working a maze. But it was like trying to figure out the maze on foot in the dark with a flashlight that only worked part of the time. Even when something seemed to add up, the end result was suspect. The ultimate truth wouldn't be known until they were able to triangulate it with other Intel the Stony Man teams would be able to provide.

Pain throbbed between Kurtzman's temples. Despite the sense of urgency driving him, he knew he was going to have to take a break soon. Otherwise, when the shit really hit the fan, he wouldn't be any good to anybody. He took a bottle of analgesics from the drawer under his keyboard and shook two out, thought about it, then added a third. He swallowed them with coffee.

"Aaron."

Kurtzman looked up at Rush, then slipped his headset on and opened the frequency linking him to Rush privately. "Yeah."

"I might have something on your clown," Rush said.

"Let's have it."

"I got it coming across your screen," Rush said.

As Kurtzman watched, a digitized image of the red-and-white jester appeared on his main monitor.

"This is the guy we're looking for."

"Yeah."

"I haven't found anything exactly like this," Rush said, "but I have tripped across some related incidents."

A window opened up beside the clown, showing another clown, this one with a bulbous nose, fiery hair and a demonic grin. A heartbeat later another window opened up, showing the front page of a newspaper, but the words were too small to be read. Kurtzman moved his mouse, clicked in the commands and made the newsprint fill the screen. The story was six years old and related the events of an attempt made against an investments company doing international business in Bordeaux, France. The news copy appeared to run for pages, followed by sequential stories relating developments.

"Want me to break it down for you?" Rush asked.

"Sure." Kurtzman saved the file, intending to read it for himself later. Rush hadn't been told everything about why he was supposed to find the jester, so it was possible he might miss something useful in the text file.

"Basically it was a case of electronic blackmail, something that was just beginning to develop back in the heyday of computer conversions that companies were beginning to make. This investment company, Gervais Horizons, had its feet solidly on the ground, turning a pretty good buck evidently. One morning they showed up at the office and were unable to bring any of their computers on-line."

"Somebody hit it with a virus?"

"Oh, yeah. And back in those days, you didn't find many programs around like Norton's Tools to fix that kind of problem. Anyway, the company turned frantic. Everything they needed to do business with was locked up. Client files, bank-account numbers, the whole schmear. While they were running around, trying to explain the problem to their clients, the computers came back on-line briefly at noon and left a message—'Pay up or your files will die.' An account number was left. Along with this cartoon clown.''

"And they paid?"

"Hell, yes, they paid," Rush said. "The guy who did this left them no choice. These days it's standard sys-op to leave backup files in a place other than your business, and the modem lines are closely monitored to keep viruses out of the system. Back then, with computer technology new to them, they didn't stand a chance."

"How much was the ransom?"

"Fifty thousand dollars."

Kurtzman rubbed his chin as he clicked the mouse and changed the monitor back to the demonic image of the clown. "Fifty thousand dollars isn't much."

"Not when you consider Gervais Horizons was the equivalent of a Fortune 500 company here in the States."

"That means the guy who did this was young."

Rush nodded. "I'd think so, yeah. Take somebody twenty, twenty-two years old, that kind of money would be a small fortune."

"The police investigated?"

"Yeah, but not until after Gervais paid up."

"How was the payment arranged?"

"Electronic transfer through Swiss accounts that belonged to real people. The money already in those accounts wasn't touched at all, so the people with those accounts weren't amenable to having their assets sifted through by any legal bodies. The reason depositors used the Swiss banks was to maneuver large sums of undisclosed cash. The last thing any of them wanted was the Feds involved."

"Right."

"Four years ago there was another clown incident." Rush entered a new series of commands on his keyboard. "This didn't make the papers. I got it from a colleague this afternoon when I began the search."

Kurtzman sipped his cold coffee and waited. His monitor blinked, then cleared, revealing a clown with a wide, happy smile and out-thrown arms.

"Recognize this guy?" Rush asked.

"Looks like Bozo."

"Yeah, I'd say that's who it's modeled on, but there are some differences. This is from a file kept by an employee of the Stuttgart phone company. The incident was hushed up right after it happened. The employee who gave me this was supposed to keep it under wraps, but she owes me a few favors. The phone company was embarrassed."

A column of figures sprouted up beside the clown, first appearing in German marks, then blurring and becoming American dollars.

"Several of the corporations keep accounts in Stuttgart, log national and international calls every day. They have large bills, and a lot of money changes hands."

"Another ransom notice?"

"No, this time the guy went strictly for nuisance value. When it came time for the monthly billing, several of the companies found their records scrambled. My friend said it took months to straighten everything out and reassure their clients that no one was being cheated."

"But there was no money involved? None this guy could get his hands on in the mix-up?"

"My friend says no. And when they started reassembling the files, this is what they found."

The clown jumped on the monitor screen, spread both hands to his sides and offered a big, happy grin. Then he yanked his pants down and revealed that he was hung well enough to make a Clydesdale turn green with envy.

Kurtzman cleared his throat. "Picturesque little son of a bitch, isn't he?"

"Maybe. I figured it might tell something more about the guy's character. This is pretty juvenile."

"Like thumbing your nose at authority."

Rush nodded.

"The phone company never found out who sabotaged their files."

"Not according to my friend."

"They tried?"

"Yeah. They were worried it might happen again the next month."

"But it didn't?"

"No."

Kurtzman reached for a pencil and scribbled a note to himself. "No money involved, designed for shock value to flaunt the powers that be in the company. Know what that sounds like to me?"

"Somebody inside the company who got pissed off."

"Yep. Can you access their employee files?"

"Not without compromising my friend, and frankly she needs that job."

"Suppose I can get you a way in." Kurtzman was thinking of Barbara Price. The Stony Man Farm mission controller had connections that amazed even Brognola at times.

"Then sure, no problem."

"I'll get it for you, and probably no one will ever know you've been there. When you're going through the files, check for someone who either terminated shortly before or shortly after this. Get a list of names. Could be a short one, but you never know. Once you have it, go back to the Bordeaux investigation and pull a list of names of students involved in the computer-science program at the university. You're searching for someone who either graduated at about the time Gervais was hit, or someone who dropped out of school about then."

"Sounds good to me," Rush said. "But for my two cents, I'd say we're looking for someone who never completed the program. If the guy was this good and he had his degree, he'd be working somewhere. Hell, even if he didn't finish and he was this good, he would have been hired by someone."

Thinking of the bloodthirsty warning the jester had left inside the Stony Man computers, Kurtzman said, "I'm sure the bastard's working for somebody. I just want to find out who."

Leipzig, Germany
5:41 a.m.

WITH THE BERETTA 93-R fisted in his hand, Mack Bolan came up out of the camouflaged hatch at the end of the escape tunnel like a ghost leaving its grave. Moonlight streamered down in slices, turning the dense forest into stripes of black and silver. He gained firm ground, caught the crashing noise coming from the underbrush behind him and spun to face it.

A maroon-uniformed security officer was in full flight, running blindly through the forest. He saw Bolan, halted against the side of a tree and raised his assault rifle to his shoulder.

The Executioner pointed the Beretta and squeezed off three shots. One of them scored a white gash against the dark bark beside the man's head. The next two took him in the face and sent him spinning away.

Tapping the transmit button on his headset, Bolan said, "Leo."

"Go, Sarge."

"Drop a flash-bang and a smoker as you get ready to come up. It might buy us some time." The big warrior reached down for Firenze Falkenhayn's hand, pulling her up easily.

She took up a position beside him, her weapon up and ready.

Turrin grabbed the side of the escape hatch and started to haul himself up. Double explosions, one on the heels of the other, echoed up out of the tunnel. A cloud of black smoke spumed into the night air and turned gray.

Wrapping a fist in his friend's shirt, Bolan helped pull him to solid ground.

Shouted commands rattled up toward the escape hatch as the Executioner lowered the door. He took an extra moment, pulled the pin from a smoker and placed the grenade with the spoon still in position so that it would fall into the tunnel and go off once the door was lifted again. It wouldn't hurt anyone, but it should buy them a few extra seconds.

A glance toward the Konigsalle Laboratories showed the Russian forces were in control. Sporadic muzzle-flashes blazed like fireflies, but the resistance was being eradicated step-by-step. Headlights of jeeps carved tunnels out of the night, splashing against the bullet-pocked and smoke-stained walls of the buildings. An Mi-24 Hind helicopter floated over the complex, moving as slowly as a zeppelin as it made its presence known. A cluster of nose-mounted searchlights arced over the battle zone.

"Those guys didn't come here looking for a fight," Turrin said tightly. "They just came here to kick ass and take names."

"They did the job, all right," the woman said.

Turrin looked at her, suspicion gleaming in his dark eyes. "What's your part in this?"

She regarded him coolly. "I called them into this area and informed them about the presence of bacteriological agents."

"You're working with the Russians now?" Bolan asked. The last time he'd seen the woman, she hadn't been sure of where her loyalties and duties lay.

She shook her head. "No."

Voices carried from the escape tunnel as the commander took control of the underground situation. The racing engines of the jeeps, and orders being issued in Russian-accented German through loud-hailers reached their position in patches.

"You know her?" Turrin asked.

Bolan glanced at the starlit sky, got his bearings and checked them against his compass. Then he took off at a jog, holding the Beretta loosely in his hand. "Yeah. Sticker, meet Firenze Falkenhayn. She used to work for West German Intelligence."

"In spite of the current German political situation, I still do," Falkenhayn said. "Although the mission I'm currently on isn't sanctioned officially."

Bolan kept the lead, grimly aware that the forest around them could be alive with enemy forces hiding from the Russian strike team. He headed for the high ground, sweeping upward in a smooth curve rather than a direct assault. The receiver cracked static in his ear.

"Striker, this is Thunderer. Over."

"Go," Bolan replied softly.

"Wanted to make sure you two were still viable, buddy. Over."

"Roger. Be advised that we're bringing a friendly in with us."

"Acknowledged."

"And make no attempts to engage the attacking force at the complex. They're Russian agents working the same angle of things we are."

"The situation here is getting knotty."

"Yeah. We'll have to take another look before we undertake any more skirmishes locally." Bolan broke the connection.

Falkenhayn jogged easily up to join him, her breathing regular. "You have a means of exfiltration?"

"Yes. And you?"

"No. Primarily I was here to bring the Russians in, point them at their target and let them do their jobs."

The warrior came to a halt below the defile of a hill and hunkered down. Falkenhayn and Turrin took refuge in the shadows with him. Taking his night glasses from his pouch, he swept the area thoroughly. No one appeared to be tracking them.

"Clean?" Turrin asked.

"Yeah."

Falkenhayn glanced from one man to the other. "Striker and Sticker. It sounds as if you two are part of a matched set."

"We've known each other awhile," Turrin said. He gave Bolan an inquisitive look.

"I met her in Germany after the wall fell," was all he said.

Bolan looked through the night glasses again. The Russian gunship still hung over the complex. Fires were spreading through the buildings now. He turned his attention back to the woman. "Where's Gustav Simmy?"

"Not in the complex."

"We already knew that."

"At this point there's not much more I can tell you."

Turrin shifted. "Look, lady, I hate to point this out to you, but we could take away those records and files you swiped back at the lab."

Falkenhayn's jaw tightened, and she changed her center of balance, adjusting herself so she could strike out more easily. The H&K VP-70 Z moved just enough to draw attention. "You'd have to take them."

Bolan studied the woman, noting the harsh lines of decisiveness that underscored her posture. Even though she'd been confused and betrayed by her Intelligence handler during the time they'd met before, he knew she had a strong sense of duty and wouldn't easily set aside the struggle even in the face of overwhelming odds.

There was a tense silence, broken by the sounds of continued carnage coming from the complex. Turrin broke the stare, leveling his gaze at Bolan.

"Let me make a phone call," Falkenhayn said. "As I told you, this mission is not sanctioned. I was told to eliminate the threat posed by the Konigsalle complex, but I wasn't given a means to do it myself. The secret messages I sent to Russian Military Intelligence were coded and through personal contacts I have. If I'd been burned or betrayed, the German government would have looked on me as a political traitor and taken appropriate steps. My own superior would have handled the details himself. He told me that." She paused. "The threat Simmy is able to wield hasn't been broken, and the Russians aren't the people for the job. Tonight will prove that to my commander. Maybe I can arrange for something."

"Sounds fine. If it doesn't work out, I don't know that I can release you with the information you're carrying because my people need it."

She lifted her hand and touched Bolan's cheek softly with her fingers. Her voice was gentle when she spoke. "I know. That's going to be one of my bargaining chips." She took her hand away.

After readjusting his equipment on the combat harness, Bolan got to his feet and aimed the small group toward Kissinger's position.

CHAPTER FIFTEEN

New Orleans, Louisiana
11:59 p.m.

"It's the goddamn witching hour," one of the booking cops said as he handed Carl Lyons a tissue soaked with cleaning solution. "I'm telling you, Lieutenant, you take a combination of the witching hour and a full moon, you got a town full of crazies prowling every alley around. Only thing that gets worse in this burg is the fuckin' Mardi Gras, and that's only because the tourism department insists on advertising for them every year."

Lyons cleaned the blank ink off his fingers with deliberation, remembering from experience how deeply ingrained the stuff could get. The tissue turned gray, then black under his ministrations. The diatribe presented by the booking officer didn't bother him. He'd heard the same song and dance for years. Only the chorus changed.

"Let's take a cup of coffee," the lieutenant suggested.

Finished with the tissue, Lyons tossed it at the wastebasket and made the shot. He trailed after the detective. None of his guns had been returned yet, and the Semmerling was over at the lab having test rounds fired through it for comparisons later. With the cover set in place through Stony Man Farm, the NOPD couldn't hold Able Team or its weapons. Detective Lieutenant Ashe Franklin had just been informed of that fact moments ago. So far, he hadn't appeared to have taken it well at all.

They walked past the holding cells and ignored the drunken invective and bravado from the men clinging to the bars or lying on the benches. The present attitude in the cells would evaporate with the alcohol by morning.

Lyons was aware of the attention he received in the homicide bullpen as they walked through. Evidently Franklin's mood was enough to dissuade anyone from trying to stop to chat about the killings at the Royal Deuce. They made a final pit stop at a hot plate holding two pots of coffee.

When the coffee was poured, Franklin jerked his head toward a darkened office and said, "In here."

"Where are my friends?" Lyons asked as he followed.

"Being released," Franklin replied, and waved at a wooden chair in front of the desk. "Trust me, somebody throws that much weight on a country cop like me, I get the message damn fast."

Lyons sat. Truth to tell, he felt compassion for the detective. He'd been shut out of a fair number of investigations himself when he'd been a member of the LAPD.

"They'll be along in a little while."

Sipping his coffee and finding it surprisingly good, Lyons waited. It was much easier waiting, he'd found, when everyone knew he had the cards all on his side of the table.

Franklin slipped the paddle holster carrying his .357 Ruger revolver into a desk drawer, making a show of making himself at home.

"This isn't your town," Franklin said in precise tones as he put his elbows on the desk and laced his fingers together. "Yet you and your buddies come here like a bunch of swinging dicks and stir up one of the biggest hornets' nests this town knows. You don't give a shit about the kind of fallout you're gonna cause. You just waltz in and throw your federal badges around and figure screw the local guy."

"That might be the way it looks to you," Lyons said, "but that's not the way this is going down."

A nerve flickered to life along Franklin's right jaw. "You want to tell me how this is going to go down, Agent Legend?"

"No."

Franklin's eyes turned hard and flat.

Lyons knew he was seated across from a no-nonsense cop who'd seen damn near every bad thing the world—especially his part of it—had to offer. The only thing that would satisfy the detective was the whole and complete truth, and that was one thing Lyons couldn't offer.

"I've been chasing Merle Spurlock and his organization for a long time," Franklin said. "Him and his people are smart. Been working this town and these docks for a lot of years. In the opinion of most people around here, a man'd have to get up awful early to catch Spurlock with his pants down."

Lyons grinned. "That's the difference between you and me. You're trying to catch the guy with his pants down, and I'm here to yank them down for him."

"You people didn't do so good tonight, though."

"It was opening night," Lyons said. "You should wait until we close the show before you pass judgment."

"You seem sure that you're going to be able to do that."

"Never a doubt in my mind," Lyons replied. "That was what I was sent here to do."

"Why the sudden interest in Spurlock from the Feds? He's always been a local problem."

"I can't go into that."

Franklin's gaze was flat, level and hard. "That G-man badge doesn't give you a blank check in my town."

"I didn't say that it did, but where Merle Spurlock is concerned, I've got a lot of latitude."

Franklin was silent.

"Could be," Lyons suggested, "that we could find a way to scratch each other's back."

After a moment the detective reached into a file drawer of the desk. "What do you know about Spurlock?"

"Runs mercenaries on an international level. Used to handle contract killings in the fifties and sixties."

"Almost got a couple of those to stick back then."

Lyons shrugged. "Happens. These guys get good, or they don't hang around as long as Spurlock. I was also told Spurlock bootlegs merchandise into and out of the States. Drugs. Guns. Even shipped Coors beer to the East Coast back in the seventies and turned a fistful of illegal dollars."

"What about the white slavery ring he's suspected of masterminding?"

"Haven't heard word about one."

"Or the voodoo stuff Spurlock's into?"

Lyons shook his head. "None of that stuff was in the files I was given." It wasn't like Price or Kurtzman to miss much.

"I'm not really surprised. The last Fed we had down here didn't know about it, either. They refuse to put it in their files because we don't have proof."

"But you know it to be true."

"As surely as I know my own name. Comes from living around this town all my life. A body gets to know things are fact sometimes without them ever becoming fact. You know what I mean?"

Lyons nodded, recalling similar incidences during his bit on the Los Angeles beat as a detective.

Franklin spread the contents of the file across the top of the neat desk. They were all colored pictures, some taken at night, others photographed in the light of day. All of them were bloody. Each corpse in the pictures had been stripped naked and painted with designs and pictographs that were haunting and disturbing, something that would live on with a man who'd seen them for a very long time.

"Spurlock?" Lyons asked as he reexamined the final picture. It was a night shot of a young woman naked and tied to a gnarled oak tree in a swamp area. The embers of the dying fire a dozen feet in front of her gleamed lambent orange lights in her sightless eyes. Her skin held a false glow of health in the places that weren't covered by blood.

"Yeah. But I could never prove it. That was from last November. Girl was seventeen. I had to go to her momma and tell her about this. Sometimes at night, when I'm alone, I can still hear her crying."

Lyons replaced the photograph on the desktop. "First time you ever handle a kid killing?" The sour taste of bile hung in the back of his throat.

"No. But it was the first time I ever had to let the killer walk."

"How do you know Spurlock was behind it?"

"There's always been a lot of rumors about Spurlock and his prize gang of cutthroats. For a while he was supposed to have headed up a witch's coven." The detective gathered the photographs and slipped them back into the manila file folder. "I scouted around and turned up a witness I was able to convince to testify against Spurlock. Going to blow the lid off the voodoo thing and the white slavery action all at one time. I worked a deal, found somebody pissed off at Spurlock enough to testify—after I applied enough leverage in the right places—and got the D.A. to agree to witness protection. I went to the Feds, the U.S. marshal's office. My informant was Edie Quoin, an ex-prostitute who used to work for Spurlock. Three days after I turned her name and her story in to the marshal's office, Edie Quoin turned up as bayou mystery meat."

Franklin rummaged through another file and opened it to a graphic picture.

A spasmodic shudder gripped Lyons's stomach when he looked at the picture. There wasn't much human that had been left behind. "You sure this was your witness?"

"Yeah. She'd been decapitated. Found her head hanging from a tree limb inside a canary cage. Warning seemed obvious enough."

"No takers for witness protection after this, huh?"

"No." Franklin closed the file and put it away. "This is the guy you're going after. I'm sure the Justice people painted Spurlock as a hardened criminal, but he's more than that. Spurlock's an animal. And if you're going to hunt a predatory animal, it's best if you know all of that animal's traits and territories."

"I agree."

"I'm still going to be watching you," Franklin warned. "You step out of line, mess things up for me and my guys in a way that I can hold you accountable for despite the influence you're packing, you and your team are history in New Orleans."

Lyons shrugged. He hadn't expected any less from the man. They might share a job, but the city was Franklin's beat. "Fair enough." The Able Team warrior rose to go.

"One other thing."

Lyons looked at the man.

"If you get a piece of Spurlock that you could use some help with, you give me a call." The detective took a card from his shirt pocket and handed it over.

"I'll do that." He put the card in his wallet and saw himself out.

Lyons got his weapons back at the booking desk, swapped artificial smiles with the guy holding down the post and made his way toward the rear of the building. The rectangular nameplate he wore kept the way clear. He thought about going to look for Blancanales and Schwarz, then decided against it. Things were strained enough between Able and the local crimebusters without pushing things even closer to the edge.

Outside, the night air was balmy, filled with the scents of the lake and fishing. In the distance the warning whistle of a tugboat sounded forlorn and lonely. Or maybe, Lyons thought, it was just the tiredness eating into his bones that made him feel that way. He zipped his Windbreaker and turned up the collar.

The Dodge van was parked across the lot, butted up against a wooden fence that sagged in places. Mercury-vapor lamps kept the area lighted well enough to chase away most of the shadows.

Blancanales and Schwarz weren't there.

Taking the key out of his pocket, Lyons crossed the lot, figuring to wait for his teammates while relaying the new information he'd gotten from Franklin to Price and Kurtzman at Stony Man Farm.

The sound of an ignition being keyed to life drew his attention. His hand dropped automatically to the .45 in the shoulder rig. His finger popped the safety strap just as a pair of headlights caught him in their glare.

Rubber shrieked, and the lights leapt out at Lyons like the baleful eyes of a jungle carnivore.

Shifting his weight, ready to break either left or right as the chance presented itself, the big ex-cop brought the Colt Commander up smoothly, flicked the safety off and thumbed back the trigger.

Shadows danced behind the windshield of the sedan.

Lyons dropped the hammer, aiming at the driver's side of the glass. The windshield starred as the heavy .45 slug smashed through, spiderwebbed out around the hole. He rode out the recoil and steadied himself for another shot, but there was no time. Throwing himself to one side, he went down, intending to come up firing. Instead, the sedan tracked him.

He heard the hiss of the tires humming across the lot surface, felt the heat of the engine hot in his face as the bumper narrowly missed him. Then the car door opened, swelled impossibly big as it filled his field of vision. He ducked to one side, trying in vain to get away.

The metal impacted against his shoulder as he twisted to protect himself, then caromed into the side of his head. Stars sparked in his brain, turning into black comets that whirled and died before his eyes. The .45 automatic dropped from his nerveless fingers as he struggled to hold on to consciousness.

The door had obviously been braced from the inside by the passenger, and it had given some with the force of the blow. The car screeched to a halt almost two lengths away, disgorging a handful of men.

Lyons sorted through the agony that filled him, forcing his motor responses to find the neurons necessary to lever an arm beneath him as he tried to get to his feet. The faces of his opponents were blurred, all but featureless. The sedan was a dark red faded by years of exposure to the sun. The front passenger door was crumpled in by a man-size crater.

"Geez, this guy's still trying to get to his feet," a man said in a thick Cajun accent. "Fucking head must be made of Mississippi mud to take a whack like that."

A hand raised over Lyons, holding something long and thick. He recognized it as a long-handled security flashlight just as it started to descend. When it landed, the pain was blinding.

He roared in agony and anger, surged up and managed to grab the man's leg. Holding on to the captured leg in one big hand, the Able Team warrior forearmed the knee from the side with his free arm.

Bone cracked. The man screamed and went down.

"Careful, damn it!" another man admonished. "Spurlock wants this bastard in one piece."

Lyons bunched his fists and turned for the next man. Then an avalanche seemed to fall on the back of his head.

Dizziness caused him to swoon. His knees buckled, and he was unconscious before he hit the ground.

Stony Man Farm, Virginia
1:23 a.m.

"ACTUALLY, MISS PRICE, I wasn't aware that you were still involved in covert espionage."

The Stony Man mission controller was taking the call in her private office inside Kurtzman's lab. She abandoned the files she had on her desk and paced the floor, watching the wall screens through her windows as they flickered through frame after frame of information the Farm's computers were digesting and sifting through.

"I never left it," Price replied. "I just went deep enough that not many people know me anymore."

The chuckle that filled the earpiece was in a deep, rich baritone that held genuine amusement. "The newer people in our line of work might not know of you, but we who have had the opportunity to test your mettle and know you for the adversary you can be will never forget you."

"You're too kind."

"On the contrary, I'm showing you how willing I am to be truthful with you."

Price smiled. "Within reason, of course."

"Of course."

The man's name was known to Price, but she didn't use it out of deference to the respect she held for him. The line was scrambled, and he knew it, but he also recognized the courtesy for what it was. The German espionage master was a true gentleman in every sense of the word. He could also be a cunning and cold opponent, and an expert player in the game of political brinkmanship. She had worked with him and against him in former positions she'd held with other American espionage agencies before joining Stony Man Farm. Enough of a history existed between them that she felt they could no longer be completely untruthful with each other.

"It is a pleasure to get to speak with you again," the German said, "but as I recall, you are a woman who doesn't make contact without some kind of agenda."

Price didn't mince words. "You have an agent in Leipzig working for you on a private matter. I thought we could discuss that."

"She told me she'd been detained, but she didn't tell me who had detained her."

"That's because she doesn't know."

"She told me she was acquainted with one of the men who're with her."

"Yes."

There was an expectant pause.

Price let it hang, then pass.

"You're not giving me much to work with here," the German said.

"You've got me, and you've got your agent's feelings. If she hadn't trusted the man she's with, she wouldn't have given you up to us, and I—in turn—wouldn't have let you know I was involved. All that remains to be seen is how much you're willing to trust me."

"You speak as though I have a choice. My agent has information that you could simply take."

"I don't want her hurt," Price said. "And I don't want my people hurt. Not if there's another way."

The line was silent for a moment.

Price looked through the window at Kurtzman's workstation and saw the killer clown's visage leering on the monitor.

"The mission," the German said, "that my agent is working on is unsanctioned. If word leaks out about my involvement, it could mean the end of a very long and precarious career."

"If we'd wanted security, we'd have taken other government jobs."

"True."

Price turned away from the window, aware of the bumps that raced across the back of her neck as she stared at the clown and felt Kurtzman's unease with its presence. "You must trust this agent very much to risk your career on her abilities and judgment."

"She is one of a kind."

"And how does she feel about her current situation?" Price already knew the answer. When she'd talked to Bolan earlier, the big warrior had explained his own perspective on the woman and the mission.

"She feels she can trust your man."

"Then if you really trust her, trust her now."

"Who is the agent she's with?"

"I can't tell you that."

His voice hardened. "I'm uncomfortable with that."

"It's the best I can do."

"You're asking me to put my agent in the hands of a cipher."

"No," Price said softly, "I'm asking you to put her in my hands. I trust the man she's with implicitly, but I don't want to make your own position any worse if this whole thing blows up in our faces."

"I see."

And Price believed the man probably did, probably even knew who Falkenhayn was with at this very moment. Mack Bolan was as well-known in espionage circles as he was in the criminal climate. "We both know how the espionage game is played. You don't send in an agent on a guessing game. You send that agent in because you know something is there, or you suspect it's there so strongly that to sit still and take no chance is more of a chance than getting caught. When you sent your agent to Leipzig, you knew what she'd find there. And she found it. Otherwise she'd have dumped the Intel on my team and gotten the hell out of there. The situation is knotty enough without adding to it. What I'm telling you—unofficially—is that I'm in a better position to do something proactive with that information than something reactive. By your own admission, you're not."

"Nowhere near that point. Much of what has been gathered is still supposition, with blame that could be tossed in any number of directions. When you lay the facts bare, you still have a former KGB terror scientist working on a biological weapon that has been forbidden under the Geneva Convention in a portion of Germany that had been under Communist rule until only a few years ago. And it's no great leap of the imagination to believe that the United States might be involved in plotting a plague that could wipe out much of northern Europe. At least, no great leap given current political feelings in Europe. My superiors want nothing to do with that. When I approached them with the unsubstantiated rumors my people had turned up, I was told to leave it alone because it might damage the new relationship between France and united Germany. But I can't. Germany is my country. Finally we are together again, as it should have been long ago. I won't see anything damage that. And the man who is behind this would let Germany fall just as quickly as any of the other nations he secretly wars against."

"Then give it to me," Price said. "Trust me to do the job you know I have to do. The documents your agent have are only part of what I need. The details you're keeping inside your head are just as invaluable."

The German laughed, low and good-naturedly. "I've always maintained that women are much better negotiators than men because they are so much better at flattery. Your male counterpart would have resorted to angry threats at this point."

"They would only be empty ones."

"Yes."

"So what does flattery buy me?"

"Nothing," the German said without hesitation. "However, your record speaks for itself. I'll contact my agent, and she'll turn the information over to you. As for my own views on what is happening, bear in mind that much of it is speculation."

Price took a notepad from her desk, sat and began taking notes. The German's thoughts and conjectures fleshed out the ones she'd been harboring herself.

New Orleans, Louisiana
12:31 a.m.

THERE WAS A CROWD in the police parking lot when Rosario Blancanales stepped out into the night. He was tired and ached from the all-day stakeouts Able had pulled, and the many cups of coffee he'd downed in the cop shop were coming back to haunt him in the form of mild jitters.

A handful of uniforms made a semicircle around three men out in an open lane of the parking area. Two of the men were old and leathery, dressed in flannel shirts with the sleeves hacked off and wearing suspenders to keep up their faded dungarees. The third man was actually a boy, clad like the two men, and looked as if he would resemble them in another four or five decades. Blancanales figured they would smell like fish, swamp and sweat if he got closer. He chose not to.

Skirting the immediate area, he headed for the van. A quick glance at the vehicle revealed Hermann Schwarz lounging in the shadows, arms crossed over his chest as he watched the group. There was no sign of the Ironman.

Two of the cops had flashlights and were playing the beams over the ground. As they moved, Blancanales recognized Ashe Franklin, the homicide cop, circulating within their midst. The three fishermen were gesturing rapidly, their voices so heavily accented by their Cajun roots the Politician was unable to understand them.

Blancanales turned up his jacket collar against the cool chill moving through the night as he fell into place beside Schwarz. "Where's Carl?"

"Haven't seen him. I thought he might be with you."

"Not me. I haven't seen him since we were separated when they took us in."

"I overheard somebody saying that homicide cop took Carl out for a private session." Schwarz's face was hard.

Blancanales studied Franklin openly, didn't look away as the homicide man's eyes met his. Franklin's gaze was hard and flat, and he glanced away only with the arrival of a small team of men carrying equipment.

"I don't think the NOPD would try a grandstand play like putting Ironman away somewhere to put pressure on Justice to give up the operation on Spurlock," Schwarz said, "but I've seen some hillbilly cops in my time that didn't recognize anyone's authority but their own."

"Not Franklin," Blancanales said. It was a gut feeling about the guy, but gut feelings about people were the Politician's stock-in-trade. "He's got that backwoods upbringing, but he's a savvy guy. Dealing with the Feds on his home turf, I get the impression that he'd try to outfinesse us before he tried anything in the neighborhood of brute force. And you can bet your ass he knows the moves to do it, too."

"Maybe." Schwarz was in a black mood.

Blancanales knew it for what it was. Able Team had been in dire straits before, came close to losing a teammate when the final cards were played in a deadman's hand. Every time one of those situations arose, he and Schwarz were reminded of the Executioner's Death Squad and how so many of their old unit had died in the trenches fighting the Mafia. It happened. No matter how good a guy was, all it took was one bullet or the quick kiss of a knife. He was hard-pressed to shake that old fear away himself, especially since Lyons wasn't anywhere around. The Ironman was impatient. It would have been more in character for Lyons to have taken the van and gone on ahead rather than being late showing up.

One of the new arrivals stepped forward, spraying the high-intensity beam of a video camera over a dark pool covering the parking lot.

Impulsively Blancanales stepped forward, drawn by that familiar shadowy stain. Schwarz was a half step behind him. When he was less than ten feet away, he recognized it as blood.

Franklin stepped in front of Blancanales, putting out a hand to stop him. The Politician grabbed the hand, giving silent testimony to the fact that the lone hand wouldn't stop him if he didn't want it to. The NOPD detective didn't try to exert any pressure, but he didn't step away, either.

His gaze hard and level, Franklin said, "They got your friend."

The lab technicians continued working the area. Two of the uniforms started marking off the vicinity with yellow POLICE—DO NOT CROSS tape. Another man brought over a set of keys, carrying them at the end of a ballpoint pen.

"Spurlock?" Blancanales asked.

"Looks that way." Franklin glanced at the key ring. "Recognize those?"

Schwarz inspected it. "Yeah."

Blancanales recognized the key ring, too. It was the Ironman's, bearing keys to the van, as well as to the equipment cases inside the vehicle. "What happened?"

In terse, professional sentences, Franklin relayed the fishermen's stories, described the kidnapping and the getaway car. "We found the car a few blocks from here," the homicide detective went on. "It was abandoned, but it looks like Legend was able to get at least one round off before they put him down. That agrees with the story I got here. We're going to match up the blood we found in the back seat against what's on the ground, and find out what kind of chance there is that your friend's still alive. Could be he wounded somebody and the blood isn't his at all."

Even though the NOPD man's impassive face gave nothing away, Blancanales could tell by the swirling glints deep in those dark eyes that the man was sure the blood did belong to Lyons.

"According to these men," Franklin said, jerking a thumb over one broad shoulder, "it appears the people who took your partner were trying to take him alive. Goes against Spurlock's nature to do something like that."

Blancanales swapped looks with Schwarz, knew the other man was thinking the same thing he was. Spurlock would question Lyons, get what information the Ironman had concerning the efforts of the rest of the Stony Man teams, then relay it to whoever was behind the organization. Although the communiqués between Able and the Farm concerning Bolan's and Phoenix Force's movements had been limited, Lyons's Intel could still prove damaging. A covert action worked best when an opponent didn't know exactly what or how many he faced. Once tactical numbers could be assigned, the fear lessened. And fear and uncertainty were major weapons in a small unit's arsenal. After those were gone, the shift from hunter to hunted was an almost immediate response.

"How did Spurlock's men know to wait on our guy?" Schwarz asked.

Franklin moved his gaze over to Gadgets. "Spurlock gets his information through the department probably faster than I do. I'd guess he made you people as Feds before I could confirm it. The thing that interests me is that he would want your partner alive."

Neither Blancanales nor Schwarz offered a comment.

"Makes me wonder if you guys aren't merely the tip of the iceberg where this thing is concerned," the homicide man speculated.

"I got to make a call," Blancanales said.

Schwarz nodded, making it clear he was going to stay at the investigation scene in case anything else turned up.

"You going hunting for your partner?" Franklin asked.

Blancanales faced the homicide cop, reading the man's body language. If the NOPD tried to hold them, the political clout rolling down from the Justice Department could free them in time. But it could be hours spent that would be costly to the mission and to Carl Lyons. Franklin was a no-nonsense, straight-ahead kind of guy from what Blancanales had seen, so the Politician went with that. "Yeah."

"This is a big city. Lot of sinkholes around that a new guy could drop into if he wasn't careful. Might be nobody'd ever hear of you people again."

"I didn't get into this business for a free ride," Blancanales said.

"Me, neither." A grim smile twisted Franklin's lips. "Make you the same offer I made your friend. If you need somebody local to show you the way, you call me. I figure you guys carry more weight in this town right now than one lone detective squeezing between crime and political favors."

Blancanales nodded but didn't reply. More pictures were being taken as he turned away. The harsh flashes rammed home the fact that the Ironman was missing with every spark. He walked to the pay phone snugged into the side of the police building and dialed a number from memory. The line clicked twice, signaling the cutouts programmed into the connection that would keep it from being traced in any way.

Barbara Price answered on the second ring.

"It's Pol," Blancanales said. "It looks like Spurlock and his people have taken Ironman. We think he's alive. At least there's evidence they tried to take him that way, but you know how the big guy can get. They might not have been able to."

"Have you got anything to work with?"

Blancanales looked at Ashe Franklin's back. The homicide cop was pointedly not looking in his direction. "I got a homicide cop who's got a ferocious itch to scratch where Spurlock's concerned. What he's got off the record might be a hell of a lot more than we had to work with when we rolled into this town. We spent most of the day working the streets and turned up zilch until we got onto the Royal Deuce. Now we don't have the time to be wrong often."

"I agree. Who's the cop?"

"A guy named Ashe Franklin. Seems local."

There was a brief pause. "He is local. And he's stand-up people, Pol. You couldn't ask for anyone better down there, and if I'd had someone who knew the area, you guys would have already had him. Ask Franklin if he'd like to work for the federal government for a few hours."

"Recruitment's going to be easy. Guy's already volunteered."

"Take him up on it," Price replied. "And get Ironman back as soon as you can. We just turned some new Intel here, and things are moving at a more accelerated pace than we'd at first thought. If you don't get him back soon, you'll have to go on without him."

Blancanales knew it hurt Price to have to say that, but he also knew she wouldn't have said it if it wasn't so. He broke the connection and walked back to Franklin and Schwarz. "Can you get away for a few hours?" he asked the lieutenant.

"Yeah. I've been working on my own time for the past three hours. Spurlock's been a major interest of mine for a long time. Once I found out you guys were breathing down his neck, I came in to see what would happen."

"Well, for the next few hours, until we get our guy back, you get the chance to see how the other half lives."

Blancanales led the way to the van, followed by Franklin as Schwarz brought up the rear. The Politician unlocked the side door and zipped the panel back with a clang, revealing the stacks of electronic hardware and heavy ordnance Able had drawn for the mission. "One way or another, we're going to get our man back." He let Franklin see the commitment on his face. "If you're not willing to go the distance with us, now is the time to say so."

The homicide detective's face was impassive. "Like I said, I figure you guys got all the smoke screen you need to pull Spurlock's little mob down without getting burned in a court of law. Legend as much as told me that. I'd like to be a part of that. You get to wondering how far I'll go with you, look over your shoulder. That'll be me covering your ass."

Blancanales grinned and climbed inside as Schwarz slid behind the steering wheel. The Politician broke out a cut-down Remington Model 870 police shotgun and passed it forward. Schwarz took it, bracketed it in the clips mounted on the dashboard, then released the clutch and got under way, creeping around the lab team still working the parking lot.

Franklin closed the side door with a bang that echoed inside the van, then took a seat.

"What do you carry?" Blancanales asked as he rummaged through the weapons cache.

The detective showed him the .357 Ruger in the paddle holster by his left kidney.

Unlimbering an Uzi machine pistol, Blancanales held it up. "You know how to use one of these?"

"I've shot one a few times."

"It's fully automatic. You'll learn how to caress a short burst out of it as you go along." The Politician passed over a bandolier with extra magazines. "You get thirty-two 9 mm rounds in a mag, but you can go through them damn quick. Practice loading that thing while we drive and talk."

Franklin seemed slow at first, but the movements came more naturally and faster as Blancanales provided instruction. Once he was satisfied, he gave the homicide cop a few additional pointers.

"You check your badge at the gate on this one," Blancanales said. "The only way we're going to get our guy back is to hit these people hard and often. Make it seem like we've gone ape-shit and the only chance they have at damage control is to keep our guy alive. You know the places where Spurlock will most likely be. We'll provide the firepower and the threat once you direct us." He looked at the NOPD man. "This ain't gonna be police work, son. This is purely guerrilla action behind enemy lines."

CHAPTER SIXTEEN

Leipzig, Germany
8:11 a.m.

"We've got company."

Mack Bolan shifted, standing only inches from the office-building wall as he swept the city terrain around him. He lifted the foam cup of coffee to his lips to mask his reply as he tapped the headset's transmit button. "Where?"

"Ten o'clock," Leo Turrin replied. "There's a dark blue BMW that pulled up to the curb a few minutes ago. Guys inside have a pair of field glasses."

Bolan studied the traffic flow cutting through the city and found the BMW parked against a curb, aerials sprouting from its top and trunk. Three men were inside, all lean and hard, and all determined not to get caught looking at him. "Do they seem more interested in my friend or me?"

Falkenhayn was at one of the public phones under the gaily striped awnings of Hotel Merkur. She was wearing black jeans and a denim shirt with the sleeves rolled up to reveal a hot pink T-shirt underneath. Her automatic was hidden away inside her purse, which was never allowed out of one hand or the other.

"The woman," Turrin replied. "But maybe it's only because they know her by sight."

Bolan was fifteen feet away, enough of a distance that if Falkenhayn bolted and ran, things could be difficult. The backpack containing the Intel from the Konigsalle Laboratories was at her feet, braced against her shins. It was possible that she could make the car before he could stop her. He glanced at the woman and saw that she was still talking animatedly on the phone with her supervisor.

The open square in front of the towering hotel held a landscaped garden and fountain area. Water glinted and sparkled as it sprayed back into itself, and the verdant growth showed off the bright red blossoms. A dozen poles sporting multicolored flags stood straight and tall as the material snapped and unfurled ceaselessly in the brisk wind. People walked along the sidewalks on all sides.

Bolan was grimly aware that the site was no place for a battle zone. He was dressed touristy, wore Levi's jeans, a charcoal turtleneck and a stone-washed denim jacket that covered the Desert Eagle and its shoulder rigging.

Falkenhayn finished her phone call, grabbed the straps of the backpack and turned toward him with a smile on her face. The smile wavered, as she sensed his unease. She took a pair of sunglasses from her purse and covered her eyes. "Trouble?" she asked in a voice that carried only a few feet.

"Maybe." The warrior indicated the BMW with a small nod. There was no sense disguising the fact that he was with Falkenhayn. The watchers had seen the woman's move toward him enough to know they were together.

As she turned, she opened her purse and dropped her hand inside. "They're Russian Military Intelligence agents."

Bolan took her at her word. Since the fall of the KGB, a lot of new players had been brought onto the field, and they frequently changed. He'd had no chance to get to know the espionage troops as well as Falkenhayn, and this was her part of the world.

"How long have they been there?" she asked.

"Minutes."

"I knew there was a possibility the tip I put within their reach would be traced back to me. I just didn't expect them to find me so quickly."

Bolan knew that if she hadn't encountered the Stony Man forces, Falkenhayn would have already gone to safe ground rather than risking exposure as they'd done. "Can we deal with them?"

She looked at him. "I can't. Can you?"

The Executioner shook his head.

"We don't need them along," Falkenhayn said. "I just received a green light on your end of the mission, but it calls for a small unit. If we cut the Russians in, well, you've already seen how they want to handle it from last night's events."

"Yeah."

The headset buzzed for attention.

Bolan tapped the transmit button. "Go."

"Looks like they've decided to take a more active part, Sarge," Turrin said.

Glancing in the direction of the BMW, Bolan watched as the three men inside got out, taking time to make adjustments under their coats. "Copy, Sticker. Cowboy?"

"Go," Kissinger said.

"You're on the vehicle. Make sure it doesn't move again."

"Ten-four, buddy."

Bolan took Falkenhayn by her elbow, then started threading their way through the sidewalk crowd in front of the Hotel Merkur. A quick glance over his shoulder showed the Russians stepping up their pursuit. He hit the headset button again. "Sticker."

"Go."

"Is that the only interested party?"

"Negative, Sarge. I just made two flankers working the ends of the street."

"On foot?"

"One team. The other's staying with the vehicle."

Bolan cut the corner, walking faster now and forcing Falkenhayn almost into a run. "This has to go down quietly. No encounter. No engagement."

"These boys don't look quite so amenable," Kissinger commented.

"Then we don't give them a choice."

"This car's down," Kissinger said, "but that won't keep them from buddying up."

"Inside," Bolan said to Falkenhayn. He guided her into the main lobby of the hotel, slowing to a brisk walk that took them across the plush red carpet toward the bank of elevators. The morning traffic was light for the cages. Two of them pinged open at the same time.

The warrior stepped inside, held the doors open and watched the reactions of the trailing Russians as they entered the hotel lobby. Four other men had joined the first three. Immediately a pair moved off in the direction of the fire escape at the side of the lobby. The others went for the elevators.

Bolan let go of the door and punched the button for the ninth floor. The panels closed, cutting the view of the lobby.

"They have walkie-talkies," Falkenhayn pointed out. "They can follow us."

"For a time." Bolan reached into his pants pocket as the elevator cage slid smoothly upward. He took out a knife, flicked it open and hit the emergency stop button when they were between the third and fourth floors.

Falkenhayn took out her pistol.

Working quickly, knowing the Russians might even now be closing in on them, the warrior forcibly popped the stainless-steel plate over the elevator controls. He checked the wiring inside, made his selection and started to cut. When he finished, the elevator was wired in such a way that it would no longer respond to any commands not issued by the control panel itself.

He pressed the emergency stop button again, then hit the button for the lobby.

"They'll have a man waiting there," Falkenhayn said as the cage dropped. "We'll have gained a little time, but it won't be enough to evade them."

Bolan gave her a tight smile. "I'm not through maneuvering yet, and I'm counting on the guy in the lobby." He unleathered the Desert Eagle and held it out of sight by his leg. He waved her to the other side of the cage.

Shouldering her purse beside the backpack, Falkenhayn took up her position and gripped the H&K VP-70 Z in both hands.

When the elevator doors slid open, Bolan made out the lobby guard at once. The man was speaking into his walkie-talkie and stood only a few feet from the doors. His arm was under his jacket.

"They're here!" the man said in Russian. "They came back down!" His hand started to emerge from his jacket, gripping a pistol.

Bolan lunged, grabbed the man's jacket in his free hand and yanked him back into the elevator cage. Working off the forward momentum, the Executioner controlled the Russian's velocity and direction, smashing him into the back wall of the elevator with enough force to cause the man to drop his pistol and the walkie-talkie. Dazed, the Russian agent sank to his knees.

The warrior stomped on the walkie-talkie, destroying it. He hit the elevator control panel, signaling for the top floor. The cage creaked and started up at once.

The Russian tried to scramble for his weapon, but froze when Falkenhayn prodded the back of his neck with the barrel of her pistol. He put his hands on the top of his head when she told him to.

Tapping the headset's transmit button, Bolan said, "Sticker."

"Go."

"How free are we?"

"Don't know what you did, Sarge, but the guys out here are acting like a hornet's nest has been stirred up."

"Have they made you?"

"No."

"Where's Cowboy?"

"We're together again, just like Butch and Sundance."

"You're moving when I tell you. Until then, sit tight."

"You got it."

Bolan slapped the control panel again, halted the cage at the fifth floor and checked the corridor. A young couple with two children was waiting by the elevators but quickly moved away when they saw Falkenhayn's gun. It would only be a matter of minutes before hotel security was involved, as well.

Gripping the Russian by one arm, Bolan moved the guy bodily out into the corridor. By taking the pointman out of the action, he'd slowed down the pursuit. The teams would have to double back on themselves to cover everything, and that was almost impossible now. While Falkenhayn kept the Russian covered, the Executioner reached up over the elevator doors and smashed the floor-indicator panel. Glass and colored plastic rained against him, but when he was finished, there was no way their cage could be traced from that floor. It would buy them a few more seconds.

"Come on," he growled.

Falkenhayn stepped back into the cage.

When the elevator doors closed, Bolan hit buttons for the remaining floors in quick succession. The cage stopped at the sixth floor, and they waited tensely to see if anyone had made them.

A small crowd had gathered in front of the elevator, and started forward expectantly.

Bolan pointed to the control panel, hanging loosely. He gave them an apologetic smile and spoke in German. "Sorry. This elevator is temporarily out of order."

A universal feeling of resignation passed through the crowd, and they all stepped back.

The elevator moved on. Bolan and Falkenhayn got out on the seventh floor. No one was waiting for them. The warrior led the way, jogging toward the fire escape. He halted at the door, then pushed on through. They waited silently for a few seconds, then heard men's voices drifting in echoing whispers above them. Quick moments later they were at the lobby level again and made their way outside the building.

The warrior tapped the headset again. "Sticker."

"Go."

"Meet us behind the hotel. We're outside."

"Roger."

Bolan snugged the Desert Eagle into leather again as they made the corner and waited in the alley behind the hotel.

"So where do we go from here?" Bolan asked.

"Rügen," Falkenhayn replied. "It's where Gustav Simmy is being held."

Bolan searched his mind for geographical reference to the name, but came up empty.

"It's an island in the Baltic Sea. There are a number of seaside resorts there. My Intel is that Simmy is being kept there, awaiting transfer to somewhere in France."

"When is he supposed to leave?"

"Tonight. There is a seaplane coming to get him."

Bolan nodded and glanced at his watch. It didn't give them much time. And they still had to be debriefed over the latest information Stony Man Farm had turned up regarding Falkenhayn's visit to Konigsalle Laboratories.

A gunmetal gray Jeep Cherokee turned into the alley and came toward them. Leo Turrin sat behind the steering wheel while Cowboy John Kissinger rode shotgun. The 4X4 pulled to a rocking stop behind a delivery van, drawing the driver's attention for just a moment while Bolan and Falkenhayn clambered into the rear seat.

"Company?" Turrin asked as he shoved the stick into first gear.

"Probably footsteps behind us," Bolan replied. The warrior leaned over the back of the seat and pulled his personal duffel closer. He unzipped one of the pouches and took out his map case and pocket atlas.

The Cherokee accelerated, weaving out around the delivery van.

Three men came dashing through the hotel kitchen area, knocking over one of the hand trucks and sent the deliveryman sprawling. They didn't look happy as they watched the Cherokee race away.

"You got a destination in mind?" Turrin asked as he made the turn onto the street.

"We make the link with Jack at the airfield. We're going to make a quick jump." The warrior's mind was already occupying itself with the logistics of the next step of the mission. He found Rügen in the atlas and began penciling the island's rough shape into a blank page inside his map case. Better topographical maps would come from Stony Man Farm, but he could lay out a lot of the preliminary groundwork along the way before he got to the meet in Berlin. "Where on the island?"

"The northeast coast," Falkenhayn said. She touched the map with a delicate finger. "There's a private estate with a dock out on the beach. At this time of year, there will still be a few vacationers. But any direct approach on the estate is going to be immediately noticed."

Bolan had already figured on that. An air approach was definitely out. He turned his mind to the other avenues left open to him as Turrin settled into the rhythm of the traffic flowing out of Leipzig toward Berlin.

Stony Man Farm, Virginia
1:31 a.m.

"WHAT IS IT?"

Aaron Kurtzman glanced up from his computer monitor and looked at Barbara Price. "It's the jester. He's trying to make contact with our systems again. For the moment we're holding him off." He worked his right hand over a tennis ball, kept squeezing it and forcing away the tension that filled him.

Price settled a rounded hip onto one of the few bare spaces left across Kurtzman's workstation.

The big cybernetics specialist sighed in exasperation. "The bastard's probably only trying to contact us again so he can thumb his nose at us. By rejecting his attempts, I'm trying to buy Akira some time to trace the transmission."

"Won't he get suspicious?"

Kurtzman shook his head. "No. This guy's a games man. Keith and I have turned up some of his background. At least, we're pretty sure it's his background. From what we've seen, this guy doesn't operate with a cash flow in mind. He's there to screw with the system as much as he can. Right now he views the Farm as the biggest authoritative system he's ever encountered. He gets his rocks off dancing around us. He won't back away until he's delivered the message he has for us."

The monitor fuzzed over, then broke into rainbows that splattered all over the screen.

"Persistent, isn't he?" Keith Rush called from his computer. He was intently watching the action on his own screen.

"Yeah," Kurtzman growled. He raised his voice. "Akira."

"I'm working it, boss man," Tokaido called back.

Kurtzman glanced at the younger man. Tokaido was hunched over his computer, one hand poised above the keyboard while the other worked the mouse. Frame after frame of schematics bounced across the huge wall screen in front of him.

"He's gone ballistic," Tokaido said. "I'm through some of his defenses, got him tracked all the way to a communications satellite hanging over Great Britain. He's riding as a carrier on the MTV network."

"Stay with him," Kurtzman said. He sat forward in his wheelchair, muscles tense and taut between his shoulder blades. He dropped the tennis ball into the carryall at the back of his chair because it was doing nothing to relax him.

Kurtzman forced himself to breathe. Everything he and Rush had turned up indicated that if they could break through the jester's defenses and access the files he no doubt kept, they'd be able to penetrate the infrastructure of the organization the clown was working for.

Without warning, the wall screen in front of Tokaido exploded like a blue sun going nova. The glare was intense, trapped inside the room. Despite the protective dampers programmed into the system, the light was still bright enough to hurt.

Kurtzman turned his head away and blinked back black spots that threatened to envelop his vision.

"Squid grease," Tokaido said. "He found me."

"No shit," Rush muttered.

When the screen cleared, a frozen tableau remained. It was a cartoon landscape of a myriad of people doing dozens of different things in various sections of a crowded city. Some people were digging dinosaur bones from a manhole while others stood around watching. In another sector skiers were slaloming down the snow-covered sides of skyscrapers. Another cityscape showed a handful of children clinging to balloon strings that lifted them from the ground as worried parents chased after them. Carmine letters slashed their way across the screen, bled out into rounded shapes. When it finished, it read, "Where am I?"

Tokaido leaned back in his chair in obvious disgust. "He's gone, Aaron. He slipped me before I could tag him."

"It's okay, kid," Kurtzman said. "You gave it your best shot. But you'll get another. This guy isn't going to be satisfied with just disappearing."

Tokaido held up his hand, forefinger and thumb less than an inch apart. "I was this close. Another heartbeat, and I'd have had him by the balls." He glanced quickly around the room. "Sorry about that, ladies."

Kurtzman accessed the file Tokaido had been pursuing, tapped the keyboard and found something. "He left a gif file behind." He brought it on-line, ran it through the virus-detecting programming he'd created for the Farm. It checked out clean. He stroked the keyboard again, feeding the file into his computer.

On-screen the myriad of figures under the "Where am I?" message came to life. They worked animatedly at everything they were doing. Then one of the figures fishing inside an oversize goldfish bowl dropped its pole and started doing back-flips, seemingly creating a third dimension and giving the appearance of being on the brink of coming out of the wall screen.

The figure landed on its feet, overshadowing the collage of moving cartoons with a flourish, hands palm up at shoulder level. A mocking smile twisted the clown's face as he tilted his head at a roguish angle. A word balloon floated out of his mouth: "Here I am, hackers!"

"Geez," Rush said with real respect. "This guy really goes in for detailed graphics."

"He's an artist, all right," Tokaido added with reluctant admiration.

The clown waved and the background disappeared, leaving him standing against a background of smoky black clouds. He reached inside his suit and brought out a globe at least eighteen inches in diameter, set it spinning in the palm of his hand. The oceans and land masses turned into a whirl of blues, browns and greens. Within seconds a happy face etched in stark black lines formed over the whirling globe. Then clock hands sprouted from the face's nonexistent nose, raced madly around the perimeters of the globe and came to a rest at twelve o'clock.

With a mocking leer, the clown pointed the forefinger of
his free hand at the globe and pulled an imaginary trigger.
A flag shot out of his fingertip at the globe, with the word
"Bang!" written on it. The happy face turned sad as the
clock hands disappeared. Then the globe shrunk in on itself until it was a shapeless blob hanging loosely in the
clown's palm.

"There's nothing subtle about this guy, either," Rush
said.

The clown placed his fists on his hips, squatted and
started dancing in hops and skips. The crotch of the fes-
tive-colored pants ballooned out until the material hung
loosely between his knees. A pair of dark glasses popped out
of his eyeballs and covered his gaze. He continued dancing,
then a word balloon leaked from his mouth: "You can't
touch this!" He reached down, grabbed his toes and flipped
himself backward, disappearing as if falling down a long
tube that made him look smaller and smaller until he was
gone.

"Okay," Kurtzman said as the screen blanked, "the
show's over. Let's get back to work and figure out a way to
nail this son of a bitch."

His team moved automatically back into their routines.

Price reached out and squeezed his shoulder in silent
support.

He patted her hand in appreciation. "Can't help thinking," he said, "that if I could just get through to this character, we could find out where Carl is and put Able one step
closer to him."

"We'll get Carl back," Price said with a surprising confidence. "That's a matter of time. Pol and Gadgets have
their own way of doing things. If we can get them some Intel that will help them, so much the better. But until then,
our job is to shake down this organization before time really does run out."

Kurtzman looked up at her. "We're really that close to the
wire?"

"I think so." Price stood and took the cellular phone
from its place at her belt. "The information I got from the
German connection is pretty solid. He had a little more than

we did. Added to what we've already got, the picture is definitely getting clearer. And they know we've got the pressure turned up. They can't ignore us. It's just a matter of how quickly they can move up their timetable.''

Kurtzman glanced back at the blank computer screen. "We'll break this, Barb. There's nothing we've failed at before. And we'll take this apart, too. I just can't give you a time frame."

"Give me your best, Aaron. That's all I've ever expected." She turned and walked away.

For a moment Kurtzman watched her, amazed at how well she handled everything. He knew she was getting pressure from the President, despite Brognola's efforts to block it, and Lyons was among the missing in New Orleans. Phoenix Force and Striker were on different legs of the mission, with no sure idea of how those pieces were going to fit into the cohesive whole. One thing he was sure of, he decided as he turned back to face his keyboard once more, Stony Man Farm would never have a more capable and sure hand at the helm.

He shoved the jester's latest outing to the back of his mind, determined to deal with it when he had the time. For now he had to set up the information feed Price had prepared for Phoenix Force and Striker. The jester would make a mistake. He knew that. It showed in the clown's history. The guy liked the game too much, liked to stay too close to the fire. This time, though, the fire was too big. Kurtzman intended to turn it up at the right time and send the guy down in flames.

New Orleans, Louisiana
12:50 a.m.

THE INITIAL TARGET WAS a flophouse located along the strip of wharves and boats that lined Lake Pontchartrain north of the city proper. Hermann Schwarz knew they didn't call them flophouses anymore, and that his use of the term probably dated him as being older than he was. But the word suited the ramshackle collection of aging buildings sinking into the swamps of the bayou land.

The flophouse was a motel with a neon sign that held only a bare flicker of former glories. The glass tubing read Seaview Motel, but Schwarz had had to be within a dozen feet of it to read it.

Taverns lined the wooden walkway behind him, and the footsteps of the passersby echoed along the weathered timbers, floated out over the lake and were gone. Raucous singing tumbled from one of the bars nearby, a dirty, tuneless ditty that picked up a couple extra voices from nearby fishing boats to carry the chorus.

"Show you a good time, sailor?" a feminine voice inquired from the shadows by the motel.

Schwarz turned to face the woman. He carried a rolled green duffel over his shoulder that didn't look out of place along the dock area. The cut-down Remington 12-gauge was tucked inside so that it would come away easily if he needed it. "I'm no sailor, but I could use some company."

The woman stepped from the murky embrace of the night, and Schwarz realized she was little more than twenty, if that. Her dark hair was cut short, looked boyish and failed to cover her ears. She was clad in a purple spandex leotard with red stripes that ran from her shoulder to her opposite hip, almost uninterrupted by her small breasts. The leotard disappeared at the waist where it was covered by a wraparound red miniskirt that hugged her slim hips. Her eyes were dark and smoky, set in an elfin face that looked ivory against the oversize black earrings she wore. "Gonna cost you," the girl warned.

"What's the going rate for a mere slip of a girl?" Schwarz asked, playing out the role he'd chosen for himself.

"Cost you three hundred for the night."

"How about I take an hour's worth?"

A lighter flared in her hand, igniting the cigarette thrust between her lips. She kept the flame on for a moment, removed the cigarette and smiled saucily at him. The attempt at humor never even came close to her eyes. "What's the matter? Afraid you can't handle a mere slip of a girl for a whole night? Big man like you, you ought to still be going strong when the cock crows in the morning."

Schwarz gave her an easy grin. "Honey, save your ego-threatening sales pitch for somebody who's still young enough to think he can live on loving. Us full-grown men realize we got to have some sleep if we're gong to pull the next shift in the morning." Part of him didn't want to talk to her. But the Seaview Motel was a place where a man checking in alone who wasn't a regular would draw more attention than he wanted. He needed her as part of his cover.

The headset earphone buzzed slightly in his ear. "Don't make the mistake of marking her off," Ashe Franklin whispered. "Girls half her age learn how to start turning tricks on the docks from their mommas. You give her your back, thinking she isn't anything to worry about, she could just carve herself a piece of it to take home."

Schwarz clicked the handset once, signaling an affirmative. It was something he didn't have to be told. While he'd been in Vietnam with Bolan, he'd learned all about the way children could be used.

"You're lucky," the girl said, snapping off the lighter. "You got a nice face and you shave regular. Don't smell bad, neither. An hour'll cost you a hundred."

"Expensive," Schwarz said.

"But worth it. Make you sleep like a baby when you're through."

"Okay."

She held out her hand. "I get the hundred up front."

Schwarz opened up his wallet and withdrew the money in crisp twenty-dollar bills.

"It's a good thing Carl's not here to see this," Blancanales said over the walkie-talkie. "He'd never let you hear the end of it."

The girl made the money disappear somewhere inside the spandex.

"You got a name?" Schwarz asked.

She slipped her arm through his. "You got a favorite?"

Schwarz adjusted the duffel roll, making sure he had instant access to it in spite of the girl's presence. "Mae."

"Ain't that a coincidence?" the girl asked. "Mae's my name." She tightened her grip on his arm in open flirtation.

"On your way," Blancanales said. "Like the man said, the guys we're after might break up their little meeting early if Spurlock's called them in."

Clicking affirmative again, Schwarz guided Mae into the motel.

The light was muzzy and dulled yellow, reflected from the stained alabaster walls. A Norman Rockwell calendar two years and three months out of date hung beside a pegboard with keys behind the desk. The young guy behind the counter was obviously suffering through a hangover, and informed them in soft tones that the bill had to be settled in cash and paid in advance.

Schwarz paid the money and received a key to a room on the third floor. He ignored the uncertain elevator and took the stairs up. Surprisingly Mae didn't complain and took the exercise easily.

On the second-floor landing, Schwarz said, "Why don't you go on up to the room and wait for me. I want to see a friend first."

Mae looked at him quizzically, but nodded without a word and started up the next flight of stairs.

Walking away from her, Schwarz stared through the gloom filling the hallway, reading the room numbers off in quick succession. Halfway down, he reached the one he wanted. Seeing no one in the corridor, he leaned forward and pressed his ear against the wood. Voices carried through the thin planks. He identified three, maybe four men. It tallied with the estimate Franklin had given them.

He took the mouthpiece for the headset out from under his collar and hit the transmit button. "They're here." Movement behind him attracted his attention, and he realized he'd been so focused on the room and the men inside that he'd missed the big man coming up behind him.

The guy was big and burly, dressed in overalls and a flannel shirt with the sleeves ripped away. He was bald and heavily bearded, and matted strands of hair poked errantly from his armpits.

As he ducked back, Schwarz realized he should have smelled the guy coming.

A big, beefy haymaker floated over the Able Team warrior's head, followed at once by an eruption of bellowed warning.

"I'm blown," Schwarz said into the mouthpiece.

"We're there," Franklin replied.

Unable to completely escape the next blow, Schwarz caught it on his chin and stumbled backward to land in a skidding heap on his butt. He struggled to free the Beretta, but felt it hang inside his jacket pocket.

The man pulled a .357 with an eight-inch barrel. The pistol looked like a toy in his mammoth fist. Before the guy could level the revolver, even as Schwarz was slipping the safety on the Beretta to fire through the Windbreaker, a metal sliver glinted between them as it sliced through the air.

A knife hilt suddenly sprouted from the big man's chest and seized his attention. He bellowed again in pain and surprise.

The door behind him opened, and a man stuck his head cautiously around the corner.

Schwarz freed the Beretta by ripping out his pocket and brought the pistol up in a two-handed grip.

The big man continued to bellow and charged Schwarz, leveling his .357 again.

Deliberately Schwarz punched two rounds through the man's left knee, not wanting to kill him. Everything had gone to hell in a handcart in a matter of seconds, but they still needed at least one man alive to question.

When the bullets crunched into his knee, the bellowing giant went down.

Schwarz pushed himself up against the wall as the thunder of the bullets' detonations rolled up and down the hallway. He kicked out, caught the big man's wrist and sent the .357 spinning away. Then bullets ate into the wall around him.

He turned his profile toward the gunner standing in the open door, presenting a smaller target. He squeezed off a half-dozen rounds as fast as he could, aiming at the center of the face. All of them missed, but they came close enough to send the guy ducking back inside.

During the lull, Schwarz slipped the Beretta into his belt and slid the Remington free of his duffel bag. As he flicked off the safety, he glanced over his shoulder and saw Mae standing on the stairway, another knife already in her slim hands. "Get back," he ordered.

She shook her head stubbornly, her short locks flying. "No way, mister. If you're taking those boys down for the cash they've got on them, then part of it is mine. I saved your life."

Unable to debate the situation, Schwarz looked back at the door as the gunner returned. He squeezed the trigger and sent a round of double-aught buck storming into the doorframe. Pine splinters created a brief fog that slammed into the opposite doorframe.

The window at the end of the hallway shattered inward, the jagged pieces and broken wood followed by Franklin and Blancanales. Schwarz gave them a rueful grin. It wasn't going according to the plan, but it was workable.

Moving into sync, Blancanales came up along the wall, his Uzi pointed upward, held in both hands. When he reached the door next to the one occupied by the gunners, he pivoted and slammed a heavy boot into the panel beside the doorknob. The lock gave way, and the door banged against the inside wall.

Schwarz racked the slide on the pump gun, chambering another round. The big man was still groaning, holding his knee with bloody hands. When the gunner stuck his head out the door this time, Schwarz hit it dead center. The double-aught load yanked the man from the threshold and spilled his corpse into the corridor.

Franklin and Blancanales disappeared inside the second room, moving on the adjoining door. Gunshots erupted immediately.

Easing forward, Schwarz kept the shotgun at the ready, took a second for himself to push replacement shells into the magazine tube and work the slide. He heard soft footsteps behind him, turned and found the young prostitute hefting the loose .357 Magnum with both hands. She eared the hammer back expertly.

"You just go on, mister," she said with quiet confidence. "I got your back covered."

Schwarz found his attention divided, which wasn't a good thing. Before he realized what was happening, one of the men in the target room made a break for it, legging out into the corridor with an Ingram MAC-10 roaring in his fist. The submachine gun jerked and jumped in wild abandon. The .45 rounds dug softball-sized holes in the plaster walls, showered the corridor with a white, powdery haze.

Aiming for the man's chest, Schwarz stroked the trigger and put the guy down.

The flat crack of the .357 sounded behind him, and for a moment he thought he'd been shot. He turned and saw the girl lining up her next shot at two armed men taking advantage of the cover provided by the stairwell. He brought up the Remington pump gun, fired a round through the narrow rails of the stairway, racked the slide and aimed again, unleashing the second load through the opening blown through the railing.

The double-aught buck caught the lead man in the shoulder and spun him into the wall. He hung for just a moment, then went tumbling back down the stairs. The other man got off two rounds that split the air above Schwarz's head, then Mae's proficiency with her borrowed weapon proved itself. A .357 slug took the man in the thigh only inches from his groin, jerked his leg back and knocked him back down the stairwell.

A cocky grin covered Mae's face. "Aim for the big pieces," she said with authority, "and with a big enough bullet, it don't really matter where you hit 'em."

"That's the way I see it, too," Schwarz said. "You get much practice at this?"

"Nope. I make do when I have to."

"Right." Schwarz hit the transmit button on the headset. "Pol?"

"Go."

"We got some action coming up from down below, too."

"Expect it," Franklin said. "This is one of Spurlock's local cash-collection centers. Any time there's a payday in this town, he keeps the buildings full of enforcers. Makes for less trouble."

"This room's clear," Blancanales said.

Schwarz peered around the corner cautiously.

Three bodies were scattered over the broken remnants of a table and a sway-backed metal-framed bed. A naked light bulb hanging from a frayed cord swung and spun from the center of the room. A battered metal suitcase containing a large amount of cash in small bills was upended on the floor.

Mae inhaled loudly as she followed Schwarz into the room. "Sweet Mother of God. Looks like our ship has done come in."

Schwarz looked at her, remembered the skill she'd shown with the throwing knife and her willingness to shoot first. He wondered what the hell he was going to do with her, and what a hundred dollars bought.

Ashe Franklin came through the splintered adjoining door with the Uzi in his fist. A handcuffed man with blood streaming from a cut on his forehead trailed in the homicide cop's wake, pulled by Franklin's other hand.

"Shit," Mae said with real feeling.

Schwarz spared her a curious glance, then checked the halls for any more action. Nothing moved except the big man holding his mangled knee. The Able Team warrior showed the guy the business end of the 12-gauge and said, "If you know what's good for you, you won't try to move from that spot." Schwarz stayed in the doorway so he could cover the man. When he glanced back into the room, Blancanales had joined Franklin.

Mae was busy scooping the loose bills into the suitcase, her eyes wary and focused on the detective.

The homicide cop looked at her and said, "Katya, what the hell are you doing here?"

The girl shrugged, finished up the money and closed the clasps on the suitcase. "Guess this means we won't be splitting this four ways."

"You two know each other?" Schwarz asked.

"Yeah. She works the docks. A nickle-and-dime thief. At least, that's what I thought she was before tonight."

"Still am, and proud of it," the girl said. "I wasn't about to get into bed with him. First chance I had, if I couldn't get at this guy's wallet, I was scooting through a window—and me with a fast hundred dollars in my hand." She smirked. "Then I saw him taking down Spurlock's guys. Figured maybe I could cut myself in for part of the pot."

"Toss the gun and get out of here. You've earned a free one. Move!"

She didn't ask any questions. The .357 hit the wooden floor with a solid thump, and by that time she was already in motion. She paused at the door to blow Franklin a kiss.

It was only after she'd gone that Schwarz realized he was still out his hundred dollars. He figured it was a wise thing not to bring up again because the Politician wouldn't let him live it down.

"Your name's Walsh," Franklin said to his prisoner. "I know you. You know me. You start lying, I'll know that, too. You believe me?"

The man nodded.

"These people are Feds. It was their partner that Spurlock's goons made off with tonight. They want him back, and they'll do whatever it takes to get him that way. So far, you're hurt but you're alive. It doesn't have to end up that way. Like I said, these guys are Feds, and that gives them a blank check around New Orleans. A lot of guys died here tonight. One more isn't going to make a hell of a lot of difference in the long run."

"Bald Gator Bayou," the man said. "They're supposed to be taking him there."

"Why?"

"Because Spurlock told them to. Ain't no other reason to do anything."

Franklin reached up, grabbed the man by the hair and softly thudded his head against the wall. The man's eyes blinked in rapt fear. "If you send me on a snipe hunt, Walsh, I'll look for you till I find you, then I'm gonna stomp a mud hole in your ass and walk it dry."

"They'll be there. I just don't know when."

Looking back at Blancanales and Schwarz, Franklin asked, "Anything else?"

Without a word, Blancanales stepped forward and put his face only inches from Walsh's. After a few tense heartbeats he said, "I know your face, amigo. If you lied to us and we lose our friend, you'll never see me coming and never know you've breathed your last breath."

"He'll be there. So help me God, that's what I was told."

Franklin produced a key to the handcuffs and freed the man. "If I was you, I'd think about the fastest way out of town tonight. Spurlock's not going to like it that you lost a few thousand bucks here, and he's going to like it even less that you gave him up to us."

Blancanales kept rear guard as Franklin led the way out of the building through the back door. The homicide man seemed more strained than ever, and Schwarz wondered if the guy was thinking about how much of tonight's activities would come back to bite him on the ass afterward. The detective didn't have faith yet in Barbara Price's abilities to smooth troubled waters.

Schwarz stuffed the Remington back into his duffel as they made their way to the van parked a few blocks away. A crowd had started to gather in front of the Seaview Motel.

"Tell us about Bald Gator Bayou," Blancanales said as the van got under way and merged with the traffic heading away from the wharf area, riding west along the lakefront.

"I've linked it to Spurlock before," Franklin said. "There've been a number of ritual murders in that area. Voodoo, maybe. I never could get anything on Spurlock concerning them. Nothing that would stand up in court. But I know he's involved."

"No shit," Schwarz said, and a coldness tingled along his spine as he thought about Lyons held powerless by Spurlock and his people.

"No shit. If your partner is anywhere near that area, he's in big trouble."

CHAPTER SEVENTEEN

"My superior has been suspicious of the Franco-German economic union for some time," Firenze Falkenhayn said. "Months ago he had me start investigating it, feeding me tidbits along the way that let me know I was only physically covering ground he'd mentally sifted through previously."

Standing in one corner of the room his group had been assigned by the American forces on the NATO air base in Berlin, Mack Bolan peeled an orange and divided it into wedges. His attention was focused on the woman's words, but part of his mind was occupied with the topographical maps and satellite pictures faxed over from Stony Man Farm. They were spread out, along with color and black-and-white photographs from the American Air Force files, across the low bookshelves filled with international legal tomes that lined two of the walls. He moved among them restlessly, looking for the keys to his planned assault.

"So the whole thing is a scam?" Jack Grimaldi asked. The pilot lounged at the long table that had been set up in the middle of the room. A mug of coffee steamed before him.

"No." Barbara Price's voice, carried by the satellite linkup with Stony Man Farm, was clear and decisive. "The original intent behind the economic union was a good one. Look at the talk that's being done at home between the United States, Canada and Mexico. It's not the situation. It's the corrupt people behind it who can turn it sour."

"Any ideas on who that might be?" Yakov Katzenelenbogen asked. The Israeli's grim visage was on another computer monitor. McCarter and Encizo could be seen in the background, arranging equipment Phoenix Force would need when they made Venice.

Bolan glanced at the monitor with Price's image. The mission controller seemed strained, but he guessed it was more from the lack of sleep than any sudden surprises that might have erupted from the mission.

"For the moment," Price said, "we're keying on Barnabe Siffre."

"Why him?" Cowboy John Kissinger asked on his way back from the coffeepot. He set a cup before Falkenhayn, received a polite thank-you and kept one for himself.

"Because certain businesses Siffre owns through parent corporations have been linked by Kurtzman and his team within the past few hours to Fauborg and Fawcett."

"The guys Phoenix and Able took down," Leo Turrin said.

"Yes."

"But you don't have enough on Siffre to proceed with the investigation on him?" Katz asked.

"At this point, no. Hopefully that will change. Siffre is also keeping a very low profile now."

"And people expect that," Turrin said, "because of the attempt made on his life."

"Yes."

"Even his partners," Bolan said. "It's more than just a headline grabber espousing pro-European dogma. And it allows him to do more than dodge the camera's eye after he's drawn all the attention. His own partners in the Franco-German push won't expect him to come out of hiding when his life is so obviously in danger. It gives him a freer hand to put the finishing touches on whatever it is that he has planned."

"Hal and I think so, too," Price replied. "We've got to think that our moves now are putting pressure on him—if it is Siffre we're ultimately hunting. Something will break, and when it does, we'll be there. After everything that's happened, there's no way this thing is going to go away quietly."

"What about the Intel Striker and his team liberated from the Konigsälle Laboratories?" Katz asked.

"It confirmed what we'd already feared. The bacterial agent manufactured there was designed only with killing plant life in mind. And the virus was genetically encoded to not only pass in fluids such as rainwater and rivers, but to be airborne, as well."

"What about oceans?" Bolan asked.

"According to the notes we were able to decipher, salt water is supposed to sterilize it. Even if a spore made it across the Atlantic or Pacific, it wouldn't be able to reproduce or infect."

"So it has natural barriers once it's been released," Bolan said.

"Yes. It also can't withstand an Arctic cold front. The virus would never make it through the northern Canadian reaches."

"Is there an antivirus?" Falkenhayn asked.

"The notes suggest that Simmy was working on one. However, the records we have weren't conclusive about whether one was created."

"Perhaps we should consider turning around," Katz suggested.

"No." Price was adamant. "I have a feeling about Crivello. The information you forwarded to the Farm suggests that Crivello keeps his bases covered. His whole career and lack of prosecutions suggest that. Accepting that he has been working with Siffre or whoever is pulling the strings on this operation, I'd be willing to bet that Crivello knows more about what is really going on than anyone would want him to know."

"You *are* betting that," Katz said gently.

"Then prove me right," Price replied, "or prove me wrong. Crivello—at least from the way I see him in his files—is an opportunist, and I don't think he would have let something like this pass him by untried."

"Personally," McCarter said from off camera, "I'll take the lady's intuition and give three-to-one odds on this little jaunt."

There were no takers.

"I'll take that as a vote of confidence," Price said. "Siffre will still be wherever he is when you and your people get back, Yakov. Except when you get back, perhaps we'll have more to work with.''

Katz nodded.

''How soon before Phoenix is ready to move?''

''Two hours, we'll be on the ground. I'd say another two to recon and get Crivello in a position where we can bring him in and debrief him.''

Price made notes off camera, then checked her watch. ''If you can cut the time somewhere, get it done. But keep your team intact no matter what. For the moment Able Team is one member short. The Ironman was taken down by his assignment before their mission got a chance to get going. The general consensus is that he's still alive, but it isn't known where they're keeping him. If something comes through in your own contact points with this mission about a federal agent being kept prisoner, get back to Aaron or me pronto.''

Katz cleared the channel with a somberness that echoed the feelings Bolan sensed in the room. Now he knew why Price seemed so stressed. He acknowledged the possible loss of Carl Lyons and put it away. As long as he was on a potential battlefield with a clear-cut objective in his sights, he was a soldier. Grieving could come later.

''Striker.''

Bolan looked at the video camera's lens. ''Yeah.''

''Is there anything your team needs that you can't get there?''

Bolan considered the only method of getting onto Rügen that he was willing to trust. ''A sailboat.''

Price didn't bat an eye. ''How soon do you need it, and where?''

''Off the northern coast of Germany, somewhere in the Mecklenburger Bucht. We can be there in an hour by chopper.''

''It'll be waiting for you. How soon before you're able to make the attempt to retrieve Simmy?''

Running the times and figures through his mind, which he'd arrived at after careful study, Bolan said, ''It'll roughly coincide with Phoenix's moves on their target.''

''Good.'' Price consulted her notes. ''Since their target is going to be on the move and perhaps harder to finesse, once you and your people lock into your final approach, hold off. If we're going to be that close in field operations, let's make it official and take these people down at the same time. It'll have more effect that way."

Bolan nodded. "Agreed."

"Anything else?"

The warrior smiled. "A good tail wind."

For a moment the stress lightened in Price's face. "That's not my department, big guy. Good hunting, people." She blanked the screen.

"All right," the Executioner said to his three comrades, "let's saddle up and move out."

Grimaldi, Turrin and Kissinger headed for the door, picking up their duffels from under the table and stopping long enough to get a final coffee refill.

Firenze Falkenhayn faced the Executioner with her level hazel gaze. "Can you outfit me for this operation?"

"You're out of it," Bolan said. "Your superior doesn't want to risk you any further than this."

"I didn't come this far only to go halfway."

Seeing the resolute fire in her eyes and knowing her the way he did, Bolan said, "No, I guess you didn't."

The Oval Office, Washington, D.C.
6:17 a.m.

"Do WE EVEN KNOW how much of this stuff there might be floating around, Hal?"

Brognola looked at the President and gave him the most truthful answer he had. "No."

"And we don't know who's behind this?"

"Not for certain." Brognola kept his cool on the outside as he unwrapped his cigar with fingers that were exceptionally steady. But inside, his guts were churning. It wasn't that the man sitting on the other side of the desk might blow up and decide to take him to task for everything that was happening. It was just knowing for himself how critical the situation could be without them having any knowledge of it.

Across the room, the TV-VCR combination continued whirring silently through stock footage of the events in France that had been assembled since the opening volley in the current crisis. Barnabe Siffre's memorable profile was significantly displayed.

"We're working this situation from a number of angles," Brognola said. He stuck the unlighted cigar in the corner of his mouth, wishing he could light it up, but refusing to give in. "Able's got the bases covered in New Orleans. Phoenix is about to break new ground in Venice. Striker's getting set to pull Gustav Simmy out of enemy hands. And the Stony Man cybernetic teams are tracing paths these people have cut across the globe. The organization can't stay buried and hidden much longer."

"But maybe long enough."

"I don't think so."

The President pushed himself back in his chair, steepled his fingers under his chin and met his gaze. "Why?"

"Because he hasn't contacted us."

"What makes you think he will?"

"Instinct."

The Man didn't look convinced.

"With something this big, this well planned out," Brognola said, "the guy's going to want to talk about it. To twist the knife if nothing else. He knows we're on to it. At least a part of it. That's why he came after us so hard. He knew you would be putting Farm personnel onto it."

"If he knows about you people, that's saying a lot."

"It is saying a lot. But a number of people know that you and your predecessors have turned to me and the Sensitive Operations Group in the past. Only makes sense that you would turn to me and SOG for this. I'd say right now our guy is holed up, trying to get a fix on how badly he's hurt. Maybe he's even running scared. Able and Phoenix have already chopped a couple of legs out from under him. He knows *we* know about him, too. If he gives us another few hours, Striker and Phoenix will cut down another couple of tiers of his organization."

The phone rang.

Betraying the tension that filled him, the Man picked it up before the first ring stopped sounding. "Yes." He looked up at Brognola. "It's Ms. Price." He told the secretary to put the call through, then activated the speaker phone.

"Hello, Barb," Brognola said.

"Aaron turned up something interesting when he correlated the package Striker got from Germany with the one Katz got from his contact in Paris," the mission controller said without preamble. "I'm putting it through on video now."

The President reached into his desk, took out a remote control and changed television channels to the one designated to receive incoming E-mail from Stony Man Farm.

Brognola looked at the screen as the image formed.

"This came from the Konigsalle Laboratories," Price went on. "Aaron broke the simple code Simmy was keeping his notes in. According to this, a series of shipments of the bacteria went out of the lab on these dates."

The image changed, scrolling down a list of entries that was almost a year old.

"Notice the discrepancy every three or four shipments. Usually a whole month or six weeks elapsed before more shipments were taken out of the complex."

"Maybe it took that long to create more of the virus," Brognola said. He looked at the number of canisters, tried to imagine how much damage would be unleashed if they were set off, and only made his headache worse.

"Most viruses reproduce themselves within twenty-four hours," Price said. "However, Hunt Wethers came up with the hypothesis that the bacterium reproduction was intentionally kept small so the operation could be moved quickly if they were discovered."

"So it took a while to generate a full shipment."

"That's what we think."

"Aside from those conjectures, Ms. Price," the President said, "do you know where those shipments went?"

"Not for certain." Price's voice held no note of embarrassment. "Apparently Simmy didn't know, either, and it bothered him."

"It bothered Simmy?" Brognola asked.

"Yeah. Judging from the personal notes, Simmy wasn't enamored of his work there and was probably being held against his will."

The image on the television screen changed again, became sheets of paper bearing Mossad espionage agency markings.

"These are copies of bills of lading," Price said. "All of these ships are owned through a half-dozen small corporations owned in turn by Pasquale Crivello."

"Crivello's the man Phoenix is assigned to in Venice?" the President asked.

"Yes."

Yellow lines highlighted specific dates. All of the listings were scheduled stops at the East Frisian islands in the North Sea.

"The dates," Price said, "coincide closely with the dates the bacteria left the Konigsalle complex."

"So Crivello's shipping lines transported the bacteria," the President said.

"We think so."

"What about a destination, Barb?" Brognola asked.

"At this point, it's unknown. We're hoping when Phoenix manages their talk with Crivello, he might shed some light on things."

Brognola stared hard at the last entry in the Crivello papers. It was dated two months ago. "If your groundwork is right, the next shipment is two weeks overdue."

"There might not have been a next shipment," Price replied. "The bacteria produced in the last two months is probably what was supposed to be discovered in those canisters in LeCourbe vineyards."

"And the Konigsalle lab?"

"Not the trail of bread crumbs we thought it was after all," Price said. "It's just part of the packaging, to let us know these people do have what we were only thinking they might."

A cold knot formed in Brognola's stomach as he considered the ramifications. There was no point hashing them out with Price. Undoubtedly she'd already covered them, and probably some he hadn't even thought of yet. She was good at her job. "Okay. Stay in touch as things develop."

Price said she would, then cleared the phone.

The President's gaze was fixed on the damning facts and figures frozen on the television. He sighed. "You were speaking of hours, Hal. From the way this situation is shaping up, we might not even have minutes."

Brognola gave the Man a tight nod. "I know. But I know, too, that the men we've got out there are the best chance we've got. If anyone can pull this thing off, they can." And he hoped it was true.

CHAPTER EIGHTEEN

Carl Lyons heard a cock crow somewhere in the distance. It was a defiant sound, one full of vinegar and promise, and the noise echoed inside the tree-lined confines of the bayou. When he looked up at the slice of sky visible through the skeletal limbs of the swamp trees, he figured the rooster to be one overly expectant son of a bitch. The sun wasn't up yet, and only a bruised purple shone from the east, not even enough yet to blot out the stars.

He let his head drop back down to his chest, relaxing cramped and strained muscles. He was sore all over from the beatings he'd been given earlier as Spurlock's men tried to get answers from him. Even though he'd been half out of his mind with pain, he hadn't given them anything.

Lifting his head again, Lyons watched the activity around the campsite. His bare back chafed and stung whenever he moved, rubbed raw by the bark of the tree he'd been tied to. The baling wire wrapped around his wrists dug into his flesh enough at times to bring blood. The rust on the wire made it rougher, and brought with it thoughts of tetanus.

He grinned in spite of his situation. At the moment, tetanus was the least of his worries.

A two-room frame home was butted up against the tree line to Lyons's left. A warped porch was attached, covered by screens that had been patched with other pieces of screen and more baling wire. Electric lanterns were hung inside the house and on the porch area. Another hung outside the door from a long nail.

At least fifteen men were at the house. Spurlock was among them, inside the dwelling so the mosquitoes from the brackish water wouldn't bother him. A shaky dock extended out over the bayou, and three small powerboats were moored to it, occasionally bumping up against the pilings with hollow thunks. Two vehicles were parked in front of the house, both of them four-wheel-drive rigs with oversize tires covered with globs of black mud. Another arrived, winding through the narrow trail that snaked back for miles before reaching a blacktop single-lane road that was even more miles from any kind of civilization.

A thin old black woman got out on the passenger side of an ancient Ford pickup as it rattled and died near the other two vehicles. She was dressed in a shapeless white cotton dress that fell down to her knees, and she carried a large white chicken under one of her arms. Without a word she walked toward Lyons.

Lyons watched her, seeing the grim purpose that glinted in her eyes.

When the woman was three feet from Lyons, she took a carving knife from her pocket. She spit on its keen edge, then wiped it clean on her dress.

Spurlock walked up behind her, an evil grin twisting his face. His men drifted in his wake, pulled like moths to a dark, cold flame. "This here's Lulu," he announced. "She's a priestess to a lot of folk around these parts. Supposed to be a handmaiden to old Damballah himself. Of course, you being a heathen and all, that probably don't mean duck shit to you."

The woman smiled, exposing a mouthful of rotting teeth.

"She here to tell my fortune?" Lyons asked, trying not to look at the knife in the old woman's hand.

A sadistic chuckle circulated within the crowd.

"You like being a smart-ass, don't you, boy?" Spurlock asked. "You Yankee Feds are all alike. You think a little schooling makes you better than anyone living down here. But just you remember who's tied to that tree right now, and who's standing here watching."

Lyons didn't say anything. Whatever was going to happen, he couldn't do anything about it. Grimly he pulled himself inside his own head and started to will away whatever pain might come.

"She isn't here to tell your fortune," Spurlock said. "That'd be an awful short study, seeing as how you don't exactly have a future right now. Lulu's here to sacrifice you, going to give you up to a loa that's friendly to her." He turned to the woman. "You go on ahead and do what you have to do, Lulu. Me and the boys will just watch."

For a moment Lyons thought the woman's presence might be an elaborate ploy to get him to talk. Spurlock was intelligent enough to use the swamp setting and leftover childhood fears of the dark and the unknown to his advantage.

The woman stepped forward, bared the chicken's neck and gnawed through the flesh as the bird kicked, squalled and tried to get away. As it jerked through its death throes with blood pumping out the lacerations on its neck, the woman grabbed it by the feet and shook it over Lyons's head.

When he felt the hot blood spill over his chest, Carl Lyons knew it was for real. He tensed in spite of himself, waiting for the knife.

"POL." SCHWARZ'S VOICE sounded tense over the headset frequency.

"I got it," Blancanales said. He sat in the fork of the tree, wrapped his wrist in the sling of the M-14 and put the Star-Tron scope over the old woman's face as she advanced on Lyons, the dead chicken hanging from her other hand. He hesitated, unwilling to shoot the woman, and moved the cross hairs to the bright shimmer of the knife blade.

The aiming light attached to the assault rifle threw out an invisible infrared beam that put a red dot on its intended target through the lenses of Blancanales's night-vision goggles. When he had it settled onto the blade of the carving knife less than an inch from where it joined the wooden haft, he squeezed the trigger.

The rifle recoil interfered with his field of vision for a moment, and the explosion of gunfire bounced around inside the seemingly impenetrable barrier of trees and water surrounding the bayou. A harsh, shrill wail of terror split the night on the heels of the rifle shot.

Focused back on the target zone, Blancanales saw the old woman go stumbling back, waving her numbed hand. He put the sights over the nearest man in the crowd, saw the infrared disk light up an eye, then caressed the trigger and put out the light.

A heartbeat later a 40 mm round from Schwarz's grenade launcher landed in the middle of the three parked 4X4s and overturned the Ford pickup. A gaseous explosion spread out from the overturned vehicle in a foggy cloud of rolling blue flames that swallowed the other two trucks.

A handful of men raced for the vehicles, bellowing in fear and cursing.

Blancanales squeezed the trigger again and put another man down with a round through the heart. He ignored the men running for the parked trucks, staying with the small group that posed a threat to Lyons. Most of them had backed off and were running for cover.

Schwarz fired his M-203 again, and a second 40 mm grenade took one of the surviving trucks dead center. The resulting explosion was filled with flying shrapnel, consisting of glass from the windshield and metal fragments. Four men went down immediately, lost in the sudden maelstrom.

Return fire started to streak through the branches near Blancanales's position, and he knew the gunners were tracking his muzzle-flashes. He lined up his last objective, knowing he would have to abandon the sniping roost.

He aimed at the baling wire twisted into a half-inch braid that bound Lyons to the sycamore tree, increased the magnification and laid the aiming light at a spot less than six inches from the Ironman's right hand. He breathed out, holding the rifle steady.

Blancanales fired, the M-14 bucking solidly against his shoulder. He was sure he'd hit the wire. Before he had a chance to check, bullets whined over his head and split the bark from nearby branches.

Knowing he had no choice now, the Able Team warrior dropped from the tree to the spongy earth twelve feet below. Then he jogged off left, moving on to the next spot he'd already chosen to cover Lyons's escape. If the shot had been successful.

THE WIRE JERKED TIGHT around Lyons's right wrist and hurt like hell. He stifled a groan as he scanned the developing battle zone. There was no question in his mind who was on the attack.

He flexed the wrist, trying to work out the creeping numbness, and discovered the slack in the wire. Gritting his teeth against the effort, he pulled and felt the wire part. Once he knew he was free, he threw himself toward the bayou, intending to take advantage of the quick camouflage provided by the dark water.

Bullets dug gouges in the tree bark where he'd just been. A muffled explosion hammered back from the parked 4X4s, showering clods of loam over the bayou.

Lyons broke into a full run, ignoring the painful twinges in his leg joints and back, the legacy of his being tied up so long. A man came up off the ground, holding a pistol in front of him.

Without missing his stride, Lyons ducked, felt the heat of the bullet as it whipped by his cheek, then hurled himself at the gunman. His shoulder caught the guy in the chest, crushed the lungs empty of air. His forward momentum carried them both into the swamp water.

Greasy mud, snarled with tree roots and waterborne vegetation, gave way under Lyons's bare feet. He blindly seized the guy's gun arm in one hand and his neck in the other. The man struggled in his grasp, flailing and thrashing about.

Grimly Lyons hung on, keeping them both underwater. The fight on both parts used up the oxygen more quickly in their lungs. Feeling as if his chest were about to burst, the Able Team warrior felt life leave his opponent.

He plucked the gun from the dead man's hand and broke the surface, gulping great drafts of fresh air.

At Lyons's quick estimate, there were perhaps seven guns left operational under Spurlock's command. He lifted the pistol in his hand and discovered it was a 9 mm Taurus PT-99 with thirteen rounds left in it, counting the one chambered. He pushed himself up onto the bank, keeping low.

A man broke from the small group trapped behind a pile of logs. He lowered his head between his shoulders, raised his M-16 in defense and ran for the water, coming straight at Lyons.

Five feet from the man, moving at a run himself, Lyons raised the 9 mm automatic and put five rounds through the guy's chest as the man cut loose with the M-16. The 5.56 mm tumblers shredded the thick carpet of dead leaves and moss, but didn't touch their intended target.

The men hiding behind the logs turned and tried to bring him into their sights.

Lyons took a Weaver stance and ran through the rest of the magazine in the Taurus, knowing he put two more of the men down before return fire drove him to ground. He dropped the automatic and rolled, aware of the bullets digging holes around him. Taking shelter behind the body of the man he'd dropped, he ran his hands along the corpse. The assault rifle was empty, and extra clips—if any—weren't easily found in the clothing. He settled for the S&W Model 25 .45 revolver. The wheelgun sported a 6-inch barrel and felt hard and reassuring in Lyons's hand.

A figure broke from the brush and skirted the bayou, working the shallow end.

Lyons tracked it instantly, recognized Schwarz a heartbeat after he'd thumbed back the hammer on the .45. A cocky grin split Gadgets's face.

"I count four hardmen behind those logs," Lyons said.

"I got something here that might take the fight right out of them," Schwarz promised. He opened the breech of the M-203 slung under his M-16 and thumbed in a 40 mm cartridge. He raised the weapon to his shoulder, whirled from cover and fired the grenade launcher.

The missile struck the top tree, impacted with enough detonation to send the logs spinning. Startled yelps mixed quickly with cries of pain.

Rolling the dead man over, Lyons reached for the guy's thick rubber galoshes. Judging from the man's build, there was no way they would fit, but Lyons figured the oversize boots might provide him some protection. They pulled free with wet sucking noises.

Schwarz worked on clearing the logjam with controlled 3-round bursts. Return fire was minimal.

"You got another round for that launcher?" Lyons asked.

"Oh, yeah."

"Put one through the window of that house. I thought I saw Spurlock waddling his fat ass in there."

"Smoker?"

"Hell, no." Lyons pushed himself into a crouch and fisted the .45 from the ground. "Put a kicker in there. Bring the house down."

"You got it." The M-16's chatter died away as Schwarz took aim with the M-203. A moment later the frame house came apart.

Merle Spurlock emerged from the ruins with his hair and beard on fire. The merc broker threw himself to the ground and rolled furiously until the flames were out. Then he got uncertainly to his feet and disappeared into the swamp brush.

"There goes Spurlock."

"I'm on him," Lyons said. "You and Pol finish things up here."

"That homicide cop, Ashe Franklin, is here, too. Just so you know. He's working with us and helped us find you."

Lyons nodded, then set off after Spurlock. He ran with his free hand in front of his face and upper chest, blocking out the branches that clawed for his eyes. He carried the .45 low and behind him so it wouldn't get caught in any of the foliage.

He listened for Spurlock, heard the big man smashing through the brush twenty feet to his right. He altered course, homing in on the noise, and forced himself to go faster. "No way, fat man," he muttered. "No way are you going to outrun me even if you do know the territory."

Spurlock continued to crash through the tree and brush barriers in his desperate bid to outdistance his pursuer.

Ten seconds more, and Lyons was close enough to hear the man gasping for his breath. He slowed, kept pace, not hurrying now because he knew he had Spurlock on the ropes.

The crashing stopped when Spurlock reached a clearing that edged another water-covered section of the bayou, leaving him nowhere to run. He turned and raised the MAC-10 in his fist, aiming in Lyons's direction.

Wanting to take the man alive if possible, the big ex-cop fired two shots that knocked small limbs off the tree above Spurlock's head.

The merc broker roared curses and fired toward the muzzle-flashes.

But Lyons had already moved, circling to the right within the protective embrace of the swamp forest. He fired again, gouging a broken stump beside Spurlock.

Whirling to face the new position, Spurlock squeezed the MAC-10's trigger again, emptying the clip this time.

Lyons raced toward the man and leapt into the air in a flying front kick as Spurlock tried to slip a fresh magazine into the Ingram. His foot collided with the man's head, hurling Spurlock backward into the water. The MAC-10 pinwheeled away.

The Able Team leader abandoned his handgun and launched himself after Spurlock once he regained his balance. He splashed through the black water, catching the merc broker as he came spluttering to the surface.

Spurlock spotted his adversary and swung an overhand blow. Lyons blocked it with his left arm, then followed through with two short hooks to the rib section with his right, forcing his opponent back.

But Spurlock hadn't risen to his position of power by being easy to take. Even with the years of easy living under his belt, the man was as hard as nails. He bellowed his rage and swung again, flailing with both arms.

Evading the blows, Lyons fired off a series of jabs that set up a left cross that sent Spurlock into the water. Snarling his fingers in the man's hair, Lyons pulled him from the swamp. Scarlet threads of blood dripped from the man's mouth with the muddy water.

Something alive and moving hit the bayou.

Staring through the darkness, Lyons found the source of the movement. An alligator coasted through the water like predatory flotsam, only its eyes and nose visible above the surface. It was fifteen feet away and closing.

"Gator," Spurlock mumbled. "It's a goddamn gator."

Lyons controlled the man's frenzied attempts at escape with a choke hold from behind. He forced the man around, faced him toward the slowly approaching reptile. "Do alligators really eat people?" he asked in a harsh voice.

The alligator held back, as if reconsidering its decision to attack. The cold eyes never blinked, giving the impression they could see in the dark.

"Hell, yes, they eat people," Spurlock yelled.

Lyons applied more pressure, bent Spurlock over until the man's cheek and chin were in the water on a level with the alligator. He held the man there, and the gator paddled in closer. "Who do you think is faster?" Lyons asked. "Me, or that floating mouth?"

"Get me out of the water, you crazy son of a bitch! You can't do this!"

"You don't sound very confident," Lyons said. "Keep those negative thoughts coming, and you might break my concentration. I don't think either one of us wants to lose his head right now."

Spurlock slapped the water with his free hand, causing the alligator to freeze again.

"You give me a name," Lyons growled. "Somebody bigger than you. Somebody you report to. And I'll see to it that you walk out of this swamp in one piece."

Warily the alligator came on, cutting through the water as if it were greased.

"Come on, Merle. We don't have all night, and we don't have anything in the way of appetizers."

Spurlock slapped at the water again, but the alligator ignored him. Obscenely the giant jaws cracked open and revealed its cavernous mouth.

"I don't have a gun," Lyons reminded the merc broker. "I tossed it away before I came in after you."

"You're going to get us both killed!"

"Nah. I think after he eats you he'll be filled for a while." For a moment Lyons thought Spurlock was simply too scared to speak.

Then he said, "Huneke. Kirby Huneke."

Shifting his weight in the mud, Lyons pulled back and waded back to shore, wondering if he was going to make it before the alligator caught him. An explosion of sound from the bank caused the alligator to let its jaws snap closed on empty air, and it used its webbed feet to paddle away.

Lyons looked up and saw Ashe Franklin standing nearby with a cut-down shotgun resting easily in the crook of his arm. He gave the Able warrior a tight smile.

"Got to give you high marks for inventive interrogation methods," the Cajun cop said. "Can't say that I've seen that one before."

Lyons pushed Spurlock ahead of him, reached down and picked up the .45. All the fight had gone out of the merc broker. "One of these days I'm going to do a book on interrogation techniques for the adventurous lawman."

"I'll look forward to it," Franklin said dryly.

CHAPTER NINETEEN

Versailles, France
1:24 p.m.

"Come in." Barnabe Siffre turned to face the door of his private study. He hated being bothered here, where there was so much of his future for him to think about.

Paxson von Kleist didn't appear in the least bit apologetic. The ex-German military commander turned corporate executive walked into the large room with the very correct posture Siffre had come to expect in the man. He doffed his gloves and offered his hand without hesitation.

Siffre took it, feeling the man's strength despite his sixty-plus years. "Welcome to my home, Colonel," he said in flawless German. Although Kleist had been out of active service for over ten years, everyone who knew the man was aware of how much he liked to be called by his military rank. If they didn't, Kleist quickly let them know.

"You have a beautiful estate," Kleist said. He rested both hands on the polished silver head of his cane and gazed about the study with a discerning eye.

"Thank you." Siffre felt slightly uncomfortable with the man. Only a handful had been allowed into his private sanctum over the years. It was where he kept his most precious of dreams, and he didn't trust them to anyone he didn't have complete control over.

The room was furnished in late seventeenth century furniture. A handful of paintings adorned the walls in gilt frames. Three of them were more than two hundred years old, showing the palace of Versailles as it had been during its heyday under Louis XIV.

The centerpiece of the room was the scale model of the palace that covered more than ten square feet. The buildings were reconstructed in great detail, showing off the gardening and craftsmanship that had astounded the world during its day.

Kleist eyed the model speculatively, one hand touching his chin in interest. "Château de Versailles," he mused, "the palace of the Sun Emperor. Louis XIV was truly king of all he surveyed during his reign." He glanced at Siffre. "I never knew you had a passion for the man."

"Not the man." Siffre poured drinks at the recessed wet bar that opened up from the wall, a Perrier with a twist of lemon for himself, a peppermint schnapps for his guest. He handed the drink to Kleist. "His ability to get things done. What you see before you was the greatest achievement of its time."

"Perhaps, if all you're looking at is material assets."

The remark stung, but Siffre refused to let it show. He waved a hand at the model. "What you're looking at is a touchstone of history. Do you know how many great things were accomplished within its walls?" He gestured toward the model. "The treaty that ended the American War of Independence was signed there in 1783. Bismarck united the German states, took Wilhelm, king of Prussia, and molded him into the emperor of Germany. That was in the Hall of Mirrors in 1871. The treaty ending World War I was signed there."

"And Mirabeau came calling to the gates during the reign of Louis XVI, saying, 'We are here by the will of the people and only the power of spears can remove us!' A few months later, the day of the guillotine ran rampant throughout France. I know my history."

Siffre turned away from the man and looked out over the miniature palace. "The main palace is almost two thousand feet long," he said in a soft voice. He looked up at Kleist. "Did you know that?"

"I've seen it." He seemed reluctant to say more, as if sensing that he'd committed a faux pas.

"Architect after architect labored to fulfill Louis XIV's dream. Gabriel. Le Vau. Mansart. Le Brun. Coustou. They all had a hand in its creation. The palace holds an opera hall, a congress hall, paintings and statues of kings and queens. The upper south wing holds the Gallery of Battles. Delacroix's *Battle of Tailleborg*. Gerard's *Battle of Austerlitz*.''

Kleist remained silent, watching carefully.

Siffre didn't care. Things were coming to a head anyway. The false face he had worn for so long was about to come off. He could be himself and glory in his excesses for a change. His dreams were on the verge of becoming a reality.

"While at its peak, the palace housed thousands. They were served by ten thousand cooks, assistant cooks, gardeners, engineers, maids and stable men. There were fourteen hundred fountains designed by Le Nôtre, fed by an underground system of canals. Every year gardeners planted one hundred fifty thousand flowers. It was a grandness that has never seen its like since.''

"It was also folly," Kleist said. "Louis XIV's indulgences split the chasm between the indolent rich and the starving poor even wider, resulting in the death of his grandson and a tyranny that shadowed France for years.''

Siffre smiled easily. "Ah, but my dear colonel, if it wasn't for follies in this life, what would life be? A grind, that's what." He sipped his drink. "You and I are both financially independent. We don't need anything the world has to offer. We take what we want. The only things that interest us are the games we can make up for ourselves, and the only rules that we recognize are the ones we choose to challenge ourselves with.''

"What are you talking about?''

"I'm talking about the future," Siffre said. "Isn't that what you and the other representatives of the Franco-German community came here to talk about?''

"We came here to discuss our next moves regarding American interests in European affairs." Kleist hesitated. "Are you sure you're feeling well?''

"I'm feeling fine. But what if I was to tell you that soon the whole of the American and Russian military machines were going to be for naught?''

Kleist's eyes narrowed in suspicion. "The bacteria doesn't belong to them, does it?''

Siffre held up his glass in a silent toast. "I always said you were a clever man, Colonel."

"You're mad."

"No, I'm a master strategist. If I go to the table to risk money or wealth, I'm damn well going to know what every other player is holding in his or her hand. Right now I'm in the game for the highest stakes imaginable." Siffre looked at the miniature palace. "All my life I've wanted to live there, to be what Louis XIV was to his century. Now I can be, and I can live there, too." He took the small remote control from his pocket, pointed it at the side wall fronting the rest of the house and pressed a button.

The wall opened, revealing a large-screen television that flickered with instant life. From the opening few frames, it was obvious that it was aerial film shot of the Château de Versailles. The palace reflected the state of disrepair in some areas.

"This is what it looks like now," Siffre said in reverence. "But this is what it will look like." He pressed another button. The screen changed, becoming a computerized picture showing a rebuilding process that took only seconds. When it was finished, a fortress stood in the palace's place, equipped with state-of-the-art defenses and offensive capabilities. "Louis XIV only thought the known world revolved around him. I'm going to make it so that it does revolve around me."

"You *are* insane."

"No," Siffre declared quietly, "I'm only hours away from making my vision into the future. I'm offering you a chance to become part of that future."

"Why?"

"Because every court needs its hangers-on. At times you amuse me."

Kleist drew himself fully erect. "We believed in you. Not only your fellow countrymen, but we Germans, as well. We thought you could help us bring about an economic equality with the rest of the world."

"You've already got an economic equality, and it's getting more equal every day. The Americans and Russians recognize that. Germany has got potential it hasn't even tapped yet. Japan had a lot going for it, but no natural resources. Germany—with a little salesmanship—can become the figurehead for the emerging Eastern European market. Don't sell yourselves short.''

Kleist shook his head sadly. "My God, Barnabe, and you held such promise." He put his drink on the edge of the display and started for the door.

"Colonel."

Kleist halted, then looked over his shoulder.

"The Americans are on to me. Just as your own espionage units were. Wessel knew. That's why he was killed."

A nerve jumped high on the German's jaw.

"You were a military commander. You tell me. What kind of move should I do next to throw my enemies off the track and put more pressure on the units they have fielded onto what can become unfriendly soil?"

Realization slipped over Kleist's face. He swung the cane up, pointed it at Siffre and started to turn the silver head.

A rapid double-tap of a large-caliber handgun rolled thunder inside the room. Two invisible fists punched Kleist in the chest and stomach, ripped bloody holes and smashed him against the open door.

Siffre sipped his drink and glanced over his shoulder.

Trudaine stepped from a hidden door and pulled earplugs from his ears, rolling them gently in his palms as he smiled. Beside him was a steely-eyed man in black cammies with a pistol in his hand.

"You were cutting it damn close," Siffre accused.

"You have a flair for the theatrical," Trudaine insisted. "I thought you would feel better if you had your moment in the sun." He knelt, pressed the back of his hand against the German's throat, then nodded to the waiting gunman.

Without a word the assassin left the room.

Trudaine hefted the cane and inspected it. "Nasty little thing."

"What was it? A sword or knife?"

"Hardly." Trudaine pointed the bottom of the cane at the door and finished twisting the head. The detonation was tremendous, and wooden splinters peeled back from the door. "Single round, 12-gauge. Double-aught buckshot from the appearance." He looked at Siffre. "You'd have been a dead man."

Siffre didn't know how many times he'd wished he hadn't had to depend on Trudaine, but he added another to the count. The man was just too unpredictable, too wild, too much into his own unknown agenda. Perhaps once the initial response from the United States and Russia was over, Trudaine's skills with the computers wouldn't be so necessary. Siffre fervently hoped it was so. He put his drink down so the other man wouldn't see it shaking in his hand, and moved to the windows overlooking the courtyard one floor below. The acrid smoke of the gunshots burned in his nostrils.

Below, the major players of the Franco-German effort to rebuild a flagging European economy were gathered for a day in the sun. They lounged by the pools, soaked up drinks under patio umbrellas and flirted with the "comfort" girls Siffre had hired. All around them were security people supposedly posted for their protection.

"Well?" Trudaine prompted. He held out a walkie-talkie, his smile warm and gentle.

Taking the communications device, Siffre keyed the frequency and said, "Kill them." He tossed the walkie-talkie back to the cybernetics man, who stood gazing raptly at the landscaped lawn.

The security people moved, drawing their weapons. Staccato bursts ripped into the gathered French and German financiers. Bodies dropped into the pool, staining the turquoise water with blood. The women weren't spared, either. A few tried to fight back or escape, but they weren't successful.

Siffre stood behind his bulletproof glass and watched. Part of him was sickened by all the death, but it was necessary for his plans. The Americans were getting too damn close.

Beside him Trudaine stood with his hands over his chest, a satisfied smile on his lips.

"You like this, don't you?" Siffre asked.

Trudaine shrugged but didn't stop smiling. "It's just different, that's all. I play in a world every day that most people don't even think exists, work with things that don't necessarily ever become tangible. But this—'' he nodded at the killing as the firing rate slowed ''—this is physical.''

''Maybe you'd like to go down and take a hand.''

Trudaine looked back at Siffre in wry amusement. ''Don't mistake my interest for anything more than what it is. Those people down there, they kill for you when you give the word.'' He nodded at the digitized representation of the reconstructed Château de Versailles. ''I build empires. Big difference.'' Nonchalantly he turned and walked away, stepped over the dead man in the doorway without giving the corpse a second glance. By the time he reached the hallway, his hands were in his pockets and he was whistling off-key.

Retreating to the wet bar, Siffre fixed himself something stronger to drink. It wasn't the killing that bothered him as much as Trudaine's coldness. Much as he wanted to get rid of the man, he knew Trudaine would probably know when he'd outlived his own usefulness and would be gone before Siffre could ever do anything to him. Siffre wasn't sure if he wanted to create a new world that held Trudaine in it. It was something to think about.

CHAPTER TWENTY

The Baltic Sea, North of Rügen, Germany
2:09 p.m.

Mack Bolan stood in the bow of the thirty-foot ketch under the yellow-and-blue-striped spinnaker bellied out in full bloom from a westerly breeze. Dressed in khaki sailing shorts, a white knit shirt with an abbreviated collar and deck shoes, he held a pair of Bausch & Lomb field glasses to his eyes and scanned the island's northern shore from a quarter mile out.

So far, he'd spotted two armed motor launches that were trying to pass unnoticed.

Other pleasure craft dotted the area, colorful sails spread out to catch the wind. But none ventured too close to the house on the hill.

Using the mast and jib as cover, the Executioner scanned the summerhouse again, fixing the details in his mind. With the way the sea fronted the tan hills of the island, any move they made on the house would have to be a quick one. Armed response would no doubt be immediate.

Driftwood and gray, white and brown stones worn smooth by the ocean's tides made a carpet over the small beach. Near Bolan's chosen point of debarkation was a twenty-foot-long tree trunk. The roots stuck out as much as five feet, resembling twisted, arthritic fingers. Near the top of the tree, gray ash spilled out over the sparse sand, giving silent witness that someone had once used it for a camp fire.

"There will not be much time once our intentions are known," Firenze Falkenhayn said.

"No," Bolan agreed.

The woman stood beside him, a hand on the bow railing as the ketch rolled with the motion of the water and wind.

She seemed completely at home on deck. Her skin was a soft golden brown from exposure to the sun. The neon tangerine bikini she wore was striking, and drew more attention than the three men on board, providing an enjoyable camouflage.

Kissinger was in the stern of the ketch making sure the jet bikes were tethered and ready to go. The equipment bags holding the munitions for the assault had already been specially packaged and were secured to the underside of the jet bikes. Within minutes they could be armed and moving. Turrin held the wheel.

Jack Grimaldi hovered some miles in the distance, piloting a CH-53E Super Sea Stallion. Once the exfiltration signal went out, Grimaldi could be in place with the big chopper within minutes.

The marine phone rang.

Bolan handed the field glasses to Falkenhayn and padded along the deck, ducked inside the cabin and lifted the phone from its cradle.

"We are go," Barbara Price said calmly. "Phoenix has its quarry in sight."

"Affirmative," Bolan replied. "Striker team likewise. We are go."

"Good luck," Price said. "You stay hard out there."

"No other way to be." He hung up the phone. "John."

"Yo."

"We're going in." Bolan went astern and unlashed the boom, bringing around the mainsail to redirect the ketch's run. The spinnaker lost none of its speed as it took on the new course. The bow crested the waves just a moment, then settled in. Satisfied with the cut of the sail, the warrior reached inside the cabin, moved the false panel he and Kissinger had put in and retrieved the handguns they'd stashed there. Then he stepped into the tiny berth and lifted the mattress from the built-in frame.

An electronic detonating device, loosely mocked-up to resemble a spare generator, lay beneath. Enough plastic explosive to turn the ketch into kindling was tucked under the mattress supports. Bolan flicked on the arming sequence, then took up the remote control and slid the leather strap over his head. It bounced against his chest lightly as he went up on deck.

Falkenhayn was standing beside Kissinger and Turrin, her eyes shaded with one hand. "They've seen us."

Binoculars were no longer necessary. The two armed speedboats were closing rapidly. At least a half-dozen men were on each vessel.

Turrin kept a steady hand on the wheel, letting the ketch follow the blustering winds propelling it on the run. The trio of jet bikes bobbed in the stern, occasionally leaping from the whitecapped blue waters and smashing back down.

Bolan glanced at the shoreline, estimating the distance at four hundred yards. The ketch had enough of a lead and the speed to get within striking distance of the beach before the two powerboats caught up with it.

A man carrying a loud-hailer came up on the bow of the closer boat, clinging desperately to the railing. "Turn that boat around!" he screamed in German. "You're approaching private property!"

The ketch cut through another fifty yards of ocean as the powerboats closed the distance, leaving whitecapped wakes behind them.

Bolan passed out the handguns. They were in military-styled holsters with the flap buttoned down. Spare magazines were in pouches placed before and after the holster.

Falkenhayn buckled her weapon around her slim hips, then buckled Turrin's for him just as a piece of wooden combing the size of a playing card went whirling away from the top of the cabin. A heartbeat later the sound of a rifle shot pealed over the ketch.

"Guess we're going to skip the 'This is your final warning' part," Kissinger said dryly.

Two more rounds slammed into the stern of the boat, only a few inches above the waterline.

Once his pistol was securely buckled around his waist, Bolan drew his survival knife from its sheath on his right calf. He looked up at the approaching boats, which were within a hundred yards. The beach was less than two hundred yards away. There was no way to better their proximity to the island without chancing his plans. "Okay, Leo, turn her broadside."

Falkenhayn moved toward the stern of the ketch and took one of the sets of bubble visors Bolan handed her. She slipped a rubber band from her wrist and quickly bound her hair in a ponytail.

A half-dozen rifle bullets crashed into the ketch.

Moving quickly, Bolan slashed the support lines that held the spinnaker. The big sailcloth came boiling down in a loose spill of material, some of it catching on the bow while some of it flowed into the water. The ketch slowed.

Turrin cut the wheel, turning hard to port to present a broadside to the approaching powerboats. The ketch reared up out of the sea like a marlin hitting the end of a fishing line. Instead of hardening up onto a reach as an experienced sailor would have done in the same situation, he helped Bolan swing the boom around in full port tack rather than trimming the mainsail.

The knife in Bolan's hand flashed again, scything through the ropes holding the jet bikes to the ketch. They bobbed free, cresting the white roil of the ocean as the vessel continued to spill away.

"Jump!" Bolan yelled. Off balance, he managed a shallow dive that cleared the ketch. He hit the water smoothly, aware of the crack of bullets splashing into the ocean around the sailboat. The undertow created by the ketch taking on water touched him only for a moment, then he was free. Stroking strongly and kicking out hard with his bare feet, he swam for the surface, peering through the visor until he saw the first of the jet bikes. Adjusting his direction, he reached the craft and pulled himself up.

Falkenhayn was a beat behind him, grabbing another jet bike and tipping it over so she could heave herself aboard.

The ketch was partially submerged, the colorful sails spread out lifelessly across the water. The hull, turned on its side as it was, blocked the view of the powerboats, but the Executioner heard their engines throttle down. He touched the remote control around his neck, making sure it was still there.

Kissinger broke the surface. He swiped his wet hair from his visor, then kicked out for the remaining jet bike. Turrin made it a moment later.

Bolan keyed the ignition, heard the craft's powerful engine whir to life. The other jet bikes switched on behind him. He leaned into the turn as he powered up, the jet bike rising up out of the water to skim across the surface and reduce the drag of the ocean, as salt spray spumed up over him.

Releasing the throttle on the jet bike, Bolan pulled the remote control from his neck and armed it with a flick of his thumb. He held it aloft so Kissinger, Turrin and Falkenhayn would see it.

Someone shouted aboard one of the powerboats, drawing the attention of both crews. Guns turned in Bolan's direction. Both of the vessels were partially blocked by the floating corpse of the ketch. The pilots stayed back, working to keep their propellers from the snarling mast lines that floated across the water like the tentacles of a jellyfish.

Rifles cracked viciously. A round skidded over the rear section of Bolan's jet bike.

The throttles of both powerboats opened up as they headed around opposite ends of the ketch, both of them cutting the distance as closely as possible.

The Executioner glanced over his shoulder and waved with the remote control. Falkenhayn, Turrin and Kissinger released their throttles, cut their bikes around in a semicircle and went turtle, turning the bikes upside down and plunging into the water.

Bullets speared into the ocean around Bolan. He triggered the remote control as he threw himself to the side, flipping the jet bike over with him. A flickering image of the ketch exploding scattered across his field of vision as he went underwater. For a brief instant he felt the heated air splash over his exposed skin. The concussive wave that followed was blunted by the sea, but the warrior still felt some of the effects.

Through the visor, holding his breath as he maintained a hold on the jet bike, he saw the flaming debris of the sailboat as it geysered into the air. The initial explosions had taken out both of the powerboats, as well.

When the Executioner surfaced, both boats survived only in broken hunks that were rapidly taking on water. Corpses littered the sea, and here and there a survivor moved weakly in the debris.

Glancing toward the summerhouse on the hill, the warrior saw activity boiling out onto the beach. He counted nine men as he hoisted himself back into the saddle of the jet bike and keyed the ignition. Taking out the opposition in the powerboats had been set up to take place in one fell swoop. Getting through the land-based guards was going to be harder. After making sure the other bikes were moving into position behind him, he opened to full throttle and streaked toward shore.

Less than fifty yards from the beach, he cut the engine and came around in a sharp arc that threw a wave of water at the shoreline. He slipped off of the jet bike and went into the sea, stroking to get himself under the surface.

Using his survival knife, he slashed the nylon ties that held his equipment bag to the side of the bike. The bag came free and he slid it over his shoulder. Thirty feet southwest of his position, he saw Turrin, Kissinger and Falkenhayn freeing theirs.

He unzipped one end of his bag, took out a pair of fins and put them on. Then he squeezed the pocket empty again and zipped it so it wouldn't create any additional drag. He surfaced beside the floating jet bike for a quick breath of air and swept his gaze over the beach.

The security teams had arrived and were deploying around two Isuzu Troopers that had carried them across the sand.

The warrior sank back underwater and finned for the objective he'd chosen along the shoreline.

Bullets chopped into the fiberglass-and-metal body of the jet bike, the impacts sounding like dulled thumps underwater. More rounds twisted through the ocean around Bolan, searching blindly for a target. White streamers mixed with tiny bubbles marked their flight path until they faded from sight or buried themselves in the loose silt on the seafloor.

Lungs aching from the need for air, Bolan put his feet down and stood up. His head and shoulders came out of the water. A quick look told him he was within eight or nine yards of the beach, westward of the security teams' positions by sixty yards. His hands moved to the equipment bag, unzipped the main compartment and took out the M-16/M-203 combo he'd packed.

Two of the gunners spotted him, shouting warnings as they turned in his direction.

With steady hands, knowing he was only heartbeats from being fired upon with no real margin of safety, the Executioner opened the grenade launcher's breech and thumbed in the first 40 mm round. Concentrating totally on his target, knowing it was an all-or-nothing gamble with only his skill shading the odds, he raised the assault rifle to his shoulder and fired the grenade launcher from the point. The buttstock shoved against his shoulder. He was already reaching for the next round before the first hit.

The warhead slammed into the lead 4X4, covering it in flames and sending the men around it diving for safety.

Snapping the breech closed, Bolan fired again, putting the second round in front of the remaining vehicle. It was an HE round designed to disorient flesh-and-blood troops. Return fire was sporadic.

"Striker!"

Bolan looked over his shoulder as he put a third grenade into the M-203, saw Kissinger managing his heavier pack and taking long strides toward the beach. "Go. I've got your back."

Kissinger hunkered down, brought his knees up high and drove his legs hard into the water, powering toward the beach.

Keeping the M-16 on 3-round burst, Bolan went through the clip. Two men went down, and he knew they wouldn't be getting back up. Three others were wounded. When the clip fired dry, the Executioner triggered the grenade launcher. The 40 mm round landed behind the security teams. He heard the detonation as the warhead blew, saw the thick strands of red smoke roil out as the smoker spewed its contents into the air. A crimson cloud followed the westerly breeze, forming a pall that hung over the security forces.

"Move," Falkenhayn called out.

Bolan wheeled, dropped the straps of his equipment bag over his shoulder and reloaded on the run. Falkenhayn's H&K MP-5 snarled harshly, sounding flat as the noise traveled across the water. Turrin's CAR-15 joined in. The smoke wouldn't hold for long, but they didn't need it to.

Kissinger headed up the hill that overlooked the summerhouse and the beach, stripping away the nylon covering from his weaponry. The Barrett M-82 Light Fifty weighed thirty-five pounds. The big gunsmith carried it cradled in his arms, with the equipment bag hanging over one shoulder. He wasn't considerably slowed by the length and bulk of the weapon, and was already almost to the top of the hill.

On the beach Bolan dropped his bag behind the driftwood tree he'd spotted earlier, wrapped the M-16's sling around his left arm as he took up a seated shooting position and settled his sights over his first target.

The cross hairs of the M-16 settled over a cheekbone of a man running out of the smoke cloud. He stroked the trigger, firing a 5.56 mm tumbler that caught the gunman in midstride. The man was dead before his legs knew it, and his body dropped awkwardly.

The smoke cloud started to lift.

Falkenhayn ran toward the beach, fighting against the water more than Bolan because she'd come up in a deeper area. She moved too slowly. Turrin was a full step in back of her.

Settled behind the assault rifle's sights, Bolan kept both eyes open, let his left eye keep watch over the entire field, then focused on the right as he brought each target up close and personal. A gunman lying prone on the beach was drawing a bead on Falkenhayn. The Executioner shot the man through the throat, the bullet passing through to strike the gunner's H&K 770 target rifle's stock and foul the shot. He put the next round through an exposed ankle, then fired four more rounds to keep the gunners interested in their own survival before he found another flesh target. His next shot took a man in the chest, stretching him out beside one of the burning vehicles.

Out of the deep water now, Falkenhayn joined him in a long dive that left a skid mark across the sand of the beach and scattered pebbles and rocks in all directions. She coughed for a second, trying to regain her lost breath. Turrin picked a spot behind a ridge ten yards away.

Bolan reached for the woman, caught her arm in his hand and pulled her to cover.

"I'm okay." She rolled over, stuck a foot through the strap of her equipment bag and dragged it to her. When it was close enough, she reached inside for a fresh magazine for the subgun, charged her weapon and slid into position at the other end of the tree.

Bullets slapped into the tree, kicking up sand and rocks. Driftwood splinters whirled into the air.

The Executioner finished the clip in the assault rifle, managing to put down two more men. His mind clicked through the scenario he'd figured would go down once his team had secured a beachhead. Grimaldi's earlier flyby had indicated that there were three vehicles at the summerhouse. Two of them had been taken out in the initial confrontation, which left one. And one was enough to get Gustav Simmy to another part of Rügen until transport could be arranged. That was the up side. The down side was that if the covert force no longer needed the scientist, they would kill him outright. The numbers on the hard probe were definitely slim.

He slammed another magazine home, then reached into the equipment bag for the rest of his gear. He pulled on a pair of high-top running shoes with Velcro straps and snugged them tight. A Kevlar vest followed, then the combat harness and pouches carrying grenades and extra ammo for the M-16/M-203, and the Desert Eagle at his hip. He fitted the radio headset into place, secured the walkie-talkie to the combat harness, flipped the mouthpiece forward and snapped it on. It hummed to life in his ear, and he modulated the frequency and the volume. Satisfied, he thumbed the transmit button. "G-Force, this is Striker. Over."

"Go, Striker. You have G-Force. Over."

"Move into your primary parameter, buddy. We're on the beach. Over."

"Affirmative. G-force is moving in, awaiting your signal for the pickup."

Return fire from the east end of the beach was sporadic. Bolan's sniping ability had taken a lot of the security teams' confidence about an easy victory, and the chain of command seemed disrupted.

Falkenhayn pulled on her own gear and nodded her readiness. At her side Turrin gave him a thumbs-up.

Bolan tapped the transmit button again. "Come in, Thunderer. Over."

"Thunderer's here, Striker. Over."

"When you're ready. Over."

"I'm ready. Over."

"Then let's get it done. Striker out." Pushing himself to his feet, Bolan stayed low as he went around the end of the dead tree. He carried the M-16 in his left hand and drew the Desert Eagle with his right. On the run as he was going to be, the pistol was easier to point and shoot, and the massive .44 rounds made sure whatever he shot stayed down.

A gunner moved to Bolan's right, taking advantage of the burning hulk of a nearby Isuzu Trooper, and aimed through the flames. The Executioner tracked the big .44 Magnum in the guy's direction, firing two rounds that sheared through the vehicle's body but missed the gunner. He ran, trusting in Kissinger's skills. The numbers were falling damn quick now, and the thought of the third vehicle seared his mind.

An invisible hand seemed to grab the gunner and throw him backward, hurling him onto the burning wreckage of the other truck. Then the noise spilled out over the beach, sounding as if the sky had opened up for a sudden tropical storm. The Barrett Light Fifty was an awesome weapon with a powerful muzzle velocity and it packed quite a punch.

Bolan caught sight of Falkenhayn's flashing arms and legs as she followed in his wake, taking advantage of cover as she found it.

Kissinger blasted through the remaining .50-caliber rounds in the 11-round box, the noise reverberating above the beach. The big loads punched through anything in their way, cored through the metal of the Isuzu Troopers as the security people still viable tried to hide. Three more men dropped under the gunsmith's hand.

By that time the Executioner had raced by the stalled vehicles, the summer home holding Gustav Simmy dead in his sights.

CHAPTER TWENTY-ONE

Venice, Italy
2:18 p.m.

"Phoenix Five, this is Two. Over."

"Go, Two. You have Five. Over."

"I've got your bogey in sight, mate. Down you go. Give me a buzz when you and Four are ready. Over."

"Roger. Two out."

David McCarter stood at the left end of the bridge spanning the Grand Canal and gazed through the compact field glasses he kept hidden in his hand from passersby. His headset was mostly camouflaged by a dark green beret.

"One, did you copy? Over."

"One copies," Yakov Katzenelenbogen replied. "Standing by."

The Grand Canal was the main thoroughfare cutting a backward S through the heart of the city. As Katz had planned, once Pasquale Crivello had left the *Jade Falcon* in the harbor near the Lido, the man had to come along the canal. The buildings rose four and five stories on either side of the waterway, most without benefit of landscaping or paved sidewalks. Wrought-iron terraces jutted from the centuries-old brick, more for show than for any place of relaxation. Television aerials swayed at various angles from the rooftops, dulled from their exposure to the salty sea air. Cast in grays, browns, reds and stained whites, the buildings carried no hint of bright color except for the occasional flower box and clothing hanging from lines strung between buildings in the alley-canals.

The Grand Canal was at low tide, and marks showed along the building foundations where the highs had been riding for the past few months. The water was dark teal blue and was amazingly clean for an area in the heart of a city. But then, most of the city's livelihood depended on tourist trade. An effort had to be made to keep the view spectacular. Red-and-white-striped mooring posts that reminded McCarter of American barber shops stood in the water in front of most of the businesses along the canal.

Crivello's craft was a sixty-foot yacht that loomed imposingly as it powered into the city. A few people stopped on the sidewalks to watch its progression.

From the observation Phoenix Force had maintained on Crivello, McCarter knew the man was security heavy. A dozen men were spread across the boat in chaise longues, or stood at the railings. Despite the heat and humidity, all of them wore some kind of jacket. The Briton didn't doubt that each and every one was armed under the loose clothing.

Crivello stood beside the pilot and talked on a telephone. The man gave the appearance of being at ease. He wore white duck pants and a purple knit shirt. His unruly hair fluttered in the breeze, and gold chains glinted at his throat, echoed by the yellow flashes of gold sequins mounted in the black patch over his right eye.

McCarter put the pocket binoculars away when the yacht was within fifty yards of his position. It moved slowly, keeping up with the traffic of native gondolas and *vaperetti* that cruised back and forth around it. The ex-SAS commando knew Calvin James and Rafael Encizo were moving on the vessel beneath the water, setting up the preliminary strike.

Tourists and citizens passed along the bridge behind McCarter as he coolly waited. His hands dipped under his jacket and attached the buttstock to the Colt Government Model .45 he carried in a web sling. His Browning Hi-Power was snugged in a shoulder leather. The buttstock fastened easily to the .45, and he threaded a silencer to the barrel. The buttstock's addition would give him greater accuracy over the distance while maintaining a weapon more easily hidden than a rifle.

Katz and Gary Manning were similarly equipped. Their part in the operation was to take out as many of the guards as they could and generate a smoke screen of confusion. They were settled in a powerboat moored under the bridge, ready in case Encizo and James ran into problems they couldn't handle. Their overlapping fields of fire would tilt the numbers on the extraction in heartbeats.

The yacht drifted to within thirty yards.

At the other end of the canal, a funeral procession came into view. The hearse boat was mantled in flowers and sheathed in sable silk. The coffin was covered in shrouds. At least a dozen other boats decked out in funereal black trailed behind. Dirge music drifted over the water, punctuated by the voice of the mourners singing hymns.

"Bloody hell," McCarter cursed, then thumbed the transmit button on his headset. "One, this is Two. We've got trouble, mate. Over."

"I see them." Katz's voice was cool and dispassionate. "We've got no choice. Five, are you people ready? Over."

"Negative." James was communicating through the UTEL built into his frogman's mask. "We've got two of the explosives planted, but if this thing is going to work the way it was set up to do, we need the other three. Over."

McCarter watched as the yacht approached the funeral party. "One, if we have to wait on them to clear the funeral, they're going to be out of range for us to do this cleanly. Over."

"Affirmative, Two. But we can't allow innocents to get caught up in this. Make your way to the next bridge. Over."

McCarter wheeled and jogged to the end of the bridge, cut left and headed along the narrow sidewalk, drawing curious gazes. "And if our target decides to tie up somewhere along the way? Over."

"We're screwed," Katz said simply.

But that wasn't the case, and McCarter knew it. Even if Crivello and his people docked before making the next bridge, Phoenix Force would have to successfully take Crivello down. The man had too many answers for them to just let him go.

Even at a jog, McCarter wasn't able to keep pace with the yacht. Against his better judgment he broke into a run, drawing more attention. He kept his arm folded over his

Windbreaker, conscious that two or three inches of the silencer were showing beneath the hem. If anyone happened to see it and know it for what it was, things would become even more complicated.

Perspiration filmed his nape and his back as he made the corner at the bridge only yards ahead of the yacht. He glanced back along the expanse of blue water, saw Manning and Katz drifting along in the powerboat behind the yacht. His hand slid under his Windbreaker and covered the .45 as he hauled himself up the flight of steps around two teenage girls engaged in an animated conversation. He fell into position as he locked on to his target.

The last boat of the funeral procession cleared the yacht. Crivello put down the telephone receiver and reached into his pocket.

A hundred yards down from the bridge, a group of men walked out of a tavern and headed for the dock. Their attention was locked solely on the yacht, and they waited expectantly beside one of the mooring posts.

McCarter hit his transmit button. "One, this is Two. We're going to have to step lively, mate, or we're going to hang ourselves in our own little trap. Look under the bridge at two o'clock. Over."

"I see them," Katz said. "Four, do you copy? Over."

"Four copies. We're finished here. Start your surface action. Counting down now. Ten . . ."

McCarter flipped the Windbreaker away from his weapon, brought the pistol's buttstock up to his shoulder and braced the barrel across his forearm. He stroked the trigger and sent a subsonic round crashing through the temple of the man standing at the portside railing. The 230-grain bullet smashed into its target, caused the man to stagger for a moment, then spilled the corpse over the side. Two other men jumped to the railing and yelled warnings to the pilot.

Crivello moved forward slightly, drawing a big silver pistol from under his shirt.

Shifting his aim, following the pattern he'd already chosen, McCarter loosed two more rounds that took another man in the chest and sprawled him across the deck. Crivello's gunners couldn't hear the gunshots with the silencer attached, but they recognized the bullet wounds for what they were and dived for cover.

McCarter put down two more men with the four bullets left in the clip. He switched magazines, dumping the empty on the stonework of the bridge. A bullet chiseled splinters from the railing beside his head, letting him know that at least one person had spotted him from the yacht. He worked the slide, snapping the first bullet of the new clip into place.

A quick count showed that the combined firepower of the three surface combatants of Phoenix Force had accounted for seven dead or wounded aboard the yacht. Crivello was hidden with the pilot behind the cabin.

Autofire ripped along the canal, chewing into the fiberglass hull of the powerboat that held Manning and Katz, scarring the stone bridge as McCarter moved on to take up a new position.

Harsh curses and screams erupted from the pedestrians as they vacated the open places and took refuge in stores and down the high, narrow alleys. Crivello's land-based crew split, most of them going for the boats in front of the tavern while another group headed for the bridge.

McCarter took aim at another target, putting a round through the shoulder of a man firing on Manning and Katz. The guy's gun bounced, slid under the railing and over the side.

The yacht's pilot shoved the throttles open, and the vessel's tail twisted as the power kicked the screws into high gear.

"Five!" Katz barked over the frequency.

"We're on him," James responded. "It's going... *now!*"

A series of explosions, sounding no louder than a sledgehammer slamming into a metal fifty-five-gallon drum, rippled through the yacht. A hush seemed to fall over the vessel as McCarter watched, then it came apart in the middle, both halves cresting waves that spumed from the middle of the canal. The fury that had ripped away the underside of the vessel never touched the decks with more than vibrations, merely playing on the vessel's own structural design faults to send it slithering into the water.

A bullet plucked at McCarter's Windbreaker, drawing his attention back to his own plight. He pushed himself up and ran. Bullets chased him, whizzed by his head and clipped fragments from the stones at his feet. One punched into his Kevlar vest over his right kidney, making him stumble and lose his breath. He almost had his balance back when another crunched into his upper left shoulder. The body armor blocked penetration, but left a bruise that went bone-deep and promised interesting colorations, provided he survived.

Driven by the force of the second round, he skidded to his knees and felt his jeans rip and flesh tear. He forced himself up, got his feet moving and sought cover behind one of the decorative posts along the bridge railing. The .45 was in the middle of the bridge, out of reach.

He freed the Browning Hi-Power from its shoulder leather as he put his back to the stone post and selected a grenade from the assortment in his buttpack. Another burst of autofire scratched stone splinters from the post. He closed his fingers around the grenade, pulled the pin and held the lever with his thumb. "Hey, look at this, mates!" he yelled, shoving his fist out with the grenade held in it, then peering cautiously around the corner.

On the sidewalk behind the knot of men, citizens and tourists were still scurrying for cover. Seven armed men took refuge where they could find it, brandishing their weapons.

"He's got a grenade!" someone screamed in English.

"Yeah," McCarter shouted, "I've got a grenade, and I intend to use it if I have to. At this distance, it'll bugger us all up. I'm ready to meet my maker. How about you gents?"

CALVIN JAMES HUNG suspended in the dark blue water of the Grand Canal, riding out the concussive waves streaming from the yacht as best as he could. Wispy ribbons of bubbles whirled in all directions.

He was dressed in a blue-and-green neoprene skin-suit that would make him hard to see from the surface. A Lambertson Amphibious Respiratory unit was packed on his back and midsection. Due to its unique design, the LAR V emitted no telltale bubbles and recycled the air he breathed. His Beretta 92-F was sheathed on his lower right thigh in an airtight holster that was part of the suit, and two diving knives were secured to his calves. He carried the extra LAR V and mask in his right hand, and the force that shoved into him made it dance in his grip.

He righted himself instinctively, let his body make the moves he'd learned while a Navy SEAL. He saw Encizo only a little above him and ten feet away, a dark shadow cut out of the sea by the sunlight glinting almost straight down overhead.

The Cuban stroked confidently as the concussions rolled over him. He was dressed like James, but carried a speargun instead of an aqualung.

James adjusted his mask, switched to the secondary frequency in the UTEL. "You okay up there?"

"Yes," Encizo replied. "Let's move before we lose our man."

"Right." James finned toward the yacht, reading appraisal of the damage automatically. The boat was taking on water quickly in both halves. As usual, Gary Manning's work left little to fault.

"Purple shirt, white pants," Encizo said.

"I remember." McCarter's description had come moments ago. "The eye patch would be hard to miss, too."

Boards, fiberglass and furniture continued to pour out of the belly of the boat like coils of intestines, drifting toward the bottom of the canal.

James clipped the extra aqualung to his belt and felt the drag at once, but knew there was no more need for speed. He'd arrived at his target zone. Now it was just a matter of finding his quarry.

The stern section of the vessel drifted lower in the water. A small galley cookstove tumbled loose, ripping free of the propane lines running from the tank on board. James had to shove it away as it fell slowly toward him, buoyed somewhat by the water. It took him down for a moment, the hissing flurry of gas escaping from the propane tank creating an underwater cloud that erased visibility until the pressurized contents were gone.

"Calvin."

"I'm okay," James told Encizo. The ex-SEAL regrouped and renewed his assault on the sinking boat. He pushed flotsam out of his way, sent a seat cushion spinning to the side. The boat's stern section took another dip, losing four more feet to the rising water.

A leg in white pants dropped through the water. James seized it and pulled hard. The body followed the leg, its face pasty white against the sun-sparkled blue of the water. There was no eye patch, and the shirt was red. The man fought in James's grip, dragging a .38 pistol from his waistband and trying to line it up for a shot.

James reached to his calf, pulled one of the knives in a trained flicker and shoved it through the underside of the man's chin until the point crunched against the inside of the skull. The man lost motor function immediately, his eyes freezing in a thousand-yard stare. Blood cut scarlet ribbons through the sea as it pooled to the surface. Unable to free his knife, James pushed the corpse away.

Pasquale Crivello clung to the bridge of the stern section, a silver Detonics .45 gripped tightly in his fist. His feet repeatedly slipped on the wet decks as he tried to find purchase.

"Rafael," James called.

"I see him, amigo. Take him. I have you covered." Encizo floated behind him, two-dimensional and hard in the teal-colored sea.

Finning hard, James closed in on Crivello, reached up and grabbed the man's ankle. He heard the man bellow even through the water. Braced against the submerged section of the deck, James yanked. Crivello held for a moment, managed to turn and fire the Detonics. Neither shot went near James. Then the black marketer's hand slipped from the railing, and he went under.

James grabbed the man's other ankle and swam for the bottom, dragging Crivello down as an alligator would its prey. Crivello struggled, but the Phoenix Force warrior held fast, his fingers sinking into the thick muscle of the man's legs.

Crivello managed to lock a beefy fist around one of James's legs with crushing force. James kicked free, letting the man go.

Immediately Crivello swam for the surface. The Detonics had evidently been lost somewhere on the way down. A body rolled over in the water as it began its descent, and Crivello recoiled from it. A speargun arrow jutted from the dead man's chest. Encizo was already firing again, taking out another man who'd made it into the water and was trying to stay afloat and fire his handgun.

"Calvin," Encizo said.

"I have him," James replied. "Just letting him use up some of that precious oxygen in his system." He drew his other knife, then finned in pursuit of his prey.

Smooth and easy, swimming much faster than his opponent, James caught up to Crivello. He snaked his free arm around the man's head and laid the knife at the man's throat. For a moment Crivello froze, but the need for oxygen pushed him past the point of fear and he fought anyway.

James maintained a choke hold, determined not to let the man drown despite Crivello's best efforts. The man's arms and legs moved more slowly, finally floated at rest. "Rafe."

"Coming."

The Phoenix Force warrior clamped Crivello's nose and mouth shut with one hand and used the other to pull the LAR V from his hip. Encizo joined him, his dark hair floating free in the water. Bits and pieces of the yacht continued to filter down around them like snowflakes in a winter paperweight. When Encizo had the full face-mask ready, James released the unconscious man's face, shoved Crivello forward and let the mask seal. Once Encizo had the mask tight, James triggered the air-release valve and blew the water out of it. He swam down, looking into the face mask to make sure it was clear. Since their prisoner was intended to be unconscious most of the trip, they hadn't been able to use the usual regulator that went with the LAR V. James had cobbled one together that fit over the man's entire face, but he wasn't sure about the seals. Everything seemed to be holding up well.

On the other side of the face mask, Crivello's eyelids fluttered open, revealing eyes that looked glassy and dull. His arms moved slowly, reaching for James.

"Hit him with the gas."

Encizo tapped a red plunger button on the small tank James had mounted on top of the air tank and hooked into the main feed lines. Anesthesia cycled through the line, just enough, James had calibrated from Crivello's personal statistics, to put the man under and keep him there for a while.

A heartbeat later Crivello's eyes rolled up into his head.

James took one side of their prisoner's shirt in his fist while Encizo took the other. Together they finned for the mouth of the Grand Canal with Crivello facedown between them.

After changing frequencies on the UTEL, James hit the transmit button. "One, this is Five. Over."

"Go."

"We've got our cargo. Over."

"Acknowledged, Five. Two is under some duress. We're going to try to help. Make your objective. We'll rendezvous with you there. One out."

James fell into a relaxed stroke, mirrored by Encizo, drifting low against the silt clogging the canal's floor. He checked Crivello and found everything functioning perfectly. Then he wondered what kind of duress McCarter could be facing.

FOR A MOMENT indecision reigned supreme along the stone bridge.

McCarter had tucked his hand back behind the decorative post once Crivello's land-based gunners had recognized the threat of the grenade in case any of them happened to think they were sharpshooter enough to erase that threat. He thumbed the transmit button on his headset with his gunhand. "One, this is Two. Over."

"Go, Two."

"I've got a situation. Over."

"Acknowledged, Two." Katz's voice sounded calm and reassuring even though the Israeli and Manning were under fire themselves. "Have you got any suggestions? Over."

McCarter glanced at the gunners, knew their fear of the grenade wouldn't hold them at bay forever. Sooner or later he'd have to use it, and then they'd find out he wasn't willing to endanger civilians. "A flyby, mate. Either I make it or I don't, and devil take the hindmost. Over."

"Agreed. You look sharp up there. We're on our way. One out."

A gunner broke cover and dashed forward, trying to gain ground at the urging of someone who'd decided to call the shots.

McCarter fired four rounds in quick succession that straightened the man up, then sprawled him along the bridge. The shots rang out unchallenged. "Any more of you bloody fools looking to become dead heroes?" he shouted.

There was no answer.

He peered along the bridge, then glanced back at the canal, listening to the sharp exchange of gunfire trapped between the lines of buildings.

Manning had the powerboat fifty yards away, turning it tight, sliding the stern section around to face back toward the bridge.

One of the speedboats parked in front of the tavern had moved into the kill zone. The gunners were improving their aim with every round. Bullets stopped making whitecaps in the water and chewed into the fiberglass hull of the boat.

Katz dropped out of sight for a moment, then appeared with the MM-1 they'd secured for a backup on the mission. It wasn't exactly an admission that the extraction had turned more ballistic than expected, but Crivello's disappearance now would definitely make major news reports.

The Israeli braced himself as the boats raced toward each other, and fired three 38 mm high-explosive rounds from the multiround projectile launcher that took the approaching speedboat just above the waterline on both sides of the bow. A fourth round missed by inches.

With the prow of the craft virtually destroyed, the speedboat dug its nose into the water and capsized, spilling the hardmen it carried into the canal. Manning skirted the hazard easily, juking through the flotsam left from the destruction of Crivello's yacht.

"All right, Two," Manning called out. "You've got your pass, and you only get one try at the brass ring. Over."

"Roger, mate. You blokes just watch out for falling bodies below. Two out."

The gunners on the bridge knew something was happening as the powerboat glided toward them. They tensed, shifted and two experimental rounds chipped rock from the post.

Measuring the distance the powerboat was covering, McCarter balanced his weight on his knees and readied himself for the quick jump. Then he flipped the grenade into the middle of the bridge.

Shouted curses signaled the hasty retreat of the gunners.

The grenade popped loudly, then spewed white smoke out in a thick fog that rivaled some of the ones McCarter had seen roll into London on particularly bad days.

"Haul ass, buddy," Manning shouted. "The engines are going full reverse, *now!*"

McCarter spun around the post and pumped three rounds into a man whose leg and shoulder were hanging out past concealment. The 9 mm bullets caught the guy and jarred him backward.

Before the thunderous roll of the Browning died away, the Briton was sprinting for the opposite side of the bridge, hoping his timing was close. The white smoke obscured his form to a degree. Bullets smacked into the stonework as he ran, but none touched him. His breath came hard, pulling at the bruises caused by the earlier rounds the Kevlar vest had stopped.

He leapt to the railing, never stopping his forward momentum, and pushed off. As he fell, the smoke cleared, revealing the teal blue water of the canal twenty feet below and the cabin roof of the powerboat six feet above that. He waved his arms to catch his balance, knowing he was going to make it if he didn't hit and bounce off. He dropped feet-first, readying his legs to take the impact.

Instead of trying to land standing, he fell backward in a tuck and roll that left him sprawled across the cabin roof, his feet dangling over the side. Bullets scarred the roof, punching holes through the wood just heartbeats later. He heard the MM-1 cut loose and spun in time to see the results of the 38 mm warhead as it slammed into the bridge. A thick yellow cloud swarmed over the gunners, driving them back coughing and choking.

"Tear gas," Katz said. "I didn't want to injure the bridge if I didn't have to." He turned to Manning. "Gary, get us the hell out of here."

"On our way."

McCarter dropped into the stern as the powerboat surged forward at full throttle. He scanned the water behind them as Katz pulled the MM-1 out of sight. No one followed them. The Briton put his pistol away after filling the magazine. He shook out a Player's cigarette and lighted it. The wind caught the smoke and whisked it away. "Kind of rough around the edges, mate, but I've always said that any kind of escape a bloke could walk away from was a good one."

Katz nodded but didn't say anything as he took up a scouting position beside Manning.

McCarter kept watch from the bow. It was possible that Crivello's people might have another team waiting near the Lido. Plans called for dumping the powerboat along one of the side waterways, but interception could come at any moment. And there was still plenty of time for things to go wrong before they made the rendezvous with James and Encizo.

CHAPTER TWENTY-TWO

Rügen Island, Germany
2:32 p.m.

Pulling a grenade free of his combat harness, Mack Bolan lobbed it toward the front of the summer home and dived behind the low dune thirty yards in front of it as autofire scratched jagged tears in the patch of sand he'd just vacated. He rolled, came up with the M-16 in his hands and sighted across the front of the house. Someone pulled back from one of the large picture windows, and he tracked it through the scope. It was an armed man, not Gustav Simmy. He squeezed the trigger, aiming for the center of his target's chest, and sent the man reeling back against the far wall.

Another burst of autofire raked across the top of the dune, and bullets whined over the warrior's head.

Bolan looked over his shoulder and saw Falkenhayn tucked into the defile that led back to the beach area where they'd left the mobile troops. Her H&K MP-5 roared in full-auto, scattering both picture windows as she took them out. She went to ground immediately when sniper fire from a new location threw bullets only inches from her face and hands.

The Executioner looked up, saw the pair of snipers who'd crawled out on the summerhouse and were partially hidden by the peaks and valleys of the rooftop. Moving into a prone position, he targeted the lead man, settled the cross hairs over the man's face and squeezed the trigger. As he rode out the recoil from the assault rifle, he felt the wind from a bullet burn his temple.

The long, loud crack of Kissinger's Barrett M-82 rolled over the beach from the hilltop where the gunsmith had positioned himself. The second sniper caught the .50-caliber round in the chest and jerked like a puppet yanked by its strings as he flew from the rooftop.

"Striker," Kissinger said.

"Go."

"I got movement at the back of the house. They're making for the attached carport."

That explained where the missing vehicle was. Bolan sat up behind the safety of the dune and rummaged through his web gear for the ordnance he needed. "Stay with them."

"If I do, I'm going to lose you."

"No choice," Bolan replied. "If we lose our target, we've wasted time we didn't have."

"I read you." Kissinger didn't sound happy about the situation.

"If our guy isn't aboard, let it go. If he is, see if you can stop the car."

"Right."

Bolan glanced at Falkenhayn's position, then Turrin's. The woman shifted back into place with a determined look. He tapped the transmit button on the headset. "Can you cover me?"

"Yes." She drew her VP-70 Z pistol and laid it beside the submachine gun.

"Go for it, Sarge," Turrin encouraged.

In quick succession, the warrior lobbed three grenades toward the summerhouse, forming a loose triangle. Moving smoothly into the buttstock of the M-16, he pushed the fire selector into single-round mode and began squeezing the trigger as fast as he could aim. His targets were the hinges of the door. Six 5.56 mm tumblers banged into the top-hinge area and splintered the wood. Grenades popped as he hammered the next three shots into the bottom-hinge position.

Red smoke from the grenades whirled up and became a massive cloud. Gunfire from the summerhouse sprayed into it.

Bolan dropped the almost empty clip from the M-16 and shoved another one into place. He pushed himself to his feet and ran, skirting the outside edges of the smoke cloud and using it for cover rather than plunging into the heart of it. The gunners never slowed their pace, and even staying away from the smoke cloud brought him close to a number of wild rounds.

He made the corner of the house, listened to the roar of Falkenhayn's subgun die away, then heard the steady beat of her pistol. Turrin's CAR-15 paused only long enough to switch magazines. He went down in a slide that brought him up against the front of the house. Gunfire was thunderous over his head. From the sound of the weapons, he figured there were at least three men inside the front rooms, perhaps as many as five.

Wrapped in the blinding coils of the smoke cloud, he found the door by feel, getting to his feet as he fixed its position in his mind. He rocked back on one foot and kicked out with the other, two stun grenades in his hands. The hinges tore through the splintered wood with long screeches.

Some of the gunfire died away, including Falkenhayn's and Turrin's now that they could no longer see him. The men inside the house screamed frantic questions at each other as the door flew inward.

The Executioner dropped the grenades inside, watching as part of the drifting smoke tracked inside, as well.

Startled exclamations were drowned out when the grenades exploded.

On the move instantly, Bolan wheeled and cut inside. His eyes burned from the smoke as he scanned the room from left to right, putting bursts through two men who turned to fire at him. A third man standing beside the door grabbed for the warrior.

Unable to use the assault rifle, the Executioner jabbed a fist into the man's face that rocked his head back. Given a little breathing space, he kicked the man in the crotch and tried to clear him as he focused on the remaining man in the room. Instead of going down, the guy grappling with Bo-

Ian locked his hands on the M-16, screaming curses in a pain-racked voice filled with fear.

The fourth man raised his shotgun and aimed it at the Executioner.

Bolan used the man fighting him as a shield and heard the roar of the shotgun trapped inside the house. The man holding on to the warrior's M-16 stiffened suddenly and slowly fell backward. The double-aught pellets had gone through the man in a tight pattern because of the proximity, and cut a large hole in his back that made an even larger hole in his abdomen. Bolan's Kevlar vest registered some of the impact as the buckshot passed through.

The hardman lifted the shotgun to fire again, taking an instinctive step back when he saw that his enemy hadn't gone down.

Bolan drew the Desert Eagle and raised it into target acquisition, touching the trigger twice as soon as he had it. The first 240-grain round took the man in the chest, and the second hit him between the eyes.

The shotgun dropped from nerveless fingers as the corpse came to a sitting position against the wall.

Leathering the .44 Magnum, Bolan took up the assault rifle again and followed the drifting smoke into the back of the house.

"Striker." It was Falkenhayn.

"Go," he said softly. He pushed the bat-wing doors to the kitchen open but found no one inside.

"Are you clear?"

"Clear."

"We're coming in."

The first bedroom was empty, too, but the unmade bed and scattered clothing gave the impression that it had just been vacated.

"Striker," Kissinger called.

"Go."

"The third vehicle just took off. Our guy's aboard. I'm going to try to take it down, but we're talking about a thousand yards here and a moving target."

"You've got the gun that can do it."

Kissinger grunted an affirmative and cleared the channel.

The dining room was empty, as was the kitchen. But movement flickered at the back door.

The Barrett began a steady metronome of rolling thunder.

Bolan stepped to one side of the utility-room doorway as a gunner swung around and fired his Uzi on full-auto. Nine-millimeter parabellum slugs raked the doorway.

When the crash of autofire died away, signaling the Uzi's empty magazine, the Executioner drew the Desert Eagle and leaned around the doorway. With no target in sight, remembering which side the man had come from, he triggered the last five rounds from the big .44 across the back wall at a level of four feet, knowing the 240-grain rounds would smash through the thin wall. As he was dropping the empty magazine, the hidden gunner fell forward, his right shoulder bleeding profusely.

The man struggled for a moment, then lay still.

As Bolan stepped over the body, he heard footsteps behind him. When he looked, he saw Turrin covering his back.

Outside, a dirt trail ran through sparse grass toward the interior of the island. Dust clouds spumed up behind the fleeing Isuzu Trooper.

Bolan took out his field glasses, hearing the basso boom of the Barrett as Kissinger kept hammering out rounds. He focused on the 4X4 and saw the big bullet holes that had torn through the metal body and the windows around the driver. He tapped the transmit button. "G-Force, this is Striker. Over."

"I read you, buddy," Grimaldi replied. "Over."

"Bring it in. You have a quick pickup at the target site. Three people. We'll be returning for Thunderer. Over."

"Affirmative, Striker. Over."

"Stand by to deploy the boarding ladder," Bolan instructed. "You won't have time to touch down. Striker out."

The 4X4 melted in the distance, fuzzed by the dust. It was at least twelve hundred yards away, bumping over the rough road.

Bolan watched through the field glasses. He keyed up the headset again. "Thunderer. Over."

"Go."

"You're going to lose them for a moment in the terrain, but they'll be bobbing back up. See the knoll east of their present position? Over."

"Affirmative."

"They're going to have to come up that. That gives you one shot, but they'll be facing you at a better angle. Over."

"Got it."

The last booming echo of the Barrett faded away.

Bolan turned to glance at Turrin and Falkenhayn and found the German agent tightening the cinch on a water-proof canvas satchel.

"I got everything out of Simmy's personal effects that I could. They had him stashed in the back room. I found a pair of handcuffs chained to the bed. From the looks of things, he might not have been a willing accomplice."

Bolan nodded, then looked up at the sky as the sound of whirling rotors filled the air above them. The long bulk of the CH-53E Super Sea Stallion drifted into view with a rope ladder trailing from the bay doors. The warrior fitted the binoculars to his eyes again as Grimaldi lost altitude.

Thirteen-hundred-plus yards away, the Trooper climbed to the top of the ridge, the tires working furiously in the loose sand. Figuring the .50-caliber round's velocity at nearly 2800 feet per second, it would take the bullet almost a second and a half to reach its intended target. Taking into consideration the Trooper was moving at an unspecified speed with no real time to figure out a lead distance, it was a hell of a shot.

The Barrett boomed. For a moment Bolan thought Kissinger had missed. The Trooper continued on its way, rolling down the steep incline.

Then white smoke blossomed from under the hood, followed by twisting spirals of oily black tendrils, indicating that the round had not only punched through the radiator, but had done massive damage to the engine block, as well. The Trooper jerked and stuttered, then came to a rolling stop. Men poured out of the vehicle, two of them dragging a smaller man with them.

Bolan caught the trailing rope ladder of the Sea Stallion as it drifted by, motioning Falkenhayn up first. She went quickly, not slowed by the satchel she carried. Turrin was next. The warrior followed, stepping onto the first rung and signaling Grimaldi to take them skyward.

The chopper hugged the contours of the ground, racing toward the stalled 4X4. Eight men lay scattered around the vehicle ready to fight. A bullet starred the Plexiglas nose of the battle chopper.

Bolan hailed Grimaldi. "Before we get any closer, let them know what they're up against."

"You got it." Under Grimaldi's expert hand, the Sea Stallion came to a halt in the air, revolved slightly and brought the 2.75-inch rocket pods to bear. A blistering dozen rounds shook the earth around the gunners. Before the smoke and debris had cleared, all of the men had thrown their weapons down and placed their hands on their heads as they got to their feet.

Bolan clipped his gear to the ladder, then had Grimaldi lose enough altitude to allow him to drop to the ground. He fisted the Desert Eagle as he jogged toward the men. All of them watched him in grim fascination.

Gustav Simmy was nearest the Trooper, standing uncertainly without his cane.

The warrior penetrated the loose ranks of his enemy and walked boldly into their midst. He gestured toward the scientist. "Simmy, come here."

Obviously afraid for his life, Simmy came forward.

Without warning, a man near Bolan lunged at him. The warrior didn't hesitate. He lifted the .44 and shot the man point-blank in the face. The corpse dropped to the sand.

Wounding would have been preferable because there was no reason for these men to die, but any sign of weakness on his part inside their ranks would detract from the threat Grimaldi posed by hovering overhead. He swept the pistol around meaningfully. "Nobody else here has to die. You make your choice to live. Now. If you want to live, back off."

A moment of hesitation ran through the men, then they turned and walked away. By the time they reached the ridge, they were running.

Bolan took Simmy by the arm and led him slowly toward the waiting helicopter.

The White House
10:01 a.m.

HAL BROGNOLA STOOD at the bulletproof window of the Oval Office and looked out over the White House lawn. Despite the bad press about American and Russian interests in Europe, it was business as usual in the nation's capital.

A tour guide stood in front of a crowd of people who'd come to see the public rooms on the lower floor of the building. They'd be gone by noon, none the wiser for what was really going on inside executive offices.

Unless, Brognola reflected, a major snafu resulted from present operations and it all hit the networks' news.

The President paced the floor, his hands behind his back as he worried over the decisions he'd made in the past hour. There hadn't been any choice. Information was still coming in from Stony Man Farm from the debriefs Mack Bolan and Phoenix Force were giving their subjects. The one thing both parties had agreed on was the culpability of Barnabe Siffre as the driving force of the frame-up. The President had assigned a covert NATO team to pick up Siffre at his home in Versailles and quietly finish building their case before presenting it to the United Nations. The bacterial agent could loosely be defined as a threatening drug, and as such it empowered American military units to operate on foreign soil. Operation Just Cause and the various strikes against the Colombian cartels had already laid the legal foundations for the international actions the NATO unit would be taking.

At least, Brognola hoped that was how the world would view the situation. There was no way to know until the dust settled. And their asses were hanging way out on this one. He just wished Phoenix Force or Bolan had been close enough for the Versailles insertion themselves.

The phone rang, and the President flicked it on to speaker function. "Yes."

"It's Ms. Price. She has a satellite relay set up," the secretary said.

The President thanked her, then retrieved his remote control, aimed it at the TV-VCR combination mounted into the wall. The screen cleared, showing Barbara Price at her office inside the Farm's computer lab.

She looked weathered and worn. "We've gotten all we're going to get from Crivello and Simmy," she said without preamble, "and it doesn't look good."

The President faced the screen where the video camera mounted on top relayed his image back to Price. Brognola came around the desk and joined him. "What is it?" the head Fed asked.

"As you already know, Crivello was the main transport person for the bacterial agents. Evidently he was the man Siffre felt most able to buy off. Of course, Siffre hadn't planned on us getting our hands on him, or that Phoenix could be as persuasive as they were."

Brognola nodded.

"Besides helping move the bacterial agents, though, Crivello was also responsible for shipping three large computer systems. Second-generation Crays."

"We used those ourselves in Desert Storm," the President said.

Brognola knew about the pinpoint accuracy of the cybernetics systems. With them, allied forces had been able to send and receive pages of coded information in heartbeats, and provide bombing patterns that were nothing short of astounding. "Where were they shipped to?"

"Baton Rouge, Louisiana, Brighton, England, and Megève, France."

"Baton Rouge," the President repeated. "That's where the man Able Team turned up is."

"Yes. We've since been able to complete our research on him."

The television screen flickered and altered views. A sandy-haired man with a lantern jaw stood in front of a small building along a street, smiling at the camera. He wore a black business suit with an expensive cut.

"Kirby Huneke," Price went on. "He's a self-made millionaire who's one step ahead of the IRS on some semi-legitimate deals he cut over the years on his way to the top. He owned some land in Louisiana, as well as some leases in oil and natural-gas wells. He got his start in real estate, parlayed it into a healthy portfolio during the oil-boom days and got out of the business months before the bottom dropped out."

"You said 'owned,'" Brognola pointed out.

The picture changed back to Price. "Yes. Over the past eight months, Huneke has been liquidating his assets in the States."

"And reinvesting them in the European market."

"Right. And before you ask, yes, he's connected to Siffre. It took some searching before Kurtzman and his people turned it up, but the connection's there. They're together and as thick as thieves. The only thing Huneke has hung on to in Louisiana is the small television-radio station he acquired back in 1983."

"That's where the Cray computer turned up?"

"Yes."

"Is the station wired for satellite?"

Price nodded, consulting a notepad. "According to the license agreement, KBOB-TV rents satellite time as they need it to broadcast away-games for Louisiana State University's basketball and football programs. For the past three years, KBOB let the agreements lapse, citing that the cash outlay for the rights was too much. They renewed the license again this spring.''

''Have they shown any of the college games since then?'' Brognola asked.

''No.''

''For a guy who watches the bottom line, Huneke's not going to make much of a return on his investment.'' The big Fed rubbed his chin, feeling the five-o'clock shadow under his fingers as his mind probed the dark possibilities. ''But it does give him access to satellite systems with the Cray.''

''That's what it's for,'' Price replied. ''During Striker's debrief of Gustav Simmy, we learned that Siffre had Simmy run tests on the experimental bacteria concerning weightlessness and vacuums.''

''Space,'' Brognola said in a quiet voice.

''That's what Simmy thought, but Siffre never said one way or the other.''

''Is it possible that Siffre has launched the bacteria into space?'' the President asked.

''Not only possible,'' Price replied, ''but probable, as well. Before bringing the bacterial agents through in Russian canisters to be found in French vineyards, Crivello transported shipments from Konigsalle Laboratories to Tokyo. Agents already in place took the crates from there. Leaving no stone unturned when blackmail could be in the offing, Crivello had the people trailed on different occasions. Each time the trail led back to the Japanese space agency.''

''Crivello had no idea of what he was transporting?'' Brognola asked.

''He says no. Striker believes the guy.''

''The Japanese space agency,'' the head Fed repeated. His stomach churned at the implications, and he shook two antacid tablets out into his palm.

''Their security isn't as tight as ours,'' Price said. ''Their space programs operate like a business. If someone has the money to shoot something up there, they'll provide the service."

"But how could Siffre get the bacterial agents past the inspection?"

"We don't know that part yet. For now we're going on the assumption that it was done. According to records Aaron pried his way into, the space agency has placed nineteen satellites in orbit for a company solely owned by Barnabe Siffre under a half-dozen false identities."

"They're using the Crays as tracking stations," Brognola said.

Price nodded. "Siffre's people could link into the satellite system through KBOB and give directions to the nineteen satellites. They're all self-powered models operating off of solar cells. Whenever Siffre's ready, he can direct them to drop into the earth's gravitational well and cause them to fall wherever he wants to."

"Can nineteen satellites carry enough of the bacteria to cover the continent of North America?" the President asked. "How big are they?"

"According to the paperwork we recovered, the biggest satellite is slightly smaller than a midsize car. The smallest is as big as an easy chair. Another thing you have to keep in mind is that it won't take much of the bacteria to defoliate the continent. Once it takes hold, it'll spread like wildfire."

"What about an antitoxin?"

"Simmy hasn't found one yet," Price said, "and I for one am not planning on any last-minute saves from the laboratory. Our only real option is to take Siffre down as quickly as possible and deep-six his play."

The President glanced at his watch. "Siffre's capture should be only moments away."

Brognola quietly hoped so, but he could tell by the familiar look in Price's eyes that the Stony Man mission controller wasn't expecting things to go quite so easily, either. "What's in Brighton, England?"

"A communications company owned by J. David Sandlier, who also happens to be a friend and business partner of

Siffre. Since the three Crays were all delivered as part and parcel of one overall package, Aaron believes they've already been programmed to be symbiotic and act in tandem to bring the nineteen satellites down to their various targets."

"And in Megève?"

"The Jura Mountains," Price replied. "Tax records show that Siffre owns a hundred acres of property in those mountains outside the city. Satellite pictures confirm that structures have been built there, some of them dug right into the sides of the mountains. There's a Stony Man blacksuit unit on standby in Paris, ready to link up with Striker.

"I figure Megève is where we'll find Siffre," Price said. "He'll have to be a part of it at the end. It's in keeping with the man's character."

"Siffre's at Versailles," the President said. "I have it on the best authority that the man was there not even twenty minutes ago."

"Twenty minutes," Price pointed out, "is a long time."

"Where are the teams?" Brognola asked.

"Able's already staked out KBOB in Baton Rouge. I can have Phoenix in place in two and a half hours for a parachute drop into Brighton. They're already en route. Striker can be in the Jura Mountains in forty-five minutes. He's also en route, but he and his team will have to pack it in. Brighton can be managed with a surprise attack from the air. Aaron has already pulled building and warehouse plans from public records concerning Sandlier's business. But Siffre will be dug in at Megève. It'll take time for Striker and the blacksuits to infiltrate the area. Even then, they might be forced to move before they're ready, and those mountains aren't an easy climb."

"If we can get Siffre at Versailles," the President said, "we can nip this thing in the bud."

"Maybe." Brognola turned to face the Man. "Even if we got our hands on Siffre, those satellites could be the biggest blackmail threat this country has ever faced. The only sure way is to take down the man and his organization, make sure it doesn't come back to haunt us."

The President nodded. "Still, if we have Siffre, maybe we can get him to talk."

The phone rang again, and the President answered it. As the Man listened, his face drained of color.

Brognola watched as the President hung up the phone and turned around.

"Siffre wasn't at Versailles. He beat us to the punch. Ms. Price, you can access this incoming scrambled eyes-only transmission. You'll need to see this, too."

Price's face cleared off the television, and a new scene took its place.

The setting was a mansion with carefully landscaped grounds. Dozens of people lay dead around a pool. The film was jerky from the cameraman's movements as he panned in on face after face. A moment later it went inside the house, showing more death in room after room.

The President cleared his throat. "Ms. Price."

"Yes."

"This footage is only minutes old. They're patching it through almost as soon as they get it. From the looks of things, Siffre wasn't at home when the massacre happened. Some of the weapons found at the scene seem to be checking back to ordnance supposedly under lock and key at Fort Benning in Georgia. I don't know any of these people. Neither do the soldiers on the grounds."

Price's voice was calm and icy when she spoke. "They're Siffre's partners in the pro-European trade movement, his French and German partners. It looks like he was making a clean sweep, getting them out of the way while pushing more guilt onto the United States with the planted weapons. I wouldn't be surprised if there's a corpse on the grounds that bears a remarkable resemblance to Siffre."

The death's gallery of male and female corpses continued to pile up. Brognola lost count, felt a cold spot in the bottom of his gut that he knew the antacid tablets would never touch until Barnabe Siffre was no longer a threat.

"It's started," the head Fed stated. "Siffre is one step ahead of us even now. He knows we've got him figured, and by now he knows we have Simmy. When he gets ready to deliver his ultimatum, he also knows his words are going to carry more weight because we know what he can do."

"Ms. Price," the President said in a hard voice, "according to your own estimation of how long it would take you to put your counterstrike into operation, you've got two hours and twenty-three minutes left. Is that still a viable time limit?"

"Yes. And we're working on another angle that might buy us some more time. We've got reason to believe there's more dissension in Siffre's camp than what we've already seen. If we can drive the wedge in where we want to, Siffre's operation can become more complicated than he's ready to handle."

"Get it done," the President said. "And if there's anything I can do for you, don't hesitate to call."

Stony Man Farm, Virginia
10:13 a.m.

"HIS NAME," Keith Rush announced, "is Dumichel Trudaine."

Seated at his console, Kurtzman studied the unmasked face of the jester on his monitor. Trudaine looked young, and his round-lensed glasses gave him an unexpectedly innocent appearance. "You're sure?"

"Oh, yeah." Rush tapped the monitor. "This is the guy. Believe me. I checked him out seven ways to Sunday. When the insurance job at Gervais Horizons went down in Bordeaux, undergraduate student Dumichel Trudaine had been gone from university for two weeks."

"He was already working on the job."

"Looks that way." Rush clicked Kurtzman's mouse, moving through the file. Text pages, including a job application and final interview sheet from WesLink Communications, zapped into place across the monitor. "Two years later Trudaine turned up working for the phone company in Stuttgart. He lied on his application, put down that he'd earned a master's degree in computer programming in Marseilles.''

"Did he ever go to Marseilles?"

"No. I'm guessing that he was keeping a lid on the Bordeaux rip-off in case inquiries had been made."

"So maybe after he scored, he never went back home again."

"Yeah. If he did, he never applied for a driver's license or paid any taxes there. I've checked him through every government agency I could think of, and Carmen came up with a few I hadn't thought of. If he was there, he lived like the invisible man."

"Fifty thousand dollars wouldn't have lasted long," Kurtzman pointed out. "Trudaine was either working or he was scamming money some other way. He shows all the signs of a local boy wanting to get out into the real world."

"A lot of these guys heavily into computers," Rush said, "don't know how to open up. They talk about programs, techniques and never mention personal feelings. From the read I get on Trudaine, he's got a strong personality. He likes to control people and things, but from a safe distance."

"He was egotistical enough to put that he had a master's degree on his application."

"Yeah, and he was well-trained enough to pull it off. Take a look at this." A page swelled into view on the screen, followed by two more. "These are quarterly reviews conducted by the phone company on his job performance. He consistently got superior markings."

Kurtzman scanned the pages. "But he had a lousy attitude that only got worse."

"He fell in love with another employee," Rush said. "I got the scoop from my friend working there. Once I could narrow the field down to Trudaine, she remembered him. He'd been at the top of the list of suspects for the computer foul-ups regarding customer billing. Trudaine had been terminated four days before for failure to show up for work. His girl jilted him, and he was having a rough time with it. Instead of working things out with his employers, he vented his frustrations at the workplace, became a real asshole, as my friend put it.''

Kurtzman looked up. ''I like it so far.''

''Then let me administer the coup de grace.'' Rush clicked the mouse. ''Here are a series of gif files over the past seven years. Notice how the list drops off halfway through, then almost completely fades by the last two years. These are files I found through my contacts on the BBS.''

''They're Trudaine's?''

''I believe they are. His old girlfriend used to talk about the systems they broke into while working their computers. Trudaine appears to have been addicted to the thrill of it. The girl wanted out when Trudaine started screwing with German national-security files. She couldn't get him to back off. That was the main reason they split up, according to my friend.''

''He likes playing with fire.''

''Yeah, and he liked working with new programs. Most of the gif files I received were highly detailed games and archiving programs. A number of businesses logged on and used the stuff Trudaine generated.''

''He didn't get paid for them?''

''Not that I know of. Here's the interesting thing—Trudaine never used his name on the files he created. He used a symbol. You want to take a guess at what that was?''

''A clown?''

''Close.'' Rush touched the mouse, and a rogue's gallery of innocent and evil clown faces flipped by as timely as a metronome. ''Faces. Every gif file was accompanied by a face. I've been able to come up with fourteen so far.''

''How many people knew these faces were associated with Trudaine?''

''Only a handful. Trudaine didn't meet people in the flesh, but some of my contacts got curious about him. The people on the BBSes love to work on problems. You know that. I've seen you tinker with some of them yourself."

Kurtzman nodded. The BBS systems could be almost totally impersonal, allowing users to hide behind names of their choice, never be seen by anyone or ever get to know anyone. But for some people, it was the only way to ever get their ideas across.

"People get curious these days," Rush said. "Sometimes the guy you start up a correspondence with isn't what he says he is. I've known three guys who nearly got caught up in an FBI sting operation ferreting out foreign agents getting Intelligence through the BBS. Their only crime was in not knowing who they were talking to."

"So someone got curious about Trudaine."

"Yeah. He was hyper on the BBS, filled with anger and resentment, from what I've been told. People checked him out, found out what they could, but it wasn't as much as we have here. Everybody who's come in contact with this guy remembers him once I bring him up."

Kurtzman looked at the last entry on the list. It was eighteen months ago. "He's been keeping a low profile for a while."

Rush nodded.

"Can you get me a list of companies that had access to those gif files?"

"I should be able to."

"Try to put one together for me." After Rush left the console, Kurtzman flipped through the rest of Trudaine's file, putting the pieces of the guy's psyche together as well as he could. Price was better at psychological warfare than he was because she knew the players better in the espionage field. But with Trudaine, Kurtzman sensed a familiar if not kindred spirit. Trudaine was egotistical, sure of himself, cocky. And to get the full rush of the bizarre game he was playing behind Siffre's back, Trudaine would have to be playing both ends against the middle.

Kurtzman surveyed the computer lab floor, saw Tokaido and Wethers at their posts while Carmen Delahunt took a short break.

"Problem?"

He turned in his wheelchair and found Barbara Price back at the ice bins pulling out a container of orange juice. "No, just thinking. We found the jester."

Price went to his monitor, her brows knitted together in interest as she surveyed the screen. "This is him?"

"Yeah." He quickly filled her in on the pertinent facts. "This guy is an adrenaline junkie, which makes him dangerous to others, as well as himself. Most of the outlaw hackers I've known love living life on the edge. They get addicted to the pump of going where they're not supposed to go. All of them have the idea that cyberspace and whatever creatures might be living out there are waiting for them to arrive. I have to ask myself, once Siffre's party has run its course, what's this guy going to do next?"

"It's possible that Siffre won't need him anymore."

"That's a given," Kurtzman replied. "And this guy isn't going to like being expendable at all. Everything I've seen on him suggests that he thrives on chaos. It's possible he's done something to double-cross Siffre at some point, hoping to stay one step ahead of any repercussions. Each time he struck back at someone or something in his past, he was able to be gone before anyone came close to him."

"If he has programmed something in Siffre's systems, things could get even more complicated."

"Trudaine will be betting on it. He'll try to be gone before the dust settles."

"Aaron. I've got that list for you."

Taping the keyboard, Kurtzman accessed the file Rush had put together after programming it into a sort file with a list of business holdings Siffre had that they had assembled. Eight matchups were left, the frequency of the files coming closer together until they disappeared.

"What's that?" Price asked.

"Proof that Siffre and Trudaine found each other." Kurtzman glanced back at Rush. "If this guy was as addicted to BBSes as you say he was, I'm betting that he couldn't stay away from them even though he was supposed to be secluded."

"I wouldn't bet against you."

"See if anyone knows a BBS around Paris or Megève that are the type that would interest Trudaine."

Rush nodded and returned to his computer.

"We'll find him," Kurtzman told Price with confidence. "He'll be there somewhere, and we'll know him from his programming style and interests the way a fingerprint man knows whorls and loops."

"And when you do find him?" Price asked.

"Then," Kurtzman said with a grim smile, "I'm going to complicate his life for him, and hopefully put a little more distance between him and Siffre."

CHAPTER TWENTY-THREE

Jura Mountains, France
5:59 p.m.

Mack Bolan wiped the sweat from his eyes and adjusted his leather climbing gloves. He peered up the mountain, so steep in places it seemed that nothing could grow on it. But here and there patches of grass, a gnarled tree root and sometimes a clutch of wildflowers grew in spite of the harsh terrain.

The ground was twelve hundred feet below the lowest member of the party, lost to view. A chill had come in with the approaching dusk, bringing with it a thin gray fog that swirled around the climbers.

The Executioner was third man in line, following two men experienced in mountaineering. They were working together ahead of him, building a way around a sharp outcrop with air-driven pitons and carabiners.

The lead man shot another piton into the granite side of the mountain, and the sound echoed across the open space covered by the fog. The climber secured the kernmantle rope, then stepped off onto the rope stirrups to reach for his next grip. The air-pressure gun dangled by a strap from his waist as he rocked loosely from the carabiner. He seemed unruffled and unhurried as he pulled another piton from the bag at his hip and loaded the gun.

Bolan peeled back the sleeve of his black parka and his nightsuit to check the time. They had to be in place in twenty minutes, no more than twenty-five. Even then, they might be too late. There was no way to know once they'd started up the mountainside. Satellite communications wouldn't resume until they reached the top, some hundred fifty yards distant if the telemetry readings Kurtzman had come up with meant anything.

Glancing down, he saw Falkenhayn grimly hanging on to the mountain. The woman's grit and determination was evident. She'd quietly insisted on seeing the mission to its conclusion. He hadn't put up an argument, because she'd earned it. And Price hadn't questioned his decision to involve the German agent. Kissinger and Turrin followed behind her. Grimaldi held a stationary position in an attack helicopter miles away below radar level.

Like the other members of the assault force, the warrior was weighted down with more than just mountain-climbing gear. The Desert Eagle was holstered at his back, leaving his hands untangled at his sides. The Beretta 93-R was sheathed in a holster attached to his boot, also so it would be out of the way. A rifle holster was cinched across his back, holding the Steyr AUG he'd chosen for the unit's lead weapon. The bullpup design and overall compactness of the weapon had made it a natural selection.

The Stony blacksuit unit from Paris had rendezvoused with him in the forest below and begun the climb up immediately. Nine out of the twelve had had previous climbing experience, and four of those were certified experts. After checking the mountainside with binoculars and using the pictures Kurtzman had faxed, the four had decided bringing the new people up was possible in the time frame allowed. Facing a potential of forty to fifty armed men, having three more guns along was certainly worth the extra work.

"On belay?"

Bolan looked at the man above him. "Belay on." He pushed himself up the side of the mountain until he was beside the guy, then belayed himself to the piton there.

"Climbing," the man called out, and swung with a monkey's ease out onto the pitons left by the first man.

"Climb on." Bolan kept the rope taut in his leather-covered fists, his weight into the act and not just his strength. The climbers' shorthand had been easily learned by the three neophytes.

The man easily negotiated the outcrop with the pitons, working along the rope held by the man waiting above.

Loose pebbles struck Bolan's face and goggles as he watched the man pull himself onto the outcrops and get to his feet.

"Off belay."

"Belay off," Bolan replied. He tested the rope and found some slack. "Tension."

"Tension," the man called back as he took the slack out. The lead man was already moving into position, looking for a way up the wall of granite.

"Climbing." Bolan moved into position.

"Climb on."

Swinging out onto the first piton, the warrior experienced one dizzying moment, then squelched it and got on with the crossing. A moment later, he was standing on the outcrop, belaying the next climber while the second man moved up after the lead man.

He was aware of the minutes passing as the group moved. The outcrop slowed them, but the ascension gradually eased.

Sixteen minutes later, two minutes into the ten-minute safety margin Bolan and Price had allowed, the group came to a momentary pause on a ledge big enough to hold thirteen of the eighteen. The other five were on another ledge twenty feet down, a ladder made of pitons already hammered into place so they could negotiate the climb without help.

The lead climber was already at the cliff's edge fifteen feet overhead, in position and ready to belay the rope to the top once he clambered over.

Bolan called over the communications man and told him to go up next and set up the LST-5C satellite radio that would give them direct access to the Stony Man Farm frequency.

They went up in quick order.

A thin layer of snow crusted the ground at the top of the cliff, making the thick copse of trees west of the complex stand out stark and sharp against the white. The stars in the night sky overhead were obscured by the fog.

Bolan took up point position, choosing Kissinger and one of the blacksuits to act as his wingmen to cover him, and faded into the dark forest. Falkenhayn was at his heels. Turrin stayed back with the rest of the crew to get them organized.

Twenty yards into the trees, Bolan saw the first security camera mounted on a branch, the electronic umbilical cord stapled to the bark until it disappeared under the snow.

He paused, using hand signals to point it out to his companions. The camera moved on a tight rotation but slowly. Each member of the team slipped across the field of view when the chance presented itself.

The warrior stopped at the edge of the tree line fifty yards from the upper limits of the complex. He took a pair of night-vision glasses from his equipment pouches, squatted and began to survey the area.

The terrain in front of the complex was rolling and rough. The security fence in front of it stood ten feet tall and had Y-strung barbs at the top. Unlighted security floods were at regular intervals on poles inside the fence.

Taking advantage of the cliff face behind it, the top of the complex looked like a rectangular metal box almost the same color as the rock it was built into. There was only one door, and it looked heavily fortified. Two guards were visible in the shadows at the sides of the building.

"In and straight down?" Falkenhayn asked.

"It looks that way." Bolan tapped his headset transmit button. "Rover Leader, this is Striker. Send Compass up now."

"Affirmative, Striker," Turrin answered.

"How soon before we have communications in place?"

"I've got a green light now."

"Good." Bolan peered back in the forest and watched as the team member he'd designated as Compass came forward to his position. "Secure the freq and get Stony Base on-line."

"Roger."

Compass was the team's tactical-information specialist. When the team had formed at the base of the mountain, the man had debriefed the members in a professional manner that had impressed Bolan.

The Executioner locked eyes with the man. "When we kick that front door in, it'll be just like we discussed. There'll be at least two ways in. With all the heavy equipment they had to install, one of them is probably a freight elevator. There'll also be at least one stairwell, in case the power goes out. And as soon as we find the generator, the power's history in that installation."

Compass nodded, reached into his pack and brought out an artist's sketch pad and a fistful of sharpened pencils.

"The squad will split on the ground floor," Bolan continued. "One crew on the elevator, the other on the stairs. As they go down, they'll call out directions and rooms. It's your job to keep up with those people and make sure they don't get cut off. It'll prevent us from getting turned around in there when everything goes to hell in a handcart, and it'll cut down on duplication of effort. You should have some kind of map of that installation in minutes."

"Yes, sir."

"If you get confused about where somebody is, you let them know then. Don't play guessing games."

"No, sir."

"And dig in out here. Once we open the ball, there could be a few who get by us."

"Yes, sir." Dismissed, the man went away to take up his position.

"There are three guards outside the fence." Falkenhayn pointed them out.

Bolan had already spotted two of them on either side of the fenced-in lot, but the third man in the cliffs with the sniper rifle wasn't a surprise. He tapped the transmit button, getting Kissinger's attention. "We go in quietly and take them out. Alive if you can get them, dead if there's no other way."

"Right."

"I've got this one," Falkenhayn said, nodding toward the other man at ground level.

Bolan nodded, then headed out. His watch showed that they had only five minutes left of the safety margin that had been allowed. He went quickly despite the treacherous terrain, locking in on his target. He climbed the steep incline easily, the Beretta 93-R in his fist.

Two minutes later he was behind the guy. The guard sat cross-legged on a dark woolen blanket with his rifle across his knees, no chance at all for a last-minute save.

The Executioner screwed the pistol's silencer into the guy's neck. "Not a sound," he said in a graveyard whisper.

The man stiffened but let the warrior slide his rifle and pistol away.

Taking a pair of disposable handcuffs from his pack, Bolan cuffed the man's hands behind his back, then put a strip of surgical tape across his mouth. After checking to make sure his prisoner was breathing okay, he rolled the guy up in the woolen blanket and tucked him up against the cliff.

He walked out on the ledge overlooking the top of the buried complex, staying low so his shadow wouldn't stand out from the others. The rooftop was thirty feet below. He ran his hands over his gear, finding the things he needed right away, and getting equipment ready that he would need in a few moments.

He keyed the headset. "Thunderer, this is Striker. Check."

"Check," Kissinger replied, signaling that he'd taken down his guard, as well.

"Sparrow?"

"Check," Falkenhayn answered.

The perimeter guards were out of the picture, and if radio contact was maintained by the security teams, they were already working on borrowed time. According to the warrior's watch, the team had beaten zero hour for the operation by twenty-three seconds. "Rover Leader, this is Striker."

"Go," Turrin said.

"Bring the troops up to the tree line and patch me through to Stony Base."

"Patching."

The headset clicked and whistled as the headset freq matched with the one being used by the LST-5C. When it cleared, Bolan said, "Stony Base, this is Stony One. Over."

"Go, Stony One. Over." Barbara Price's voice was tense.

"Be advised that Rover Group is in final approach. Over."

"Roger, Stony One. Stand by for green light from Stony Base."

Bolan waited, shook out the nylon cord from his pack and set the folding grappling hook so that it would take his weight when he was ready.

The sharp squeal of the guard's radio echoed against the cliff face, and a voice demanded in French for the guard to check in.

TRUDAINE STARED at the monitor screen, which listed the E-mail at the BBS he accessed in Paris. According to the files, there was a message for the jester logged on.

His fingers hesitated above the keyboard as he thought about breaking the modem connection and leaving the message unread. Chances were, the sender had tagged the E-mail with some kind of virus, maybe something that would destroy his mainframe. If it had been him, Trudaine knew he would have done it. He was sure he knew who the sender was, and he had a lot of respect for the guy.

Working off a hunch, trusting to it because so much of his work was intuitive, he opened another window and accessed the BBS in Megève. Once he had it on-line, he checked the E-mail and found another letter waiting for the jester.

He stared hard at the two windows, willing the messages to go away. But they didn't.

Trudaine forced himself to exhale. He was on the verge of hyperventilating. It had been such a grand game, playing cat and mouse with his unseen opponents. The playing of the game had made life so much more interesting than it normally was. He was sad to see it go, but the sharp edge of fear that thrilled through him let him know he had no choice.

Steeling himself, he pushed back from the desk and averted his gaze from the computer monitor. He had his own room on the third floor of the underground complex. Privacy had always been a top priority in his life, and he had enough power in Siffre's organization to not only demand it, but to get it, as well.

He walked to the room's dorm-sized refrigerator and took out a bottle of soda pop. He screwed off the top and drank half the contents, waiting for the sugar rush to help clear his head.

The split screen of the monitor across the room signaled him with a silent siren call.

He set the bottle aside, took his backpack from the closet and began stuffing in clothes. As he packed, his mind worried about where he'd made a mistake and what kind of mistake it had been. With the way he had set things up, he figured when he had to abandon Siffre, he would have been able to simply walk away. Siffre knew nothing about him beyond the name Trudaine, and that could have been a given name or a surname.

And Trudaine knew he would be leaving that name behind when he left. There was enough money in the secret Swiss account to take care of his needs for a very long time—provided money meant anything when Siffre finished rebuilding the world in the warped image the man had designed. The thing that worried Trudaine most was that there might not be another game to play for a very long time, or that the players might not be as sharp as the ones he was being forced to leave. He regretted that.

With a sigh of discontent, he took off the dress shirt and slacks he was wearing, picked a long-sleeved fleece sweatshirt and jeans from the closet and put them on. He pulled on two pairs of thermal socks to protect him from the cold outside, then his favorite pair of cross trainers.

His parka was drab gray, chosen ahead of time in case he had to make the kind of departure he was making. He would blend in with the mountain and the forest as he made his getaway. Robbing the cache of chocolate bars he had under his bed, he filled the pockets of the parka, then zipped them up.

Trudaine started to put the parka on, but his eyes cut to the monitor screen and saw the E-mail files again. Suddenly he realized the game wasn't really over. This was a challenge, perhaps a final gambit on the part of his unknown player.

There was no way he could leave without finishing this game. It had been the best one ever.

He dropped the parka onto the bed beside the backpack, returned to the desk and sat down. He flexed his fingers, cracked the joints, then tapped the keyboard.

When he accessed the file at the Paris BBS, the screen evaporated into a thousand gleaming shards. The audio clicked on, making a terrific whoosh. The red-and-white clown walked onto the screen, then took a big pratfall that left a half-dozen bluebirds swirling around his head in a cartoon parody of being knocked nearly senseless. Dazedly the clown got to his feet and swayed drunkenly.

"You son of a bitch," Trudaine swore as the dark anger claimed him. His fists shook and he pounded the desktop. He'd created the jester as a thing to be feared and respected. His opponent had no business ridiculing his creation.

The clown suddenly shimmered and split into two people. The one on the right was obviously a digitized and animated photograph of Trudaine as he was in the flesh, letting him know his opponent had figured out who he was. A bulbous red nose suddenly appeared on the clown's face, sparking a look of horror as the clown grabbed it with both hands. The nose writhed like a live thing, swelling bigger until it became softball sized, then it sucked the clown inside. When the clown was gone, the rubber nose dropped to the bottom of the screen and rolled for a moment as if sizing up the real Trudaine.

Words appeared at the bottom of the monitor, and the ball hopped from one to the other as calliope music played "Send in the Clowns."

"Dumichel Trudaine. How do you think you're going to look on a wanted poster?"

The screen wavered, and the bouncing nose disappeared. When it cleared, the monitor showed a split screen depicting Trudaine in a full-frontal head-and-shoulders shot beside a profile shot of the same. He wore a striped and numbered prison shirt.

"Or maybe as part of a matched set?"

This time the monitor showed the same shots, only Barnabe Siffre had been added in the frames.

The intercom buzzed harshly. "Trudaine, what the hell is going on with the computers?"

Trudaine's intestines suddenly felt like ice-cold pythons twisting inside him as he realized the E-mail had been programmed to integrate itself into the rest of the mainframe's infrastructure, as well. Every monitor in the complex was seeing what he was seeing.

He jumped up, grabbed his parka and backpack from the bed, and ran for the door. In the hallway he avoided the freight elevator, heading instead for the nearest set of stairs.

"Trudaine!"

He ignored the voice, knowing Siffre was behind him, and concentrated on the stairway door. Before he reached it, an armed guard stepped out, a pistol leveled before him.

Trudaine held up his hands and turned around.

Siffre's face was suffused with blood. "You betrayed me."

"Not really. I just got beat by a guy who's very good."

"How much do they know?"

"I'm not certain."

"How much did they pay you?"

"Nothing."

"Then why did you do it?"

"You wouldn't understand."

"You led them to me."

"Not hardly. They already knew about you—that's why the NATO team hit your estate in Versailles. You've been in the public eye all along, and you've cut the details with the Japanese, Gustav Simmy and Crivello. You were known. They didn't know about me, but now they do. The only thing that's been compromised here is my anonymity."

"And my trust in you."

"You never trusted me. You only needed me."

"Now," Siffre said, "I think it's evident to both of us that that is no longer true." He gave a short nod to the man standing at his side.

Trudaine threw the backpack at the man and hurled himself to one side. He slammed into the side of the corridor with his palms and pushed himself toward the stairway. There was nothing but open space between him and the door. Bile cloyed the back of his throat. For a moment he thought he might even make it.

Then a thunderclap sounded behind him, and it felt as if someone had driven a steel fence post through his back. He came to a stop against the door, tried to make his hands work but they wouldn't. He pushed back and looked down, searching for the fence post that had impaled him. Blood smeared the door in front of him, and he realized that it was his own. He saw the scarlet strands winding through the sweatshirt. His legs buckled, and darkness claimed him as he saw the floor coming up to meet his face.

The White House
12:32 p.m.

BARNABE SIFFRE'S CALM veneer was starting to crack. Hal Brognola could see it on the television screen relaying the satellite communication. A muscle jumped in the man's jaw. Behind Siffre armed men moved into a predesignated response, telling the big Fed that Bolan's attack on the complex promised to be hard going. Huge chrome-and-gray hulks of computers were against the back wall, with technicians scanning them and making adjustments accordingly.

"You know who I am," Siffre said in a voice that showed signs of forced calmness. "And you know what I can do. If you don't get your people the hell away from here, I'm going to do it."

The President stood in front of his desk, arms folded across his chest. He looked tough and uncompromising, and Brognola knew it was no act. The Man was prepared to go down fighting to defend his country. "I don't know what you're talking about."

Brognola nodded. They'd agreed on the strategy before Siffre ever placed his call. It was a sure bet that the transmission was being taped at Siffre's end just as much as it was at the White House. Besides maintaining a position of being able to disavow the Stony Man operation, it also allowed the President to increase stress on Siffre by refusing to deal with him in any fashion.

"I have nineteen satellites in orbit around this planet, and I'm prepared to drop them all across the North American continent if my demands aren't met. I know you're aware of the bacterium aboard those satellites."

"No, I'm not. And if I was, how would you convince me any kind of bacterium is out there? No one would knowingly send that in space with a chance of it returning God only knows where."

Siffre grinned and shook his head in obvious disbelief. "Are you trying to bury your head in the sand on this thing? Is that what you're trying to do?"

The President made no answer.

"Because if it is, you're a bigger fool than the one I just had killed."

Brognola's stomach churned, settling only a little when he forced himself to remember that if anything had happened to Bolan or his team Price would have notified him.

"The Japanese space agency didn't know the bacterium was in those satellites," Siffre said. "It was placed in the walls of the satellites themselves. They went through x-rays easily, and were never even exposed to air. Until they crash into the ground on your side of the world, the bacterium will remain dormant."

"Without contesting your hypothesis," the President said, "there's no guarantee you can give me that will make me think you won't drop those satellites from their orbits at your earliest convenience. You can't hold a gun on a man without having to use it sooner or later. If you've got it, you're going to have to use it. Until then, I don't believe you."

Siffre laughed, but it was strained. "You pompous idiot."

The President ignored the derisive remark. "As for men under my control in your area, there are none. If you've got any further threats to make against this country, I'll be glad to convene with Congress this very afternoon regarding them."

"I hope you can teach your countrymen to eat dirt," Siffre said, "because in a few months, that's all you people are going to have."

Without another word the President broke the relay connection.

Brognola unwrapped a cigar and shoved it between his teeth. Then he reached for the phone and dialed the number for the Farm.

Stony Man Farm, Virginia
12:35 p.m.

"I'M IN," Kurtzman said.

Barbara Price watched the big man work at the computer console, taking confidence from his actions. The numbers had fallen away on the play to the last handful, as leaden as tombstones striking wet clay.

The three wall screens around the big room were active, cycling information. The first screen showed the noon horror show being broadcast from station KBOB in Baton Rouge, Louisiana. Black-and-white images scattered across the screen, depicting women in 1950s hairstyles biting their knuckles and screaming in open-mouthed terror.

The second wall screen held a satellite view of Sandlier Communications in Brighton, England. It wouldn't get any closer, nowhere near enough to show Phoenix Force's attack on the corporation, but it felt good to know that she could be there in a sense.

On the third wall screen news footage of the massacre at Siffre's Versailles estate was still unfolding, being interspersed with footage from the LeCourbe vineyards. Even though the news team hadn't cited any connection between the events, it was apparent they were willing to let their audience jump to conclusions on their own. International cover-ups were big business in the reporting circles, even if they were eventually found out to be unsubstantiated.

Price paced, trying to walk off the nervous energy that always filled her at the culmination of an operation. So many chances had been evaluated and taken to get them this far, when the time they were down to the wire on a mission, it seemed as if they were playing against the odds. She knew it was the same for Siffre and his people. But in this field, Death owned the house and took odds right out of the middle.

"Kid was smart," Kurtzman growled. "When I tried to spring a virus inside his mainframe through the E-mail, he had some cutouts waiting. I never made it past the first parameters. But once I had the phone line he was using, I found a secondary fax line open under the same fake ID. I appropriated it, skated past the defenses there and got into Siffre's main computer systems."

"Can you shut the satellites down?" Price asked.

Kurtzman looked at her. "I can now, but only after those three tracking stations are brought down. I've programmed the Farm in as a secondary station, but I can't override the primary control."

"Once they're gone, you can stop the satellites if they've already been pulled out of their orbits?"

"As long as they're not so deep in the earth's gravitational well that they can't pull back out under their own power."

Price squeezed the big man's shoulder.

"Barbara." Carmen Delahunt was acting as the mission controller's communications board, fielding all forms of communications through the computer into the headset Price wore. "I've got Stony One on two."

Price nodded and switched over. Immediately she heard Klaxons in the background, sounding far away. A picture of the mountain from Kurtzman's satellite recon flashed through her mind, and she imagined the team stranded there under hostile guns. "Stony One, you have Stony Base. Over."

"We have a situation," Bolan said. "We can't hold our position. We have to go in now. Over."

"Acknowledged, Stony One. We are go here. You are go there. Good hunting. Stony Base out." Price always surprised herself at how composed and taciturn she could be when the chips were down. She certainly didn't feel that confident. She called out to Delahunt and asked the woman to bring Able and Phoenix on-line in that order. She walked away from Kurtzman, letting the big man work out the logistics of his own cybernetic strike.

"Stony Base, this is Able One. Over."

"Able One, you have your go. Repeat, you have your go. We are confirmed here. Stony Base out."

Lyons cleared the channel, and Katzenelenbogen checked in, receiving the same message.

"Barbara, I've got Hal on one."

Price switched over. "Yes."

"Siffre just contacted us," Brognola said.

"That," Price assured him coldly, "was only the nerve spasm of a dead man."

CHAPTER TWENTY-FOUR

Baton Rouge, Louisiana
11:37 a.m.

"That's the *House of Frankenstein*," Schwarz said as he switched off the portable black-and-white television in the back of the Dodge van Able Team was using as transport. He grabbed the SPAS-12 from the rack beside the sliding panel door, made sure his Kevlar vest was zipped, then pulled down the brim of his navy-colored SWAT hat. The Windbreaker he wore identified him as a member of SWAT, as well.

"It's the *Son of Dracula*," Blancanales insisted. "I've seen it a hundred times." He checked his gear, smoothed his hair back under his cap and picked up his Ingram MAC-10.

Carl Lyons swung from the driver's seat and switched on his headset. He ignored the byplay of his teammates. In the past half hour that they'd been sitting outside the station, he'd heard more about horror movies, Lon Chaney and special effects than he ever cared to know.

The team drew attention at once as they crossed the four-lane street. Cars slowed as they passed, and pedestrians turned their heads and pointed.

Lyons took the lead, hit the door at a run and dropped his Remington Model 870 pump gun into target acquisition on the potbellied security guard standing in the foyer. "Don't," he growled.

Reluctantly the security man put his hands on top of his head.

"Down on your knees."

The guy complied.

Lyons took a pair of disposable cuffs from his equipment belt and fastened the man's hands behind his back. A couple of quick loops of ordnance tape secured his legs. "You stay quiet," he advised as he got to his feet. "We might have to come back this way."

"You're not cops," the guard said. "I retired from the force. I know the SWAT guys around here."

Lyons didn't reply. It was their choice to cut the local law enforcement out of the play. Ashe Franklin had stayed behind in New Orleans to book Merle Spurlock and close down that end of the operation. But if they'd had to bring in any of the home team, things would have gotten too knotted with priorities and territorial disputes to have allowed the strike to come off quickly.

Blancanales took the stairs two and three at a time. His booted feet made muffled thuds on the thick carpet. Then he turned the corner and disappeared.

Lyons trailed after Schwarz as they headed for the control booth. They found a door at the end of the hall. According to the blueprints provided by Kurtzman and Price, the sound booth was on the other side of the room. The adjoining corridor led to rest rooms and the ad seller's office. Schwarz opened the door and took up a position beside it as Lyons rushed through.

The secretary in the waiting room was an older woman with peroxided hair and heavy green eye shadow. She sat lounging at the desk, leaning back in her chair with a healthy expanse of calf showing. She had her legs crossed at the knee and obviously knew she held the interest of the four hardmen inside the room.

That interest was held a heartbeat too long.

Lyons had the Remington up by the time the first man reached for his shoulder rig. The big Able Team warrior had an impression of blued steel, then he squeezed the pump gun's trigger. A burst of double-aught buckshot caught the man in the chest, blowing him back onto the overstuffed couch resting against the wall. Lyons racked the slide and searched for his next target.

Schwarz's SPAS-12 boomed beside him, and another man went down.

Springing for all he was worth, the third man reached for the screaming secretary.

Lyons saw the move and, trusting his back to Schwarz's skill, threw himself at the man, unable to bring the shotgun into play for fear of hitting the woman. He slid across the paper-strewn desktop and wrapped his free hand around the man's ankle. Falling away from the woman, Lyons maintained his hold on the man's ankle and twisted viciously.

A yelp of pain ripped from the guy's lips as he tried to keep his balance. His headlong plunge toward the secretary came to an abrupt end.

Instead of pulling his leg away from Lyons, the man kicked out, catching the Ironman on the side of his face. Lyons tasted blood and momentarily lost his vision as the man pulled free. Instinctively he gathered his feet under him and pushed up.

His vision returned in patches, and he saw the man desperately trying to bring up his pistol. Lyons screamed to intimidate the man, succeeded in freezing him for half a beat, which was long enough to launch a high roundhouse kick.

The kick caught the man in the head, pushing him backward. His gun fired and put a round into the desk. When the guy rebounded off the wall, Lyons was waiting for him. He raised the buttstock of the 870 and used it to crack the man's skull. The body slumped to the floor.

Schwarz was making tracks to the back door, the SPAS-12 canted off his hip. "Bastard got through while you were in the way."

Lyons turned to the secretary. "Get the hell out of the building. There's a bomb."

"A bomb?" She seemed rooted to the chair.

He grabbed her by the arm, trying not to be too rough but definitely in control. "Call the cops. Tell them there's a bomb in the television studio. Hurry, lady, and you might get to tell your grandkids about this." He propelled her toward the door, then followed Schwarz.

He ran, caught up with his teammate and came to the main corridor of the first floor. The sound booth was to the right. A meeting room was to the left, the door opening to disgorge three men with guns.

"Company," he said.

Gunfire sounded from overhead, letting them know Blancanales was engaging the enemy, as well.

"I see them," Schwarz said. "I figure we can always stay and fight. Right now we need to find out if the sound booth is where that damn Cray mainframe is." He pulled a grenade from his webbing.

Lyons pointed the Remington at the meeting-room door and pulled the trigger. The charge of buckshot caught the lead man in the chest and knocked him into the water-cooler. The five-gallon glass container sloshed over onto the hard floor and shattered with a crash.

In their haste to get back inside, the two survivors smashed into other people trying to get out of the room.

Lyons fired two more loads into the walls to slow down any would-be heroes.

Schwarz tossed the grenade underhanded, bouncing it off the wall to land only a few feet from the meeting room. It went off with a sharp report, covering the walls and ceiling with the coiled-spring-mesh shrapnel.

While Schwarz cleared the door to the sound booth, Lyons emptied the Remington into the walls. He wheeled inside, thumbing fresh rounds from the bandolier across his chest into the 870.

"Hey," a technician said as he turned in his swivel chair, "you guys can't come in here like that. We're taping a god-damn show." He pulled off his earphones, then noticed the guns in their hands.

Lyons secured the door behind him. It wouldn't hold the security team out for long, but it would make them pause to wonder what was on the other side.

"I told you I heard somebody shooting, Larry."

Lyons looked through the sound booth glass and saw Arabella, Seductress of the Night, sitting on her casket in the center of the stage. The horror-show hostess was supposed to be a vampire, but at the moment her fake vampire teeth were sitting in a glass of water beside a 7UP can. Her blond hair was poofed up and ran in platinum terraces down her shoulders, playfully covering the prodigious amount of cleavage allowed by the tight-fitting black leather vest she wore instead of a shirt.

She hopped off the casket with a jiggle that Lyons found more intriguing than the plot of the old black-and-white horror flick she'd been hosting. "So, big guy, you want to tell us what the hell is going on? You're screwing with my ratings. I need to be focused when I do the intros after commercials." She placed her hands on her hips.

"It's not here," Schwarz said. He was leaned over the equipment, looking at the keyboard in particular.

"It's got to be upstairs, then." Lyons hit the transmit button on his headset. "Pol."

"Go."

"We're clear down here. There's no computer."

"I haven't found it here, either. Damn it!" There was a whine of a bullet striking a hard surface and ricocheting. "But I haven't had a chance to check all the offices."

"We're coming up."

"I'll bake a cake."

Movement caught Lyons's attention, and he saw a side door open inside the sound stage. Two gunners stepped into the room carrying Uzis. Lyons raised the Remington to his shoulder and aimed it at the glass and roared "Get down!" to the television host.

Arabella hit the deck like a pro, covering her hairdo with hands that had impossibly long nails.

Lyons pulled the trigger and watched the sound-stage window shudder and come apart as his hearing fuzzed over. He racked the slide, aimed from the point and fired again. One of the gunners took the load below his knees, knocking him from his feet.

The other man fired, rattling 9 mm hail across the top of the sound booth.

Schwarz opened up, catching the man in the shoulder with his first round, and shot him again before he fell.

Careful of his hands, Lyons waded through the open space where the big window had been and ran to Arabella's side. He gave her a hand up as Schwarz climbed through the window after him.

"You okay?" Lyons asked the woman.

"Yeah." She appeared shaken, but she was holding it together. She reached up and took the long earrings from her ears, dropped them to the floor, then kicked out of the stiletto heels.

"Ironman."

Lyons glanced at Schwarz, who was pointing the SPAS at the door to the corridor. The door was jumping, straining against its hinges and the lock. Schwarz touched the trigger, and a tight pattern of holes appeared in the door. The door stopped moving for a moment, then shook and shuddered as gunfire ate more holes in it and scattered splinters over the sound equipment and cameras.

"That's not going to hold them long."

Lyons nodded and headed for the side door. The blueprints showed a juncture with the stairs just around the corner. Arabella was close behind him. He pulled up short at the doorway, listening for a moment for anyone who might be waiting outside. He looked at the woman. "We need to find a place to lose you."

She shook her head vehemently. "No way, sugar. I'm sticking closer to you than Tonto stuck to the Lone Ranger. Any way out of here is through them, and the damn place is lousy with them. I just hope you're one of the good guys, because those guys are real pricks when it comes to the way they treat a lady."

Lyons shoved more shells into the 870. "We are."

"Figured you were. You guys shoot straighter than they do."

Lyons grinned in spite of the situation, warming to the gutsy lady and her skewed logic. Schwarz joined them at the door, and the big ex-cop swung around the corner, the 870 lowered before him. Nothing moved. He took the lead, heading for the stairs with Arabella and Schwarz close behind.

Three men were coming down the staircase with drawn weapons. They opened fire at once.

Cutting back, Lyons flung his arms out and tackled Schwarz and the woman, knocking them out of harm's way. Bullets chipped the corner of the wall, while others dug holes in the ceiling and the opposite wall. Lyons freed a stun grenade from his rig, armed it and tossed it around the corner. "Close your eyes," he warned.

It went off, starting a whole new wave of autofire that raked the hallway. During a lull, he and Schwarz swept around the corner and fired point-blank. The double-aught buckshot plucked one of the gunners from his position against the wall and knocked down the man left on the stairs. The third man was prone on the floor, dropped by the grenade blast.

Three hollow pops sounded in rapid succession behind Lyons. He turned and saw Arabella with a Raven Arms .25 automatic clenched in her fists as she faced back the way they'd come.

"Guys back there are nipping at our heels," she said.

Lyons moved out, the woman at his side as he went up the stairs over the dead body. "You do this a lot?"

"Hell, no. But my momma taught me how to take care of myself. This here's a big city. If a lady don't watch out for herself, no one else will. I've used my pistol a few times to back Larry down when he was feeling a little frisky, but I never shot at nobody before."

Lyons reached the landing, turned and ran up the stairs.

"What are you guys looking for?"

"A really big computer."

"That Cray that Huneke has?"

Lyons looked at the woman as he made the top landing. "For a girl who sounds like she's just in off the farm, you sure know a lot."

"Pays for a woman to keep her eyes peeled."

"Right. Where's the Cray?"

"Huneke's office."

Lyons moved down the hall, hearing sporadic gunfire farther down the corridor and listening to the distinctive detonation of Schwarz's SPAS-12 as Gadgets covered the stairs. He hit the transmit button on his headset. "Pol."

"Go."

"The Cray's in Huneke's office."

"Can't be. I've already been there."

"I've got someone here who says it is."

"It's behind a false wall," Arabella said. "Huneke owns the apartment against this building."

"I copied that, Ironman," Blancanales said. "Where are you?"

Lyons told him.

"I'm on my way back now. I'll join you there."

"This way," Arabella said, taking the lead.

"How do you know about the false wall?"

"Huneke figures himself to be some sort of Romeo. He invited me up once, showed me around. Besides the Cray, there's a really nice adult playroom, if you know what I mean. He uses it when he wants some hanky-panky behind his wife's back. He tried to cozy up to me, but I told him I had the clap. That was right after I got this job. He gave up for a little while, but he tried again later. That time I had a microcassette recorder so that I had his advances toward me on tape. Threatened to fire me if I didn't come across. I didn't. But I phoned him later, played him some of the tape and told him how I didn't think his wife or the state labor board would cotton to him firing me. Instant job security."

Blancanales joined them outside and they entered together.

Lyons was trying to get his bearings in the darkened room, wondering which wall was shared with the apartment building, when the wall to his right opened up with the suddenness of a sprung trap.

Autofire lighted up the office's interior, and a burst of 5.56 mm rounds chewed through the expensive furniture as

Able Team went to ground. Lyons wrapped his free arm around Arabella and pulled them both behind the eight-foot-long couch on their side of the room. Bullets slammed into the wooden framework.

"Lucky this guy has expensive taste," Lyons said. "If that was a regular couch, we'd have been chopped to ribbons."

Arabella stayed low, her hands over her head. "Between you and me, I'm glad I missed out on the experience."

Moving into a position beside the couch, Lyons lifted the Remington and pumped two rounds into the yawning cavern of the trick wall. Five-point-fifty-six-millimeter rounds chased him back down. He tapped the transmit button. "See anything?"

"Four, maybe six guys," Blancanales said. "They've got guns that shoot really fast."

"Terrific. Any ideas?"

"Well," Schwarz stated, "they did make one mistake."

"What's that?"

"We don't necessarily need that room."

Lyons peered around the couch again, raised his Colt Government Model .45 and brought down a man who tried to invade the room. It kept the opposition apprehensive. He couldn't see very far into the room. "How big is that apartment?" he asked Arabella.

"I don't know."

"Give me something to work with."

"Forty feet by thirty feet. Maybe a little bigger. Those apartments are small."

Lyons keyed the headset. "Gadgets, we got a room maybe forty by thirty. Trick is you have to leave the walls standing around it."

"Figured you'd make it hard, Ironman. Give me a minute."

Lyons reloaded the Remington, wondering if the other team was booking out the back door while they waited. Since they hadn't already, he assumed it was because Siffre was trying to make his play. If the man had already made it, the defensive team would have already been gone. It gave him hope.

They exchanged bits of gunfire, each side letting the other know it was still there.

"Ready," Schwarz called out.

"Do it now!" Lyons said. He got to a kneeling position and shouldered the shotgun, racking the slide immediately after he shot. He fired from the point at everything on the other side of the room that moved. Blancanales's Ingram kept up a steady chatter.

Schwarz appeared from behind the desk briefly. He threw a rectangular package like a bowler, scooting it across the carpet. Gunfire caught him before he could take cover, driving him back in a stagger step.

A foot appeared to kick the package back as it skated into the hidden room.

Lyons put the final double-aught burst into the foot, ankle and knee, sending the guy attached to them spinning away.

Then an explosion shook the building, echoing like a big drumbeat throughout the office. The concussive force swept across the room, taking out the window behind the desk and toppling the couch onto Lyons.

Shoving the couch back, Lyons got to his feet with the .45 in one hand and the .357 in the other. He rushed across the room, noticing Schwarz already trying to get up. Blancanales was at his heels.

A quick check confirmed that there were no survivors, only seven dead men. Kirby Huneke was among them.

"The computer?" Lyons asked Blancanales as the man surveyed the Cray.

Blancanales turned around with a triumphant smile on his face. "Toast, amigo."

Schwarz limped into the room, his left pant leg bloody from the thigh down. Arabella had his arm draped across her shoulders.

"You okay?" Lyons asked.

"Took a couple rounds in the thigh and calf. The vest kept the rest of them away."

"Any other signs of Huneke's goon squad out there?"

Schwarz shook his head. "I guess we convinced them this wasn't a healthy environment."

Police sirens screamed outside the windows in the street.

Lyons knew that the bomb scare the secretary had hopefully reported would slow the police long enough for Price to run interference through Justice Department channels. He looked at the blackened walls of the room and found them all intact. There hadn't been much in the way of furniture except for the big round bed at the opposite end of the room. "You do damn fine work, Gadgets," he said in congratulation.

Schwarz slit his pant leg open while Blancanales took a small first-aid kit from his pack. Arabella was on her knees helping, playing the most seductive nurse Lyons could ever remember having had the pleasure of seeing.

He changed the frequency on his headset to the Stony band, waiting for the radio in the van outside to pick it up and amplify it to the Farm.

"Hey, cowboy."

Lyons looked at Arabella.

"If you get the time, maybe you'd like to stay around a few days and help me plan my unemployment." She gave him a shy smile that seemed out of character for the personality she'd portrayed as the Seductress of the Night. "Maybe even get to know me a little better."

"If it can be arranged, I'd like that."

"Hey, look, Pol," Schwarz said, "the Ironman has a ghoul friend."

That kind of humor, Lyons reflected, wasn't out of character at all.

CHAPTER TWENTY-FIVE

Brighton, England
6:39 p.m.

Adjusting his shroud lines, Yakov Katzenelenbogen continued sailing silently through the night, moving back onto the tracking pattern the team had worked out before jumping from the C-130 Hercules over the English Channel. The jump had been a high-altitude, high-opening one from fifteen miles up.

Price had determined to go for the jump versus a land-based attack for two reasons besides the limited amount of time involved. One was that any entry made through customs even under diplomatic immunity was bound to draw attention from informants at Heathrow whom Sandlier or Siffre had working for them. Another was that landing in the middle of the manufacturing plant after working hours were over would keep the team from having to bust through perimeter defenses. Aside from the security guards, who weren't supposed to be armed in the country, the only people they might meet who had guns could be safely assumed to be the enemy.

"Okay, mates," David McCarter's calm voice said, "you can dump the oxygen gear. We're at a safe level."

Katz stripped the mask and tank away, letting it slip through his fingers. He watched it for a moment as it spiraled down toward the dark channel, then looked back at Brighton. He made out the lights of the city, burning along the coastline. A moment later he was over the beach, still falling and gliding toward his target. He keyed his headset. "Phoenix One to Phoenix Force. Count off. Over."

The team counted off quickly.

Katz was close enough to make out the streets and buildings now, the wind a steady push against his face. He opened his chest pouch, took out his night-vision goggles and put them on. The world disappeared. He was still too far from the ground for them to be used. Loosening the strap, he dropped them into position around his neck.

He checked his gear by touch. The SIG-Sauer P-226 was leathered under his right arm. A Beretta M-12 S submachine gun was on a sling and hung at his hip. Web gear held extra clips for both guns, as well as incendiaries and an assortment of grenades. More equipment was in the heavy pack secured at the bottoms of his legs.

"Thirty-five seconds until we achieve ground zero, lads," McCarter told them. "Make sure you drop those packs before you hit. It's bloody well hard to tuck and roll with your ankles tied together."

Katz marked the time on his watch, saw the luminous second hand sweep around. He took a few deep breaths, charging his system with oxygen he'd need once they touched down.

Sandlier Communications was laid out in a triangle along two streets on the outskirts of Brighton. At the corner flush with the streets, a security fence was built around a landscaped terrace of flowering plants and vines beside a brick wall bearing the company name. Another fence was inside that one, with barbed wire strung across the top. Diagonal from the landscaped corner was the main building where the factory was located. To the left was the corporate garage housing transport vehicles for repairmen and delivery vans. To the right were the corporate offices. All of the buildings were single story.

Katz adjusted the parachute again and swung toward the offices. He could see the ground clearly now, and it was coming up quick. He pulled the goggles back into place and flexed his legs as the landscape brightened.

A truck with flashing yellow security lights braked to a stop thirty yards from his position, its taillights flashing bright ruby.

He tapped the transmit button. "Phoenix Four, this is Phoenix One. Over."

"Go, One. Over." Encizo sounded relaxed.

"We've been spotted. You are to disable the truck occupants quickly, quietly if at all feasible. Over."

"Acknowledged. Phoenix Four out."

The pickup wheeled around cautiously, coming back toward the descending parachutists.

Katz freed the pack between his feet, felt his descent slow a bit, then hit the quick releases on the parachute. The nylon billowed away from him, no longer constrained by his weight. He hit, and even though he was prepared for the sudden impact, it drove the air from his lungs.

He rolled, flailed an arm out and stopped on his feet in a crouched position. The Beretta M-12 S came easily to his hand. He flicked off the safety, put the fire selector on full-auto, then raced for the equipment pack less than ten yards away.

Encizo touched down free of his parachute and rolled to his feet, his silenced Beretta 92-F in his fist as he ran toward the security truck.

Katz ran after the Cuban, ready to supply firepower if necessary.

The pickup halted, then tried to back away.

Before it could go more than a few feet, Encizo had gripped the side mirror and stepped up onto the running board. The driver stopped the vehicle.

"It's okay," Encizo reported. "The guy's regular security."

Katz jogged to his teammate and covered Encizo while he cuffed his prisoner. Glancing around the perimeter, the Phoenix team leader checked off his group. McCarter and Manning were already headed for the main factory. Keying the headset, he said, "Phoenix Five, this is Phoenix One. Over."

"Go," Calvin James responded.

"Are you in position? Over."

"That's affirmative, Phoenix One. Phoenix Five has the high ground. Over."

Katz cleared the channel and looked on top of the corporation's garage but couldn't find James. It was the tallest building in the area. With the Galil sniper rifle, a Star-Tron scope and a clear field of fire, the ex-SEAL would be a decided advantage in their assault.

The discarded parachutes continued to blow across the empty pavement like giant black amoebas.

"The pickup will give us a certain amount of camouflage," Encizo pointed out. He pulled the security guard to his feet.

Katz nodded. "Take it." He jogged around to the passenger side as Encizo slid the guard into the truck and climbed behind the wheel.

The pickup started easily, and the Cuban put it into gear and headed across the open lot to the terraced landscaping.

"Is Sandlier still here?" Katz asked.

The guard hesitated only a moment, his eyes cutting to the submachine gun in the Israeli's hand. "Yes. Him and them other rough-cut blokes are back of the office talking. Looked like they was getting ready to go someplace."

"How many men?"

"Couldn't be more than ten of them. But they got some blokes inside the factory, too. Got some kind of big to-do going on tonight. They got guns, and don't look like somebody you'd want to tangle with."

Encizo stopped the truck in the shadows of the landscaped terraces and took the guard by the arm.

"You ain't going to kill me, are you?" the man asked in a voice as dry as chalk.

"No," Encizo replied. "We just need a place to leave you for a few minutes. Over here, you'll be out of the way. Just keep your head low."

While the Cuban put the guard on the ground so he couldn't be seen in the shadows, Katz hit the transmit button on his headset. "Phoenix One to Phoenix Two. Over."

"Go, mate."

"The factory has an unspecified contingent of armed men inside. Over."

"Roger, One. We'll step lively, try not to open the show too soon. Two out."

Finished securing the guard's legs, Encizo clambered back into the truck and drove toward the office building. The flashing yellow lights threw streaks across the pavement around them.

Katz keyed the headset again. "Phoenix Five, this is Phoenix One. Over."

"Go," James responded.

"We're en route to the rear of the office. How much help can you be? Over."

"None. From here I can't see a thing. If you go inside the building, I can cover the front row of windows, give you a little relief if you get into a jam. Over."

"Roger. One out."

Encizo cut the wheel, giving the office building a wide berth. "We go behind?"

Katz nodded. "If David and Gary don't find anything in the factory, we'll need Sandlier."

The headset squawked for attention.

"Phoenix One, this is Five. You've got movement coming from the back of the building. I see two, no, three vehicles coming from there. Confirm on three. They're rolling your way. Over."

"Are they going to the factory? Over."

"Negative. Looks like they're headed for the gates. Over."

Encizo pressed his foot harder on the accelerator and twisted the steering wheel. He shrugged his M-16/M-203 combo off his shoulder and got it ready for action.

Katz rested the muzzle of the Beretta subgun on his open window, ready to drop his arm over the side when the time came.

Lights pooled around the alabaster sides of the office buildings, flicked quickly through the groomed hedges at the sides of the building and splashed across the security pickup's grimy windshield. The lead car was a black sedan, either a Jaguar or a Mercedes, from the quick look Katz had of it. A large four-wheel-drive van followed, trailed by an unmarked sedan.

"We have the element of surprise on our side," Katz told Encizo, "for only a moment. We need to make the best use of it we can. Drive toward the cars slowly."

Encizo complied, one hand on the wheel while the other gripped the assault rifle.

"I figure Sandlier for the Jaguar," Katz said. "It seems to fit the personality profile Barbara sent us. The other two vehicles doubtless contain Siffre's agents."

Encizo nodded.

"When I give the word, stop the truck and use you grenade launcher to take out the van."

"Right."

Keying the headset, Katz said, "Phoenix Five, when this engagement starts, take out the lead car's tires. Sandlier is probably inside, and I don't want him hurt. Yet. Over."

"Roger. Five is standing by."

"Ready," Katz said, shifting in the seat.

The cars were twenty yards away when autofire cut loose inside the factory, shattering the stillness of the night.

The caravan slowed, then stopped as if the drivers were confused. The car in back peeled off and headed for the factory. Armed men climbed out of the van and milled around for a moment before their commander ordered them toward the plant.

"Now," Katz growled, "while we still have a chance at keeping them together."

Encizo brought the pickup to a rocking halt and slid out the door. Katz went out the other and was bringing up the

Beretta M-12 S when he saw the group from the van turn and notice him. Bullets spanged off the metal sides of the truck as he dropped into position beside the fender and peered around the front of the truck.

The Cuban's grenade launcher whumped loudly, and a heartbeat later it looked as if a sun had gone nova on the side of the van. Flames from the 40 mm incendiary warhead splashed over the closer of the men and set their clothes on fire. The van rocketed from the impact.

Katz raked a full 32-round clip from his subgun, putting four of the men down. Others dug in, trying to take shelter in the burning and twisted hulk of the van.

The Jaguar's driver came alive with the sudden recognition that he was parked near a battle zone. The tires spun as it shot for the gate.

Katz couldn't hear James's Galil fire, but he saw the Jaguar's right front tire go suddenly flat and the car go momentarily out of control. Before the driver could regain mastery over the vehicle, the other front tire was blown, as well. The door opened on the driver's side, and the glass was blown out by at least two 7.62 mm rounds. After that the driver didn't seem inclined to try to get out.

Fifty yards away, the remaining sedan pulled to a stop with the rear bumper facing the truck. Four men piled out and took cover behind the car. Their assault rifles chipped away at the security pickup.

James's sniper fire accounted for one of them, then the others knew they were being fired on from behind and above and shot at the rooftop of the garage.

Flicking the Beretta subgun to a single-fire, Katz pushed himself into a standing position beside the door of the pickup. He squeezed off round after round, aiming at the rear of the sedan, going for the gas tank. After the fifth bullet, he saw a trickle of gasoline drip onto the pavement and waited for it to build.

Encizo had already rearmed the grenade launcher and he fired an HE round through the hole made by the incendiary grenade. The van jumped when it went off inside, and the weaker structure of the rooftop peeled back like a sardine tin.

Aiming for the pool of fuel under the sedan, Katz fired on single-shot mode again. As sparks from the bullets hit the pavement, the gasoline caught on fire, and a twisting claw of flame slithered into the holes in the tank. The ensuing explosion blew open the trunk and knocked the back end of the sedan to one side. Two of the gunners were caught in the blast and went down. The Israeli put a round through the surviving man's head as he tried to run.

With Encizo in control of the action at the van, Katz sprinted to the stalled Jaguar. Quick movement inside the car alerted the ex-Mossad agent that someone was taking the offensive initiative. He threw himself to one side a heartbeat before the window blew out, the fragments framed in the harsh white-yellow of the pistol flash.

Slinging the subgun, Katz rolled, came up on his knees with the SIG-Sauer P-226 in his fist and the hammer rolled back for less trigger tension and a surer shot. The muzzle-flash flamed again, and the Israeli put a round four inches above it, where a man's forehead would be if he was sighting along the barrel in a two-handed grip.

He moved on the car quickly, the P-226 resting on his prosthesis. There were no other shots.

Inside the car, Sandlier was sitting next to a dead man and not looking very happy about it.

Katz yanked the door open and pulled the man out. He shoved Sandlier up against the Jaguar, holding the man in place with his metal hook at the man's throat. A glance at the burning van showed that Encizo had things well in hand. Only dead men littered the pavement as the Cuban completed a quick survey.

The sound of gunfire coming from the factory was intense, and bright explosions from the flash grenades Manning and McCarter had carried lit up the long row of windows set into the middle of the building.

"Where's the computer system tying you in with Barnabe Siffre?" Katz demanded.

"I don't know what you're talking about."

Katz shoved the heated muzzle of his pistol against the man's cheek just below his eye. "Then I don't need you."

"Wait." Sandlier developed a nervous tic that caused him to wink repeatedly. "I know where it is, but you're too late. Siffre has already initiated the satellite sequence."

"Where is it?"

"Inside the factory. There's a room built underground, under the machine shop."

"Show me." Katz grabbed Sandlier's collar and yanked him toward the pickup. "Where's the sending dish?"

"A mile away."

"The lines connecting it?"

"Buried. I'm telling you, you're too late to stop Siffre."

"You might spend some time in the next few minutes praying that you're wrong."

Encizo jogged up to join them. He was bleeding from a bullet wound in his left forearm, and bloody furrows had been plowed along his cheek by shrapnel.

"The factory," Katz said as he motioned Sandlier into the truck bed, then followed. He sat the industrialist against the cab, sheathed the SIG-Sauer and recharged the Beretta M-12 S. "Let's go."

The Cuban nodded and settled himself behind the steering wheel of the pickup.

Thumbing the headset, Katz said, "Phoenix One to Phoenix Two. Over."

"Go," McCarter responded after a moment.

"The computer's inside the factory. There's an underground room beneath the machine shop. I've got a guide. Over."

"Acknowledged, mate, but we've got a rat's nest here we haven't been able to clean out yet. Over."

The pickup lurched as Encizo stepped on the accelerator.

"Give me your location," Katz said. "Over." McCarter did, and the Israeli was able to place the positions of the two Phoenix Force members inside the factory. He gave directions to Encizo, then called for James.

"Go," the ex-SEAL said. "I'm already en route, One. I should be there shortly after your arrival. Out."

The factory wall swelled into view. The gates were closed, padlocked shut. Katz stood up in the rear of the truck and got the Cuban's attention. "Drive through. Let's not waste time with the gate."

Encizo nodded and lined the truck up on a more direct course.

The rolling gate was built to slide sideways, and the metal of the tracks built into the ground gleamed with years of use. It was reinforced to carry the weight and the rough handling, but it was never intended to be a barrier against a vehicle on the attack.

Katz ducked and settled his back against the truck's cab only instants before the vehicle slammed into the gate. Metal sheared and shrieked, and came apart. The truck rocked with the impact, bouncing from side to side as Encizo put his foot heavily on the brake. It slid sideways, crumpled up against a plastic extrusion machine half the size of an eighteen wheeler.

Bringing the subgun around, Katz fired into the mass of gunners who'd almost succeeded in pinning down Manning and McCarter. He burned through a full clip as Encizo pushed himself from the cab. Two men went spinning away, then some of the hostile guns turned toward the pickup. Sandlier wasted no time in throwing himself prone in the truck bed.

Katz reloaded, palmed a grenade from his web gear, armed it and threw it into the enemy position. He came around, firing on the point as eight men scattered from the grenade. The subgun chattered at 550 rounds per minute, emptied in a shade under eight seconds. The grenade blew in the middle of the autofire and further disoriented the gunners. Between the cross fire provided by the four Phoenix guns, there wasn't a man left standing when the smoke cleared.

Calvin James jogged into view holding his Galil rifle at the ready, but there were no targets left.

Fisting Sandlier's shirt, Katz dragged the man from the truck bed and said, "The machine shop."

The man nodded and pointed. "This way."

Katz released Sandlier, following close behind in case the man tried to bolt.

For a moment Sandlier acted as if he was lost, then got his bearings. The machine shop was off to the side. It took McCarter only a moment to slip the lock, and they were inside.

"There," Sandlier said, indicating a section of the floor.

"How do they get it up?" McCarter asked as he dropped to his knees and examined the half-inch-wide crack.

"Chain hoist. There's a ring to put into the floor over there."

James retrieved the ring and screwed it into the floor while Encizo and McCarter maneuvered the chain hoist.

"Gary," Katz said softly.

The demolitions man was working with components he'd gotten out of his equipment pack. "I'm on it. I'm looking for something neat and effective, trying to implode the computer rather than destroying everything. The President is going to need some kind of proof of a conspiracy after this thing hits the news."

Katz nodded and turned to Sandlier. "How is the computer accessed?"

"From the office. Worked through the modem. But once Siffre initiated the programmed sequence, the computer cut off all other input."

Katz discarded any ideas of cutting through the supply line feeding into the Cray II. It would have to be reached manually.

Encizo worked the crank on the chain hoist, and the links clinked rapidly as the slack came out. The heavy concrete-and-steel door opened with a whine of metal on metal. A set of concrete steps was revealed.

James reached inside and found a light switch.

"I've only been in there once," Sandlier said. "Right after it was built."

Katz passed the man off to McCarter, then descended the steps. The room was small, large enough to hold the massive Cray with no room left over. It was a tight fit once Manning joined him. The big Canadian slapped an explosive device onto the center of the Cray as the computer's indicator lights blinked coldly.

"We're out of here," Manning said, charging back up the stairs.

Katz followed him, Sandlier's warning that they were already too late nagging at the back of his mind. At the top of the stairs, Manning thrust a remote control into the Israeli's hands.

"Lower the door," the Phoenix leader ordered.

Encizo released the hoist brake, and the heavy door slammed shut like the door on a tomb.

"Will that signal transmit through all that concrete?" James asked.

Manning gave him a tight smile. "If I did it right, yeah. Otherwise everybody for a mile around who owns an automatic garage-door opener is going to be upset."

Katz pressed the button. The resulting detonation shook the door in its moorings, and spiraling tendrils of gray smoke rose toward the ceiling.

With great pulls on the chain hoist, using plenty of shoulder muscle, Manning lifted the concrete door again. Smoke belched out in a large cloud, tainted with the acrid taste of an electrical fire and yellow vapor. Trying to master a coughing fit caused by the smoke, Manning said, "I think we can say the garage doors in the neighborhood are safe."

"Good job, Gary." Katz switched channels on the headset to the frequency used by the C-130 Hercules circling out of sight overhead. The communications officer waiting there for his signal could relay it to Stony Man Farm. If the team had arrived too late, perhaps Price knew how late they were. Maybe the situation could be salvaged.

CHAPTER TWENTY-SIX

Jura Mountains, France
6:40 p.m.

A dozen armed men erupted from the compound and began to secure the fence. They moved efficiently, their leaders barking orders in authoritative voices. There were three groups of four men each.

Mack Bolan lay prone on the cold mountain rock, the Steyr AUG's buttplate resting against his cheek. He confirmed the leader of each group, marked their positions in his mind, then thumbed the headset's transmit button. "Rover Leader, this is Stony One. Over."

"Go, Stony One," Leo Turrin responded without hesitation. "You have Rover Leader. Over."

"Hold your positions until I give the word. We need to cut ourselves a neutral zone out there if we expect to hold this mountain. Over."

"Roger. Rover Group is standing by."

Sighting in on his first target, Bolan put the Steyr's crosshairs over the man's face and took up the trigger slack. All of the enemy forces were wearing Kevlar battle vests, which would be protection against the assault rifle's 5.56 mm rounds. Taking in a quick half breath, he held it, then squeezed the trigger. He rode out the rifle's recoil, letting the motion help move him into his next target acquisition. The Star-Tron scope pulled the man's features up close. He squeezed the trigger again and got a brief impression of the second target going down, as well. The third man was in motion when the Executioner found him. The warrior's first round took off the lobe of the man's ear, streaking the side of his face with blood, then the next one took him in the forehead.

The three groups froze, suddenly uncertain about what to do, realizing the first defense had already been breached.

Bolan put down two more men before return fire drove him to ground. Stone chips buzzed over his head, and sparks from the bullets smashing into the rocks flared against the night. He tapped the transmit button. "Okay, Rover Leader, take down the fence. Stand by with the Armbrusters. Over."

"Affirmative."

Rolling to a new position, Bolan peered over the cliff face and took a fresh hold on the nylon cord attached to the grappling hook secured on the mountain.

"The fence is going," Turrin called out, "now!"

Kissinger and Falkenhayn had been busy mining the fence line with plastic explosives after taking out the perimeter guards. When the fence line suddenly went ballistic, twisting and spinning as if it was caught in a cyclone, the warrior knew it had been time well invested.

The survivors in the outside grounds of the complex tried to make it back inside the above-ground structure under the covering fire of two .50-caliber Browning machine guns that blistered the forest. Small-arms fire from the blacksuit team continued to pelt the complex's metal walls.

The fence came down in sections, rattling from the trees and boulders.

Bolan knew the defenders were expecting a charge and were preparing to deal out a mass slaughter with the Brownings. He hit the transmit button. "Rover Leader, over."

"Go."

"First gunner."

"In position."

"Fire."

"Firing."

The Armbrust was a shoulder-fired disposable antitank weapon that carried a 67 mm warhead. It was capable of penetrating tank armor at more than three hundred yards.

At the distance involved, Bolan didn't think there would be any problems at all with the reinforced sides of the above-ground building.

He heard the distinctive cough of the Armbrust, but there was no signature muzzle-flash because the firing pistons at each end of the tube worked to seal in the gases and flash. A heartbeat later the warhead impacted against the complex walls and blew a hole through them.

The retreating men dug into their positions as the smoke and flames roared out over their heads.

Bolan hit the transmit button again. "Second gunner."

"In position," Turrin replied.

"Do you have your target?" From his position Bolan wasn't sure how big the opening was.

"That's affirmative. Plenty of room."

"Fire."

"Firing."

The second Armbrust went off, louder than the first in the deathly quiet that had descended over the immediate vicinity. The impact was muffled, rolled around inside the complex and was punctuated by screaming yells of mortally wounded men. The second Armbrust had been loaded with an antipersonnel fragmentation round that guaranteed few survivors.

"Rover Leader," Bolan said as he got to his feet and prepared to rappel down the side of the cliff, "take the high ground."

"Roger."

As he dropped down the length of nylon rope, kicking out strongly with his legs, Bolan saw the advancing wave of blacksuits take up covering positions for one another as they swarmed the complex. Counting Kissinger, Turrin and Falkenhayn, the group consisted of fifteen guns. If anyone had been taken out of the play during the exchange earlier, Turrin would have let him know.

One of the men in the neutral ground rose up to fire his assault rifle.

Shooting from the hip as he descended the rope, Bolan ripped a long burst through the man from the side, putting him down before he could fire on the Stony Man team. The other three threw down their weapons without any further trouble.

Bolan kicked loose of the rope two yards from the ground and landed on his feet. Kissinger and Falkenhayn were almost within arm's reach of him as he went through the gaping hole in the complex wall. He scanned the room, then tapped the transmit button. "Compass."

"Here, sir."

"The ground floor."

"Ready."

"Three rooms. Room one, twenty by twenty. Checkpoint usage only. Elevator to the right on the west wall. Freight size. It's open, maybe eight foot by ten. Stairwell to the left on the west wall."

"Compass copies."

Bolan jogged behind the room, past the bodies the Armbrust had left behind. The numbers were falling inside his head now, soft and deadly. There was no way a man could beat a satellite signal.

Kissinger and Falkenhayn checked bodies but found none alive. Turrin came in with an H&K MP-5 in his fists, barking orders that brought his group hard on their marks.

"Foxtrot Group," Bolan called.

"Here, sir." Four men stepped forward, their faces tight and hard.

"You have the strong point position here. No one goes up or down without my say-so or Rover Leader's. Stay clear of the freq unless you're up to your ass in alligators."

"Yes, sir."

"Baker Group."

Falkenhayn and four blacksuits moved toward Bolan.

"We have the elevator shaft." The Executioner glanced at Turrin and Kissinger, who were lining their team up for the descent down the stairwell. "Stay hard down there."

Turrin nodded and sent his pointman through the door. They disappeared quickly, and seconds later the sound of small-arms fire echoed in the enclosed space beyond the door.

Bolan drew his combat knife and crossed the room to the elevator doors, slammed it between them and twisted. The doors popped open, revealing the empty cage. When he checked, the panel showed three floors, but there was also a slot for a magnetic key card. Baker Group made their first room, and he heard Turrin calling out the description to Compass. Bolan punched the first button, letting the elevator doors close long enough to allow the cage to drop to the first level. He opened them back up and said, "Get some thermite over here."

A blacksuit hustled forward and affixed the thermite charge to the hoist cables. "Clear," he said as he backed away.

Bolan turned, making sure his team was looking away from the elevator. "Clear."

The stench of burning metal filled the room, and cables spanged loudly as individual strands were torn apart by the weight before they could burn. With a creak, the elevator dropped, slamming loosely against the sides of the shaft on its way down.

Bolan turned around just before the ringing gong of impact sounded. A mushroom of dust belched out into the room. He hit the transmit button as he peered down and counted floors. "Compass, this is Tango Group."

"Ready to receive, Tango."

"The elevator shaft has been breached. There are three underground stories."

"Roger that, Tango. Three stories confirmed."

Slinging the Steyr over his shoulder, Bolan waved forward a man holding an M-79 grenade launcher. "Hit the cage."

The man nodded tightly, leaned over the edge and fired his weapon. The 40 mm warhead struck the cage and sent a gout of flame racing up the shaft.

When Bolan looked down again, the roof of the elevator cage had been torn away. He pulled on his night-vision goggles, left them hanging around his neck and climbed into the elevator shaft. Falkenhayn started to climb down the other side.

The doors at the first level opened and a head poked through.

Lashing out with a booted foot, the Executioner caught the man flush on the chin. The guy's head slammed into the closed door.

Bolan stopped at that level, grabbed the door with his hand and pulled it open. Braced and standing on the elevator shaft's exoskeleton, he reached behind his back and fisted the Desert Eagle. Falkenhayn was to his left with a spherical fragmentation grenade in her hand.

Turrin talked to Compass, calling out the rooms Baker Group was searching on the first level with crisp authority. Bolan broke in long enough to apprise Baker Group of the situation at the elevator. Turrin directed his team toward a rendezvous. Nearly every room they'd turned up on that level had been supply oriented; there was no sign of the Cray computer or a generator.

Leaning around the open door, Bolan glanced down the corridor. Three men stood there holding assault rifles. The lead gunner was already approaching the elevator and calling out to the unconscious man.

Firing left-handed, the Executioner aimed above the man's rifle barrel and fired two 240-grain boattails into the man's face. The heavy .44 Magnum slugs punched the corpse back at the other two men.

They fired and tried to retreat at the same time. Bullets from the assault rifles raked the front of the elevator and blew lights from the ceiling.

Coolly tracking the two men, Falkenhayn fired four shots that knocked another gunner off his feet and took him out of play.

"Disengage, Tango," Kissinger called out. "Baker's got the deck."

Bolan lifted his pistol as the big gunsmith came around the corner. The Steyr AUG blazed in his hands, cutting down the remaining man as he turned to shoot. The Executioner gave Kissinger a brief salute, then said, "You have the deck, Baker. Good hunting." Then he continued down the shaft.

He bypassed the second floor. It stood to reason that Siffre would have located his headquarters at one extreme or the other. The second floor would primarily be for troop deployment and munitions.

He dropped the last four feet to the wrecked top of the elevator cage, landing on one of the surviving narrow strips of roof. With a lithe bounce, Falkenhayn joined him.

Eighteen inches of door stood out above the crumpled top of the elevator cage. Glancing inside, Bolan estimated that the floor of the cage extended perhaps a foot below the third-floor ground level. It could work to their advantage.

"Stony One, this is Rover Leader."

"Go," Bolan said as he knelt and took two flash-bang grenades from his web gear.

"We've got control of the ventilator shafts," Turrin said.

"Give us twenty seconds," Bolan replied, "then drop the gas."

"Affirmative."

"Mark."

"Counting down. Twenty..."

Bolan took his own gas mask from his pack. "Foxtrot, do you read?"

"Foxtrot copies, Stony One. We're ready."

Tucking the mouthpiece of his headset into the specially prepared fitting, Bolan tightened the straps and went back to the grenades. There was a chance Siffre and his shock troops had gas masks. If not, the CS gas would prove extremely debilitative in the closed quarters of the tunnels. A few seconds later the gas flooded into the elevator shaft at an astonishing rate, looking like fog blowing in from the sea.

"Take the bottom of the elevator," Bolan told Falkenhayn. He had to raise his voice to make himself heard

through the gas mask. "When I open the doors, it'll give us
two fields of fire."

She nodded and dropped through the giant rent in the top
of the elevator cage.

After peering down to make sure the woman was in position and using the twelve inches of floor space as protection, Bolan popped the elevator doors open, armed the
grenades and shoved them through.

Bullets hammered the steel frame, penetrating the sheet-
metal doors and passing through the wall beyond, missing
Falkenhayn entirely. A heartbeat later the grenades went off,
roaring with the crackle of vibrant thunder.

Bolan used his foot and one hand to kick the elevator
doors open. Falkenhayn had her Steyr in action before he
could unlimber the Desert Eagle. A knot of men tried to
hold their position behind a thick wooden office table despite the blindness and deafness that hampered them.

Falkenhayn's short bursts chewed splinters from the tabletop but failed to penetrate the wood. She raised her aim
to compensate.

Bolan fired as quickly as he could, knew the heavier .44
Magnum rounds would have no problem with penetration
and knockdown power. He emptied the clip, pulled back
and grabbed the Beretta 93-R from his boot holster.

"Grenade!" Falkenhayn yelled.

The warrior caught a brief glimpse of the spherical grenade bouncing across the tiled floor and thudding against
the table. A man made a wild grab for it, but the explosive
detonated before he could reach it.

Exhaling to deflate his chest, Bolan slid through the
opening with the Beretta in his fist, the pistol set at 3-round
burst. Two men were still moving after the explosion. Both
threw their weapons away and put their hands on their
heads.

Bolan kept the Beretta on them as he stepped through the
tangled remains of the table and bodies. He waved to one of
his group to handcuff the prisoners. Ahead of him, the
tunnel was filled with the CS gas, impairing his already

strained vision through the gas mask. He came up to the computer-lab door almost before he knew it was there.

The entrance was heavy, steel and had a huge locking mechanism.

Falkenhayn eyed the door in dismay, her hazel eyes tense on the other side of her glass visor.

Bolan hit the transmit button on the headset. "Stephens."

"Sir."

"Front and center."

"Yes, sir." A young man over six feet tall, with long blond hair poking out the back of his gas mask, came forward.

"I need this door taken out."

Stephens gave a low whistle and shrugged out of his pack. He dropped it with a thud at his feet, knelt and began rummaging through the contents. "That's a hell of a door, sir." He worked plastic explosives in his big, scarred hands, preparing the charges.

Bolan split up the other three team members to firm up their position. There weren't any other tunnels going anywhere. The staircase Turrin and his group were descending had to end somewhere on the other side of the steel door, probably at just the same kind of dead end they were facing now.

He glanced back at Stephens, watched the man roll out the plastic explosive with experienced precision.

"Little plastic champagne glasses," Stephens said as he pulled a stack out of his bag and snapped the stems off. "God, I love 'em." He shaped the charge around the champagne glasses, then slipped them inside soup cans. "Cans are about two inches in diameter, so you want to set the explosives back about three inches from the surface to get the maximum effect." He produced a cordless drill gun, self-starting screws two inches long and straight pieces of aluminum with a bent flare at the end. "You know how to place them?"

"Yeah." Bolan took the drill gun and hunkered down.

Taking a grease pencil from his kit, Stephens marked six
Xs, three on each side of the door. "Do the bottom first.
We'll work our way up to the top."

Bolan worked the drill, set the screws, then secured the
shaped charges in place with strips of masking tape. He felt
the numbers hiss by in his head, wondered if they were already so far behind the clock they couldn't make it. He
called to Compass and had the man patch him through to
the Stony Man Farm frequency on the headset's other
channel. "Stony Base, this is Stony One. Over."

"Go, Stony One. You have Stony Base. Over." Price
sounded cool, collected.

Bolan took that as a good sign. With Price, though, he
was sure he could never tell by her voice, but he chose to
believe it was good. "How are we doing on time? Over."

"We're inside the mainframe," Price replied, "and Able
and Phoenix have neutralized their targets. But the satellites have been pulled from their orbits. According to the big
guy, if we can't put that final Cray out of commission in the
next two minutes, we're going to lose this one. Over."

A screw bent, snapped in Bolan's hands. Without a break
in his movements, he fitted a new one to the bit and set the
aluminum bracket. "We'll make it. We're taking down the
final barrier now. Stony One out."

"Wait," Price called out. "There's something else I've
got to tell you. Stony One, do you copy? Over."

"Stony One copies. Over." Stephens passed Bolan the last
shaped charge and set to work building a bigger one.

"When we got into the mainframe computer, we found
out from the complex schematics that your target has that
whole mountain complex mined with explosives. If he's already set the computer in motion and thinks everything is
proceeding as planned, he might skip out early and try to
drop the mountain on you people. Over."

"We're not leaving until that computer's down," Bolan
said grimly. "There's no other choice." He saw Stephens
give him a thumbs-up after setting the last charge near the
top of the door. "Stony One out." He clicked out of the

frequency, checked back into the operational one for the mission inside the mountain and heard Turrin breaking down the second floor for Compass.

"We need to move back," Stephens said as he stuck remote-control detonators into the shaped charges. "This thing's gonna make a hell of a bang when it goes up."

Bolan waved the group back around the corner, then hit the transmit button on the headset. "Rover Leader, this is Stony One."

"Go."

"We've got a fire in the hole down here, guy. You'll probably feel some of the waves."

"We'll ride them out when they come," Turrin said.

Bolan put the thought of the mountain being mined out of his head. Once they got to Barnabe Siffre, all threats could be neutralized.

Stephens flattened into position along the wall with the detonator in his hand. He looked at Bolan. "The bottom ones blow first, just to loosen everything up. Then the top two go to get the initial thrust going that we need. Before the door has a chance to settle, the big one in the middle goes. Should kick that son of a bitch in slicker than bird shit on a pump handle."

"Do it."

Stephens pressed the detonator.

The series of explosions started at once, filling the hallway with debris and smoke that looked dark and dirty as it mixed with the CS gas.

Bolan pushed himself off the wall and ran. When he reached the door, he found it lying halfway inside the room and tilted at a crazy angle. He brought the Steyr forward on its sling as he stepped through the smoke and gas.

The room was filled with computer hardware. Walls of data banks were on two sides, balanced with an array of computer monitors, workstations and supply racks on the others. Two rows of computer data banks ran down the center of the room.

A man rose up out of the smoke and debris with an Uzi in his hands.

Bolan squeezed the Steyr's trigger and put three 5.56 mm tumblers through the man's face. He drew target acquisition on a second man before the first hit the ground. He fired again, stitching a burst into the man's chest and cutting him down.

Falkenhayn and the rest of his group followed him into the room and spread out immediately. There was only a short resistance, then Siffre's people threw their guns down and their hands up.

"Cuff them," the warrior said as he turned his assault rifle on the Cray computer. He emptied his clip into the data banks, drilling the full-metal-jacketed rounds into the computer's central processing unit. Sparks jumped and flickered as the system died.

He recharged his weapon, turned and walked to the men lying on the floor as the blacksuits finished securing them. He hit the transmit button and was patched through to Stony Man Farm. "Stony Base, this is Stony One. Over."

"Roger, Stony One. We have control of the satellites now. The big guy's putting them back into orbit until a cleanup crew can be fielded to retrieve them. Have you got your target neutralized? Over."

Bolan looked at Falkenhayn, who'd followed him during his inspection of the men on the floor. She shook her head. "Negative, Stony Base. He's eluded us for the moment. Over."

"Striker, you've got to get out of there. Over."

"He can't be far."

"You can't take that chance."

"It's the only chance we have. Even if we're headed down the mountain when he detonates, the avalanche could take us all out. We've got to fix the situation from the inside. Stony One clear." Bolan broke the connection. He stopped beside the nearest prisoner and yanked the man to his feet. "Where's Siffre?"

"I don't know."

"Don't play games with me," Bolan said in a graveyard whisper that carried to the other prisoners. "Siffre has this whole mountain wired with explosives. Do you think he's going to hesitate about using them because you people got left behind?"

"I don't know. He was just here. I lost him when the gas hit."

"Over there," another man said. "There's an emergency exit behind that bank of computers."

Turrin and Kissinger and their team came through the stairwell after a blacksuit inside the computer lab let them in.

The Executioner crossed the room and shoved the machines out of the way. They clattered as they tumbled to the floor and shattered. The door was unlocked when he tried it, and opened outward. He turned to Turrin. "Evacuate the complex and do it now. Siffre's got this place wired, and he's loose."

Turrin nodded and began barking orders. The blacksuits hustled to comply.

The warriors stepped through the door into a corridor with a low roof and walls cut from stone. He pulled off the gas mask and got only a taste of the CS gas as he held his breath and pulled the night-vision goggles over his eyes. The corridor lightened enough to see by and freed him from using a flashlight that would have announced his presence to Siffre.

He pushed himself into a sure-footed jog as Falkenhayn came through the door and tossed her own gas mask aside. She tried to keep up, but his longer stride made that impossible.

He ran hard, driving his legs with all his strength. The air inside the tunnel was cold and wet. He slung the Steyr and used his hands to keep him from stumbling and falling.

Thirty yards on, the tunnel led out of the complex and onto a ridge covered with swirling snow. The warrior paused, tuning into his combat senses as he searched for Siffre. The high ground was out. Once the explosives were set off, there'd be no more high ground. And it wouldn't be safe below, either, because of the falling rock. That left Siffre with only one option: to get off the mountain.

There had been no aerial support. Grimaldi would have called that in when he spotted it on radar.

Examining the ground, he found a set of footprints that had been punched through the frozen crust of snow that already covered the mountain. He unslung the Steyr and continued his pursuit.

The cold surrounded him, battered him with icy fists and tore at his face with blistering daggers. The temperature had dropped more than twenty degrees since the last sunlight had faded from the sky.

The footprints led up over a ridge almost a hundred yards away. From the distance between each print, he knew that Siffre hadn't been running when he'd made his escape.

The Executioner made the ridge and saw Siffre about two hundred yards away at the edge of a sharp drop-off. The Frenchman had secured a harness around his waist, then hooked it onto a thick cable that was bolted into the side of the mountain.

The cable ran nearly a hundred fifty yards over a chasm that had to have been a half-mile deep. It hooked into another part of the Jura Mountain range. When the mountain complex blew—provided Siffre was standing on the other side—the man would be on safe ground.

It wasn't much in the way of an escape plan, but the warrior knew Siffre hadn't been planning on losing. It had just provided the psychological advantage of having a back door. Only now, with the Stony team trapped inside the belly of the mountain, that steel strand was all that was needed.

Knowing there was no way to reach the man in time, Bolan dropped into a prone position, ignoring the sudden chill of the snow as it pressed up against him. He used the range finder and found that the shot would be about three hundred twenty-five yards—just as Siffre swung out onto the cable.

The tracked handwheel needed no effort. The downgrade pulled it along at increasing speed. The hissing of the wheels singing along the cable made an audible sound that carried.

Bolan took up slack on the trigger, bringing Siffre's face into his sights.

The man twisted and looked back at the mountaintop, sliding away.

When their eyes touched for a fleeting instant, Bolan knew the man had somehow sensed him and now saw him lying in black against the white of the snow.

Siffre reached for his jacket pocket.

The Executioner concentrated on his shot, allowed for the windage and squeezed the trigger.

For a moment Siffre hung there, slack and immobile. Then his grip slipped on the handwheel, and the harness didn't hold his shifting weight. He spilled out into the thin air and began the half-mile plunge to the rocky ground.

By the time Bolan reached the cliff, Siffre was a broken and twisted corpse at the bottom of the chasm. He used his binoculars to confirm it.

"It's over, then?" Falkenhayn had finally caught up to him.

"Yeah."

"Those men that Siffre had murdered at his home in Versailles," she said, "had a lot of dreams for themselves and their families. They weren't bad men. They didn't deserve to die like that. New worlds are being born every day politically. We can't continue to be afraid of them."

"I know." Bolan stared up at the starlit sky. "But just because a dreamer dies, that doesn't mean that the dream has to die, too."

She took his hand and held it. "So where will you go next?"

He shook his head. "Somewhere. To protect someone else's dreams."

"Don't you have any dreams of your own?"

"Yeah, but they only come in the impossible size. My dream is for the day when the world doesn't need someone like me."

"Do you have to go right away?"

He smiled at her, touched her face with his fingers and saw the promise in her eyes. "Maybe not."

"I'd just like to go somewhere for a few days and be held by someone who could really care about me if things were different."

"Now that," Bolan said as he guided her away from the chasm, "is the stuff dreams are made on."

Join Mack Bolan's latest mission in

THE TERROR TRILOGY

Beginning in June 1994, Gold Eagle brings
you another action-packed three-book in-line
continuity, the Terror Trilogy. Featured are
THE EXECUTIONER, ABLE TEAM and
PHOENIX FORCE as they battle neo-Nazis
and Arab terrorists to prevent war in the
Middle East.

Be sure to catch all the action of this gripping
trilogy, starting in June and continuing through to
August.

Book I:	**JUNE**	**FIRE BURST** **(THE EXECUTIONER #186)**
Book II:	**JULY**	**CLEANSING FLAME** **(THE EXECUTIONER #187)**
Book III:	**AUGUST**	**INFERNO** **(352-page MACK BOLAN)**

Available at your favorite retail outlets in June
through to August.

**Don't miss out on the action this summer—
and soar with Gold Eagle!**

TT94-1

BATTLE FOR THE FUTURE IN A WASTELAND OF DESPAIR

EARTH BLOOD

AURORA QUEST

by JAMES AXLER

The popular author of DEATHLANDS® brings you the gripping conclusion of the Earthblood trilogy with AURORA QUEST. The crew of the U.S. space vessel *Aquila* returns from a deep-space mission to find that a devastating plant blight has stripped away all civilization.

In what's left of the world, the astronauts grimly cling to a glimmer of promise for a new start.

Available in July at your favorite retail outlet.

A new warrior breed blazes a trail
to an uncertain future in

JAMES AXLER

DEATHLANDS®

Twilight Children

Ryan Cawdor and his band of warrior-survivalists are transported
from one Valley of the Shadow of Death to another, where they
find out that the quest for Paradise carries a steep price.

In the Deathlands, the future looks terminally brief.

Don't miss out on the action in these titles featuring
THE EXECUTIONER, ABLE TEAM and PHOENIX FORCE!

The Freedom Trilogy

Features Mack Bolan along with ABLE TEAM and
PHOENIX FORCE as they face off against a communist
dictator who is trying to gain control of the troubled
Baltic State and whose ultimate goal is world supremacy.

The Executioner #61174	BATTLE PLAN	$3.50	☐
The Executioner #61175	BATTLE GROUND	$3.50	☐
SuperBolan #61432	BATTLE FORCE	$4.99	☐

The Executioner ®

With nonstop action, Mack Bolan represents ultimate
justice, within or beyond the law.

#61178	BLACK HAND	$3.50	☐
#61179	WAR HAMMER	$3.50	☐

(limited quantities available on certain titles)

TOTAL AMOUNT	$	
POSTAGE & HANDLING	$	
($1.00 for one book, 50¢ for each additional)		
APPLICABLE TAXES*	$	_____
TOTAL PAYABLE	$	_____
(check or money order—please do not send cash)		

To order, complete this form and send it, along with a check or money order for the
total above, payable to Gold Eagle Books, to: **In the U.S.:** 3010 Walden Avenue,
P.O. Box 9077, Buffalo, NY 14269-9077; **In Canada:** P.O. Box 636, Fort Erie, Ontario,
L2A 5X3.

Name: _____

Address: _____ City: _____

State/Prov.: _____ Zip/Postal Code: _____

*New York residents remit applicable sales taxes.
Canadian residents remit applicable GST and provincial taxes.

GEBACK5